P9-BYD-649

Also by Debbie Macomber

Blossom Street Books
THE SHOP ON BLOSSOM STREET
A GOOD YARN
SUSANNAH'S GARDEN
BACK ON BLOSSOM STREET
TWENTY WISHES
SUMMER ON BLOSSOM STREET

Cedar Cove Books
16 LIGHTHOUSE ROAD
204 ROSEWOOD LANE
311 PELICAN COURT
44 CRANBERRY POINT
50 HARBOR STREET
6 RAINIER DRIVE
74 SEASIDE AVENUE
8 SANDPIPER WAY
92 PACIFIC BOULEVARD
A CEDAR COVE CHRISTMAS

The Manning Family
THE MANNING SISTERS
THE MANNING BRIDES
THE MANNING GROOMS

Dakota Series
DAKOTA BORN
DAKOTA HOME
ALWAYS DAKOTA

Heart of Texas Series
VOLUME 1
(Lonesome Cowboy and
  Texas Two-Step)
VOLUME 2
(Caroline's Child and *Dr. Texas)*
VOLUME 3
(Nell's Cowboy and
  Lone Star Baby)
PROMISE, TEXAS
RETURN TO PROMISE

Midnight Sons
VOLUME 1
(Brides for Brothers and
  The Marriage Risk)
VOLUME 2
(Daddy's Little Helper and
  Because of the Baby)

Christmas Books
A GIFT TO LAST
ON A SNOWY NIGHT
HOME FOR THE HOLIDAYS
GLAD TIDINGS
CHRISTMAS WISHES
SMALL TOWN CHRISTMAS
WHEN CHRISTMAS COMES
THERE'S SOMETHING
  ABOUT CHRISTMAS
CHRISTMAS LETTERS
WHERE ANGELS GO
THE PERFECT CHRISTMAS
ANGELS AT CHRISTMAS
  (Those Christmas Angels and
  Where Angels Go)

THIS MATTER OF MARRIAGE
MONTANA
THURSDAYS AT EIGHT
BETWEEN FRIENDS
CHANGING HABITS
MARRIED IN SEATTLE
(First Comes Marriage and
  Wanted: Perfect Partner)
RIGHT NEXT DOOR
(Father's Day and
  *The Courtship of
  Carol Sommars)*
WYOMING BRIDES
(Denim and Diamonds and
  The Wyoming Kid)
FAIRY TALE WEDDINGS
(Cindy and the Prince and
  Some Kind of Wonderful)
THE MAN YOU'LL MARRY
(The First Man You Meet and
  The Man You'll Marry)
DEBBIE MACOMBER'S
  CEDAR COVE COOKBOOK

DEBBIE MACOMBER

Midnight Sons

VOLUME 3

MIRA®

Recycling programs
for this product may
not exist in your area.

ISBN-13: 978-0-7783-2754-7

MIDNIGHT SONS VOLUME 3

Copyright © 2010 by MIRA Books.

The publisher acknowledges the copyright holder of the individual works
as follows:

FALLING FOR HIM
Copyright © 1996 by Debbie Macomber.

ENDING IN MARRIAGE
Copyright © 1996 by Debbie Macomber.

MIDNIGHT SONS AND DAUGHTERS
Copyright © 2000 by Debbie Macomber.

www.MIRABooks.com

Printed in U.S.A.

For Bailey and Carter Macomber
Who both make their Grandma and
Grandpa Macomber so very proud

Dear Friends,

Welcome to Hard Luck, Alaska, and the last volume in the MIDNIGHT SONS series. If you read Volumes 1 and 2, you've become familiar with the families living in this rugged tundra town. These books were originally published in 1995 and 1996 and led me to write the six-book HEART OF TEXAS series and eventually its sequel, *Promise, Texas*—which was my very first title on the *New York Times* bestseller list.

My husband worked on the pipeline in Alaska back in 1982. In fact, Wayne was in Purdue Bay when I received word that my first book had sold. It was a phone call that changed our lives. Because Wayne had loved working in Alaska, we traveled north—many years later—in order to do the research for this series. If anyone from the IRS inquires, the *entire* trip was for research purposes! It was work, work, work!

I remember we were in Fairbanks for the summer solstice. When they say Alaska is the land of the midnight sun, that's no exaggeration. We ended up propping a chair against the drapes to keep the light from shining into our hotel-room window. (See? It's all research.)

Our trip was quite an adventurous one. Wayne and I were able to fly over the Arctic Circle on a "mail run" and visit a town called Bettles (which bears an astonishing resemblance to Hard Luck). In the name of research I interviewed bush pilots, panned for gold, dined on moose meat and talked with anyone and everyone willing to share their experiences. It ended up being a trip Wayne and I would long remember. Although it *was* strictly work! (In case that IRS agent is lurking over your shoulder reading this.)

I like to think of myself as a "value-added" author, and my publisher shares my desire to give readers a bonus whenever possible. Included in this volume is the novella titled *Midnight Sons and Daughters,* originally published in 2000 in a Harlequin Superromance book celebrating the line's twentieth anniversary. It's a follow-up story many readers had asked me to write. This is a great opportunity to find out how some of the children you met in these books turned out.

I hope you enjoy *Falling for Him* and *Ending in Marriage,* plus the bonus novella.

Warmest regards,

Debbie Macomber

P.S. And remember Wayne's and my trip was *just* for research purposes. By the way, I love hearing from readers. You can reach me at www.debbiemacomber.com or P.O. Box 1458, Port Orchard, WA 98366.

CONTENTS

FALLING FOR HIM   13

ENDING IN MARRIAGE   189

MIDNIGHT SONS AND DAUGHTERS   371

The History of Hard Luck, Alaska

Hard Luck, situated fifty miles north of the Arctic Circle, near the Brooks Range, was founded by Adam O'Halloran and his wife, Anna, in 1931. Adam came to Alaska to make his fortune but never found the gold strike he sought. Nevertheless, the O'Hallorans and their two young sons, Charles and David, stayed on—in part because of a tragedy that befell the family a few years later.

Other prospectors and adventurers began to move to Hard Luck, some of them bringing wives and children. The town became a stopping-off place for mail, equipment and supplies. The Fletcher family arrived in 1938 to open a dry goods store.

When World War II began, Hard Luck's population was fifty or sixty people, all told. Some of the young men, including the O'Halloran sons, joined the armed services; Charles left for Europe in 1942, David in 1944 at the age of eighteen. Charles died during the fighting. Only David came home—with a young English war bride, Ellen Sawyer (despite the fact that he'd become engaged to Catherine Fletcher shortly before going overseas).

After the war, David qualified as a bush pilot. He then built some small cabins to attract the sport fishermen and hunters who were starting to come to Alaska; he also worked as a guide. Eventually he built a lodge to replace the cabins—a lodge that was later damaged by fire.

David and Ellen had three sons, born fairly late in their marriage— Charles (named after David's brother) was born in 1960, Sawyer in 1963 and Christian in 1965.

Hard Luck had been growing slowly all this time and by 1970 it was home to just over a hundred people. These were the years of the oil boom, when the school and community center were built by the state. After Vietnam, ex-serviceman Ben Hamilton joined the community and opened the Hard Luck Café, which became the social focus for the town.

In the late 1980s the three O'Halloran brothers formed a partnership, creating Midnight Sons, a bush-pilot operation. They were awarded the mail contract, and also delivered fuel and other necessities to the interior. In addition, they served as a small commuter airline, flying passengers to and from Fairbanks and within the northern Arctic.

In 1995, at the time these stories start, there were approximately 150 people living in Hard Luck—the majority of them male....

Now, almost fifteen years later, join the people here in looking back at their history—particularly the changes that occurred when Midnight Sons invited women to town. Women who transformed Hard Luck, Alaska, forever!

FALLING FOR HIM

Chapter
1

Late July 1996

THE WOMAN DROVE him crazy. Christian O'Halloran had given a *lot* of thought to Mariah Douglas lately and had compiled a long list of reasons to fire her. Good reasons. Unfortunately he had to get his stubborn brother to agree. According to Sawyer, Mariah could do no wrong.

According to him, she could do no right.

It astonished Christian that his brother was so blind about this. As a rule, Christian valued Sawyer's opinion. In fact, he considered both his older brothers—Charles, too—excellent judges of character. Christian couldn't understand it, but they'd been hoodwinked by Mariah. Not only that, they'd accused *him* of being arbitrary, unfair, unkind.

Mariah gave the impression of being sweet and gentle. Unassuming. Efficient. But he knew otherwise. Mariah Douglas was not to be trusted. She was, to put it simply, a klutz. Whenever he was around, she lost messages, misfiled documents, dropped things. None of that ever seemed to happen when Sawyer was in the office, so Christian had to conclude that she had it in for him, and him alone. Now, he didn't believe she'd ever *intentionally* do anything to undermine their business. If she managed to sabotage Midnight Sons, he was convinced it would be purely accidental. That, however, didn't make her any less dangerous. There was definitely a negative chemistry between them. He nodded to himself, pleased with the term.

Sitting at his desk in the mobile office for Midnight Sons, the flight service the three O'Halloran brothers owned and operated in Hard Luck, Alaska, Christian wondered exactly what it was about Mariah he found so objectionable—aside from her clumsiness, of course. He'd never really figured that out.

It wasn't her looks. The woman was attractive enough—medium height, medium build with medium-length red hair and brown eyes. Some might even think she was pretty, and Christian wouldn't disagree. She *was* pretty. Sort of. Nothing that would stop traffic, mind you, but reasonably pleasing to the eye.

Duke Porter, one of his pilots, apparently thought so.

Christian's mouth thinned at the memory of walking in on them recently and finding Mariah and Duke locked in each other's arms. It irritated him no end that they hadn't kept their romance out of the office. If they wanted to smooch and carry on, they could do it on their own time. Not his.

This sort of behavior wasn't what he'd had in mind when he convinced Sawyer that they should bring women to Hard Luck. In his view, the plan had a practical business purpose.

Midnight Sons had been losing pilots. And he'd hoped that persuading women to move to Alaska would solve their problems.

Instead, it had created more—Mariah Douglas being one of them.

Abbey Sutherland was the first woman to arrive. From the moment his levelheaded brother laid eyes on her, Sawyer hadn't been the same. In less than a month, he and Abbey were engaged.

In Christian's opinion, Sawyer lost more than his heart when he met Abbey; since then, his brain hadn't functioned properly, either. Charles wasn't much better once Lanni Caldwell showed up. The two of *them* were engaged by the end of the summer. They'd set up house this past April, and all the common sense Charles used to have had flown right out the proverbial window.

Christian appeared to be the last of the three in full possession of his wits.

Shortly after he'd found Mariah and Duke embracing, Christian had approached Charles. He'd hoped his oldest brother would help him convince Sawyer that the time had come to replace Mariah. She'd been their secretary for a full year now, and there was only so much a man should have to take. They'd signed a one-year agreement, and as far as he was concerned their responsibilities toward her had been met.

Charles had proved to be a major disappointment. It wasn't that his brother had sided with Sawyer over the secretary issue; however, he hadn't said what Christian had been hoping to hear. Charles seemed to feel that Sawyer and Christian should settle this matter between themselves.

That would never work, because Sawyer didn't have the same problems with Mariah that Christian did. His brother was in favor of keeping her as long as she was willing to stay on.

Every time Christian brought up the subject, Sawyer reminded him that *he'd* been the one to hire her. What his brother failed to remember was that Christian had never wanted Mariah as their secretary in the first place. He'd wanted Allison Reynolds.

Even now, the image of the tall, beautiful blonde stirred his blood. He'd met her in Seattle and been immediately captivated. It had taken a lot of fancy footwork to get her to give Hard Luck a try.

Allison had come to Alaska, but after viewing the town and seeing the living quarters allotted her, she'd experienced a sudden change of heart. Unfortunately Christian hadn't been in Hard Luck at the time, and once she'd decided to return to Seattle, he didn't have the opportunity to talk her into giving the town another chance.

Disheartened after her departure, he'd pulled out the next job application in the pile.

Mariah Douglas.

Christian had rued that day ever since. He'd wanted Allison Reynolds. She'd affected him the way Abbey had affected Sawyer, the way Lanni affected Charles. If he hadn't been so dismayed with Allison's decision to go back home, he'd have done a better job of choosing her replacement.

"Christian, could I speak to you for a moment?" Mariah approached his desk in her usual timid manner, as though she expected him to leap up and bite her.

He raised his eyes. It had taken her six months to call him by his first name, instead of Mr. O'Halloran. Didn't she realize he and Sawyer had the same surname? He sighed. And Sawyer wasn't even in today to help with damage control; he'd gone to Fairbanks with Abbey and the kids.

"Yes," he muttered, barely hiding his impatience.

"Before he left, Sawyer said I should talk to you...." She bit her lower lip. From her expression, you'd think he was some kind of ogre. Christian saw himself as considerate and intelligent and hoped he behaved that way. Obviously Mariah didn't agree. He sighed again.

"Talk to me about what?" he asked, more kindly this time.

"I've been with Midnight Sons for a whole year now."

No one was more aware of that than Christian. "Yes, I know."

"I'd like to take a week of the vacation I'm allowed according to my employment contract."

Christian straightened. A week without Mariah. A week of freedom. A week of peace.

"I'm meeting a friend in Anchorage," she explained, not that he needed to know or particularly cared.

"When?" The sooner she left the better, in Christian's opinion. This would be his chance to prove to Sawyer once and for all that they didn't need a secretary. Or—and this was his own preference—that they should hire someone else. Someone more like Allison and a lot less like Mariah.

"If it's possible, I'd like to take next week," she said, her eyes hopeful. "Early August is the perfect time to see Alaska."

"Next week'll be fine." Christian was so excited it was all he could do not to grab her by the shoulders and kiss her on both cheeks.

She hesitated, lingering at his desk.

"Is there something else?" he asked.

"Yes, there is." Her eyes flashed briefly, but with what he couldn't quite guess. Anxiety? Resentment? "I wanted to thank you for giving me this time off on such short notice. I realize it puts you in a bind, but I didn't decide to go until last night after I got Tracy's letter and—"

"Tracy Santiago?"

Mariah nodded.

Tracy was an attorney hired by the Douglas family soon after Mariah's arrival. Tracy had flown up to inspect the living conditions and review Mariah's contract with Midnight Sons. Through all of this, apparently, Mariah and Tracy had struck up a friendship.

With any luck Tracy would convince Mariah to forget about Alaska and return to Seattle where she belonged. One thing was certain: Christian wanted her gone.

"I'll be leaving on Saturday," she said, again providing him with more information than he wanted or required.

"Fine."

"And I'll be back the following Saturday."

"Fine."

She backed away from him. "I just thought you should know."

"Will you be flying out of Fairbanks?"

"Yes." She nodded enthusiastically. "Duke's offered to take me into the city."

Duke. Christian should've known he'd relish a chance to spend time alone with Mariah. Duke was welcome to her, although Christian would insist they keep their romance out of the office and out of his sight. The problems with having one of his pilots dating the secretary were obvious—weren't they? Well, maybe he couldn't articulate all of those problems this very minute, but he knew instinctively that it wasn't a good idea. For reasons he couldn't entirely explain, Christian did not want Duke flying Mariah into Fairbanks.

"Duke's going to be busy next Saturday," Christian announced suddenly. He wasn't sure what he'd assign the pilot, but he'd come up with something.

"But I checked the schedule, and there wasn't anything down for Duke. He's already said he'd do it, and—"

"Then I suggest you check the schedule again," he snapped, "and have one of the other pilots fly you in."

"All right." She agreed readily enough, but Christian could see she wasn't pleased.

He'd no sooner resumed his paperwork than Mariah approached him a second time.

"Yes?" he said, realizing he sounded annoyed but unable to help it. Then he reminded himself—in a few days he'd be free of her for an entire week. The thought cheered him considerably.

"I've gone over the list, and there's only one other pilot available this Saturday but—"

"Fine." Christian didn't care who flew her into Fairbanks, as long as it wasn't Duke.

"But—"

He clenched his jaw, growing impatient. "Mariah, I have more important things to do than discuss your travel arrangements. Someone other than Duke will be available to fly you out in plenty of time to catch your flight to Anchorage, and that's all that matters."

"Yes, I know," she returned, just as impatient. "That someone is *you*."

THE MAN WAS IMPOSSIBLE, Mariah decided as she left the Midnight Sons office that afternoon. Nothing she did pleased him. What she should've done was look Christian O'Halloran right in the eye and tell him he could take this job and shove it.

She would've, too, if she wasn't so much in love with him.

Mariah didn't know when it had happened, possibly the first time they'd met. He'd been in Seattle interviewing applicants for a variety of positions in Hard Luck. She'd been excited about applying for the job, although as claims adjuster for a large insurance company, she had limited office experience.

Her meeting with Christian had been short and to the point. He'd asked her a list of questions, but his mind seemed to be elsewhere. She'd gone home discouraged, assuming he'd already made his decision and wouldn't be giving her the job.

When she learned she *had* gotten the job and told her friends, no one seemed to understand her reasons for wanting to move to a remote town north of the Arctic Circle. If she was doing it to escape her family, they told her, there were any number of places that would've been more suitable.

Her friends' doubts were nothing compared to her family's reaction. When she'd informed her parents that she planned to move to Hard Luck, they'd feared the worst.

She couldn't make them understand that Alaska appealed to her sense of adventure, her need to experience a different life. She'd suspected she would grow to love this land, and she'd been right.

Her friends had teased her unmercifully. She still grinned whenever she remembered a comment of her friend Rochelle's: "I hear your odds of finding a man in Alaska are good—but the goods are odd."

Mariah hadn't come here looking for a husband. No one seemed to believe that. She'd come because she wanted a life of her own, a life away from her family. She wanted to make her own decisions and her own mistakes. For the first time, she didn't have her mother or one of her aunts hovering over her constantly, ready to leap into the middle of her life and arrange everything.

Two important occurrences had shaped her year in Hard Luck. First and foremost, she'd fallen in love. Head over heels. Hook, line and sinker. The whole nine yards.

The problem was that the object of her affections was Christian O'Halloran and he didn't even seem to *like* her. He thought she was a major klutz, and in the past year she'd done everything possible to prove him right. Not intentionally of course. The man flustered her. Whenever they were in close proximity, she said or did something stupid. She couldn't help it. And now he seemed to think she was infatuated with Duke. The man had to be blind.

The second occurrence had been set in motion by her family. Mariah should've realized they'd have a difficult time accepting her decision to move away. The ink had barely dried on her contract with Midnight Sons when her parents had hired an attorney.

Tracy Santiago had turned out to be a blessing in disguise. At first Mariah was afraid the woman would jeopardize her position with Midnight Sons, but her fears had been ground-less.

Shortly after Mariah's arrival in Hard Luck, Tracy flew up to meet her, and while she was there she interviewed several of the other women. In the year since then, Mariah and Tracy had become good friends.

They'd kept in touch, with letters and phone calls and the occasional brief visit. In that time, there'd been a number of unexpected events. Marriages. A death. A new enterprise— the revived Hard Luck Lodge. And soon the community would see a spurt in population growth. Abbey O'Halloran was pregnant, as was Karen Caldwell. Both were due in mid-winter.

Tracy had enjoyed receiving Mariah's letters, updating her on life and love in Hard Luck. Romance abounded. The two older O'Halloran brothers had fallen for women in no time flat. They were both married now. Pete Livengood, who operated the general store, had married Dotty Harlow, the health clinic nurse. Then Mitch Harris, the public safety officer, and Bethany Ross, the new schoolteacher, had fallen in love. Some women had come to Hard Luck and stayed; others had quickly moved on. Those who did stay became so integrated in the community it was sometimes difficult to remember who was new to this rugged, beautiful place and who wasn't.

Mariah liked writing long, detailed letters about the happenings in Hard Luck as much as Tracy liked reading them. She appreciated Tracy's friendship and support more than ever.

Mariah's family had been convinced she wouldn't last six months. But her parents had underestimated her tenacity; Tracy hadn't.

Mariah continued walking toward her small cabin. As she strolled past Hard Luck Lodge, Karen Caldwell stepped out onto the porch. Karen was four months pregnant, and radiantly happy.

"Mariah," she called. "I hear you're going on vacation. That's great. Where are you headed?"

This was one thing about living in a small community that still astonished Mariah. There were few secrets, although people did seem to respect each other's privacy. It wasn't as though they were eager to spread gossip; it was more a matter of genuine interest and concern. News was passed along in a friendly sort of way, often at Ben Hamilton's place. Almost everyone in town stopped in at the Hard Luck Café at least once during the week, and some more often.

Mariah joined her friend on the front porch of the renovated lodge, which had once belonged to the O'Hallorans and was now owned by Karen's husband, Matt.

"Who told you about my vacation?" she asked, curious to learn how the news had made the rounds.

"Matt. He had coffee with Ben after John Henderson was in this morning."

That explained it. John Henderson was Duke Porter's best friend. Duke had obviously mentioned he was flying her into Fairbanks, then John had told Ben and Ben had told Matt.

"I'm meeting Tracy Santiago in Anchorage," Mariah said. "I've been in Alaska over a year now, and I thought it was time I played tourist."

"Have a great trip," Karen said. "But don't let the bright lights of the big city dazzle you."

"Not to worry. This is my home." And it was. Mariah had no desire to stay in Anchorage—or return to Seattle. Her commitment had been for one year, but she fully expected to settle in Hard Luck permanently. The cabin, for whatever it was worth, and the twenty acres of land promised her in the contract had been deeded to her. Mariah had achieved what she wanted. Nothing held her in Hard Luck now except her love of the community and those in it.

Especially Christian.

CHRISTIAN WALKED into the Hard Luck Café and slid onto a stool at the counter. Ben Hamilton was busy writing the dinner special on the blackboard. Moose pot roast in cranberry sauce with mashed potatoes and gravy. Christian studied the board intently.

"A little early to be eating, isn't it?" Ben asked.

"Of course it is." It was only four-thirty, and he generally didn't have dinner until six or later.

"You just ate lunch three hours ago," Ben reminded him.

Christian knew exactly when he'd had lunch. He hadn't come into the café for food. He wanted to complain. Sawyer had barely left, and already Christian felt at the end of his rope. Between dealing with Mariah and the increased workload, he'd completely lost his composure. He sure hoped Sawyer didn't stay in Fairbanks longer than a couple of days.

"You got something on your mind?" Ben asked, leaning against the counter.

"Yeah."

"Well, I'll tell you what I said to young Matt not so long ago. If you want advice, it doesn't come free. Not anymore."

"What do you mean?"

"Did you come in here to eat or to talk?" Ben asked curtly.

Christian had noticed a difference in Ben's temperament ever since he'd started his frequent-eater program. Apparently he'd decided that from now on, nothing was free. Not even speech. Christian was almost surprised Ben wasn't charging him for sitting on the stool.

"How about some coffee?" Christian muttered.

Ben's mouth formed a slow grin. "Coming up."

Christian righted the mug and Ben promptly filled it. Staring at it reminded him that Mariah had made coffee for him nearly every morning for a year. He couldn't count the number of times he'd told her he liked his coffee black. Some days she added sugar, some days cream, some days both. But he could count on one hand the days she'd gotten it right.

"So what's bugging you?" Ben asked.

Christian shook his head. Now that he was here, he didn't feel inclined to share his woes. More than likely, Ben would side with Mariah the way his brothers had.

"If you've got a problem, spit it out," Ben said.

"You going to charge me?" Christian asked jokingly.

"Nah, I'm just trying to sell a little coffee."

Ben probably sold more coffee than some of those all-night diners in Anchorage, but Christian didn't say so.

"If you've got something on your mind," Ben pressed, "best thing to do is get it out."

"It's nothing."

Ben's laugh was skeptical. "My guess is it involves Mariah."

Christian glared at the older man. "What makes you say that?"

The cook lifted one shoulder in a casual shrug. "Whenever I see you frown, it usually has to do with her. After all, you've been complaining about Mariah for over a year."

"Not that it does me any good," Christian said with ill grace. "According to everyone else, the woman walks on water. Is there something wrong with me?" he asked, not really expecting an answer.

"She's a sweetheart, Chris."

"Not to me, she isn't." She might be as wonderful as everyone said, but Christian doubted it. "We can't seem to get along," he mumbled.

"Have you ever stopped to consider why?"

"I have, as a matter of fact," Christian said. "I read an article in one of those airline magazines—oh, it must've been three or four years ago. It was about a man who walked from one end of the continental United States to the other. Took him months. People from all over asked him what he'd found the hardest."

Ben frowned. "Are we still talking about Mariah?"

"Yes," Christian insisted. "The writer who was doing the interview suggested the hardest part must've been the heat of the desert or the cold of the mountains."

"Was it?" Ben asked, obviously curious now. He folded his arms and waited for Christian to respond.

"Nope."

"You sure we're still talking about Mariah?"

Christian ignored the question. "After deep thought, the man gave his answer. The most difficult thing about the long walk had been the sand in his shoes."

"The sand in his shoes?"

"Yup. And that's what's wrong between Mariah and me."

Ben's face broke into a network of lines as he frowned again, and Christian could tell he assumed Mariah had been pouring sand in his shoes. "It's the little things about her that drive me nuts," he explained. "The fact that she ruins my coffee every morning. The way she loses things and just…irritates me." Christian paused, then said grudgingly, "I'm sure she's a perfectly capable secretary—or would be for someone else. But she hasn't worked out for me."

"Sawyer doesn't seem to have a problem with her." Christian had heard this argument from Ben before; he wasn't surprised to be hearing it now.

The door of the café opened just then, and he glanced over his shoulder and saw Duke. The other man's eyes narrowed as he caught sight of Christian.

"What's this all about?" Duke demanded, waving the note Christian had slipped into his mailbox.

"I'll be flying Mariah into Fairbanks on Saturday," Christian told him calmly. He didn't expect the other man to argue, since he was the boss.

"*I* offered to do it," Duke said.

"I know, but there are other, uh, more important things I need you for."

"You're sending me out on a wild-goose chase and you know it. I could make the flight into Barrow any time next week, and all of a sudden you decide I have to do it Saturday."

Christian wasn't proud of his little subterfuge, but his justification was that he didn't want Duke and Mariah furthering their romance on company time. What they did on their own time was entirely up to them, he told himself righteously. But when it came to Midnight Sons…that was another matter.

"You seem to think I'm interested in her," Duke said angrily.

Christian's hands tightened around the coffee mug. He didn't want to get into this.

"Are you?" Ben wanted to know, his eyes eager.

"No," Duke growled. "I've got a girlfriend in Fairbanks I was planning to see."

"You've got a girlfriend in Fairbanks?" Ben repeated. "Since when?"

"Since now."

Christian wasn't sure he should believe him. "What about the other day when I saw you and Mariah kissing?"

Ben's eyes widened. "You saw Duke and Mariah kissing?"

"Sure did." Whenever Christian thought about walking into the office and finding them in each other's arms, he felt a fresh wave of fury. "Right in the middle of the day, too."

Duke knotted his hands into fists. "I *wasn't* kissing Mariah."

Christian wasn't going to sit there and let one of his pilots lie to him. "I saw you with my own eyes!"

Duke shifted his weight from one booted foot to the other. "Since it's so important to you, I'll say it again. I *wasn't* kissing Mariah."

Christian glared at the man. This was a bold-faced lie; he knew what he'd seen.

Duke lowered his gaze and muttered, "*She* was kissing *me*."

Chapter 2

August 1996

ON SATURDAY Mariah was at the airfield well before the allotted time of departure, eager to see Tracy again and make their plans for the week. They'd already decided to take a glacier tour and visit some of the other sights in and around Anchorage.

Fierce, dark clouds puckered the sky, filling the morning with shadows and gloom. Not a promising start to her vacation.

"You ready?" Christian marched past her toward the two-seater Luscombe. It was the smallest plane in the Midnight Sons fleet and used the least often.

Mariah picked up her suitcase and hurried after him. "I want you to know how much I appreciate this," she said, holding on to the case with both hands. She didn't understand why Christian had insisted on doing this himself, especially when it was so obvious that he considered it an imposition.

Because of the heavy suitcase, she couldn't keep pace with

him. Eventually he seemed to realize this. He glanced at her over his shoulder, and then, without a word, turned back and took the suitcase from her hands.

"What did you pack in here, anyway? Rocks?"

She didn't bother to answer.

When they reached the plane, Christian helped her inside. He stowed her bag, then joined her in the cockpit. She was surprised by how small and intimate the space was; their shoulders touched as Christian worked the switches and revved the engine.

Mariah snapped her seat belt in place and gazed anxiously at the threatening sky. She wondered if she should tell Christian she wasn't all that keen on flying. She found small planes especially difficult. Give her a Boeing 767 any day of the week over a tiny, little Luscombe.

For the sake of peace, she gritted her teeth and said nothing. No need to hand him further ammunition.

The ever-darkening sky didn't bode well. Mariah noted that Christian was watching it closely. He radioed Fairbanks and wrote down the necessary weather information.

"Is there any chance we'll run into a storm?" she asked once they'd started to taxi down the gravel runway.

She expected him to make light of her concern, but he didn't. "According to the flight controller, we should be able to fly above the worst of it. Don't worry, I'll get you to Fairbanks on time."

Or die trying, Mariah mused darkly. She gritted her teeth again and held on for dear life as the single-engine furiously increased its speed. Soon they were roaring down the runway, and at what seemed the last possible second, the plane's nose angled toward the sky and the wheels left the ground.

As soon as they were airborne, Mariah relaxed slightly. The flight would take the better part of an hour, possibly a bit longer, depending on the winds.

Within a few minutes, they were swallowed up by the unfriendly clouds. Mariah couldn't see two feet in front of them, but that might have been just as well.

Trying to relieve her tension, she closed her eyes.

"If you feel yourself getting sick," Christian said, "let me know."

"I'm fine," she assured him.

"Your eyes are closed."

"I know." Her fingers gripped the edge of the seat cushion as she concentrated on breathing evenly.

"Why?"

"Because I don't want to look!" she snapped.

Christian chuckled and seemed to enjoy her discomfort. "I haven't crashed in more than a year," he teased. "But now that you mention it, I'm probably due for a big one."

Suddenly the plane began to pitch first to one side, then the other.

"Don't, *please,*" Mariah begged.

"I'm not doing this on purpose," Christian muttered.

Mariah opened her eyes and saw that he was actually struggling to maintain control. "I'm trying to get us above the clouds. Don't worry, everything's well in hand."

The plane pitched sharply to the right and she swallowed a gasp. Although she'd flown in small planes a number of times since coming to work for Midnight Sons, she remained nervous about it—more than ever now, when they were flying directly into a storm.

"Are you all right?" Christian asked a minute later.

"Just fly the plane," she said over the noise of the engine.

"You're pale as a sheet," he said.

"Stop worrying about me."

"Listen," he returned, "I'm not going to be able to fly the plane *and* revive you."

"If I pass out—" she squeezed her eyes shut "—don't worry about me."

The plane heaved. She gasped aloud and covered her face with both hands.

"Mariah," Christian said gently. "Everything will be fine in a few minutes. Trust me." He patted her arm reassuringly.

Usually when he spoke to her, Christian was impatient or sharp. Half the time she wasn't even sure what crime she was supposed to have committed. But for reasons she'd probably never understand, today, when she needed it most, he'd chosen to reveal this softer side.

Judging by the feel of the plane, Mariah knew they were increasing altitude. Within minutes they'd be above the squall and everything would be fine. Just as he'd promised.

"You can look now," Christian told her.

She splayed her fingers and peeked through. Bright sunlight greeted her, and she sighed deeply, relaxing in her seat. The weather couldn't be more perfect.

They traveled in silence for a while.

"Does your boyfriend know you don't like to fly?" Christian's question startled her.

"My boyfriend?" she asked, genuinely perplexed until she remembered that he'd seen her with Duke.

"In case you're interested, lover boy made quite a stink when I told him he wouldn't be flying you into Fairbanks." The disapproval was back in Christian's voice.

Mariah looked out the side window. "No matter what you think, Duke and I are not involved."

"Yeah, that's what he said, too." The skepticism in his voice was plain.

"It's the truth," she insisted.

"Duke claims *you* kissed *him*."

He appeared to be waiting for her to deny or confirm the statement. "I did—in a manner of speaking."

Christian snorted a laugh. "I'll say. You seem to forget I walked in on the two of you with your lips locked."

"It wasn't like that," Mariah said heatedly. "I'd been on the phone with Tracy—"

"On company time?"

"Yes," she admitted reluctantly. He could dock her pay if he wanted.

"Go on," he encouraged.

"Tracy and Duke don't get along."

Christian laughed again. "That's putting it mildly."

"She, Tracy, thought it would be fun if I kissed Duke and said it was from her, and that's what I did. It was all teasing—a joke."

Christian didn't comment.

"Do you believe me?" she asked. It was important that he do so. They had their differences, but trust was a vital factor in any relationship, whether it was work or personal.

"Yeah," Christian admitted grudgingly, "I guess I do. But you should know something in case you have any, uh, romantic feelings for Duke. He's got a girlfriend in Fairbanks. And he swore to me he's a one-woman man—one at a time, anyway."

"It doesn't matter to me how many girlfriends Duke's got."

Although Mariah was surprised. This was the first she'd heard of Duke being romantically involved with anyone. But then, he was a private person and not inclined to share such things with her.

Just when she'd finally relaxed enough to be comfortable, they approached Fairbanks. As soon as the plane descended into the clouds, Mariah stiffened.

"Hey, you aren't going to tense up on me again, are you?"

"Yes, I am." No point in denying it. She closed her eyes as her fingers reshaped the upholstery.

"Don't worry, we'll be down in no time." He was busy after that, communicating with the tower and manipulating the controls.

True to his word, they touched down in a textbook-perfect landing a few minutes later and taxied to the hangar where Midnight Sons kept a truck.

Neither of them seemed ready to leave the plane. "That wasn't so bad now, was it?" Christian asked, and his gaze settled on her. All at once the atmosphere was charged with excitement. Never had Mariah been so physically aware of him, and he seemed to be experiencing the same reaction to her.

"You're right. The flight wasn't bad at all," she said, realizing how breathless she sounded. "Thank you," she murmured.

She meant to open the door and climb out, but Mariah found that her body refused to function. Suddenly Christian leaned close, so close the distance between their mouths became too slight to measure.

She wasn't sure what to think, what to do. She stopped breathing and was convinced Christian did, too. Gradually he eased forward until his mouth grazed hers. His touch was tender. Light. And all too brief.

The effect was, somehow, more devastating than if they'd engaged in a lengthy, passionate kiss.

Christian reared back as if she'd slapped him.

Mariah savored the exquisite sensation of that kiss. This was what she'd wanted from the first, what she'd been longing for.

Christian opened the door just then, and a rush of air instantly cooled the interior of the plane.

Mariah didn't wait for him to come around and help her down. She did notice that he couldn't seem to get her luggage out of the plane fast enough.

Once they were inside the truck and headed for the terminal, Christian cleared his throat. "I don't want you to attach any... importance to what happened back there," he said brusquely.

"I...won't."

"I didn't mean to do that. It...well, it just happened."

Regret. He had to go and ruin the most perfect moment of her life with regret.

STUPID, STUPID, STUPID. Christian didn't know what in the world had possessed him to kiss Mariah. Four days later, and he couldn't keep from dwelling on their last moments alone in the plane.

Although he'd analyzed the kiss over and over, he couldn't make sense of it. Not once in the entire year Mariah had been employed by Midnight Sons had the thought of kissing her even entered his mind.

Yet in those awkward moments after they'd landed and taxied off the Fairbanks runway, Christian could think of nothing else. The temptation had become too much for him.

Nothing like complicating his life—and he had no one to

blame but himself. True, he'd made an effort to put it behind them, but only a blind man would've missed the stars in Mariah's eyes.

That was the trouble with women. You kissed them a time or two, and they seemed to think it *meant* something. Well, he wanted to make one thing clear right now. He was not—repeat, not—interested in Mariah Douglas. He didn't even like the woman. If he could find a legal means of getting her completely out of his life, he'd leap at the opportunity.

"You aren't looking too happy," Sawyer announced as he walked past Christian's desk to his own.

"I'm fine!" he snapped. The last thing he wanted was for Sawyer to learn about that stupid kiss.

"If I didn't know better, I'd say you missed Mariah."

Christian snickered loudly. "Have you noticed how well everything's gone this week?" he asked. He hoped to convince Sawyer that the office had run like clockwork without her. Maybe, just maybe, Sawyer would see reason and agree to do away with the position.

"It's been hectic," Sawyer argued.

"Well, we've been busier than usual," Christian conceded. "But have you stopped to notice how peaceful it is around here? And how we've had no major problems?"

Sawyer nodded.

Perhaps this wasn't going to be as difficult as Christian had assumed. "We don't need Mariah."

His brother sent him a disgusted look. "Don't need Mariah? Sure, we've managed without her, but I have to tell you, this place has been hopping. We're getting more business all the time. If everything's running smoothly, then it's because Mariah oiled the gears before she left. I don't know about you, little brother, but I'm counting the hours until she returns."

Christian cursed under his breath. He was counting the hours himself, but not for the same reason.

"Don't need Mariah?" Sawyer repeated in the same tone of disbelief he'd used a minute earlier. "Tell that to Abbey and the kids. I've been late for dinner every night this week. I don't like working this hard. I've got a wife and family I'd like to see once in a while."

The phone pealed, and Sawyer glared at Christian, who was concentrating on tallying a row of figures. "Since you've got so much free time on your hands, you can answer that."

Christian scowled and reached for the telephone.

"DUKE'S GOT A GIRLFRIEND?" Tracy Santiago asked Mariah as they sat outside the Kenai Lodge and enjoyed the sunshine. "You've got to be kidding." Tracy didn't bother to disguise her shock. "What woman would put up with that chauvinistic character for more than five minutes?"

"I don't know. I'm just repeating what Christian told me. It's funny, though," she said, thinking out loud. "Duke's never mentioned anyone."

Tracy raised her face to the sun and grumbled something Mariah couldn't make out.

"Duke's not so bad."

Tracy straightened and sipped her margarita. "The man's a public nuisance. Let's change the subject, okay? He has a bad effect on my blood pressure."

Mariah lay back in the lawn chair. They'd spent four full days sightseeing. Every minute of every day had been full, and Mariah was exhausted; so was Tracy.

Now was the time to relax. Mariah didn't want to think about Hard Luck—and particularly not about Christian. This was her vacation, and she was determined to make the most of it.

"Mmm, this is the life," Tracy said, closing her eyes and smiling into the sun. "A woman could get used to this."

Mariah smiled, too. Although most of their communication had been by phone and mail, she knew her friend all too well. Tracy would soon grow bored lazing around a swimming pool; before a week was past, she wouldn't be able to stand the inactivity. She'd be eager to get back to her job.

"You surprise me," Tracy said out of the blue.

"I do?" Mariah asked. "How?"

Tracy grinned sheepishly. "Well, when your parents first contacted me, they described you as this delicate hothouse flower who didn't have a clue what she was letting herself in for."

"That's how they see me." It saddened Mariah to admit that. Her family's attitude was the very reason she'd left Seattle. They considered her helpless and inept, and if she'd stayed much longer she might have come to believe it herself.

"You really love it in Hard Luck, don't you?"

"Oh, yes. This has been the most..." Mariah hesitated, unsure how to explain what her year in the Arctic community had been like. She felt proud of her own ability to survive in difficult surroundings, especially during the winter when the temperature dropped to forty below. True, there were times she'd been lonely and confused. Depressed. At other times she'd felt a new confidence, a newly developed sense of self that was unlike anything she'd ever experienced. After a year in the Arctic, she knew she was capable of handling any situation. She'd learned to trust her own judgment and to take pride in her achievements.

But her nonrelationship with Christian continued to baffle her, although her attraction to him grew more potent with each passing month. Unfortunately he didn't seem to share her feelings. But then again, perhaps he did… The kiss gave her hope.

"When you told me you'd decided to stay in Hard Luck, I admired you," Tracy said with a thoughtful look. "I admired you for taking charge of your life and for not being afraid to do something risky."

Mariah squirmed under her praise. "It's no more than the other women have done—Abbey and Karen and Lanni. Bethany Ross and Sally Henderson."

"You're good friends with them, aren't you?"

"It's like they're part of my family," Mariah said. But better. The women who'd come to Hard Luck were a close-knit group, out of necessity but also genuine liking. They relied on and supported each other in every possible way. In the dead of winter, when sunlight disappeared and spirits fell, it was the women who brought joy and laughter to the community. She'd known these women for only a year, but her friendships with them were closer now than the friendships she'd left behind.

"What do you miss most?" Tracy asked next.

That question took some consideration. She wouldn't lie; there were certainly aspects of city life that she yearned for, services and stores and all kinds of things that weren't available in Hard Luck.

Things like first-run movies, her favorite junk food, shopping malls… But how much did any of that *really* matter?

"What do I miss most?" Mariah repeated slowly. "I'm thinking, Trace…"

"That, my friend, is answer enough," the attorney said. She sounded almost wistful.

CHRISTIAN SET ASIDE the murder mystery he was reading and forcefully expelled his breath. He couldn't seem to concentrate, although the author was one of his favorites.

Tomorrow evening, Mariah would be back, and frankly he dreaded her return. Despite his warning, he was sure she'd be foolish enough to put some stock in that stupid kiss. He tried to put her out of his mind, something he'd been struggling to do all week.

Mariah wasn't the only woman who'd been on his mind lately. Funny that he'd be thinking of Allison Reynolds now. But again and again he found himself comparing his current secretary to the one who got away.

Every time the statuesque blonde drifted into his thoughts, Christian felt his heart work like a blacksmith's bellows.

In the year since she'd gone home to Seattle, he'd never called. More fool he. When they first met, they'd dated— nothing serious, just a couple of dinners while he'd been in Seattle conducting business and setting up job interviews. He remembered those evenings with Allison in a haze of pleasure.

He was due to go back to the Northwest, strictly for business purposes, anytime now. He'd been discussing the trip with Sawyer just that morning. Generally they took turns going to Seattle to arrange for supplies, but with Abbey pregnant and the kids getting ready to head back to school, Sawyer wasn't eager to leave Hard Luck. Christian was.

For one thing, he'd have a chance to visit his mother, who

lived in Vancouver, British Columbia. He had a special bond with Ellen. While Charles and Sawyer were more like their father in looks and temperament, Christian had always been closer to his mother.

As a boy, he'd spent eighteen months with her in England. The years before the separation had been difficult for his parents. Christian, only ten at the time, hadn't understood what was happening to his family.

All he knew was that his mother was desperately unhappy. More than once he'd found her weeping, and in his own way had attempted to comfort her. When she told him she was leaving Alaska, Christian had known immediately that he should go with her. His mother would need him, he thought—and she had.

Saying goodbye to his father and brothers was hard, and he'd missed them far more than he'd dreamed possible. In the beginning, he'd enjoyed living in England, but that hadn't lasted long. He missed Alaska. He missed his home, his brothers and the life he'd always known, and he suspected his mother did, as well.

After a year and a half, they'd flown back to Hard Luck, and for a time, a very brief time, they'd been a family again, and happy.

Christian had never fully understood what had shattered that fragile joy, but he realized Catherine Fletcher was somehow responsible. She was gone now and his father was, too. A few years ago Ellen had remarried; her second husband was a wonderful man who shared her passion for literature. She'd moved to his home in British Columbia.

Ellen had come to Hard Luck twice in the past year. Nevertheless, Christian intended to visit her and her husband,

Robert, in Vancouver. He knew she was delighted with her new grandchildren, and if he could coordinate the flights, he might be able to bring Scott and Susan with him. A nice way to end their summer vacation. And Abbey and Sawyer could have a second honeymoon.

While he was in Seattle, Christian decided, he'd look up Allison Reynolds. The thought cheered him. Yes, that was what he'd do. He'd give Allison a call and they'd go out on the town.

Content, Christian picked up the novel and started reading again. Then it struck him. It seemed unfair—and a bit unrealistic—to arrive in Seattle unannounced and expect Allison to be free.

Maybe he should call her now. Besides, talking to a woman who was as close to perfect as any human had a right to be would lift his spirits.

In another moment, he'd dug out her phone number.

The phone rang three times. "Hello."

It was Allison. She sounded…silky. Yes, that was the word for her voice—silky. Soft and a little breathless. A man could get light-headed just listening to her.

"Allison, this is Christian O'Halloran."

"Christian!" Her elevated voice said she was pleased to hear from him. "Don't tell me you're in Seattle? Why, I was thinking about you the other day."

Forget light-headed, he was almost ecstatic. "You were?" Life was good. Very good.

"Are you in town?" Her voice was definitely silky.

"No, but I will be."

"When?"

He couldn't believe how eager she sounded. "I'm not sure

yet. I, uh, thought I'd arrange my schedule around yours. Are you going to be available this month?"

"I'm available any time you want." Her voice dipped in a playful whisper. Christian's chest tightened. This was one way to get Mariah out of his mind.

EARLY SATURDAY EVENING, Christian flew into Fairbanks to meet Mariah. He'd dreaded this moment all week, but now that it was upon him, he discovered that his earlier anxiety had vanished. He credited Allison with this. Knowing that a week from now he'd be spending time with the most beautiful woman he'd ever seen left him with a euphoric sense of well-being.

As he waited at the gate for Mariah's flight, he realized, somewhat to his surprise, that he was looking forward to seeing her again.

Sawyer was right; the office had been hectic without her to run interference, take calls, organize schedules and perform the dozens of other tasks she'd taken on. He suspected he'd become accustomed to having her around—and truth be told, he'd actually found himself missing her once or twice.

The gate where she was due to land was directly across from a gift shop. Deciding this might be a good time to mend fences, Christian wandered inside. The instant he saw the small jade figurine he knew it was the perfect welcome-back gift. No larger than a child's building block, the green jade had been skillfully sculpted into a bear, gripping a salmon between its teeth.

On impulse Christian bought it, then stuffed it in his pocket.

The flight landed on schedule, and Christian watched the passengers file out one by one. Mariah stepped out of the jetway and glanced around expectantly, her arms filled with packages. She looked tanned and rested. When her gaze happened on him, she hesitated, as if uncertain of her reception.

Christian moved forward. "Welcome home," he said, grinning.

"Hi. I wasn't sure you'd be here."

He chose to ignore the statement. "How was your week?"

"Fantastic. Tracy and I had a fabulous time." She shifted the packages in her arms. "I brought everyone a small gift," she said, and lines of happiness crinkled at the edges of her eyes. "Even you."

"That's funny, because I got you a gift, too. Just to say we're glad you're back." He took some of the packages out of her arms and together they walked toward the baggage carousel.

"You bought me something?" She sounded incredulous.

Perhaps he should give it to her now, seeing that he'd gone out of his way to make her life miserable for the past twelve months. He regretted his earlier behavior. Mariah wasn't so bad—once he'd gotten used to working with her. Too bad that had taken a year. "Have you had dinner?"

"Dinner," she repeated. She frowned and looked at him. "No. Are you feeling all right?"

Christian chuckled. "I'm feeling just fine."

When they'd retrieved her suitcase, he loaded that, along with her carry-on packages, into the truck Midnight Sons kept at the airport.

He was turning over a new leaf as far as his relationship with Mariah was concerned. True, she was still an irritant, but he was tired of fighting a losing battle. Sawyer thought she was wonderful, and so did almost everyone else. This week without her—and the prospect of seeing Allison—had done wonders for his tolerance.

"You're taking me to dinner?" she asked when he pulled into his favorite restaurant, the Sourdough Café. The ambience wasn't great, but the food more than made up for it.

"Sure," he said, and climbed out of the cab.

He led the way inside and selected a booth. Mariah sat across from him. Now that he'd set his prejudices aside, he realized she was a pleasant dinner companion. He laughed wholeheartedly at the tales of her escapades in Anchorage and carefully studied her photographs, which she'd had developed the day before. The most spectacular photos were of the boat tour she'd taken in Prince William Sound. Sometimes Christian forgot how impressive the glaciers were.

Mariah had captured the deep blue color of the ice with the sun glinting off the canyon's high walls. The marine-life photos—a pod of whales, several species of seals and a wide variety of birds—were as good as any he'd seen.

"These are great pictures," he said enthusiastically.

She blushed with pleasure. "I'm sort of an amateur photographer."

He'd worked with her for more than a year and hadn't known that.

Their meal arrived, and the conversation slowed while they feasted on thick roast-beef sandwiches served on sourdough rolls.

It wasn't until they were back at the airport that Christian remembered the jade bear in his pocket.

He parked the truck and turned off the ignition.

"Thank you for dinner," she said shyly.

"I'd like it if you and I could start over, Mariah," he began.

He didn't want her to place any special significance on his words, but simply to take his offer at face value.

"I'd like that, too."

"I don't know how we got off on the wrong foot."

"Me, neither."

"This last week—with you gone…" He hesitated, not sure how to continue, not wanting to say too much.

"Yes?" she asked, her voice hushed.

"It didn't seem…right."

If she was going to gloat, the time was now. To her credit all she said was, "I've missed Hard Luck and my friends. I…missed you."

He wouldn't go so far as to admit he'd missed *her,* but she'd been on his mind. Removing the plastic sack from his flight jacket, he handed it to her. "I saw this at the gift shop in the airport and thought of you."

She carefully peeled away the tissue paper and gasped softly when she uncovered the tiny statue.

"Christian," she breathed in awe. "It's lovely. Thank you so much. I got you a silk scarf—nothing much. I read that the early pilots needed them because oil used to spray into the open cockpit. The pilots cleaned their goggles with the scarves." She stopped abruptly, as if she'd noticed that she was chattering, and stared down at the jade bear.

"I wanted to apologize for being kind of a jerk the past few months," he said. "This last week, with you away, I could see what a difference you've made at the office. You've come a long way since you first moved to Hard Luck, Mariah."

She looked up at him and to his astonishment, her eyes were bright with tears.

Tears.

"I'll be the first to admit we've had our moments, but you've turned out to be an excellent secretary. You're an important part of Midnight Sons."

The tears spilled over, rolling down the sides of her face.

Christian wanted to tell her that the last thing he'd expected was emotion. He would have, too, if his mind hadn't been dominated by a more compelling thought. All at once, completely against his will, he experienced the burning need to kiss Mariah Douglas again.

Chapter
3

CHRISTIAN WAS ABOUT to kiss her. Mariah read the longing in his eyes and felt a rush of anticipation. Her hand closed around the precious jade figurine as she realized that her patience with Christian had finally paid dividends. She was about to receive her reward.

Her eyes drifted shut as she awaited his touch. She'd dreamed of this, of exchanging tender kisses, followed by passionate ones. Now the dream was about to become reality.

Mariah waited for what seemed far too long. Nothing happened. Flustered, she opened her eyes and looked at him. To her utter embarrassment, she saw Christian sitting with his hands locked around the truck's steering wheel. His jaw was clamped tightly, his mouth tense.

Mortified, Mariah swallowed and gathered her composure. Christian refused to kiss her? Well, so be it. She would resign herself to his cowardice. And her own disappointment.

Still, she had to acknowledge that he'd made progress in

the week she'd been away. He'd apologized for his childish behavior toward her and bought her a gift. For now that was enough.

The flight into Hard Luck seemed to go quickly. At first, the nonkissing incident left them both feeling awkward and ill at ease, but after a year of working in the same office, they were familiar enough with each other that they became comfortable companions once again.

By the time they made their descent into Hard Luck, they were chatting amicably, like people with a number of mutual friends and shared interests.

After Christian had parked and secured the aircraft, he piled her suitcase and other packages in the company truck. "It's good to be home," Mariah whispered with a heartfelt sigh of appreciation. Her week away had been enjoyable and relaxing, but she was grateful to get back to her normal life.

Although she insisted it wasn't necessary, Christian drove her to her small log cabin on the outskirts of town. He kept the engine running as he leaped out of the cab and carried in her suitcase. He stopped abruptly just inside the door.

"Is something wrong?" she asked nervously, stepping up behind him.

"I'm surprised, that's all," he answered after a thoughtful pause.

"Surprised?"

"You've done a terrific job with this place." Before she could ask what he meant, he elaborated. "Decorating the old cabin. It's really nice. Downright homey."

"This *is* my home, Christian." She'd worked hard to make her space both livable and pleasing to the eye. That meant more than adding lace curtains to the windows. One of the first things she'd done was get rid of the chunky, oddly shaped furniture that came with the cabin. She'd replaced it, a piece at a time, with furniture that suited her needs—not the easiest task when you lived in the Arctic. She'd bought some chairs from Matt, had her bed shipped up from home, ordered fabric and a small table and a replica nineteenth-century oil lamp from catalogs. She had an eye for color and detail and was genuinely pleased with what she'd managed to achieve in her cramped quarters.

Christian set the suitcase down in the center of the room, on the green-and-rose braided rug she'd purchased on a trip to Fairbanks six months ago. She'd also splurged on a quilt that picked up the same colors.

"Thank you again," she said, smiling. "I had a lovely evening. I appreciate your flying in for me, the dinner and… everything else."

He shrugged, looking uncomfortable with her gratitude. "I'll see you Monday morning," he said a bit gruffly.

"Monday," she echoed.

As Christian walked past her, he paused and casually kissed her on the lips. He'd gone another couple of steps before he appeared to realize what he'd done. He came to a sudden halt, shook his head as if to clear it, then continued on to the truck.

MONDAY MORNING, when Mariah entered the office, she was greeted with chaos. Two phone lines rang simultaneously and the fax had started transmitting data. Christian was frantically searching through the filing cabinet, demanding to know where she'd hidden the Freemont account.

Concealing a smile, she located the file, answered the

phone and dealt with the fax. It did her heart good to know she'd been missed.

"Welcome back," Sawyer told her two hours later. It was the first quiet moment that morning.

"Was it this hectic all week?" Mariah had barely had a chance to take off her sweater. The phone hadn't stopped ringing. Pilots had been coming and going every few minutes, and they all seemed to need something—a scheduling change, a form, some information. It hadn't helped that Christian was having a crisis of his own over the Freemont account. He spent much of the morning ranting and raving, unable to locate various crucial documents. Every time, it was Mariah who quietly and efficiently silenced him by supplying whatever he needed.

"We pretty much handled everything ourselves," Sawyer answered, "but we're sure glad you're back."

"You can say that again," Christian seconded, holding his hand over the mouthpiece. Sawyer glanced at his brother and then at Mariah. He considered them shrewdly.

Mariah sat down and turned on her computer. The hard drive had begun its familiar hum when Christian ended his telephone conversation and approached her desk.

"I'm going to need you to make travel arrangements for me," he told her.

"Of course." Christian would be traveling? Somewhat surprised, she reached for a pencil and pad.

"I'll be visiting my mother in British Columbia and then stopping in Seattle."

"That won't be any problem. How long will you be away?" Picking up the small calendar on her desk, she waited for him to give her the dates.

"Say, ten days from Friday—" he pointed to the end of that week "—until Sunday of the following week. And I'd like reservations at our usual hotel in Seattle. Oh, and Scott and Susan will be traveling with me as far as Vancouver. I'll go on to Seattle Monday or Tuesday, then back to Vancouver and home."

"I'll see to everything this afternoon," Mariah promised.

"While you're at it, could you get me the names of a couple of five-star Seattle restaurants?" Christian asked.

"Restaurants." She made a notation on her pad. "I know of a number in the downtown area that cater to businessmen." And Tracy would be happy to give her suggestions, too.

"I wasn't thinking of a business dinner," Christian said matter-of-factly. "I'm going to be seeing a…friend while I'm in town. A good friend."

A few minutes later, Mariah was on the phone with the airline when she happened to overhear the two brothers talking.

"A friend?" Sawyer asked.

"Yeah, Allison Reynolds." Even from across the room, she saw Christian's eyes brighten with what could only be described as excitement. "You might remember her," he added.

Mariah felt as if she'd been slapped. No one needed to tell her who Allison Reynolds was—the secretary Mariah had replaced.

"You're going to be seeing Allison?" Sawyer asked, lowering his voice, obviously afraid Mariah would hear. Well, it was too late; she'd already heard.

"Yeah," Christian murmured, preoccupied with a fax. "I talked to her the other night and promised to call her back as soon as I knew when I'd be arriving. I'm hoping I'll convince her to give Hard Luck a second chance."

Sawyer held on to his pencil with both hands and darted a look toward Mariah. "Do you think that's wise?"

"Why isn't it?" Christian asked, his voice equally low. He set aside the fax and confronted his brother openly. "She's beautiful, witty, charming and we'd be fortunate to have her. Let's talk about this later, all right?"

Sawyer frowned.

Mariah couldn't believe her ears. Christian actually planned on luring her replacement to Hard Luck. Furthermore, he expected *her* to make the arrangements!

"MOM, SHOULD I PACK my Barbie playhouse?" Susan called from her bedroom.

Abbey took the towel from the dryer, folded it and set it on the washer. "No, sweetheart. You can only take one suitcase each. You won't have room for all your Barbie things."

"You know my mother's going to spoil those kids, don't you?" Sawyer said, leaning against the laundry-room door.

"I know. Scott and Susan will be impossible to live with by the time they return."

"But we'll have an entire week to ourselves." Sawyer waggled his eyebrows suggestively. "I sincerely hope you intend to spoil *me* next week."

Abbey kissed her husband and nuzzled her nose against his. "I'll see what I can do."

Sawyer's eyes gleamed. "Barbie and Ken will play while the kids are away."

"Sawyer!"

Her husband chuckled and slid his arms around her waist. "It's too bad Christian will be gone, too, because that means I won't be able to get away much myself."

"We'll manage," Abbey assured him.

"A second honeymoon," Sawyer murmured, grinning provocatively. "I don't know if I'm ready for this. I still haven't recovered from the first one."

"You seem to have done pretty well for yourself!"

"Mom, Dad, you'll remember to feed Eagle Catcher, won't you?" Scott asked, poking his head into the laundry room.

Her son seemed genuinely concerned, as if he wasn't sure he should trust them with his much-loved friend, even if it was only for ten days. And even if he'd once been Sawyer's dog.

"We'll remember," she said.

"It's important, Mom," Scott insisted. "This is just the second time we've been separated, and Eagle Catcher might worry. I had a long talk with him, but I'm not sure he understood."

"I promise we'll remember," Sawyer told him solemnly.

"Good." Scott looked relieved and disappeared.

Sawyer gently patted Abbey's protruding stomach. "This time alone will be good for us," he told her, his eyes serious. "After the baby arrives, everything will change."

Abbey knew her husband was right, but it would be a wonderful kind of change. So far the pregnancy had caused her almost no trouble, physically or emotionally. No morning sickness, no drastic mood swings. She loved Scott and Susan with a ferocity only a mother could understand, but their pregnancies had drained her. It was different with Sawyer's baby. The comfort of his love, the assurance that he'd move heaven and earth on her behalf, eased her worries.

"Mom!" Susan screeched from the hallway. "Should I pack my Bible?"

Abbey sighed and pressed her forehead against Sawyer's shoulder. "I'd better go supervise those two." She called to the kids that she'd be there in a minute.

"I'll finish up here," Sawyer said, gathering the rest of the towels from the dryer.

"Sawyer."

When he turned around, she leaned forward and kissed him with a hunger they generally reserved for the bedroom.

A low rumble of arousal came from her husband as she started to leave. Sawyer caught her hand. "What was that all about?"

She offered him a saucy smile. "Just a sample of what's available later."

"How much later?"

Abbey smiled again and stroked his face. "As soon as the kids are gone, you and I can pick up where that left off." She walked out of the laundry room, but not before she noticed Sawyer staring at his watch, calculating the hours before they'd be alone.

ALLISON REYNOLDS was as beautiful as Christian remembered. Even more so. Heads turned when they walked into the five-star restaurant. He'd never realized how much a beautiful woman could improve a man's image and raise his self-esteem. He had no doubt that he was the envy of every man there. Any vague, nagging thoughts about superficial values or shallow choices were easy enough to suppress.

He hadn't been in the Seattle hotel five minutes before he made a point of phoning Allison. He'd made another phone call, too, but this one was to Hard Luck. He'd had to call Mariah regarding a variety of subjects, all of them business-related.

It might have been his imagination, but her greeting had seemed decidedly cool. He wasn't sure what to make of her chilly tone, but whatever the problem, Sawyer could handle it. As for him, he was taking a well-deserved break from the office. He was willing to admit privately that his business dealings in Seattle, however necessary, were a pretext; his primary reason for coming here had to do with the beauty on his arm.

"I have a reservation for seven o'clock," Christian informed the maître d'.

Allison smiled up at him sweetly, and it was all he could do to pull his gaze away. He'd been mildly surprised by her dress; short and slinky, it revealed every curve of her luscious body. He hadn't been able to take his eyes off her. But the front was deeply cut, and that appeared to bring her a lot of unwanted attention—unwanted, at least, by him. He was the one buying her dinner, and he wasn't all that pleased to be sharing her, even vicariously, with anyone else.

"This way," the man said, tucking two menus under his arm. The restaurant had been one of Mariah's recommendations, and she'd chosen well. He'd have to thank her when he returned. The dim interior suited him perfectly. Lights from the waterfront shimmered on the glass-smooth surface of Elliott Bay. A ferry sailed in the distance, its lights blazing.

"This place is great," Allison said once they were seated.

"My secretary chose it." He had to stop himself from telling Allison about Mariah. The stories would have them both in stitches, but he didn't want to spend the evening thinking about Mariah. Although her lack of friendliness earlier today continued to nag at him...

Allison leaned forward. "I'm so glad you found someone

else to work for you. Personally I can't imagine anyone lasting more than a day or two in that desolation."

Desolation. The Arctic? Hard Luck? Why, it was one of the most beautiful places on earth! Give him home any day of the week over the smog and traffic of the big city. Even a city as pleasing to the eye as Seattle. The noise alone had kept him awake most of the night. Street sounds had reverberated from the cluttered avenues and echoed against the skyscrapers. And in his expensive hotel, he'd heard the elevator and laughter in the halls and the TV next door. No wonder he felt suddenly tired and let down.

Christian roused himself. "What would you like?" he asked, studying the menu. He made his choice quickly. Blackened salmon, one of his favorites.

Allison's huge blue eyes met his. "I'm watching my diet, you know."

She seemed to be waiting for him to tell her she was perfect as she was and that dieting would be ridiculous. Christian didn't. He'd never understood what it was about women and their weight. They seemed to feel it was a topic men found fascinating. Well, he, for one, found it boring. Nor did he think someone like Allison needed to fish for compliments.

"I'll have a salad," she said sweetly. "No dressing. You'd never guess how many grams of fat there are in salad dressing. Someone told me just the other day that it would be less fattening to eat a hot fudge sundae than to put dressing on lettuce. Can you imagine?"

Christian smiled benignly.

The waiter came for their order, and Allison took five minutes to give hers. She explained precisely how she wanted her salad. He'd never met a woman who requested sliced cu-

cumbers on the side. And that wasn't all—she had to have her radishes cut a certain way and only on one half of the salad. He was impressed that the waiter could write it all down and keep a straight face.

While Allison was giving her detailed instructions, the memory of his dinner with Mariah at the Sourdough Café came to mind. There'd been no talk of salad ingredients with her. Nor did she drag him into ridiculous conversations about grams of fat and hot fudge sundaes.

Unfortunately the dinner conversation didn't improve. Allison discussed the color of her fingernail polish in great detail. When Christian introduced another topic, she found a way of immediately bringing it back to herself and telling him about a new skin cream on the market.

It became something of a game, watching her manipulate the conversation to reflect her own interests—such as they were. Not once did she ask about the people she'd met on her brief trip to Hard Luck.

"Oh, I've got a new job now," she said casually when he mentioned her old one. "Actually this is the second job I've had in the past year."

Christian nodded in seeming interest, and she went on, "When I met you I was working for Pierce. He was a friend of my old boyfriend, Cary. But after I got back from Hawaii and went to see you, Pierce said he needed someone he could depend on. He didn't like me taking vacation time." She pursed her lips slightly. "He didn't even pay me for my days off."

"How long did you work for Pierce?"

"About a month."

"A month. You didn't have any vacation time due you."

"That's what Pierce said. Only he sounded really mad. You know, some men aren't very nice. I worked for him one full month and his benefits were lousy."

Christian found it difficult to follow Allison's conversation from that point forward. Several times she brought up names he didn't know and didn't care to know. Instead, his thoughts drifted to the year before, when he'd first met Allison. It astonished him that he hadn't seen through her then. The woman wasn't interested in working; she was looking for "benefits," and it seemed to him she wasn't just talking about paid holidays. She wanted a free ride.

When at last they'd finished their meal and were walking out of the restaurant, Christian was once again aware of several envious stares. Only this time it didn't raise his self-esteem. Sure, he'd enjoyed his blackened salmon, and the Washington-made wine had been some of the best he'd tasted, but he'd rather have eaten at Ben's or the Sourdough Café. As for his dinner companion—the truth was, he'd become disenchanted.

Later, when he dropped Allison off in front of her apartment, she flexed her long nails over his thigh. "Would you like to come up for a nightcap?" she asked. Her beautiful eyes invited him for more.

"Not tonight."

He helped her out of the car and walked her to her door.

"When will I see you again?" Her voice rolled from her lips like silk.

Christian had made the mistake of letting her know his schedule. "I'll call you," he said.

She gave him a hurt-little-girl pout. Her eyes rounded with a practiced look of disappointment. "You will phone me, won't you, Chris? I'd be so unhappy if you didn't."

Christian couldn't get away fast enough. They'd be raising huskies in hell before he'd agree to spend a second evening with the likes of Allison Reynolds.

After returning to his hotel room, Christian sat on the edge of the bed. It was hard to believe he'd been so blinded by her earlier. Because he was restless and angry, he reached for the phone and dialed Sawyer's home number.

"Hello," Sawyer answered impatiently.

"It's me."

"Christian? What's wrong? You don't sound like yourself."

"I'm fine," he said, then wondered if that was true. Rarely had he felt so disappointed, so disillusioned, but he couldn't entirely blame his dinner date. His own willful blindness had something to do with it. "You remember Allison, don't you?"

"Of course I remember her. Listen, if you're calling to sing her praises, you've caught me at an inopportune moment. You seem to have forgotten that Abbey and I are having our second honeymoon. She's decided to re-create the night we attended the luau. Grass skirt, leis, the whole deal. D'you mind if we talk about the sex goddess another time?"

"Trust me, Allison is no goddess."

"Not you, honey," Christian heard his brother explain to Abbey. "I was talking about another sex goddess. One *far* less gorgeous than you."

"I'll talk to you when I get home," Christian said. Chuckling to himself, he replaced the receiver.

A year ago, he'd been completely wrapped up in Allison. He wasn't sure who'd changed in the past twelve months. Allison or him? But she wasn't at all how he'd remembered her.

A year ago, Christian had been thrilled when Allison had agreed, after some fast talking on his part, to give Hard Luck a try. Unfortunately, because of business commitments, he'd been unable to greet her personally when she arrived.

For an entire year he'd believed someone had said or done something to offend her. When he discovered she'd returned to Seattle after only one night in Hard Luck, he'd been furious. Not that there was anything he could do while he was on the road. He'd made one feeble attempt to contact her, but because he was busy with other things, he'd dropped the matter.

For twelve long months, he'd been convinced the people of Hard Luck had been at fault. The other women were jealous of Allison's natural beauty and had gone out of their way to make her feel unwanted. The list of possibilities had mounted—but there'd only been one reason Allison had left. A reason he hadn't seen until that very evening.

A vain, selfish woman wouldn't last more than a day in a town like Hard Luck. Allison had said it herself, although she'd meant something very different. And a day was exactly how long she'd stayed.

MARIAH THOUGHT she'd never been this miserable. There wasn't enough deep-dish pizza in the world to get her through the night, but that didn't keep her away from the Hard Luck Café.

Christian was in Seattle dining with the beautiful, sophisticated Allison Reynolds. He didn't think she knew, but she did, and that made everything worse.

Although she'd never met her, Mariah had heard everything she needed to know from the few women who remembered Allison's brief visit.

Right that moment, Christian and Allison were at a waterfront restaurant rated as one of the country's top ten. Mariah didn't want to consider what they'd do after dinner. Dancing. Stargazing. Kissing. The image of another woman in Christian's arms was just too painful to contemplate. Nor did she care to dwell on how his relationship with Allison would affect her position with Midnight Sons.

She knew that Christian would do practically anything to get Allison back in Hard Luck.

Allison was a secretary. And so was she.

Given the choice, Christian would pick Allison over her any day of the week. And she figured that, to keep the peace, Sawyer would ultimately agree to letting her go in favor of Allison.

"What can I do for you?" Ben asked.

Mariah sat at the table closest to the counter. "Do you have any pizza left?"

"The one with four kinds of cheese and all the extras?" He didn't wait for her answer. "I suspect I've got a couple tucked away in the freezer," he told her. "I generally don't bake them unless I have a special request."

"Would you be willing to consider this a special request?" Mariah asked. "It's a food emergency."

"A food emergency," Ben repeated, grinning. "Hey, I like that." He raised his hand and read the imaginary words, pointing one finger as he spoke. "Hard Luck Café, specializing in food emergencies." Then the amusement left his eyes, and he muttered, "It might go over better than my frequent-eater program."

"Could you feed me the pizza intravenously?" she joked, but it was a struggle.

Ben pulled out a chair and sat down next to her. "What's the problem, kiddo?"

Mariah knew that a lot of the men in town talked to Ben;

he was a good sounding board and a faithful friend. She liked and trusted him, but she wasn't comfortable talking about the situation between her and Christian. It didn't seem fair to unburden her soul to a friend of the O'Hallorans.

"I don't have anything one of your pizzas won't cure," she assured him.

"Coming right up." Ben stood and patted her affectionately on the shoulder. "You want anything to go with that?"

"Diet soda," she told him, knowing he'd find humor in her downing his million-calorie pizza with a diet drink.

"This could take a while," he said on his way to the kitchen. "The oven's got to heat up first."

"No problem."

There were dirty lunch dishes on a couple of the tables, and because she felt too restless to sit there doing nothing, Mariah cleared them away.

"Thanks," Ben told her as she carried the dishes into the kitchen. "I meant to do that earlier."

"Anything else you need help with?" she asked.

"Nah."

But when she'd brought in the dishes from the second table, she noticed that some of the paper-napkin dispensers were empty. She asked Ben about that.

"I've been meaning to fill those, too, but I got sidetracked."

"I'll do it," she said, eager to occupy her hands while she waited for her food.

"I've been feeling a bit tired lately," Ben admitted. "Guess I'd better stop watching those late-night talk shows."

"I don't suppose you'd be needing extra help?" she asked hopefully. "Someone to wait tables, wash dishes, fill the napkin dispensers, that sort of thing."

"You serious?"

More than he knew. If everything went according to Christian's plan, her boss was about to lure the beautiful Allison Reynolds back to Hard Luck and offer her Mariah's job.

"I'm very serious," she told Ben.

"Actually I've been thinking about getting some help for a while now. In fact, I was about to ask Christian to pass along some of the applications he collected last year."

"I thought business was, uh, down a bit." She spoke as tactfully as she could. She'd heard that a decrease in customers was the reason he'd started the frequent-eater program.

"It's not so bad lately," Ben said, leaning against the counter. "I'm here 365 days a year. You can't blame a man for wanting a break now and then. Have you got someone in mind for the job?"

Mariah nodded.

"Who?"

She didn't hesitate. "Me."

"You?"

Despite her best efforts, her lower lip quivered slightly. "Christian's in Seattle and he...he's with Allison Reynolds."

"Listen, Mariah, I don't know what he sees in that woman, but trust me, your position with Midnight Sons is safe! Sawyer isn't going to let him replace you with anyone."

"I've known for a long time that Christian would love to get rid of me."

"I'm not saying whether that's true or not, but I *will* say that his attitude underwent a...minor adjustment the week you were away."

"Well, that's nice," she murmured a little sarcastically. "But he'd do *anything* to convince Allison to move here. He's been hung up on her all year."

Ben didn't argue. Rubbing the side of his jaw, he frowned. "I don't know what to advise you."

"If you don't hire me, maybe Pete Livengood will," she said. "He might need someone to stock shelves for him."

"Now don't do anything rash." Ben patted her hand. "Sawyer's always been on your side, no matter how much Christian griped."

Which was another way of telling her that Christian had done plenty of griping.

The oven buzzed in the background. "Let me get your pizza into the oven and I'll be right back," Ben told her, scurrying to the kitchen.

She could apply for a position with the state, too, she mused while he was gone. But if she got a government job, it was unlikely she'd be able to continue living in Hard Luck, which made the idea less appealing.

"You sure you'd want to work in a restaurant?" Ben asked when he returned. His look was thoughtful.

"I'm positive." The way she saw things, she wouldn't have much of a choice.

"If you don't want to stay with Midnight Sons anymore, you can have a job right here."

Chapter
4

THE LUMP IN Mariah's throat wouldn't go away. The computer screen blurred as her eyes filled with unshed tears. Swallowing hard, she quickly typed out her letter of resignation. Every word was like the end of a dream, the end of her hopes. The printer spewed out the single sheet, and she took a few minutes to compose herself before signing it.

When Mariah was fairly certain she wouldn't make a fool of herself by bursting into tears, she brought the letter to Sawyer.

"What's this?" he asked, glancing up from his computer terminal.

"I'm giving you my notice."

Sawyer's gaze shot to hers in disbelief. "You're *quitting?*"

She nodded, then said with forced cheerfulness, "It's been a wonderful experience, but as Christian pointed out, my contract is up. I'd agreed to work for Midnight Sons for a year, and—" she shrugged "—it's time to move on."

"Is it the money?" Sawyer asked with a dumbfounded look. "Are you unhappy with the benefits package?"

"No. You've always been more than generous."

"But…" Sawyer didn't seem to know what to say. She realized she'd taken him by surprise, but that couldn't be helped. She'd made her decision and felt it was the right one.

"In that case, can I ask why you want to leave?" Sawyer asked. "Especially now?"

"For one thing, I can see the writing on the wall," she told him, struggling to keep her voice even. "I overheard Christian telling you he wants to bring Allison Reynolds back to Hard Luck. There simply isn't enough work to occupy two full-time secretaries. Allison was the one he wanted from the first. I…I have what I want—the cabin and the twenty acres of land."

"Now, listen, there's no way on earth I'm going to let my brother hire Allison Reynolds," Sawyer insisted. "Your position here is secure, I promise you." Fire glowed in his eyes as if battle loomed on the horizon and he was ready to take aim. Brother against brother.

"I appreciate what you're saying, and I thank you, but you and I both know that Christian—"

"It's not going to happen, Mariah," Sawyer said from between clenched teeth. "I won't let it."

He was making this more difficult than she'd expected. She'd assumed she would hand in her notice, and he'd put up a token fuss, then release her. What shocked her was the vehemence with which he argued.

"Thank you, Sawyer. I'm grateful for what you're trying to do, but the last thing I want is to cause dissension between you and Christian. It's pretty obvious that he'd prefer to work with Allison."

"Why don't we wait until Christian's back?" he suggested. "There's no need to jump to conclusions. I talked to him last night, and he didn't mention bringing Allison back with him." He paused and seemed to reconsider. "But then, I suppose I didn't give him an opportunity to say much."

"It's too late, Sawyer. I already have another job."

This seemed to shock him even more. His jaw dropped and his eyes widened. "Who...where?"

"The Hard Luck Café. I'm going to work for Ben."

"Since when did Ben Hamilton need a secretary?" Sawyer demanded. He made it sound as if Ben had stolen her away from him.

"Not a secretary," Mariah hurried to explain. "He needs help in the kitchen."

"You're qualified to cook?"

"I won't be responsible for the cooking," she clarified. "I'll wait tables and clean up and...and things like that. Ben's been running the café on his own all these years. It's time he relaxed and left the small stuff to someone else."

"Ben!" Sawyer said the name in a tone that implied his longtime friend had turned traitor.

"*I* asked *him* about the job," Mariah pointed out. She didn't want to cause trouble between Ben and the O'Hallorans any more than she wanted to between the two brothers.

Sawyer reread her letter and frowned anew. "You're sure this is what you want?"

Was she sure? Mariah didn't know anymore. From what Christian and the others had said, Allison Reynolds was a real beauty; he was clearly besotted with her. Mariah didn't stand a chance of winning Christian's heart. It wasn't easy to walk away from this job—or from Christian—but she had to, for the sake of her sanity. And for the sake of her pride, she had to convince Sawyer she was perfectly content to give up her duties with Midnight Sons. She had to be certain he'd never know how much it hurt.

"I'm sure," she said, revealing nothing.

Sawyer pinched the bridge of his nose. "In that case there's not much I can say."

"WHAT DO YOU MEAN, Mariah quit?" Christian shouted into the phone.

"She gave me her notice first thing this morning," Sawyer said, sounding none too pleased.

"She can't do that!"

"Why can't she?" Sawyer asked impatiently. "It's a free country. We can't force her to work for us if she doesn't want to."

Christian stood, forgetting that the receiver was connected to the telephone on the hotel nightstand. He started to pace and the phone fell with a discordant clang. For an instant he was afraid he'd severed the connection.

"You there?" he asked his brother.

"Yes. What happened?"

"Nothing. I dropped the phone." Christian rammed his fingers into his dark blond hair and winced at the unexpected twinge of pain. "You might've tried talking her into staying."

"I talked until I was blue in the face. I tried everything short of out-and-out bribery. I have to tell you, Christian, I blame *you* for this. You haven't done a damn thing to help, you know."

"How can I help when you're in Hard Luck and I'm in Seattle?" His irritation was fast turning to anger. This whole business with Mariah didn't make sense. It should've been obvious to Sawyer—to anyone with half a brain—how crucial it was to keep Mariah with Midnight Sons. She knew more about the office than the two brothers combined. True, there'd been a time, not so long ago, when he'd have willingly replaced her. But he'd undergone a change of heart in the week she'd been away. And the week *he'd* been away…

"It seems to me I'm the one stuck here with all the problems," Sawyer said, his voice hard. "As I recall, last year you were off in Seattle dating your cover model, and I had to deal with the avalanche of problems you'd created. It's the same thing all over again."

"Now just a minute—"

Sawyer didn't allow him to finish. "You'd better remember exactly whose idea it was to bring women to Hard Luck in the first place."

"Yeah, but if it wasn't for me you'd never have met Abbey." Christian played his trump card before this argument with his brother could deteriorate any further.

Sawyer sighed deeply, and Christian could virtually hear his anger drain away. "True."

"I'll talk to Mariah myself," Christian said, feeling confident he'd succeed where his brother had failed. If she'd listen to anyone, it would be him. He felt they'd come to an understanding in the last while. Mended fences and all that.

"Fine, but you should know that it's because of you she's decided to quit."

"*Me?*" Sawyer must have misunderstood. His relationship with Mariah had taken a dramatic turn for the better. Or so he'd assumed.

"She seems to think you're bringing Allison back with you, so she's stepped aside."

"You're joking! What made her think that?"

Sawyer's frustration was palpable. "You did, little brother. You managed all of this single-handedly."

"Me? How?"

"You told me you planned to talk Allison into giving Hard Luck another shot."

He'd said that? Christian pressed his hand against his brow. "Well, I didn't. She's not coming."

Christian's words were followed by a stiff silence. "That wasn't the impression you gave me," Sawyer eventually said. "And Mariah overheard the conversation."

Christian cursed.

"Mariah felt that if Allison returned to Hard Luck, there wouldn't be enough work for two full-time secretaries."

"You'd better let me talk to Mariah," Christian muttered. "I'll straighten this out."

"It's too late," Sawyer said with a heavy sigh. "She's already got another job. Apparently she and Ben have come up with this scheme—"

"Mariah and *Ben?*"

"Right. She's going to be his assistant, help in the kitchen, wait tables, that sort of thing."

"You've got to be kidding!"

"I swear it's true."

"Let me talk to her," Christian demanded again. He could foresee trouble already—for Ben, as well as for Midnight Sons. Obviously Ben hadn't remembered how clumsy Mariah was. He'd never known a woman more inclined to trip over her own feet.

"She isn't here," Sawyer murmured. "I have a feeling we're going to lose the best secretary we ever had, and frankly, Christian, I hold you responsible."

This didn't seem to be the moment to remind Sawyer that Mariah was the first and only secretary Midnight Sons had ever had.

NO ONE RESPONDED to Bethany's knock at the back door of the Hard Luck Café. She tried again, then turned the knob—the door was open. She let herself inside.

"Ben?" she called.

No answer. A sliver of light peered out from beneath the door that led upstairs to Ben's private quarters.

Bethany opened the door and peered up the stairway. "Ben!" she called again. Smiling to herself, she climbed the stairs. More than likely he was asleep in his chair.

She was right. He lay stretched out on the recliner, the television guide on his lap. His head was tipped back, and he was snoring lightly.

"Ben." Bethany pressed her hand over his.

His eyelids fluttered open, and he blinked. "Bethany? What time is it?"

"Nine."

"Nine," he repeated. "That's early yet."

"Yes, I know."

He leaned forward, yawning, then reached for the remote control and turned off the TV. "I must've fallen asleep. Guess I'm beginning to feel my age. Soon I'll be an old man."

Shaking her head, Bethany sat down on the love seat. "Not you. Never you."

She could see that her words pleased him. "It's good to see you. Now, to what do I owe the pleasure?"

She slipped off her shoes and tucked her feet beneath her. "Mitch is on patrol and Chrissie's spending the night with a friend. She's been beside herself not knowing what to do while Susan O'Halloran's on vacation. Those two have gotten so tight that Chrissie's lost without her. I think it's a good idea for her to make other friends."

"Are you ready for school?" Ben asked.

"Yes. No," Bethany quickly amended, and then because she couldn't hold the news inside any longer, she blurted it out. "I'm pregnant."

Ben's feet slid off the recliner and hit the floor. "Pregnant!"

"Mitch and I are just as surprised—almost." She nearly laughed aloud at his incredulous look.

"But you haven't been married very long."

"I know. We didn't plan to have a baby this soon, that's for sure. It was just…one of those things."

Ben's eyes lit up. "Unplanned pregnancies are sometimes the very best kind," he said, nodding sagely.

Bethany knew he was referring to her own birth. He'd had an affair with her mother before leaving for Vietnam, and because of a disagreement, he'd never known Marilyn was pregnant. He'd never known of his daughter's existence. Bethany had learned Peter Ross wasn't her biological father while she was in college, after her mother had experienced a cancer scare. As the years progressed, Bethany had become increasingly curious about the man who'd fathered her. With a bit of detective work and the help of the American Red Cross, she'd been able to trace Ben to Hard Luck.

Soon afterward, she'd applied for a teaching position in the tiny Arctic community, hoping to meet him.

Bethany had never intended to confront Ben with the truth, but she was relieved—and happy—that she had. In many ways they were very alike, and in others completely dissimilar. No one in town, other than her husband, knew Bethany's true relationship to Ben, although she wondered why no one had guessed. Ben was fiercely proud of her and staunchly protective; she felt the same about him.

"A baby," Ben repeated, grinning broadly. "How does Mitch feel about this?"

"When I first told him, he was floored, but it didn't take him long to adjust. The baby's due in the spring. We told Chrissie this evening, and she's thrilled. I can tell she's going to be a wonderful big sister."

"Have you told your mother and father?"

"Oh, yes. They're thrilled."

"I'm thrilled for you, too, sweetheart."

"It still takes some getting used to. I'm just becoming accustomed to being a wife and stepmom, and now I'm about to be a mother."

Ben chuckled. "Try finding out that you're a father at *my* age—that's what I call a bombshell. As for your little one, personally, I think of the baby as a delightful surprise."

Bethany smiled, relaxing against the cushions. "What's this wild rumor I've been hearing about your taking on an assistant?"

"It's true," Ben said. "Mariah Douglas is coming to work with me."

"But…I thought she was the secretary for the O'Hallorans."

"She is—was. What I understand, she's already handed in her notice. Sawyer's annoyed with me, but it's not my fault—Mariah approached *me*. The way I figure it, she already had her heart set on leaving Midnight Sons. I tried to convince her to stay with the O'Hallorans, but she wouldn't hear of it."

"You'd think Christian would be pleased. He's been looking

for a way to be rid of her from the moment I met him," Bethany recalled.

"Apparently he's had a change of heart."

"Isn't that just a like a man?" Bethany muttered, shaking her head. "They don't know *what* they want."

CHRISTIAN HAD never been this eager to get back to Hard Luck. In the past several days he'd talked to Sawyer half-a-dozen times. And every time, he'd hung up frustrated—and confused.

As far as he could grasp, Sawyer had released Mariah from serving out her full two-week notice, and the woman his brother had referred to as "the best secretary they'd ever had" was gone.

Scott and Susan were just as eager to be home. Christian had collected them from his mother's, and Ralph Ferris flew into Fairbanks to meet their commercial flight. The short hop between Fairbanks and Hard Luck felt longer than the flight from Vancouver to Anchorage.

By the time the plane touched down in Hard Luck, Christian had his conversation with Mariah all figured out.

Sawyer and Abbey were at the airfield waiting for Scott and Susan. The kids leaped out of the plane and raced toward their parents, full of talk about their visit with Grandma Ellen and Grandpa Robert.

Christian waited impatiently for a moment alone with Sawyer. "Where is she?" he asked abruptly.

Sawyer blinked at him, wearing a baffled expression. "Oh, you mean Mariah."

Who else would he have been referring to? "Yes, I mean Mariah."

"Ben's, I'd guess. She spends every day there, now that she no longer works for us." Judging by the edge in Sawyer's voice, he still seemed to place the blame squarely on Christian's shoulders. He'd settle the issue with his brother later, Christian decided.

"Who's minding the office?" Surely Sawyer wasn't so irresponsible as to leave it unattended. The flight service had grown by thirty percent in the past year, thanks partly to the boom in population. An answering machine no longer met their needs, and Sawyer knew that.

"Lanni's agreed to step in for now, but she's got her own work, you know. I told her it wouldn't take *you* long to find Mariah's replacement."

"Me?" he exploded. He'd left for a few measly days, and meanwhile his brother let all hell break loose, then calmly announced it was *his* responsibility to set everything right.

"Yeah, you," Sawyer returned, eyes snapping. "If you'll recall, you spent the better part of a month interviewing job applicants. I don't even know where you filed the résumés."

"I didn't file them. Mariah did."

"Ask her, then. All I can say is we need to hire someone and quick. It isn't fair to Lanni to keep her tied up at the office. She's got better things to do with her time than answer our phones."

"You might have discussed it with me first," he argued.

"I would've if you'd been here," Sawyer said in a disgusted voice.

Christian didn't deign to respond. It was clear that he wasn't going to get anywhere with Sawyer when his brother was in this cantankerous frame of mind. Sawyer unfairly blamed him for Mariah's sudden need to become a waitress. Well, he wasn't going to accept the blame!

As soon as Christian had dropped off his suitcase at home, he headed over to the Hard Luck Café. First thing he noticed when he walked in the door were the tablecloths—not plastic, either. A vase of wildflowers on each table added a touch of color and warmth. On the chalkboard, where Ben wrote the daily dinner special, someone had drawn yellow daisies.

Ralph Ferris sat at one of the tables, reading the menu, which also looked new. They acknowledged each other with a brief nod.

Christian stepped up to the counter the way he always did and pulled out a stool. He nearly slid onto the floor—the stools had been newly padded and recovered in shiny black vinyl.

It certainly hadn't taken Mariah long to leave her mark on the café.

She was busy making coffee, and apparently didn't hear him come in.

"Did you want coffee?" she called to Ralph over her shoulder.

"Please," Ralph called back.

Mariah turned with a full pot in her hand—and saw Christian sitting at the counter. She gave a start, and the glass carafe slipped from her fingers. It shattered, and hot coffee splashed across the polished floor.

"Oh, no!" Luckily Mariah had jumped back in time to avoid getting burned.

It took a determined effort on Christian's part not to call attention to the accident. He merely shook his head. Poor Ben. He didn't have a clue what he was letting himself in for when he'd hired Mariah.

"What happened?" Ben stuck his head out from the kitchen.

"I—I broke the coffeepot."

Christian waited for the cook to start bellowing. Ben wasn't known for his patience, and if ever a woman was born to try men's souls, it was Mariah Douglas.

He'd give Ben a week; then he'd be begging Christian and Sawyer to take her off his hands.

"Don't worry about it," Ben said, reaching for the mop. "I've got plenty of pots. You weren't burned, were you?"

"No. I'm fine." Her eyes flew to Christian, narrowing as if she blamed *him* for the accident. He hadn't done a thing, yet everyone in Hard Luck was ready to go for his jugular.

"Your coffee'll be just a minute," Mariah told Ralph.

"No problem," the bush pilot assured her. He unfolded the Fairbanks newspaper and disappeared behind it.

"I'll take a cup when you get around to it," Christian said, righting the ceramic mug in front of him. He might be risking his life asking her to pour it for him, but it was a risk he'd have to take.

Mariah refilled another glass pot from the large percolator. He noted that her hand shook slightly as she filled his mug. "When did you get back?" she asked conversationally. Christian wasn't fooled; she'd been the one to arrange his itinerary. She knew his travel schedule as well as he did.

"This afternoon."

Mariah pulled an order pad from her apron pocket. "What can I get you?"

"I'll have a piece of apple pie."

Mariah called back the order to Ben, who appeared a couple of minutes later with a large slice of pie. He set it in front of Christian and eyed him warily, as if anticipating a confrontation.

Christian figured he didn't need to say a word. Within a week, when Ben was out of coffeepots and patience, he'd recognize that Mariah was never cut out to be a waitress.

"How's it going?" Christian asked Ben, tipping his head toward Mariah, who was busy serving Ralph his lunch. He'd apparently ordered the day's special—meatloaf sandwich, with a bowl of beef-and-barley soup.

"With Mariah?" Ben grinned. "Great. Just great." He gestured toward the tables. "Have you ever seen my place look better? Mariah's responsible for all the fancy touches. I don't know why I delayed hiring someone for so long. She's the best thing that's happened to the café since I got in the soft-ice-cream machine."

Christian took a bite of the pie and raised his eyebrows. "Hey, this is great! What's different?"

"Mariah baked it."

"Mariah?" Ben could've knocked him over with a flick of his finger.

"It's her grandmother's recipe. Best apple pie I've ever tasted. As far as I'm concerned, she can do all the baking around here, she's that good."

Christian was confused, to put it mildly. "Are you sure we're talking about the same Mariah?"

Ben chuckled. "I'm sure." The cook drifted back to the kitchen, but Christian wasn't alone for long. Mariah hurried to bring him the small canister of cream.

"I—I forgot you like your coffee with cream, don't you?"

Christian didn't bother to correct her. "Do you have a minute?" he asked.

She hesitated. "The dinner crowd will start coming in any time now."

It was barely four; a poor excuse. "I'd appreciate it if you could sit down and chat for a few minutes."

"All right." But her reluctance was obvious. She walked around the counter to sit on the stool next to him. Folding her hands on the counter, she waited for Christian to speak.

"Allison didn't come with me," he said, wanting to clear the air about that immediately. He understood her concern and was willing to admit that he'd been sadly remiss in mentioning the other woman in Mariah's presence. He'd seen the error of his ways; now he wanted her back. They'd just begun to find their footing with each other, and it seemed a shame to end it all so abruptly. And unnecessarily.

Three months ago—three *weeks* ago—he would've cheered to see her leave Midnight Sons. But not now.

"Sawyer already told me she wouldn't be coming." Her gaze met his straight on.

"Then why'd you decide to quit?"

"It never really worked out between you and me."

"Things were improving, though, don't you think?"

"I suppose. Only you…"

"Yes?" he pressed.

"You wanted a different secretary."

"I don't anymore," he said, growing impatient. It occurred to him to tell her he'd made a mistake, to apologize, but he couldn't quite bring himself to do it.

"I'm already committed to working for Ben," she said, and she did sound mildly regretful. "Do you like the pie?"

At the moment it was stuck in his throat, but he managed to respond with a quick nod.

"So your mind's made up?" he asked, pushing back his plate.

"Yes." She eyed him expectantly, and he wondered if she was waiting for him to plead with her. Well, there'd be frost in the Caribbean before he'd grovel! If she didn't want to work for Midnight Sons, fine. There were stacks of applications from women clamoring for the opportunity to move north. He'd met a number of them a year ago.

"Fine." He stood and paid for the pie. "We're sorry to see you go, but what the hey, right? You were with us for a year and it was fun."

"Yes," she said, but she didn't sound so sure that it *was* fun.

Christian walked back to the mobile office. Their conversation hadn't gone nearly as well as he'd assumed it would. Perhaps he should've waited a day or two. Rushing over to Ben's the minute the plane landed made him look too eager; that had been a tactical error. Still, he had other options, and he planned to exercise them, starting now.

Christian opened the top drawer of the filing cabinet and sorted through a sequence of file folders, searching for the one that contained the applications he'd received the summer before. It took a while, but he eventually located what he needed, and without any help from Mariah.

With the precious folder clutched tightly in his hand, he walked over to his desk and sat down. Reading through the top three applications instantly lifted his spirits. Plenty of women had been interested in this position.

"Ramona Cummings," he said aloud, remembering his interview with the dark-haired beauty. Gleefully he punched out the phone number.

Disconnected.

Christian flipped to the second application. "Rosey Stone." A face didn't immediately come to mind, but he'd probably remember her once he heard her voice. Once again he punched in the number and waited.

A soft, feminine voice answered.

"This is Christian O'Halloran from Hard Luck, Alaska. Is Rosey Stone there?"

"This is Rosey." She sounded surprised and a little breathless. Good, Christian liked awed and breathless. This was a fine start, a fine start indeed.

"You applied for the position of secretary last year."

"Yes…yes, I remember!" she said excitedly.

"We currently have a position available, and we'd like to offer it to you." He felt smug at the thought that it would be so easy to replace Mariah.

"Are you still offering the same employment package you were a year ago?" Rosey asked.

"Ah…yes. There's a cabin you could have. Actually it isn't much," he added with a twinge of conscience. "My father built it over thirty years ago, and there's no electricity and no indoor plumbing."

"You're joking!"

Christian didn't know what had possessed him to blurt that out. "The cabin lacks modern conveniences." He smacked his forehead with one hand.

"What is this, some kind of sick joke?"

"No. The job's available if you still want it."

"No, thanks," she informed him, and slammed the phone in his ear.

"I didn't think you would," he said into the drone of the disconnected line. Sighing, Christian hung up the receiver. He wanted Mariah back.

Chapter
5

BRIGHT AND EARLY Monday morning, Christian settled down at his desk in the Midnight Sons office. Determined to make some headway in replacing Mariah, he reached for the file folder that held the pertinent applications.

Leaning back in his chair, he read over a number of résumés. Several applicants were vastly overqualified. Others had little or no relevant experience, just an eagerness for adventure. Christian decided they wouldn't work out, either. Neither he nor Sawyer had time to train a replacement.

Discouraged, he set the file aside and promised himself he'd read through it again later, when he was ready to deal with the problem. What he wanted of course, what he hoped would happen, was that Mariah would realize she wasn't cut out for the restaurant business and return to Midnight Sons. Now that she knew Allison Reynolds wouldn't be coming, there was no reason to be stubborn.

Sawyer arrived half an hour after Christian, clearly surprised to find his brother at the office so early.

"I've been working on finding a replacement for Mariah," Christian told Sawyer. What he failed to mention was that he hadn't found a résumé or application that suited him yet. Nor did he think it was a good idea to admit he was holding out, hoping Mariah would have a change of heart.

Sawyer nodded.

"You want to give me some help here?" He supposed they might as well go through the motions. "Perhaps we should try for an older woman this time, someone mature," he suggested.

"Sure." Sawyer didn't sound as if he particularly cared.

"Someone methodical," Christian said next. "I don't care how fast she types, as long as she's accurate." He wrote that down on the pad.

"Okay with me," Sawyer murmured while preparing a pot of coffee.

The coffee had always been made before they arrived at the office—by Mariah. Not that they weren't capable of making coffee themselves. But it was generous of her to do it without being asked. Christian hadn't given the matter more than a passing thought until just that moment. In fact, Mariah had willingly taken on a number of small tasks that made their lives easier.

"She should have a good attitude," Christian went on.

"I agree," Sawyer said with conviction. "I don't want someone to come in here asking what we can do for her. I'm much more interested in what she can do for us, especially since we're the ones paying her wages."

Christian added "good attitude" to the list, and with Sawyer's help came up with several other qualities. They found it vital that the new secretary be prompt and professional. Loyal and responsible. Because they did so much of their business over the phone, a pleasant phone manner was essential.

As Christian read over the qualifications for Mariah's replacement, it became obvious that—except for the "older" part—they'd described Mariah herself.

Christian felt suddenly troubled. How could he have been so...so misguided? The perfect candidate had been there all along, and it had taken him all this time to see it. For twelve months he'd been hoping she'd leave; now that she was gone, he wanted her back. Something was definitely wrong, and he had the feeling that whatever was askew had to do with him.

"Have you got someone yet?" Sawyer asked ten minutes later.

"No!" Christian snapped. "How could I?"

"Well, read through those applications, would you? The sooner we get someone here, the better. We can't expect Lanni to fill in for long."

"I understand that," Christian returned impatiently.

"Charles was against Lanni coming to work for us in the first place," Sawyer went on, "but she insisted—said a few days away from her writing wouldn't matter. She'll be in this afternoon."

Christian didn't understand why Sawyer was in such an all-fired hurry. He'd already gone through the file a second time and hadn't found a suitable applicant. Nor did he share his brother's sense of urgency. This wasn't something that needed to be done right that very minute.

Brother worked amicably with brother for the remainder of the morning. Their staff of pilots wandered in and out of the office, as was their habit, before heading out to the hangar to complete their assignments for the day.

"Who's going to make up the flight schedule?" Sawyer asked. In the past Mariah had seen to it.

"You do it this week and I'll do it next," Christian suggested in what he felt was a fair compromise.

"Oh, so you'll do it next week," Sawyer muttered sarcastically. "You'd better have hired a replacement long before then."

Before next week! Sawyer didn't actually expect someone to drop her entire life because of a phone call, did he? Christian doubted he'd find a replacement willing to move to the Arctic just like that. These things took time, lots of time.

Duke Porter was the last pilot to drop by the office that morning. He walked in, glared at Christian and announced, "Mariah's working at Ben's."

"Yes, I know." Christian studied the pilot. Although Mariah had assured him there was nothing between her and Duke, Christian couldn't help wondering.

"Why?" Duke was still glaring at him.

"You'll have to ask her." Christian wouldn't mind having the answer to that himself.

"I'm asking *you,*" Duke said in a way that laid the blame squarely on Christian's shoulders.

"I don't know why she quit," he mumbled, and realized that wasn't completely true. "I have my suspicions, but none I'd care to discuss."

"It isn't the same around here without Mariah," Duke complained, setting aside his clipboard. "A man becomes accustomed to things being done a certain way."

"What do you mean?" Sawyer asked. "It's still the same office, same business."

"Well, it's too quiet in here. A man could get, I don't know, bored."

"Bored," Sawyer repeated.

"Bored," Duke said again, with more certainty this time. "Before, it was fun to watch Mariah tiptoe around Christian. She used to make these hilarious faces at him behind his back."

"She did what?" Christian was outraged, then amused. That sounded like something she'd do, and in retrospect he didn't hold it against her. He *had* been kind of a jerk.

"Who could blame her?" Duke asked. "For making faces *or* leaving. Christian was always on her case for one reason or another, but she was a good sport about it." He turned to Christian. "Everyone knew you were looking for an excuse to fire her. But without Mariah around, it's…it's like someone dimmed the lights in here."

Christian was inclined to argue, but realized Duke was right. In more ways than one.

"Do you?" Duke pressed. "Blame her for leaving?"

"I guess I can't," Christian admitted in a grudging voice.

The pilot seemed surprised that Christian had agreed so readily. "You going to get her back?"

Christian desperately hoped so, but he couldn't guarantee it. With luck, Mariah would figure out that waitressing wasn't for her. She had all kinds of abilities that were wasted at the café, although he had to concede she baked a fine apple pie.

Duke left after a few more admonitions, and Christian started thinking about what the bush pilot had said. He wasn't going to plead with her to come back, but that didn't mean he wasn't willing to make a few subtle suggestions.

"Will you be all right if I drop in at Ben's for a few minutes?" he asked his brother.

Sawyer gave him an odd look, then nodded. "Just don't be too long."

"I won't."

He hurried across the yard and noticed a distinct chill in the air. Although it was still August and summer wasn't officially over, he could feel autumn coming on; soon the days would shorten dramatically. It wasn't unheard of for snow to fall in September or for the rivers to freeze. The wind increased as he rushed into the Hard Luck Café, almost pulling the door out of his hand. He saw Ben at the counter, but the place was otherwise empty, since coffee break was over and the lunch crowd hadn't started to arrive.

Ben offered Christian a friendly smile. "What can I do for you this fine day?" he asked.

"How about coffee and a doughnut?" Christian pulled out a stool. He made sure that when he sat down this time he didn't slide off. He looked around, wondering where Mariah was, but he didn't want to be so obvious as to ask.

"In the kitchen. Baking another pie," Ben supplied, knowing all too well the purpose of Christian's visit.

Christian pretended not to understand what Ben was talking about.

"You want me to call her out here?" Ben asked.

"No," Christian answered automatically, then regretted it.

"She's causing quite a stir, you know," Ben said conversationally as he filled Christian's mug. He piled a couple of sugar-coated doughnuts onto a plate and set it in front of him.

"You mean her apple pie?"

"Not her pies, although her recipe is excellent." He raised his fingertips to his mouth and loudly kissed them. "I mean Mariah herself. Business has really picked up since she came to work for me. Those fellows are interested in more than my moose pot roast with cranberry sauce."

This was something Christian hadn't considered. Mariah had been living in Hard Luck for the better part of a year and had caused barely any reaction among the men in town. He'd never understood it. Many a time he would've given his eyeteeth for one of his pilots to sweep her off her feet—and out from under his. It hadn't happened. Nor did he understand what was so different now.

"Who?" he demanded. He wasn't about to let a bunch of lovesick pilots pester her! Christian didn't linger on the contradictions between his attitude today and that of two months ago. If his men wanted to come in and eat at Ben's, then fine, but anything else and they'd answer to him. After all, he'd been responsible for bringing her to Alaska; he was responsible for ensuring her safety and well-being while she was here. Which was why he had to protect her from the pilots. He didn't feel completely convinced that there wasn't anything going on between her and Duke, either. She claimed there wasn't, but judging by the pilot's behavior earlier, Christian was beginning to think otherwise. Duke might well be attracted to her. Mariah needed the gentle guidance of an older brother, a good friend. Someone like himself.

"Bill Landgrin for one," Ben answered.

The name caught Christian's attention right away. The pipeline worker was a known troublemaker. Generally Christian was able to get along with just about everyone, but Bill rubbed him the wrong way. He frowned, disliking the thought of Mariah having anything to do with the likes of Bill.

"Who else?"

"Ralph asked her out," Ben murmured, dropping his voice. He glanced over his shoulder to make sure Mariah wasn't listening in on their conversation.

"Ralph Ferris?" One of Christian's own pilots. He felt not only betrayed but puzzled. Ralph had seen Mariah on a daily basis for a whole year. If he'd been interested, he could've asked her out before this. Why he'd pursue her now didn't make sense, especially if Duke had set his sights on her. *None* of this made sense.

"You don't look pleased."

"I'm not," Christian admitted. Unfortunately he wasn't in a position to do anything about it.

"Not that you have a say in the matter." Ben echoed his own thoughts, again keeping his voice low.

Christian met Ben's gaze evenly. They'd been friends for a lot of years. Frankly Christian didn't like the idea of a woman standing between them, and he stated his feelings.

"I want her back," he said.

Ben laughed.

It wasn't the reaction Christian had expected, to say the least.

Still grinning, Ben said, "I knew that the minute you walked in here. It might come as a surprise, old friend, but I haven't got her tied to the stove back there. Mariah's free to leave or stay, whichever she decides."

"Fine, just as long as you know where I—where *we* stand," he amended, including Sawyer and Charles in the equation.

"To my way of thinking, you shouldn't have let her go in the first place," Ben said. He frowned, giving the impression that he didn't understand why the O'Hallorans had been so foolish.

Christian didn't have an answer.

MARIAH WAS ELBOW-DEEP in flour as she strained to hear the conversation between Christian and Ben. She didn't mean to snoop—well, to be honest, she did. She wanted to hear what

Christian was saying and strained to make out every word. She couldn't help wanting to know if he missed her, or if he'd given her absence so much as a passing thought.

Ben's voice drifted into the kitchen far more clearly than Christian's. She heard him tell Christian about Bill Landgrin's interest in her and smiled to herself. Not that she'd ever consider dating Bill. That would be asking for trouble. Word had got around fast about Bill and his roving hands. Besides, there was only one man who interested Mariah, and he was sitting in this very café, whispering about her.

The phone rang, and she heard Ben amble over to the counter to answer it. A moment later, the cook shouted, "Mariah, it's long distance for you."

Mariah quickly dusted the flour from her hands and reached for the extension on the kitchen wall. "This is Mariah," she said into the mouthpiece.

Once he was sure she'd picked up the phone, Ben hung up.

"Mariah, it's Tracy. What *happened?*"

"Happened?" Her friend sounded upset.

"I called Midnight Sons, and Sawyer said you no longer worked there and said I should contact you at the Hard Luck Café."

"I quit," Mariah explained simply.

Tracy exhaled a sharp breath. "What did Christian do *this* time?"

Mariah loved the way her friend immediately assumed Christian was to blame. This was one of Tracy's most endearing traits—she was loyal to a fault.

"What makes you think Christian did anything?"

"I know the man. He's done everything in his power to make your life miserable."

"That's not true." Mariah found herself wanting to defend Christian. "I'd been with Midnight Sons for a year, and it seemed time to move on, that's all."

"You didn't mention it while we were in Anchorage."

"I—I didn't decide until after I returned."

Tracy wasn't about to accept such a weak explanation. "You didn't come up with this idea on the spur of the moment. I know you far too well to believe that. Christian O'Halloran drove you to it."

"No one drove me to anything," Mariah insisted. "I work with Ben now." She didn't say that she wasn't sure Ben could afford to keep her much longer. Her pies were selling as fast as she could bake them, but her waitressing skills left a lot to be desired.

Thus far, Ben had been exceedingly patient with her, but she'd already broken two coffeepots. She'd offered to have him deduct the cost from her paycheck, but he'd refused.

To Mariah's own disappointment, she had to acknowledge that she lacked the skills to be a waitress. She confused orders and had a tendency not to look where she was going. Only this morning, she'd dumped a plate of poached eggs on Keith Campbell's lap. It hadn't been intentional of course, but Keith had been annoyed, to put it mildly.

Mariah had tried to apologize, but Keith hadn't given her a chance. He'd stomped out. Ben didn't seem distressed to lose him as a customer, though, saying he'd just as soon do without Keith's business. No big loss, Ben assured her.

"I had to leave Midnight Sons," Mariah admitted miserably.

"I thought as much," Tracy said in a soothing voice. "Do you want me to file a lawsuit against them?"

"On what grounds?" Mariah demanded. The O'Hallorans

had been good to her. They'd deeded her twenty acres of their own land, plus given her the cabin. In a way she felt they'd saved her by granting her the means to escape her family's dominance.

"I'm sure we could come up with something," Tracy said.

Tracy was by nature confrontational, which made her a good attorney. But that was also the reason for her problem with Duke, Mariah realized. The pilot enjoyed saying outlandish things just to rile Tracy, and it worked every time.

"I'd never sue the O'Hallorans," Mariah stressed, wanting to make that clear.

"Christian's at the root of this, and I—"

"Tracy," Mariah said, cutting off her friend, "listen. I'm perfectly happy. Midnight Sons will survive without me." The real question was whether she'd survive without them—or without one of them, anyway. But for pride's sake she couldn't admit that, not even to her friend.

They talked for a few more minutes, with Mariah struggling to convince Tracy that she was happy and at the same time convince herself.

Working for Ben was what she wanted. She said it over and over, and once Tracy was satisfied that Mariah had been the one to initiate the change, she was less concerned.

"Promise you'll contact me if you need anything?" Tracy asked. "I'll do anything I can to help you, as a friend and as an attorney."

Mariah promised, but she couldn't imagine why she'd ever need an attorney.

BETHANY STOOD at the front of the classroom and looked down the evenly spaced rows of empty desks. In a matter of days those same desks would be filled with Hard Luck's children.

A sense of pride, mingled with responsibility, suddenly overwhelmed her. She loved her job. She loved Alaska. Although she'd never asked Ben what had drawn him to the tiny Arctic community, she thought she understood. The beauty of this place often stole her breath. She defied anyone to look over the tundra in full bloom, to smell the scent of fresh, clean air mingled with spruce and wildflowers, and not understand.

Yes, there was also the challenge of winter, the difficulty of living week upon week in almost total darkness and subzero temperatures. Not everyone was suited to this life.

Spring brought with it far more than daylight and budding flowers, she mused. With the end of winter came a sense of— she wasn't sure just what to call it—accomplishment, she decided. Bethany remembered experiencing this phenomenon the previous spring. She'd realized that she'd survived the dark and the cold of winter. She'd stood in the sun, soaking up the warmth, her arms stretched toward the bright blue sky. With that moment came a feeling of power. She'd known that with love, with determination, with the force of her own inner strength, there wasn't anything she couldn't accomplish. The feeling had never left her.

Bethany smiled, thinking of Ben, and how coming to find him, meeting this man who'd given her life, had changed her. She was grateful to him in more ways than she could express. Without Ben she'd never have met Mitch and Chrissie.

"You're looking thoughtful."

Mitch stood in the classroom doorway, his arms crossed. Tall and muscular, he was dressed in his Department of the Interior uniform. Her heart swelled with pride and love at the sight of her husband.

"I was just thinking about Ben," Bethany said.

"You're worried about him, aren't you?"

It would be useless to deny it. "I guess I am. He just didn't look good the other night."

"Sweetheart, you woke him out of a sound sleep."

"I know." Ben had been thrilled with the news of her pregnancy, and they'd chatted and laughed for an hour before she'd headed home.

Not until she dressed for bed that night had she given her visit a second thought. Something wasn't right with Ben, but she couldn't put her finger on it.

"I came to take you to lunch," Mitch told her, "since Chrissie's playing at Susan's. You'll be able to see for yourself that Ben's as cantankerous as always."

"Lunch," Bethany said, grinning. "You certainly know the way to my heart."

CHRISTIAN DIDN'T THINK he could avoid being obvious when he stopped in at the Hard Luck Café for dinner that evening. The special, barbecued elk ribs, was by no means his favorite meal. Nor was he keen on having half of Hard Luck watch him make a fool of himself. But he had no choice. Somehow, he needed to convince Mariah to return to Midnight Sons.

His day hadn't gone well. Sawyer was on his back about hiring a replacement. The phone had kept them hopping all afternoon. The pilots were complaining. Nothing seemed right. Sometimes Christian forgot what an ill-tempered bunch they could be.

He thought wryly that even when Mariah *wasn't* at the office, she managed to make his life miserable.

When he entered the café, Christian was shocked by how busy it was. The place was packed. Every seat at the counter was taken and all the tables were occupied. The last empty spot in the entire restaurant was tucked away in the far corner. Considering himself fortunate, Christian grabbed that before someone else could take it.

"I'll be with you in a minute," Mariah said as she rushed past Christian, pen and pad in hand. She'd gone two or three steps before she realized who it was. Turning back, she offered him a brief but tired smile. "Hello, Christian."

"Mariah." For an instant he had to stop himself from rising out of his chair to help her. The temptation was so strong he had to hold on to the table. She didn't belong here, doing this job. She should be with him, not a roomful of other men.

"Mariah, isn't my order up yet?"

"Mariah, I need more coffee."

"Mariah, did you forget my apple pie?"

When Christian couldn't bear to listen any longer, he left the table, hurried past her and directly into the kitchen, where he found Ben filling dinner plates as fast as he could.

"Don't you hear what's going on out there?" he demanded.

"Sure I do," Ben said, chuckling. "I'm hearing the clang of that cash register. Didn't I tell you Mariah's been a real boon to my sales?"

"They're not giving her a moment's peace!" Christian clenched his fists at his sides.

"Ben, I need—" Mariah flew into the kitchen and stopped dead in her tracks when she saw Christian standing there. "More rolls," she finished weakly.

"I want to talk to you," Christian said, holding her captive with his stare.

"I can't." She looked over her shoulder. "I've got a roomful of hungry people all wanting their food right this minute." Her harried gaze darted past him to the counter, where Ben had placed the rolls. "I'm sorry, Christian, but I just can't."

"You're running yourself ragged," he said in a tone few would ignore. His patience was gone. He'd make her an offer she couldn't refuse. He wanted her out of this café, and he didn't care what it cost him.

"She can't talk now." It was Ben who answered on her behalf. "You seem to forget Mariah works for me. If you have anything to say to her, you'll have to do it on *her* time, not mine."

"Fine," Christian said, gritting his teeth with frustration. "I'll walk you home."

"That...that won't work, either," Mariah said, biting her lower lip. "Ralph already asked if he could walk me home, and I told him he could."

"Ralph," Christian repeated bitterly. Well, he'd have something to say about that. The man was not only his employee but a personal friend. Or used to be.

Christian's mood didn't improve during his meal. He watched as Mariah fluttered from one table to another, growing more harried with every minute. It gave him no pleasure to realize he hadn't underestimated her skills. Mariah made mistake after mistake, but what astonished him was that not a single customer complained. Half the time the men didn't even bother to correct her.

If she gave someone the wrong order she never knew it; people ate what they were served or traded with someone else.

Once he'd finished dishing up the meals, Ben positioned himself in front of the cash register and gleefully collected money. He grinned from ear to ear each time the register rang.

The only person in the whole restaurant who didn't seem happy was Christian. He'd planned to wait it out, convince Ralph to let him walk Mariah home, but after an hour he couldn't sit idle anymore.

His mood soured as the men openly flirted with her. It infuriated him when they told her how pretty she looked and how her presence brightened the whole place. It was all rubbish, and yet Mariah ate it up as quickly as they downed her apple pie.

He paid his tab and left wearing a scowl.

When he got home, his mood still hadn't improved. He turned on the television for a while. Thanks to the satellite dish, he had a large number of choices. But he surfed from channel to channel, unable to find a program that held his interest.

Disgusted with himself, he turned off the set and reached for the novel he'd started the week before. He read ten pages and couldn't remember a single word. Slamming the book closed, he began to pace. Soon he was studying the clock.

Ben closed shop around eight. He figured with cleanup and all, it would take an hour or so before Ralph escorted Mariah to her cabin. His jaw tightened at the thought, but Christian knew he had no claim on her. Nor did he want one, he tried to convince himself.

It was just that he felt responsible for Mariah. Yeah, responsible, the way a man might feel toward his little sister. She needed a guiding hand, someone to advise her and caution her.

He'd definitely cleared that up in his own mind. He felt immeasurably better.

Although he'd let her know he wanted to talk to her, he wasn't sure what he was going to say. He was walking a fine line here, and he knew it. If he pressured her, she'd resist.

What he hoped would happen was that she'd openly admit she missed Midnight Sons. At that point, Christian would be free to suggest she return. But he could see this wasn't likely without some concessions on his part. If only he could figure out exactly what they should be!

Christian bided his time, counted off the minutes, then walked out of the house. He stood on his front porch and stared across the street at his brother's place.

Scott and Eagle Catcher were playing in the yard. The boy was tossing a stick, and with boundless energy the husky was retrieving it. Susan was playing dolls with Chrissie Harris on the porch steps.

The reflection of the television screen showed in the window, and Christian assumed Sawyer and Abbey were cuddled up in front of it watching the news.

A year. In an amazingly short time his brother had become completely domesticated. Christian was happy for him, but he wanted none of this for himself. His life was just the way he liked it. One thing was certain: he didn't want a woman trying to change him, messing with his individuality. He'd leave this marriage-and-family stuff to his two older brothers.

He sighed as he walked down the steps and buried his hands in his pockets. He sincerely hoped Charles and Sawyer appreciated what he was about to do. If he was successful, they'd have their secretary back. If not, well, he'd deal with that after he'd talked to Mariah.

"Where you going, Uncle Christian?" Scott asked, running to catch up with him. Eagle Catcher was like a shadow at his side.

"For a walk." He hoped the brevity of his response would give Scott the hint.

"Someone's playing cowboys and Indians," Scott said conversationally.

"Really?"

"Yup, they're sending signals." Scott stopped, hands on his hips. "They're not doing it right, though. Look." He pointed toward the cabins where Mariah lived. "See all that smoke?"

"Smoke?"

Christian whirled around, and sure enough, a trail of dark smoke spiraled upward. His heart kicked into gear. "Those aren't smoke signals," he shouted. "That's a fire!"

Chapter 6

FIRE. MARIAH'S HEART hammered against her rib cage as she fought her overwhelming panic.

At first she tried to battle down the flames, but her puny efforts only seemed to make matters worse. The blaze came out from the pipes that led from her stove and licked ravenously at the old wood.

Soon the room was engulfed in smoke. Mariah choked and coughed, struggling to breathe. Grabbing what clothes she could, she staggered outside.

Air. Beautiful clean air filled her lungs. She sucked in a deep breath and immediately had a coughing fit. With no time to spare, she dragged in another lungful, then hurried back into the burning cabin for her purse.

Blinded by the smoke, she fumbled about helplessly, seeking her important papers, plus the most precious item she owned, the little jade bear. She could *not* lose that to the fire. All at once her mind wouldn't function properly. Where, oh where, had she left her purse? And the bear—wasn't it on her night-stand?

"Mariah!"

Someone yelled her name, but it sounded as if it had come from a great distance. She felt herself weakening, needing desperately to breathe. The smoke dulled her senses, but she refused to give up, refused to leave until she'd found the jade bear and her purse.

"Mariah!" Whoever sought her was much closer now. Her name came to her, sounding frantic and fearful.

"Here." How pitifully weak she felt. Not until she saw a pair of men's shoes did she realize she was on the floor.

Strong arms scooped her up and carried her out the door.

Air again. Beautiful, clean air.

She breathed in deeply, coughed again and staggered back toward the house.

"Mariah, are you crazy?" Christian stopped her by circling his arms about her waist. "You can't go back."

"But—"

"Nothing in there is worth dying for, damn it!"

He didn't understand what she was after, so she fought him, using every ounce of strength she possessed. She tugged and pulled but made no headway against his superior strength.

"Mariah," he said, turning her around. "Stop!" His fingers dug unmercifully into her shoulders. The fire hissed and spit, the heat so fierce it was suffocating.

"My purse, the bear…"

"Bear? What bear?"

In the distance Mariah heard the fire siren, piercing the evening with its urgency, screaming tragedy to the entire town.

"My purse and your gift—I need them." She'd lost everything, but her mind focused on the two things she valued most. She was thinking less and less clearly. So little made sense.

"You mean to tell me you risked your fool neck over your *purse?*" Christian shouted.

She jerked her elbows from side to side, futilely seeking release. "Let me go!"

"Not on your life," he said, none too gently. "Not on your life."

The bright yellow fire truck screeched to a stop in front of the burning cabin. Five or six men moved with impressive agility to free the hose. Their figures blurred as they worked together.

Mariah recognized Sawyer and Mitch Harris and Marvin Gold, who were all members of the volunteer fire department. She wanted to tell them to hurry, but even as the words worked their way up her throat, she knew it was too late. All was lost— her home and everything inside it. No hope remained.

With his arm wrapped protectively around her, Christian drew her away from her cabin, which was by now fully engulfed in flames. A chill came over her as she stood by and silently watched the fire swallow up everything she owned, every possession, save the armful of clothes she'd managed to snatch.

A breathless Dotty Livengood arrived, having raced over from her home. "Is Mariah all right?" She directed the question at Christian.

"I don't know."

"Let me check her."

"Mariah." Before Dotty reached her, Christian placed his hands on her shoulders and turned her to face him. "Were you burned?"

Mariah saw his lips move and heard the words, but it was as though he was standing on the other side of a glass wall.

Nothing seemed to touch her, to penetrate her confusion and loss. The question took several minutes to register. Was she hurt? Had she been burned? She felt no pain, not physical at least. Only loss, deep and personal loss.

"Her hands." This comment came from Christian, and it seemed to her, even from this emotional distance, that he was angry, frustrated. "It looks like she blistered her fingers."

"She must have tried to put out the fire herself." Dotty's gentle voice soothed her.

"I can't believe what she just did," Christian muttered. "I had to drag her out of the house. She was after her purse and some silly figurine I gave her. She risked her life for a forty-dollar piece of jade." His anger spilled out of him like water hissing against a hot burner.

"Christian." It was Dotty again, her voice forceful. "Calm down."

"I can't!" he shouted. "Do you realize she could have *died* in there? If I hadn't arrived when I did, no one would've been able to save her. We barely got out in time."

"Take several deep breaths," Dotty said. "You've both had a fright, but you're safe now. Everything's going to be fine."

"Her purse and a figurine! She was willing to die trying to save them!" The rage in Christian seemed to intensify as the other men dealt with the fire. He began to pace, his steps awkward and abrupt as he attempted to manage his anger.

Mariah was only now beginning to comprehend what had happened. She wasn't sure how the fire had started; all she knew was that she'd lit her stove, trying to chase away the chill. It'd been weeks since she'd lit the thing, and there must have been something in the chimney, because a few minutes later the pipe started to glow. The dry cabin wall behind it caught fire and then, in almost no time, the curtains. The flames roared across the room so quickly, they'd been impossible to stop.

"Take her over to the clinic," Dotty instructed Christian. "I'll tend to those burns."

Others were arriving now, children and adults alike. Their eyes filled with sympathy and fear.

"Go," Dotty told Christian.

He guided Mariah away from the gathering crowd. She looked back only once at what had been her home.

Dotty got there a little later. "They weren't able to save anything," she said sadly.

Christian nodded. He couldn't seem to stand still. And Mariah could barely move; she didn't have the strength. It felt as though someone had sucked the very life from her. It was an effort just to keep her head up.

"Mariah," Dotty said in a gentle voice, "you've had quite a shock."

Christian paced the clinic. "She was on the floor when I found her," he said. "If I'd arrived a minute later I might never have reached her. She came so close to dying in the fire."

"Christian, you've had a scare, too."

"The woman hasn't got a brain in her head. Just how important can a purse be?" With rough, angry movements, he rubbed the back of his neck. "She shouldn't even have been *living* in that cabin. The place is a firetrap! But she was so damn stubborn, insisting this was where she had to stay—"

"Christian!"

"She should go back to Seattle!" he exploded. "I'll personally pay for her ticket. At least there she won't be dealing with fires and a bunch of women-hungry men."

She should be back in Seattle. The words penetrated the haze in Mariah's mind, and a sob erupted from deep in her throat. Christian had never made a secret of how he felt about her, but the fact that he could be so cruel now, when she'd lost everything, was more than she could bear.

"Christian O'Halloran, what a rotten thing to say!" Dotty snapped. "I think it would be best if you left. The last thing Mariah needs now is you haranguing her."

Mariah watched Christian stomp out of the health clinic.

Leaning her head against the wall, she sighed and closed her eyes. Tears were close to the surface, but she held them at bay, concentrating, instead, on the pain in her hands. They'd started to throb, and she was grateful when Dotty returned.

Soon Dotty had taken care of her burns and bandaged her hands. Shortly after that, Abbey and Lanni O'Halloran came by with Karen Caldwell and Bethany Harris to check on her.

"Are you okay?" Abbey asked, sitting next to Mariah and placing an arm around her shoulders.

"I'm fine," Mariah assured her friends. But she wasn't. The sense of devastation hit her again, bringing fresh tears. Everything she'd worked for in the past year was lost. The man she secretly loved was furious with her. Now her hands were burned and bandaged and she was unable to work. She had no home, no place to live.

"If I was smart, I'd do what Christian said," she mumbled, forcing herself to smile.

"What did Christian say?" Bethany asked, glancing at Dotty.

"He suggested she return to Seattle," the nurse answered, her lips pinched disapprovingly. "Someone needs to have a talk with that young man."

"He said *what?*" Lanni demanded, outraged.

"How dare he!" This came from Karen.

The atmosphere in the room crackled with indignation.

"Just a moment," Abbey said, stroking Mariah's back. "Let's not be so quick to condemn him. I had a chance to talk to him just now, and you know what? I've never seen Christian so upset."

With me, Mariah added silently.

"He's had the scare of a lifetime. Think about it. Christian almost lost Mariah, and he couldn't handle that."

"Then why would he say something so terrible to her, especially now?" Lanni asked, her eyes flashing at the insult.

"In my experience, a man will express what he fears most, rather than let it sneak up on him. Women do the same thing, but not as often."

"You're making excuses for him," Bethany said.

"No," Abbey insisted. "I think he'll be back to apologize to Mariah the minute he realizes what he said. Christian no more wants Mariah to move back to Seattle than he wants to live there himself."

"And if he doesn't apologize, then I know a number of women who'll be more than happy to assist him in seeing his mistake," Karen said meaningfully.

Dotty chuckled. "You know, I almost feel sorry for that boy."

"Now listen, Mariah, we've got this all figured out," Abbey assured her, again with gentle firmness.

"Right." Karen stood in the center of the room, arms akimbo. "You're going to need someplace to live until you rebuild. I'm sure that with all the new construction in town, you could find someone to do it quickly."

"Rebuild. Yes. I—I don't know what I'm going to do," she

whispered, grateful for her friends. Her mind remained confused, her confidence in the future badly shaken.

"You don't need to worry about that," Karen continued. "You're going to come and live with Matt and me at the lodge."

"The lodge." Mariah knew she must sound like an echo, but making decisions, even simple ones, was beyond her.

"We're going to take care of everything," Abbey promised. Somehow Mariah doubted that anyone could help her repair the mess she'd made of her life. It was too late for that.

"ARE YOU GOING to the Labor Day community dance?" Ben asked Christian when he arrived for breakfast a couple of days after the fire.

"The dance?" Hard Luck routinely celebrated Labor Day with a festive get-together. Because of all the problems at the office and the chaos following the fire, Christian hadn't given the matter more than a fleeting thought. "I guess," he said with little enthusiasm. He attended every Labor Day dance and didn't expect this year to be any different.

"Will you be taking Mariah?"

Christian noticed that Ben had saved that for the punch line. At the sound of Mariah's name, it was all Christian could do to keep from clenching his fists.

Every time he remembered the fire, he became so angry he couldn't think straight. The woman had nearly lost her life! A chill ran down his spine again at the realization. He averted his gaze, not wanting Ben to know how intensely all this had affected him.

"Uh, how's she doing?" Christian cut the sourdough hotcakes with his fork.

"I hear she's staying at the lodge."

Christian nodded; he'd already learned that much.

"With her hands all bandaged up, she can't work. She felt real bad about that," Ben said, "but I've been running this café on my own close to twenty years now. I told her I could manage for however long it takes her hands to heal."

"Was she badly burned?"

"Nah. Dotty seems to think she'll be good as new in a week or so."

Christian was relieved to hear it.

"I understand you single-handedly riled every woman in town." Ben chuckled as he walked to the other end of the counter, where Duke and Ralph were finishing breakfast, and refreshed their coffee.

"So it seems," Christian muttered. He wasn't proud of his outburst, but he'd been so furious with Mariah that he couldn't have suppressed the words if he'd tried. At the time, he'd meant every one. He'd never been more frightened in his life. Only last night, he'd awakened in a cold sweat, trembling. He'd dreamed about the fire, that he'd gone into the house and hadn't been able to find her. For a long time after he woke, his heart continued to race. There was no point in trying to sleep again, so before dawn, he'd dressed and gone to the burned-out cabin. He'd stood there until the sun rose, giving incoherent thanks that Mariah had been spared. *"She's safe."* He'd repeated it over and over—but couldn't quite forget that she'd almost died.

"What are you going to do now?" Ben asked.

"What *can* I do? Apologize, I guess," Christian muttered. He glanced over at the two pilots, feeling like a fool. As it was, his own brother had no use for him. Sawyer had yet to forgive him for losing their secretary, and the situation hadn't improved, since he hadn't immediately hired another. Now, to make everything even worse, he seemed to be blaming Christian for the danger to Mariah, for letting her stay in the cabin. *Letting* her stay!

"Good." Ben sighed as though the issue of Christian's apology had been weighing heavily on his mind.

After paying his tab, Christian hurried to the office. Sawyer was busy on the phone and left him to deal with the pilots and their assignments for the day. The usual dissatisfaction broke out, but he dealt with it, if rather more ruthlessly than normal.

During a midmorning lull, Christian slipped out and walked over to the lodge to see Mariah. On the way, he formulated what he wanted to say. He was so intent on putting his apology together that he didn't notice she was sitting on the front-porch swing.

"Karen and Matt are gone for the morning," she announced as he began to climb the porch steps.

Christian paused, one foot on the ground and the other on the first stair. His gaze was immediately drawn to the bandages on her hands and then to the sadness in her eyes. The need to comfort her was strong, but he knew she didn't want anything to do with him now. Personally he didn't blame her.

Mariah's hair was tied back, away from her face, and she wore a simple light green summer dress that suited her perfectly. He didn't recognize it and wondered if one of the woman in town had lent it to her. No matter; she'd never looked lovelier.

"I didn't come to see Karen or Matt," he said, finishing the climb.

It was unseasonably warm for late August, despite some cool

days the week before. The swing, a recent addition to the lodge, swayed gently in the breeze. He could hear birdsong in the distance. The sun splashed over her shoulders, glinting off her red hair, adding an aura of cheerfulness he knew was false.

He found it difficult to pull his gaze from hers. Her expression was blank, neither welcoming nor unwelcoming.

"I came to apologize for what I said," he blurted. He might as well deal with the unpleasantness right away. "I didn't mean it. The last thing I want you to do is leave Alaska."

"But you wouldn't object if I found my way out of Hard Luck." Her voice was as dispassionate as her eyes.

"No, that's not what I meant. I don't want you to leave Hard Luck." She was making this difficult, but then, he suspected he deserved it.

"Here." He dug inside his pocket and fished out her jade bear. It had taken no small effort to find the figurine in the charred rubble, and unfortunately he'd been unable to recover her purse. He'd spent hours yesterday morning, once the sun had risen, sifting through the ashes and debris.

Mariah's eyes lit up. "You found my bear!" It was the first emotion she'd shown. Her lower lip trembled, and he realized she was struggling to hold back tears. She gripped the figurine tightly. "Thank you, Christian."

He shrugged, making light of the accomplishment. "It was nothing."

Her beautiful brown eyes held his. Annoyed, Christian looked away. Not because he didn't find her attractive—he did, more so each time he saw her—but because she reminded him of what he'd been trying to forget ever since he'd kissed her. He didn't *want* to see her eyes like this, wide and beguiling.

He couldn't resist their luminous beauty or her enticing mouth or soft, pale skin. If he looked at her, he'd want to kiss her again.

He remembered when Charles had first learned about Lanni's relationship to Catherine Fletcher and how he'd avoided looking at her. But this was different, he told himself. This was Mariah, and his feelings toward her were crystal clear. She needed someone—an older-brother kind of someone—to help her. A friend to steer her in the right direction. Christian wasn't like his brothers. No, sir. Charles and Sawyer wore their hearts on their sleeves. Not Christian. Sure, he'd kissed Mariah, but that had been a…a fluke.

Yet even now, after all this time, he could remember the way she'd felt, the way her mouth had tasted. He'd done everything he could to push that memory to the farthest reaches of his mind, but to no avail.

Maybe, just maybe, he was like his brothers, after all.

Without invitation he sat down on the swing next to her. It seemed important that she realize how sincere his apology was. "I'm sorry—I don't know what came over me the night of the fire," he muttered, knowing that was no excuse, but he had none better to offer. "It's just that you could have died." His jaw tightened as a surge of anger threatened to take control of him all over again. "If you decide you never want to speak to me because of the things I said, I wouldn't blame you. But I'm hoping you won't do that."

He couldn't believe exactly what he *was* hoping. The urge, the need to kiss her, was back. And it was more powerful than before.

"I understand, Christian."

"You do?"

"All is forgiven." She smiled, as if amused by the melodramatic words. "You were angry. Upset."

His heart felt lighter. She smiled sweetly at him, and he noted once more that, while she didn't possess the striking beauty of Allison Reynolds, Mariah's loveliness went much deeper. Was so much more *real*.

He stared at her mouth, soft and moist. He recalled how her lips had melted beneath his and how…

He cleared his throat and glanced quickly away.

"Thank you for finding the jade piece for me."

"It was the least I could do." He shrugged, tried to grin, but his heart pounded like a lovelorn teenager's.

"Mariah." He whispered her name before he drew her into his arms. She seemed to understand what he was asking of her; she leaned toward him. Their mouths came together with an urgency he'd never experienced.

Christian's breathing was labored. Their previous kisses had been tentative exchanges, brief encounters. Not this one.

A noise sounded in the background, and with great reluctance, Christian broke off the kiss. A truck barreled down the dirt road, leaving a trail of dust in its wake.

If he was going to kiss Mariah, Christian decided, he didn't want the entire town looking on.

"Ben misses you," he whispered, hardly able to find his voice. He dared not dwell on how wonderful it was to kiss her, and how difficult it was to keep from kissing her again.

Mariah lowered her lashes and smiled. "I can't imagine why. I'm an even worse waitress than I was a secretary."

"That's not true." The irony of the situation didn't escape him; here he was defending her, when only a few months— weeks!—earlier he'd been the one listing her shortcomings.

"Well, it's a moot point now." Her eyes dulled—with sadness, regret, worry, he wasn't sure which.

"You'll be back in no time." What he hoped, though, was that she'd be back at Midnight Sons. Another truck sped past. Christian had no idea the road in front of the lodge was so busy. He checked his watch; Sawyer would be on his case if he stayed any longer. He thought of mentioning that he'd like her back in the office, but he didn't want to rush her. And he didn't want her thinking that kiss had anything to do with work. Besides, he'd already swallowed one serving of crow; he wasn't eager to down another quite so soon. He'd ease into the topic, be sure she understood how much they missed her, how much *he* missed her.…

"I have to go," he said, hoping his voice conveyed his reluctance.

"I know. Thanks again for finding the bear for me and for stopping by."

On impulse, he leaned forward and gently pressed his lips to hers. It would've been easy to let the kiss develop into something more than a farewell gesture, but he forced himself to make it just that.

His step was almost jaunty as he hurried back to the office. When he walked in the door, Sawyer cast him a disgruntled look.

"What took you so long?" he snapped, but Christian assumed his brother didn't actually expect him to answer.

He picked up his phone messages and sat down at his desk to return the calls. His hand was on the receiver when his brother spoke again.

"I hate to be a pest about this," Sawyer muttered, "but when can we expect another secretary?"

"Soon." He knew the minute he said the word that he'd used it one time too many.

"You've been saying that ever since Mariah left," Sawyer said impatiently. "Either hire someone else, or I will."

Christian didn't take kindly to ultimatums. "Now listen here, Sawyer. I've put up with about as much of this as I'm going to."

"You! Seems to me you haven't done a thing to find Mariah's replacement." He glared at him from across the office. "I'm beginning to think you don't *intend* to hire anyone else."

"I don't."

Sawyer's jaw fell open. "Why the heck not?"

"Because I'm going to convince Mariah to come back."

"I already tried that," Sawyer told him, sighing wearily.

"But I caused the problem, not you."

Sawyer snorted. "You won't hear me coming to your defense on that one."

"I planned to say something to her this morning, but—"

"So that's where you were!" Sawyer's look revealed his curiosity.

"Yeah. I apologized and she accepted my apology." He paused. "Ben reminded me about the Labor Day dance, and I think I'll ask Mariah. You know, get back into her good graces." He had an ulterior motive, as well. From now on, Christian wanted every man in town to stay away from her. By escorting her to the dance he was sending a silent message. Mariah was off-limits. Out-of-bounds.

Sawyer brightened. "Ask Mariah to the dance—now that's a great idea. Wine and dine her. Women like that sort of thing."

"I thought so, too." Christian felt downright smug. Everything was falling neatly into place, just the way it should.

Before long Mariah would be back at Midnight Sons.

Christian didn't want to appear too anxious, so he waited until the following evening to pay Mariah a second visit. He toyed with the idea of bringing her a small gift. Easier said than done. He surveyed the office and saw the latest issue of *Aviation News* on Sawyer's desk. He tucked it under his arm, thinking she'd enjoy reading it. Maybe it would remind her of everything she'd liked about Midnight Sons, get her back in the mood.

Humming cheerfully to himself, he strolled down the hard dirt road. The evening was chilly, and he was glad he'd remembered his sweatshirt. That way, they could sit out on the porch again. With any luck Karen and Matt would be away. He wasn't planning to kiss Mariah, but if the spirit moved them, well…

It wasn't until Christian had rounded the corner to the lodge that he noticed Bill Landgrin's truck parked outside. He stopped, frowning, then increased his pace.

He found Mariah sitting on the swing as if she'd been there all along awaiting his return. She looked as pretty as she had yesterday, but happier, more animated.

Bill was leaning casually against the porch rail, his legs crossed. He certainly seemed to have settled in for the evening.

Christian opened the gate and started purposefully up the walkway. Mariah's eyes met his, and he read the welcome in her look. Landgrin twisted his head around; when he saw Christian, he glared.

"What are you doing here?" Landgrin demanded.

"I've come to see Mariah."

"So have I," the pipeline worker said, sounding none too friendly. "You can wait your turn like everyone else."

"It's going to take someone a whole lot bigger than you to get me to leave," Christian informed the other man in deceptively calm tones. He didn't appreciate Bill moving in on Mariah, and he wanted that understood.

"Bill. Christian. Please."

Both men ignored her. They were too busy glowering at each other. By nature, Christian wasn't a violent man, but there were few people who raised his ire as much as Bill.

"You had your chance with Mariah," Bill said.

Christian didn't know what Bill was implying, but he didn't like it. The fact was, he didn't like the other man, period. One thing was certain: he didn't want Bill anywhere near her.

"She worked for you for a whole year!"

"That has nothing to do with this." The point wasn't worth discussing.

"You could've asked her out anytime. You didn't, so she's fair game for the rest of us."

From the corner of his eye, Christian saw Mariah stand up from the swing. "Will you two kindly stop? You're talking about me like...like I'm some kind of hunting trophy. Fair game!"

Christian had seen Mariah in this mood before. "Bill will apologize," he said immediately, pointing at the other man. "I believe you owe the lady an apology."

"Bill!" Mariah shouted. "What do you mean, Bill? What about *you*?"

Shocked, Christian broke eye contact with Bill long enough to glance her way. "Me? What did I do wrong?"

"How much time have you got?" Bill muttered under his breath, snickering.

Christian reverted his attention to Landgrin. "Okay, I'll say what I came to say. Then, in the interests of fairness, I'll leave."

"I was here first," Bill took pleasure in reminding him.

"Fine." Christian raised both hands in a gesture of peace, the magazine still tucked under his arm. He moved forward and handed it to Mariah. "I thought you might like this."

"Thank you," she replied stiffly.

"And…" he said, clearing his throat. This wasn't easy, especially with another man listening in. "I wanted to know if you'd attend the Labor Day dance with me."

"Now just one damn minute," Landgrin blared. "That's the reason *I'm* here."

A slow, satisfied smile unraveled across Christian's face. "I asked first."

"But I was here first!"

"Bill. Christian."

Again they both ignored her.

"She's going with me," Christian said, glancing briefly at Mariah for confirmation.

"Sorry, pal. If anyone's taking Mariah to that dance, it'll be me."

"Not on your life." Christian was willing to eat a whole lot more than crow just to get Bill out of the picture.

"As it happens," Mariah said sternly, "I won't be attending the dance with either of you. Duke Porter asked me two days ago, and I've already agreed to go with him."

Having said that, she walked past them both and disappeared into the lodge.

Chapter 7

DUKE PORTER! Christian didn't like it, not one bit. While he was playing it cool, not wanting to appear overeager—because, of course, he wasn't—Duke had gone behind his back and asked Mariah to the dance. Didn't that beat all!

However, Christian decided he wasn't *really* angry that Duke had outdone him; actually he found the whole thing rather amusing. His own pilot had shown him—and Bill—a thing or two.

Mariah weighed heavily on his mind. His possessive attitude toward her had begun to bother him. Duke didn't concern him because—well, because he knew Duke wasn't romantically interested in her. At least that was what Duke had been claiming for months, and Christian finally believed him.

Bill was another story altogether. He gritted his teeth every time he thought about the pipeline worker making a play for Mariah. What irritated him most was that she didn't see through his fast-talking style. Christian had credited her with better sense than that.

In the past few weeks, everything had changed between him and Mariah, and Christian didn't fully understand the differences yet.

Often when he was disturbed about something, he'd pull a flying assignment himself. That morning, instead of delegating Duke to take the mail into Fairbanks, Christian planned to make the run himself. He left a quick note, hoping Duke wouldn't care, and set out early.

The morning was foggy and cold for the end of August. The mist felt cool and refreshing while he was on the ground, but icy crystals formed on the plane's wings as he headed south.

En route, his thoughts were once again filled with Mariah. True, he wanted her back as his secretary, but he didn't dwell on that. His concern centered on the attention other men were giving her. Naturally, he wasn't interested in her himself, but he didn't want to see her make a mistake.

Mariah was sweet and genuine, a bit naive and too darn trusting. At times he wondered if she had *any* sense, and at others he was astonished by her insight and sensitivity.

The woman perplexed him.

He touched down in Fairbanks and collected the mail, then flew straight back to Hard Luck. An hour later, he landed on the gravel runway.

Duke was in the office waiting when Christian returned from unloading the cargo. The pilot glared at him. "You grounded me—again—because Mariah's going to the dance with me, didn't you?" His eyes fairly snapped with anger.

The verbal attack caught Christian by surprise. He finished

removing his black rayon jacket with its Midnight Sons logo on the back before he answered.

"No, Duke, of course not! Didn't you find my note?"

"That didn't explain anything. You took my run! You're angry because Mariah is going to the dance with *me*."

"Where's Sawyer?" He wasn't ignoring the outburst, but needed to know where his brother had disappeared. With the office shorthanded, this was not the time for Sawyer to be yakking over coffee with Ben.

"He stepped out for a couple of minutes. He'll be back. Now answer me!"

Christian exhaled forcefully.

"You can't, and we both know why," snarled Duke. "I've been with Midnight Sons for more years than I want to remember. Until now, I've always considered you and Sawyer to be equitable and fair-minded employers. No longer." He walked over to the desk and picked up a sheet of paper. "As of this moment, you have my notice."

"Your…notice?"

"Yeah," Duke said, his look colder than Christian had ever seen it. "I quit." With that, he grabbed his leather jacket and stalked out the door.

No sooner had Duke left than Sawyer walked in. "What's the problem with Duke? He looked pretty mad."

"He is," Christian said, and slumped down in his chair. "He just quit."

"What?" Sawyer exploded. "Quit? Why? Duke's been with us almost from the beginning."

"I know." Christian propped his elbows on the desk and resisted the urge to bury his face in his hands. Everything he touched lately turned to dust. Because of him, Midnight Sons had lost Mariah, and now he was solely responsible for Duke's leaving.

Sawyer walked over and read Duke's letter. The message was brief and to the point. Christian could picture the pilot sitting at the keyboard, tapping out the letter with one finger, swearing under his breath and getting angrier by the minute.

"What happened?"

Rather than go into a long and complicated explanation, Christian opted for a shorter version of the truth. "He's upset about me taking the mail run this morning." Christian rubbed a weary hand down his face. "Despite what he thinks, I didn't do it to punish him."

"Punish him?" Sawyer sounded more confused than ever.

"Duke seems to think that because he's taking Mariah to the dance, I—"

"What has that got to do with anything?"

"Absolutely nothing," Christian insisted, close to losing his own patience now. "Why should I care if Duke takes Mariah to the Labor Day dance? I needed time to do some thinking, so I decided to do the mail run. How was I to know Duke would consider it a personal affront?"

"I don't believe this." Sawyer walked from one end of the trailer to the other in agitated strides. "We—Midnight Sons—recruited women to Hard Luck well over a year ago, and everything's gone pretty smoothly.

"Some have come and gone, and others have stayed. The town's thriving. There's been construction all summer. New homes are going up. The lodge is repaired and open for business. John and Sally's mobile home is up, and more are ordered. Midnight Sons started all this, and now Midnight

Sons is going down the drain—just when we should be doing better than ever! Could someone kindly tell me *why?*"

"You're exaggerating."

"I don't think so," Sawyer continued, growing more impassioned. "We've had more complaints in the past two weeks than we've had in two years."

Mariah's absence from the office would explain that.

"Duke's quitting, and he isn't the only unhappy pilot we've got. I wouldn't be surprised if Ralph left with him. We might lose Ted, too."

The pilots had been good friends for a lot of years, and Christian suspected his brother was right. This could result in a mass exodus.

"I'll talk to him," he promised. "It's me Duke's upset with, not the business. I'll give him a couple of hours to settle down, then I'll approach him."

Sawyer's icy glare thawed only a little. "So you're going to take care of this?"

"I'll do my best," Christian promised.

SAWYER NEEDED to get out of the office and vent his frustration. He walked to the library, located in the log cabin that had once belonged to his grandfather. Abbey sat behind the desk, busy updating her meticulous files. She looked up and smiled warmly when he walked in.

"My, oh my," she greeted him. "Sure looks like you're having one of those days."

"Duke handed in his notice."

It was almost comical to watch Abbey's expressive eyes fill with shock. "Duke? But why? Something must have happened!"

"Christian." If it wasn't so serious, Sawyer might've laughed over his younger brother's condition. He recognized the symptoms, having experienced them himself a year earlier.

Christian was falling in love.

"What did he do this time?"

Sawyer could see from the look on his wife's face that she was fast losing patience with her brother-in-law.

"He took the mail run himself, grounding Duke. Christian claimed he needed a chance to think, but Duke figured it was a form of punishment because he'd asked Mariah to the dance."

"Was it?"

Sawyer pulled out a chair at the reading table, a recent addition to the library. "I don't know. I don't think so. Christian may not be the most sensitive guy in the world, but he'd never intentionally do anything to upset the pilots or hurt the business."

"You know what's wrong with him, don't you?" Abbey asked.

"I have my suspicions."

Abbey smiled, and for the life of him, Sawyer couldn't take his eyes off her. She grew more beautiful every day, he thought, especially now that she was carrying his baby.

"Christian's in love."

Sawyer chuckled. "Was I this bad?"

"Worse," she said primly, leaving no room for doubt.

"Oh, come on," Sawyer returned. "You know what the real problem is? Christian's the youngest of the family, and—"

"Exactly," Abbey cut in, "and his role models are you and Charles." She shook her head. "The poor guy's so confused he has no idea how to behave with a woman."

"What's wrong with Charles and me?" Sawyer demanded.

"You mean I have to explain it?" Abbey rolled her eyes. "Charles was willing to let Lanni walk out of his life—all because of an old family feud. And you, my fine husband, offered me one of the most insulting marriage proposals any woman could receive."

"I was desperate," he said quickly.

"My point exactly. With such pathetic examples, it's no wonder Christian can't decipher his feelings."

"I might not have said all the fancy words women like to read in those books," he said, gesturing toward the romance section in the fiction department, "but I got my message across, didn't I?"

Her faced softened and she grinned, patting her rounded stomach. "You certainly did."

Sawyer had known he loved Abbey and her children a year ago, but his feelings then couldn't compare with their intensity now. In retrospect, his life had been empty and shallow before he'd met Abbey. Her love gave him a sense of purpose, a reason to get up in the morning. Abbey and the children were his incentive to be the best husband and father—the best *man*—he could.

"Maybe we should...help Christian," Abbey suggested. "Subtly, of course. He'll resist any obvious attempts to steer him in the right direction."

"Christian would resent it if we intruded."

Abbey looked disappointed. "You're sure?"

"It won't do one bit of good, sweetheart," Sawyer told her. "My brother's got to figure this out all on his own, the same way Charles did."

"And you!"

"And me," Sawyer agreed with a grin.

Abbey chewed on her lower lip. "It took Charles *weeks*, remember?"

Sawyer wasn't likely to forget. His older brother had walked around town like a wounded bear, snapping at everyone in his vicinity.

"I just wonder…" Sawyer murmured.

"What?"

"If Midnight Sons will survive Christian's falling in love."

DUKE WAS SITTING glumly on the end of his bed when Christian let himself into the bunkhouse. He glanced up; as soon as he saw who it was, he looked away.

"Got a minute?" Christian asked.

Duke made a show of checking his watch. "I suppose." He stood up and crossed to his locker, pulled out a duffel bag and started stuffing things into it.

"I'd like to talk to you about leaving Midnight Sons."

"Yeah, well, I didn't think you wanted to chat about the weather."

Duke's back was to him, and Christian was having a hard time finding the right words. He was willing enough to apologize, only he wasn't sure what he was supposed to apologize *for*.

"Uh, taking your run this morning," Christian began, broaching the topic tentatively. "I should've explained why I did that. I needed to think something over, and I do that best when I'm in the air." The excuse sounded weak even to his own ears, but he'd swear on his father's grave that he hadn't been punishing Duke for asking Mariah to the dance.

Duke whirled around to face him. "Tell me, Christian, do I look like a bloody secretary?"

The question took him aback. "No. I don't understand why you'd ask that?"

"Well, what do you think I was doing for two and a half hours this morning? Answering the phone, looking for files, running errands."

"You didn't need to do any of that."

"Well, Sawyer couldn't do it all. He was rushing around all morning. What was I supposed to do, ignore the phone? I go in to complain about you taking my flight, and next thing I know I'm talking to some woman in Anchorage. She says she's a travel agent and that she's booked all these flights with us. I couldn't find a darn thing in any of the files that says she did or didn't."

"Did her name happen to be Penny Ferguson?"

"Yeah, she's the one," Duke said, narrowing his eyes.

Christian groaned and covered his face. He'd resign, too, if he'd been stuck on the phone with Penny, who was demanding and difficult.

"I apologize," Christian said. "I never intended for you to have to deal with Mrs. Ferguson."

"You mean she's married?" Duke shook his head. "My condolences to Mr. Ferguson. The woman reminded me of that attorney friend of Mariah's."

At the mention of her name, Christian cleared his throat. It was now or never. "Speaking of Mariah…" he began, uncertain where to head from there.

"What's with the two of you, anyway?" Duke asked. The anger had left his eyes, replaced with curiosity.

"Nothing," Christian said quickly, perhaps too quickly.

Duke frowned, then shrugged. "If that's what you say, who am I to argue?" He turned around and stuffed a shirt deep into his duffel bag.

"About your letter of resignation," Christian said cautiously. "I'm hoping I can get you to reconsider. You're a valuable part of our business—probably one of the best pilots in all of Alaska." A little flattery would probably help, although that statement wasn't far from the truth.

Duke didn't respond.

"I looked over the payroll file and noticed it was well past time for you to get a raise."

Duke faced him again, his interest obviously piqued. "What're you offering?"

In the last year or so, Midnight Sons had been doing good business. Very good. "Twenty percent increase in your base salary."

Duke's eyes widened. "Okay! Mariah thought you'd only go for ten." He clamped his mouth shut and flushed.

Christian raised his eyebrows. "You discussed this with Mariah?"

"Yeah," Duke answered in a way that challenged him to make something of it. "She's the one who talked me into staying. If it wasn't for her, I'd have been out of here on the afternoon flight." He shoved his duffel bag in the locker and slammed the door. "You might say I was a bit agitated when I left your office this morning. I stopped by the lodge, and Mariah and I had a long talk."

Christian would've liked to be a bug on the wall for that.

"She's loyal to you, Christian. Really loyal. The thing is, I'm not sure you deserve it."

At this point, neither was Christian.

September 1996

MUSIC BLARED from several huge speakers strategically set about the polished hardwood floor. It was Labor Day, and Hard Luck's school gymnasium was as crowded as it had been back when the state had built the school during the oil-rich years.

Linen-covered tables arranged against the wall were laden with food left over from the earlier potluck. There were salads of all kinds and desserts to tempt the saints, and a dozen casseroles redolent with onion and garlic and savory herbs. Contributions to the feast had been so plentiful that by nine o'clock, enough food remained to feed everyone a second time.

Mariah had made four apple pies, although Karen had peeled the apples. She was able to do most things for herself, although the bandages tended to frustrate her. But they'd be off soon, according to Dotty.

Duke had been a thoughtful, devoted companion all evening, and after dinner, they'd danced a number of times.

Schoolchildren raced with inexhaustible energy from one end of the room to the other. Several had removed their shoes and slipped and skidded across the slick floor.

So far Mariah hadn't seen Christian, and she was beginning to wonder if he'd make an appearance. And if he did, she wondered if he'd bring another woman to the festivities. Foolishly Mariah had dreamed of seeing Christian here; she'd dreamed that he'd take her in his arms, dance with her, kiss her… But that was all fantasy, she reminded herself.

Christian probably wouldn't even show up, but Mariah had given up second-guessing her former boss. The kisses they'd exchanged had been incredible, but as far as she could tell they meant nothing to Christian. Afterward, he'd looked repentant and even angry. Except the last time…

Because her feet hurt from her new shoes, Mariah sat out the next dance. Duke, however, became involved in an imaginative free-form dance with Angie Hughes.

"Hello, Mariah."

"Christian…hello." He'd snuck up on her. Her heart reacted with a leap of happiness.

"How's the dance going?" he asked, sitting in the empty chair beside her.

"Great." Her pulse reacted as if she'd been caught doing something illegal.

After a few minutes of silence, he said, "I understand I owe you a debt of thanks."

Her eyes opened wide in surprise. She couldn't think clearly when he was this close. The light, spicy scent of his aftershave sent her senses reeling. She considered it grossly unfair that he should affect her like this when he clearly didn't return her feelings.

"Duke explained that you'd talked him into staying," he continued.

She shrugged, making light of her involvement.

"I want you to know I appreciate it." He hesitated and rubbed his hand down his thigh. "I don't know what it is lately, but I seem to have developed a talent for making enemies."

"That's not true." As always she was prepared to defend him. "It wasn't you Duke was angry with, but Mrs. Ferguson."

He smiled and seemed grateful for her support.

"Have you eaten?" Mariah's mother seemed to think food was a remedy for all problems, social or personal, and Mariah found herself falling back on that familiar solution. "Dotty's salmon casserole is wonderful." She regretted opening her mouth almost immediately. She strongly suspected that women like Allison Reynolds didn't rave about someone's salmon casserole.

"I ate earlier," he said.

Everyone in the room seemed to be glancing their way with expressions of anticipation and curiosity. If Christian noticed he didn't comment. It was all Mariah could do not to stand up and beg everyone to ignore them.

"Would you like to dance?"

Mariah couldn't have been more shocked if he'd proposed marriage. *Her dream come true.* "Yes—that would be very nice." She forgot how much her feet hurt; at that moment she would gladly have walked across broken glass for the opportunity to be in Christian's arms.

Christian rose from his seat, then hesitated.

He'd changed his mind. Mariah recognized that look.

"Will Duke have a problem with it?" he asked, scanning the room.

"I'm sure he won't, since he's dancing with Angie Hughes."

Mariah had no idea whether Duke was or not, but it sounded good.

A ballad, a slow, melancholy song about tormented lovers, had just begun. Christian drew her into his arms and held her loosely.

"How are your hands?" he asked in a concerned voice.

"Fine. Dotty says the bandages can come off tomorrow." Her head moved closer to his, and was soon tucked beneath his chin. It seemed so perfect, so natural, to be in his embrace like this.

"Is everything working out for you at the lodge?"

He certainly seemed full of questions. For her part, Mariah

would've preferred to close her eyes and give herself over to the music. And the dream.

"Karen and Matt have been wonderful. I—I don't know what I would've done without them. Everyone's been so good to me." It was true—almost everyone had stopped by to see her, to wish her well. While she hadn't made any decisions about rebuilding, she felt the support of her friends and, in fact, the whole community.

"If you need anything..."

"I don't," and because he couldn't seem to take a hint, Mariah started to hum along with the song.

"That's a nice song, isn't it?" Christian asked next.

Mariah groaned. "Christian," she whispered. "Please shut up."

He tensed, then chuckled lightly. It was probably the boldest thing she'd ever said to him, but Mariah didn't care. This was *her* fantasy, and she wasn't about to let him ruin it with idle chatter.

If he *did* insist on making small talk, she wanted him to tell her how beautiful she looked. She'd flown into Fairbanks a week ago to buy some new clothes, and it wasn't Duke she was thinking of when she chose the denim skirt with the white eyelet hem. Nor was it the prospect of an evening with *Duke* that had prompted her to dab on her brand-new—and terribly expensive—French perfume.

Her smile sagged with disappointment. She should've known Christian wouldn't live up to her fantasy. Shaking her head, Mariah smiled softly to herself.

"Something amuses you?"

"You aren't supposed to talk," she reminded him.

He brought back his head just enough to look at her.

"This is my fantasy," she announced without thinking.

"Your fantasy?"

"Never mind."

"No, tell me," he said.

He was going to ruin everything with this incessant talking. "Just shut up and hold me."

His laughter stirred the hair at her temple, but she noticed that his arms tightened fractionally around her.

"What about kissing you?"

"Yes," she whispered eagerly. But because she didn't want to be the focus of any further attention, she added, "Not here, though."

"Is that part of the fantasy, too?"

"Yes."

"Do you have someplace special in mind?" he asked. "For me to kiss you, that is."

Anywhere but on the dance floor. She wasn't given an opportunity to say more, however, because they were interrupted by Lanni and Charles.

"Christian. It's about time you showed up. Where've you been all evening?" Charles asked.

"Around," Christian answered shortly.

Mariah saw that he attempted to steer her away, but they were trapped in a maze of other couples.

"Mariah, that's a lovely color on you," Lanni commented, gesturing at her pale blue silk blouse.

"Thanks." She cast a forlorn look at Christian.

"Listen—"

"Stop," Christian said to his brother, holding up one hand. "We don't mean to be rude, but you're interrupting a dream here."

"A dream?" Charles repeated. He apparently thought this was some kind of joke.

"A fantasy," Mariah elaborated. She wasn't sure what possessed her to keep talking but the words seemed to flow without volition. "Christian was about to kiss me, and he can't do that if folks are going to interrupt us."

Charles burst out laughing, but stopped abruptly when Lanni glared at him. "Sorry."

"There," Christian whispered to Mariah, "is that better?" He smiled down at her, and the compulsion to stand on tiptoe and thank him with a kiss was a powerful one indeed.

As Lanni and Charles tactfully withdrew, Mariah felt a moment's horror—an intrusion of reality. "I can't believe I said that—about the fantasy."

Christian blinked a couple of times. "I can't believe I said what I did, either." Then he lifted one shoulder in a shrug. "Oh, well…" He smiled roguishly.

Mariah smiled back, and awaited his kiss. Then, in plain view of his oldest brother and the entire community, Christian cupped the back of her head and eased his mouth toward Mariah's. His lips met hers with a tenderness that made her go limp in his arms. Soon they gave up the pretense of dancing altogether.

He ended the kiss with a reluctance that said he'd thoroughly enjoyed being part of her fantasy. She knew he wanted to continue—and would have, had they been anyplace else. She opened her eyes slowly and noticed that he was studying her, a baffled look on his face.

The music ended.

Christian dropped his arms and took a step back. "Thank you for the dance," he said when he'd escorted her to her chair.

Duke approached them, looking smug. "I see you're trying to steal my date." But his tone was humorous, and there was no sign of rancor.

Christian seemed decidedly uncomfortable. "Would it be all right if I talked to Mariah for a minute?"

"Are you sure all you're going to do is talk?"

"Yes." Christian sighed.

"Someone might ask me how *I* feel," Mariah suggested in a low voice. She sat down to remove her shoes, but her feet were swollen, and she had to yank the shoes back and forth to pull them off her feet.

By the time she'd finished, Christian had returned with two glasses of punch. He sat down next to her and cleared his throat. "I started this conversation by thanking you. It would've hurt Midnight Sons badly to lose Duke." He downed the entire contents of his glass in one swallow. His gaze seemed fixed on a point at the opposite side of the gym.

"I'm glad I could help."

"Would you be willing to help us again?" he asked, glancing briefly at her.

"How?"

"I offered Duke a twenty percent increase in his wages if he'd stay on. I'd be willing to make the same deal with you if you'd come back and work for Midnight Sons."

Mariah gasped. The request itself didn't shock her, but she took offense at the inducement he'd used. "Is that what the kiss was all about?" she asked, struggling to hold in her anger.

"No." He looked directly into her eyes. "I swear the kiss had nothing to do with this." His face fell. "I'm sorry, Mariah," he said, vaulting to his feet. "I really bungled that. You must think I'm a complete jerk. Forget I asked." He started to walk away and she stopped him.

"Christian."

He whirled around, and his expression was so hopeful she had to restrain herself from laughing.

"I haven't made any long-term plans yet. The fire…well, it raised a number of questions regarding my future." She took a deep breath. "I'll come back to Midnight Sons on two conditions."

"Name them."

"One, Ben has to give his permission, because technically I still work for him."

"No problem. Ben's a good friend, and he knows Sawyer and I are going crazy without you."

She smiled, agreeing that Ben would willingly let her go. Although he appreciated her help, it was all too apparent that she wasn't cut out for waitressing.

"Second," she said, "I'll only agree to work for you—"

"Great!"

"Wait, I haven't finished."

The look on his face was almost comically expectant.

"I'll work for you," she said, "but only until you can find a permanent replacement."

Chapter
8

WHEN CHRISTIAN ENTERED the Midnight Sons office Tuesday morning, he was met by the welcoming scent of a freshly brewed pot of coffee.

"Good morning, Christian," Mariah said cheerfully.

It was all he could do not to close his eyes and exhale a deep, fervent breath of relief. His life was about to return to normal. Mariah was back. The temptation to kiss her—to show her how grateful he was—nearly overwhelmed him.

"Would you care for some coffee?" she asked, automatically pouring him a cup.

"Please." Christian saw that her hands had been freed from the bulky bandages. Gauze was lightly wrapped around her palms, giving her the use of her fingers.

He sat down at his desk and resisted the urge to lace his hands behind his head and prop his feet up. He figured Mariah might perceive that as overconfidence, and the last thing he wanted to do was annoy her.

"Here you go," she murmured, setting the mug down in front of him.

Christian beamed her a smile of heartfelt appreciation. At his first sip, however, he grimaced. She'd added cream and sugar. Still, his disappointment was minimal; she could've added horseradish and he wouldn't have complained. In time, maybe ten or twenty years, she'd learn he liked his coffee black.

Mariah was back, and right now that was all that mattered.

The morning sped past with such ease it was well after noon before Christian noticed the time.

"I'm going over to Ben's for lunch," he told his brother.

"Okay," Sawyer answered distractedly. "Don't forget this is my afternoon off. I'm flying Abbey in for an ultrasound later."

"I didn't forget." Christian smiled to himself. His brother made a great father.

Ben was busy flipping hamburgers on the griddle when Christian walked into the café. "You can put on an extra burger for me," he called, and hopped onto a stool.

"You want fries with that?" Ben called back.

Christian shook his head. "Do you have any potato salad?"

"Not today," Ben told him. "How about macaroni?"

"Sure." He was easy to please, especially today.

The bell over the door chimed, and Charles walked in. He sat on the stool next to Christian. "You alone?" he asked.

Christian looked pointedly at the empty stool on his other side. "So it seems. What makes you ask?"

Charles shrugged and pulled the menu from behind the sugar canister. "I thought you might be taking Mariah to lunch," he said absently as he scanned the selections he'd seen perhaps a thousand times before.

"Why would I do that?" Christian asked, finding the question odd.

"Why not? You're the one who was kissing her in the middle of the school gymnasium. I assumed you two were an item now."

Ben walked past them to a middle-aged couple sitting at a table in the back of the café. "Be right with you, Charles."

"No problem."

"Mariah and I are not an item," Christian said evenly. The kiss meant nothing. He had half a mind to explain that he was just playing along with that little fantasy of hers, but decided against it. His explanation would only give his brother extra ammunition.

Charles arched one brow. "If you say so."

"I do," Christian said. It annoyed him that his own brother, someone whose judgment he trusted, hadn't been able to tell the difference between fantasy and reality, between a "dream" kiss and waking love.

Fortunately Ben delivered his hamburger at that moment. He took Charles's order, then promptly disappeared into the kitchen.

"I talked to Mom this morning," Charles announced.

They didn't often hear from their mother. Christian made an effort to call Ellen once or twice a month—had, in fact, visited her a few weeks earlier—but she'd remarried and lived a full life in British Columbia now. She loved to travel and took frequent trips with her new husband. Books remained an important part of her life, especially since Robert owned several bookstores. She was independent of her sons now and very much her own woman.

"She said something curious," Charles murmured thoughtfully; he seemed a bit awed, even shaken. "She was telling me how much she enjoyed having Scott and Susan with her. Then, out of the blue, she said that the three of us were her...connection to life."

Christian frowned. "Her connection to life?"

"Yes. Now that both Sawyer and I are married and Abbey's pregnant, she said she's begun to feel freer to keep in touch with us. To reach out more often. Apparently she was afraid of intruding in our lives."

"There's no need for her to feel that way."

"That's what I told her, but she dismissed it. She told me she's had to stop herself for years from playing too large a role in our lives. Frankly I don't understand it. I thought she *preferred* to keep her distance. I don't know about you, but I had the feeling the three of us were reminders of all those unhappy years she lived in Hard Luck."

"They weren't all unhappy."

"Perhaps not, but it seemed that way," Charles said. "I assumed that because she has a new life now, she's comfortable with the separation."

"Yes and no." Christian, as the son closest to his mother, spoke with a certain authority.

"I told her that," Charles said, smiling, "and you should've heard the lecture I got. It was pointed out to me that, as her children, we represent her past, share her present and form her future. That's the connection-to-life stuff she was talking about."

"Sounds as though you two cleared the air."

"Yes," Charles agreed, "only I wasn't aware we'd been at odds."

"You weren't," Christian assured him. "All you both needed was a bit of...clarification."

Charles said nothing more for a moment. Then, finally, "She loved him, you know."

"Dad?"

Charles nodded. "For a time I wondered about that, but I realize now how deeply she cared for him. It wasn't a perfect marriage, but they loved each other in their own ways."

"No marriage is perfect," Christian muttered, and bit into his hamburger. He'd leave all that happy-ever-after stuff to Charles and Sawyer. He was thirty-one and had no intention of settling down. Not for a good long while, anyway.

"I don't know about no marriage being perfect," Charles said, grinning broadly. "But I'm happy with the current state of *mine.*"

"Sure—you and Lanni are newlyweds."

Charles shook his head in a kind of wonder. "It seems like we've always been together. I'm happy, Chris, happier than I can remember being in many years."

Christian was pleased for his brother, but he reminded himself again that married life wasn't for him.

"Here you are," Ben said, bringing Charles his turkey sandwich. "Now I can take a load off my feet." He pulled up a stool and sat on the opposite side of the counter. "I've been busier than a one-handed piano player," he said with a heavy sigh.

"Do you miss Mariah?" Christian asked, feeling slightly guilty.

"What do you think?" Ben responded. "Of course I miss her. She might have confused orders and broken a few dishes, but she lent a willing hand. And the customers loved her—not to mention her pies. Fact is, I'm going to hire someone else as soon as I can get around to it."

"Good," Charles murmured between bites. "It's about time you did."

"That's what I've been saying." Ben wiped his brow with his forearm.

Christian finished his burger and slid the empty plate away. Ben reached for the dish and added it to a stack behind the counter. "People have been talking about you and Mariah all morning," he said casually. "You sure have set tongues wagging." Ben chuckled. "What's this I hear about you kissing her in front of half the town?"

Christian ignored the question. "Talking? Who's talking, and what are they saying?"

"Most folks around here seem to think you two're as good as married."

Charles burst out laughing. "That's what you get, little brother. If you don't want people to talk, then you shouldn't dance with Mariah again. Especially if you're going to take part in her fantasies."

"It's not like that," Christian told Ben, pretending he hadn't heard Charles. "Mariah and I are…friends. Good friends. Nothing more."

"Sawyer and I are brothers *and* friends," Charles said lightly, "but you don't see me kissing him."

"Very funny," Christian muttered sarcastically.

He wasn't about to get involved in a verbal battle with Charles and Ben. He'd let them have their fun. They could think what they wanted, but he knew the truth—and for that matter, so did Mariah.

Christian slipped off the stool, looked at his tab and slapped the money down on the counter. In his eagerness to make a clean getaway, he nearly collided with Bill Landgrin.

They eyed each other warily. Bill hadn't been at the Labor Day dance, and for that Christian was grateful.

"Hello, Bill," he said. Even if he didn't think much of the other man, there was no need to be rude.

Bill acknowledged the greeting with an inclination of his head. "I hear you've decided to marry Mariah, after all."

"What?" Christian exclaimed. He was getting frustrated with having to defend himself against this crazy talk. "Who told you that?" he demanded, and sent an accusing glare at Charles and Ben.

"Not those two, if that's what you're thinking," Bill told him.

"Then who?" Rumors like this had to be stopped before they did damage.

"Practically everyone I've talked to this morning. They all saw you kiss Mariah."

"Just because I kissed her doesn't mean I'm going to marry her! That's insane!"

"Everyone knows how she feels about you."

"No way!" Christian said, unwilling to listen. After all, she'd accepted Duke's invitation to the dance, which disproved *that* theory.

"Why else do you think the single men in town haven't beaten a path to her door?" Bill asked. "We knew it wouldn't do any good, because she set her sights on you from the first moment she arrived. Oh, she was nice enough to the rest of us, but we all knew we didn't stand a chance."

"If you believe she's interested in me, then why'd you ask her to the dance?"

"Because she wasn't working for you anymore. I figured she'd given up beating her head against a brick wall, pining for you, but I was wrong. She's as stuck on you as ever. Poor woman."

Christian chose to ignore the last part. "There's nothing

between Mariah and me." He was getting tired of having to explain it.

"That's not what I hear."

"And I'm saying whatever you heard isn't true." Christian had to struggle to keep his voice level.

"Then you don't mind if the rest of us pursue her," Bill asked, meeting his gaze evenly.

Christian opened his mouth to object, to tell them he felt responsible for Mariah's welfare, but then he closed it. If he did protest, Bill would discount everything he'd just said.

"Sure," he muttered, "but you don't need my permission." He'd talk to Mariah himself and offer her some advice regarding the so-called eligible men in Hard Luck.

As soon as he could extricate himself from the conversation, Christian made his way back to the office.

Duke had returned from the mail run into Fairbanks and was finishing up his paperwork when Christian stepped into the trailer. Mariah was nowhere in sight, and the pilot sat on a corner of her desk, one foot squarely planted on the floor, the other dangling. "So, how does it feel to have Mariah back?"

Christian laughed. "Like a reprieve from the warden."

Duke set the clipboard aside. "Are you and Mariah going to make a formal announcement soon?"

"A what?" Christian's patience was shot. "Listen, Duke, I wish you and everyone else would get this straight. Mariah and I are *not* romantically involved. We never have been and we never will be."

The pilot didn't bother to conceal his surprise. "You're not?"

"Absolutely not!" To Christian's relief, Mariah came out from the back room just then. "Ask her yourself," he said heatedly, gesturing in her direction.

"Ask me what?" She looked from one man to the other.

"There appears to be a rumor about us floating around town." Christian folded his arms over his chest.

"Well, if you two aren't involved, what were you doing kissing in front of the entire town?" Duke asked.

If Christian had to explain this one more time, he'd scream. "It wasn't what it looked like!"

Duke rubbed a hand across his beard with a reflective expression. "It looked obvious enough to me."

"Tell him, Mariah," Christian said.

She stared at him blankly.

"Mariah," he said through gritted teeth, "this isn't funny anymore. *Tell him.*"

"What do you want me to say?"

"The truth! That you and I are not involved. That we're nothing more than friends."

She turned to Duke, and it seemed to take her a long time to speak. "Christian and I are not involved. We're…nothing more than friends."

Christian threw his hands in the air. "I rest my case."

IT WAS EXTREMELY unfortunate, Mariah felt, that she'd lacked the nerve to empty the coffeepot over Christian's head. The man was an insensitive lout.

They were trapped together in the office all afternoon, and her anger simmered just below the surface, threatening to explode. The first time she slammed a file drawer closed, he leaped up from his chair. He looked at her and, coward that she was, all she did in response was smile. This was her problem in a nutshell. Christian O'Halloran had abused her good nature from the outset.

And she'd let him.

"I don't blame you for being angry," Christian said.

She sat back and studied him carefully. "You don't?"

"Of course not. It makes me angry, too. The whole town is talking about us, and it's grossly unfair—to you *and* me."

Mariah clamped her teeth tightly shut as her frustration mounted.

"There must be some way we can dispel these rumors."

"You seem to be doing a fine job of that," she murmured. If he noticed the sarcasm in her voice, he ignored it.

"I've been thinking," Christian said, leaning back in his worn vinyl chair.

"A painful process, no doubt."

Once again he chose to overlook her derisive comment. "I'm sure you're just as embarrassed by all this gossip as I am." He paused, laughing with what sounded like rather forced heartiness. "Bill Landgrin went so far as to claim you've been in love with me for months. Can you believe that? What a crock."

"Exactly!" She needed her head examined, and the sooner the better.

"He asked did I mind if he asked you out." He eyed her speculatively. "I couldn't very well tell him I did."

"Do you?"

"Well, yes…"

"You don't like Bill?"

"I don't trust him." Christian's eyes grew dark. "I don't think you should, either."

She knew exactly the type of man Bill Landgrin was. Never once had she seriously considered dating him, but she wasn't about to tell Christian that.

"Duke's worth ten Bill Landgrins."

Mariah didn't comment.

"Ralph's a decent sort, too," Christian said, chewing thoughtfully on the end of his pencil.

"Are you suggesting I go out with Duke or Ralph?" The man had a certain effrontery, she'd say that for him.

"Sure," he answered cheerfully. "Why not?"

"I don't happen to be attracted to either one of them."

Christian threw down the pencil. "You're right, that could present a problem. I'll tell you what," he said, brightening, "I'll take care of it myself."

"Good." She didn't know what he had in mind, but it was sure to be amusing.

Mariah liked to think of herself as an even-tempered person, but if she listened to much more of Christian's bizarre advice, she'd turn into a homicidal maniac. And her first victim would be O'Halloran brother number three.

"I'll be back in a minute," he said, purposefully walking out of the office. "I've got to get something at the house." He was halfway out the door when he turned and flashed her one of his devil-may-care grins. "We haven't got a thing to worry about. I've got a terrific idea."

"I'll just bet," she muttered, but as before her sarcasm was wasted on him.

True to his word, Christian returned five minutes later, slightly breathless. He flashed her another grin and waved a small black telephone directory at her.

"What's that?" It might not have been a good idea to ask, but she couldn't resist.

His eyes twinkled. "Exactly what it looks like. My little black book."

True to her prediction, this was going to be amusing.

Crossing her arms, Mariah sat down and waited. "What do you plan to do with it?"

"Get a date, what else? There are a number of women in Fairbanks who'll remember me."

"A date?"

"Yeah." He leafed through the pages. "Since you aren't keen on dating Duke or Ralph—"

"They aren't the only eligible men in town."

"That's right," he said, reaching for the telephone receiver and pinning it between his shoulder and ear. "But there's more than one way to skin a cat," he said, and winked at her. "Or in this case, kill a rumor."

Mariah rolled her eyes dramatically.

"Hello, Ruthie?" Christian rested his feet on the corner of his desk and wore a cocky grin. "It's Christian."

Mariah watched as the grin slowly faded.

"Christian O'Halloran from Hard Luck. Remember?"

The smile was back in place.

"Yeah, that's me. Right. How are you? Wonderful. Wonderful."

A shocked expression came into his eyes. "Married! When did that happen?"

He looked at Mariah and shrugged, free hand palm up in a gesture that said this was a complete surprise.

"Congratulations. Yes, of course. You should've sent me an invitation... Oh, you did. Sorry, we've been really busy around here the past few months... Oh, it's been a year now? That long? Well, listen, I won't keep you... Pregnant? Oh...wow. Great. Keep in touch, okay?"

Mariah had to turn her back to him to keep from laughing out loud.

"Scratch Ruthie," he said. "But don't despair. I've got plenty of other names."

"I'm sure you do." The phone rang and Mariah answered it. While she was dealing with the call, she watched Christian reach for his phone a second time. Because her attention was on the call, she couldn't follow what was happening, but from the expression on Christian's face, it seemed to be a similar experience.

Mariah took down her caller's information and replaced the receiver.

"Carol's seeing someone else, too." He flipped through the pages, muttering under his breath, dismissing one name after another. Tanya? No, he'd heard she'd gone to California. Hmm, what about Tiffany? No, they'd had that big fight. Sandra? Never really liked her. A number of times he paused and tapped his finger against his teeth as he contemplated a name. Gail? He tried the number; it was disconnected.

"It seems I've been out of circulation," he said to no one in particular. "Ruthie married." He sighed. "We used to have a lot of fun together. Where did the time go?" He picked up the phone and tried again.

Mariah didn't want to listen, but she couldn't make herself stop.

"Pam," he said in a carefree voice. "It's Christian O'Halloran from Hard Luck. It's been two years?" He sounded shocked. "That long? Really? How've you been?"

Five solid minutes passed, during which Christian didn't speak. He opened his mouth a couple of times, but couldn't seem to get a word in edgewise.

"I'm sorry to hear that," he finally said in a rush. "Married—only lasted three months. Divorce final this week…" He closed his eyes and waited. "Pam—listen, I'm at work. Gotta go. I'll call you again soon. So sorry to hear about your troubles." He replaced the receiver as if he couldn't do it fast enough.

Slowly he raised his eyes to Mariah. "Pam's been married *and* divorced since the last time I saw her."

"This doesn't sound like it's going so well." She couldn't keep the glee out of her voice. If he was having difficulty finding a date, that was fine with her.

"Vickie," he said, suddenly triumphant. "She used to be crazy about me."

"Really?" More fool she.

"I'm sure Vickie'll be available."

It didn't escape Mariah's notice that the woman who was supposedly enamored of him wasn't his first choice. Now, why didn't that surprise her?

Christian punched out the phone number, but Mariah saw that most of his cockiness had vanished. Apparently Vickie was unavailable, because he spoke a few, brief sentences in a near-monotone.

"I got her answering machine," he said. He looked mildly discouraged. "I wonder if Vickie's married," he said, and the thought appeared to sadden him.

But she wasn't; an hour later, Vickie, the smitten one, returned his call.

Christian perked up like a freshly watered flower. "*Hello,* Vickie. So how's it going?"

As best she could, Mariah tuned him out. This time, she didn't care to listen. Vickie, Mariah feared, would sound all too familiar. It would be like listening to herself.

"Saturday night?" Christian seemed pleased. "Dinner. A

movie? Sure, anything you want to see. Great. I'll look forward to it." A short pause. "I'll be in Fairbanks around six. See you then."

When he finished, Mariah glanced toward his desk. Christian sat with his fingers linked behind his head, elbows jutting out. He wore a wide, satisfied grin.

"Our troubles are over," he said, and paused as if she should thank him for the noble sacrifice he was making on her behalf.

"Wonderful," she said.

"Don't you see?" Christian asked impatiently. "Once everyone in Hard Luck finds out I'm dating another woman, the gossip will stop."

"Really? And how will people learn that, since you're flying into Fairbanks to see Vickie? Or was that Pam? No, Carol." She was being deliberately obtuse.

His smile was stiff. "Vickie. And people will know because I intend to tell them."

"Perfect," she said without enthusiasm.

"You don't sound happy."

"You're wrong. I'm thrilled." She checked her watch and realized it was quitting time. In more ways than one. Reaching for her sweater, she cast him a deceptively calm smile. "See you in the morning."

Then she walked out the door, suppressing the urge to slam it.

VICKIE. CHRISTIAN COULDN'T believe he hadn't thought of her sooner. He'd always gotten along famously with her. He wondered if she still worked at the bank.

Not until he'd started making the calls did he realize he'd been out of touch for so long.

Tucking the small phone directory into his shirt pocket, he frowned. Mariah had left the office in quite a rush. And she didn't seem to appreciate that he was putting his ego on the line, calling his former girlfriends after such a long absence.

More than a year.

Like the rest of the men in Hard Luck, he occasionally flew into Fairbanks—or he used to—for some R and R when the mood struck him.

But a *year.*

Then it hit him. Hard Luck had started bringing in women right around that time. That explained it.

Turning off his computer and the office lights, Christian left for the evening.

As he was walking home, his eight-year-old niece rode past him on a bike. She hit the brakes, skidding on the dirt.

"Did you hear?" she called back to him excitedly.

"Hear what?" Christian asked.

"Mom and Sawyer—I mean Dad—just got back from the doctor's appointment in Fairbanks."

Christian remembered that Sawyer was flying into Fairbanks that afternoon because Abbey was having an ultrasound.

"The baby's a girl."

"A girl." Christian smiled. Ellen would be delighted.

"They got pictures of the baby and everything. I was on my way over to tell Chrissie. Bethany's going to have a baby, too."

"They have a picture of the baby?" This was something Christian wanted to see. A picture of an unborn baby.

"Well," Susan said, chewing on her lower lip, "they said it was a picture, but all it looked like to me was a bunch of blurry lines."

"A little girl," Christian repeated. "That's great."

"Dad thinks so," Susan said, and laughed, "but I think he would've been happy with a boy, too."

"My brother's easy to please."

Susan tried to climb back on the bicycle, but was having difficulty. Christian walked over to give her a hand by holding the bike steady. She clambered up and grinned at him. "Thanks, Uncle Christian."

"You're welcome."

Susan took off at breakneck speed, leaning over the handlebars in her eagerness to reach her friend's house with the news. So, Mitch and Bethany were going to add to their family, too. Hard Luck was about to experience a population explosion.

Christian hadn't gone more than half a block when Scott came racing down the road. "Did you see Susan?" he asked, his face red with anger.

"What if I did?"

"She stole my bike."

"She wanted to tell her friend that your mom's having a girl."

"Well, the doctor might be wrong," Scott grumbled and kicked at the dirt with the toe of his tennis shoe.

"I take it you were hoping for a boy?"

Scott shrugged. "We got enough girls in the family already. I asked Mom if she'd be willing to have another baby, to make sure the next one's a boy—and you know what she said?"

Christian shook his head.

"She said not to count on that, but if she doesn't have a boy, then maybe Lanni would when her and Charles have babies. Or maybe Mariah after you marry her."

Chapter
9

CHRISTIAN WAS HAVING a pleasant evening, but he sensed his date wasn't. Vickie was resolutely silent as they sat across from each other in the all-night diner. They'd been to dinner and a movie, and Christian's spirits were high.

"Did I mention the time Mariah made the filing cabinet fall over?" He could laugh about the incident now, but he hadn't found it funny at the time. She'd been trying to shift the cabinet herself, just to spite him. Then when he'd hurried over to help, she'd tripped—and the cabinet had tumbled onto his foot. He'd limped for a week.

To this day the top drawer didn't close properly. Leave it to Mariah.

He relayed the story, laughing as he told it; Vickie, however, hadn't so much as cracked a smile.

Confused, Christian lowered his coffee mug to the table, and his laughter faded.

"Do you realize," Vickie asked, her gaze direct and not the

least amused, "that you've spent the entire evening talking about another woman?"

He had? No way. "Who?" he asked. Surely Vickie was exaggerating. That couldn't possibly be true. Okay, so he'd mentioned Mariah and the filing cabinet, but the only reason he'd told Vickie about that incident was because it was so funny.

"First, I heard about the fire that destroyed Mariah's cabin, followed by—"

"I was updating you on the news in Hard Luck," he broke in, defending himself. "Didn't I also tell you that Sawyer's married and Abbey's expecting? And I told you about Charles and Lanni, didn't I?"

"Sure, in passing," Vickie said, flipping a strand of hair over her shoulder. Christian had always liked her long, golden hair. Straight and silky, it reached halfway down her back.

"Then there was the story about Mariah's luggage flying open on the runway—"

"You're making too much of this." Christian didn't remember Vickie as the jealous type, but then, he didn't really know her that well.

"I don't hear from you in over a year, and now all of a sudden you can't wait to take me out. I have to tell you, Christian, your suggestion that we get together is becoming suspicious to me."

"Suspicious?"

"Like you're trying to prove something to yourself and using me to do it."

"Not true," he replied in annoyance. "There's a perfectly logical reason I haven't been in touch. You heard we, uh, invited some women to town, didn't you?"

"Of course I heard about it! Midnight Sons had the whole

state talking." She pinched her lips together in a show of disapproval and folded her arms. "Bringing in women! It's the most ridiculous thing I've ever heard. What's wrong with the women right here in Fairbanks?"

Christian wasn't wading into that muddy pond, so he ignored the question. "Well, it explains why you didn't hear from me," he muttered.

"I'd have moved to Hard Luck if you'd given me a reason to." Her look was full of meaning, and her gaze held his.

Christian swallowed. "Sure," he said, feeling more than a little uncomfortable with the turn the conversation had taken. "There're plenty of single men left in Hard Luck. You'd be welcome to move to town anytime."

She glared at him. "I'm not asking about other men," she snapped. "I want to know about *you*."

"Me?" Someone must have raised the temperature in the restaurant, because the room felt suffocatingly hot. Christian resisted the urge to ease his finger along the inside of his collar.

"Well, I'm certainly not interested in the guy who runs that café."

"Ben." Christian leaped on his friend's name. "Why, he's great."

"Get real, O'Halloran." The hair he'd recently admired flew back over her shoulder like a blast of gold. The glare returned full force. "What I want to know is why it was so allfired important to call me now, especially with all those women you've managed to bring to Hard Luck." The challenge was impossible to ignore.

Christian decided it would be poor timing to explain that

he was hoping to kill the rumors that linked him with Mariah romantically.

"I've been awfully busy lately…and, well, I figured I should renew old acquaintances."

"It wouldn't be so bad if I hadn't been so eager to see you," she said, and slapped her purse on the table. "You call good ol' Vickie, and then spend the whole evening talking about another woman."

"I don't know what you mean," he said stubbornly.

She sent him a disgusted look, then slid out of the booth.

"What are you doing?" Christian was stunned; she was *leaving*.

Vickie offered him a bright smile. "I'm going home."

"I'll drive you." She appeared to find his company objectionable, but to leave the diner without him added insult to injury.

"No, thanks," she said stiffly.

Christian hurriedly paid for the coffee and followed Vickie out of the diner. "What did I do that was so terrible?" It was embarrassing, but he suspected he was actually whining. He'd never had this kind of trouble with a woman before.

Vickie had changed in the past year; then again, maybe she wasn't the only one. Christian had the distinct feeling he'd done some changing of his own.

"What did you do?" Vickie echoed, standing outside the coffee shop. She sighed loudly. "Listen, you're a great guy, but whatever there was between us is over—and was a long time ago. I guess I needed this date to prove to myself how over you I am. It's also pretty clear that you're crazy about Mariah."

Out of habit, Christian opened his mouth to deny everything, but Vickie didn't give him the opportunity.

"I don't know exactly what you were trying to prove, but I resent being used."

"No need to get on your high horse. If you don't want to go out with me again, fine. But at least let me drive you home." It was a matter of pride, if nothing else.

Vickie agreed, and they rode silently back to her apartment complex. When he parked, she turned to face him. "I hope you manage to work everything out with Mariah."

Christian didn't bother to correct her. He wasn't "crazy about" Mariah or involved with her or anything else, but he'd be wasting his breath to tell Vickie that.

"Promise me one thing," she said.

"Sure."

"Send me a wedding invitation. I'd like to meet the woman who tagged you."

This time Christian couldn't stop himself. "I'm not marrying Mariah!"

He wanted to shout it again. He *wasn't* marrying her—was he? Yes, he found her attractive. Yes, he'd kissed her and wouldn't mind doing it again. But that didn't mean *marriage*. It shouldn't. True, he felt protective of her, but that was because…because he felt responsible. Wasn't it?

Vickie laughed softly and patted his cheek. "You protest far too much. Just remember what I said. I want an invitation to the wedding."

FIRST THING MONDAY morning, Mariah took out the file of applications Christian had collected the previous year. She was reading through the stack of them when he arrived.

"Morning," he said curtly, refusing to meet her eyes.

"Morning," she returned, her mood matching his.

The coffee was brewed and ready, but she didn't pour him a mug. He could darn well get his own, she decided. Either he was unwilling to do that or not interested, because he sat down at his desk and immediately turned on his computer.

"How'd your big date go?" she couldn't refrain from asking. This penchant for emotional pain was probably something she should investigate. Besides, even if he'd had a perfectly miserable evening, he'd never let her know.

"Fine," he growled. "Has Ralph been in yet?"

"No," she answered.

Christian glanced at her and seemed surprised by her terse reply. "What's wrong?" he asked.

"Not a thing," she assured him sweetly. She refused to give him cause for complaint, and every time he looked her way she made sure she was the picture of contentment. Not that he looked over very often.

Whatever was on the computer screen commanded his full attention. He sat up straight in his chair and peered at it for long minutes. Finally, without lifting his eyes, he asked abruptly, "Where's Ted?"

"Don't know."

"I'm going over to the bunkhouse to see if I can find him."

"I thought you asked about Ralph."

"Nope, I need to see Ted." He left as if it was a dire emergency.

He didn't close down his computer, and out of curiosity, Mariah got up to look at his screen. He'd been reviewing the flight schedule for the week. The mail runs into Fairbanks were made on a rotation basis. Ralph had made the run the previous week, but Ted was scheduled to do it this week.

Ted appeared in the office soon afterward wearing a forlorn

expression. "Christian asked me to tell you he'll be going into Fairbanks this morning."

Mariah made a note of the change. "Thanks, Ted."

So Christian was interested in flying into Fairbanks. That could mean only one thing.

He'd be seeing Vickie again.

KAREN CALDWELL SANG quietly to herself as she placed the Noah's-ark stencil along the bottom of the freshly painted wall. The baby's nursery was coming along nicely. She felt a constant undercurrent of excitement these days. Preparing the room, buying clothes, reading infant-care books—it all made the baby seem so *real*.

"Karen." Matt's voice boomed from the lobby.

"In here," she shouted over her shoulder. Unfolding her legs, she got to her feet, eager to talk to her husband. All at once, the room started to spin and she promptly sat down again.

Matt must've seen what happened because he rushed in. "Honey, what's wrong?"

She smiled up at his worried face, loving him all the more for his concern. "Nothing. I'm fine. I guess I just stood up too quickly."

"Getting dizzy like that—are you *sure* you're okay?" he asked. "What about the baby?"

"It happens to everyone now and then, not just pregnant women."

"You're sure?" he asked again. He didn't sound like he believed her.

"Positive."

He still didn't look reassured. "I'd feel better if Dotty checked you out."

"All right," she agreed, "but after lunch." Her appetite had increased lately, and Karen suspected her body was making up for the weight she'd lost during her first months of pregnancy, when she'd been so ill.

"Actually," she told him as he led the way into the kitchen, "I feel wonderful." Working on the nursery made the baby's birth seem so close. The crib and other furniture had arrived a few days earlier, and they'd assembled everything over the weekend.

"You look wonderful," her husband told her. He gazed at her intently, then the worried expression fled his eyes and they softened with love.

Karen went about making toasted cheese sandwiches while Matt opened a can of soup. "I have a feeling we're going to lose Mariah soon," Matt said as if the subject was on his mind.

Karen had been thinking the same thing. "I blame Christian for that. I swear that man left his brains behind somewhere."

"He's a stubborn one, that's for sure."

"You should know," Karen teased.

Matt made a show of protesting. He moved behind her and wrapped his arms around her middle, splaying his hands across her abdomen. "How come Abbey and Sawyer get an ultrasound and we don't?"

"Because I'm under thirty-five, so the doctor didn't think it was necessary. Besides, I'd rather be surprised by the baby's sex."

"Sawyer passed around the picture of the ultrasound at Ben's this morning, proud as could be over a few blurry lines." Matt sounded a little wistful.

"Do you want a picture to pass around, too?" she asked sympathetically.

He nuzzled her neck. "I guess I do."

"I can ask the doctor at my next appointment. But, Matt, I'd really prefer not to know if we're having a boy or a girl until the baby's born. Okay?"

"Okay." He spread kisses down the side of her neck.

Karen yawned unexpectedly. Every afternoon, like clockwork, she slept a good hour, sometimes two. Again she suspected this was her body's way of regaining strength after the first turbulent months of her pregnancy.

"I wish there was something I could do for Mariah," Karen said as she carried the sandwiches to the table.

Matt emptied the soup into two bowls. "I don't know what. She has to make her own decisions, just like Christian does."

"Maybe you could talk to him."

"Not a chance! He's got two brothers, but I imagine they feel the same way about all this as we do. If it's anyone's business to say something to Christian, it's theirs. I tried to help Lanni's romance with Charles along and—"

"You did? When?"

"Last year about this time. It didn't work, and I got myself into hot water with my sister. No one appreciates unsolicited advice."

"So what can we do?" Karen asked. She really felt for Mariah.

"Nothing."

"But—"

"I know, sweetheart, but it's not our affair, and neither Christian nor Mariah would appreciate our interference."

Sadly Karen acknowledged that he was right.

CHRISTIAN KNEW MARIAH was upset about something the minute he returned from the flight into Fairbanks. If ever there'd been a time he needed to think straight, this morning was it. That was why he'd taken the mail run from Ted.

Mariah had snapped at him earlier, and now she glared at him like a mother bear protecting her cubs—or, maybe, hoping to feed them. One glance told him the only way he was going to walk away whole would be to run for cover.

"I'm back," he said unnecessarily.

She responded by scowling at him.

He tried again, ignoring her bad mood. "Where's Sawyer?" His older brother was more accustomed to dealing with women, irrational creatures that they were; he could use Sawyer's help here. He sighed. First Vickie and now Mariah. And to think, *he'd* been the one to suggest bringing women to town.

"Sawyer's out," was the only response she gave him.

"Did he happen to mention where he was going?" he asked tentatively.

"Yes."

Mariah seemed to forget he was her employer. Just because he'd practically kissed her feet when she'd agreed to come back didn't mean she could get uppity with him.

"Do you have any objection to telling me where my brother is?" he asked, hardening his voice.

"None. He said he was going home for lunch."

Sawyer had been doing that more often lately. If Christian had been aware of the time, he could probably have figured it out himself.

"Thank you," he said coolly. He sat down at his desk and discovered a number of employment applications lying across the surface. The very ones he'd read through a dozen times the week before. The very ones he'd rejected.

"What are these for?" he asked in a way that would inform her his patience wasn't limitless.

"You didn't seem in any hurry to hire my replacement," she said without emotion, "so I took the liberty of contacting a few of the applicants myself."

He opened his mouth to object and realized he couldn't. She was right; he wasn't in any hurry to replace her. He told himself it was because he couldn't handle the idea of training a new secretary; it seemed beyond him. Perhaps he was being unfair to Mariah, but he'd hoped that in time she'd decide to come back permanently. Then everything would return to the way it used to be.

"I guess you found a number of suitable applicants," he said, gesturing at his desk.

"I called all of those. I offered the position to Libby Bozeman, who's accepted. She'll arrive in Hard Luck a week Friday. I printed up the contract and faxed it to her."

"You *hired* her?"

Mariah's back stiffened. "Yes. As I mentioned earlier, you didn't seem to be in a hurry to replace me, so I took matters into my own hands."

"Does Sawyer know?"

"Yes, and he approved Libby."

"I see." Christian knew when he was beaten. He leafed through the papers until he found Libby's application. As he read over the simple form, it shocked him to see how naive they'd been going into this project. He'd requested only the most basic information. He hadn't even asked for references.

"She looks suitable." For the life of him, Christian couldn't remember interviewing her.

"I talked to five or six of the other applicants this morning," Mariah told him in that prim voice of hers. He could always tell when she was put out, because her voice dipped several degrees below freezing.

"Mrs. Bozeman seemed the most qualified."

"She's married?"

"No, but she was—until recently."

"Was she married last year when I interviewed her?"

"Apparently so."

"I see." He did remember her now, and if his memory served him correctly, she was very qualified. Libby Bozeman was a tall, attractive woman, perhaps in her forties; she knew her mind and had no problem speaking it. A no-nonsense woman. Mariah had chosen well.

"If you have no objection, I'll have an airline ticket sent to her."

"None whatsoever," Christian returned in the same crisp tones.

Neither spoke for several minutes. Then, because he had to know, Christian asked. "What about you? Where will you go?" He wondered how Ben felt about taking her back. The café owner was fond of Mariah—for that matter, so was Christian—but it hadn't worked before and he doubted Mariah would be willing to try again.

"Where will I go?" Mariah repeated softly as if considering the question for the first time.

Christian stopped himself from making several suggestions, all of which would keep her in Hard Luck.

She looked up at him, and it seemed her eyes were brighter than normal. Slowly she released her breath, and when she spoke her voice faltered slightly. "Somewhere I won't ever have to see you again, Christian O'Halloran."

CHRISTIAN WALKED BACK to his house later that afternoon, his hands buried in his pockets. His spirits dragged along the road like an untied shoelace, threatening to trip him.

Mariah leaving. Again. Only this time she was leaving more than Midnight Sons. She was leaving Hard Luck. Leaving Alaska. *Leaving him*.

Libby Bozeman. He was sure she'd work out fine, but damn it all, he wanted Mariah. At least this time she'd agreed to stay until Libby could be properly trained.

Even Sawyer seemed to think it was best to let Mariah go. Christian had approached his brother the minute the two of them were alone, and Sawyer had shrugged and reminded him that they couldn't force her to stay.

When he reached his house, Christian noticed that Scott and Ronny Gold were playing catch with Eagle Catcher in the front yard of Sawyer's home across the street. Depressed, he sank onto the top porch step, watching the boys' carefree play. Scott and Ronny tossed the stick and Eagle Catcher dashed across the yard to retrieve it.

Christian didn't know how long he sat there taking in the scene. Soon it would be dinnertime, but he didn't have the energy to cook, nor did he feel like joining Ben at the café. The fact was, he didn't seem all that hungry.

Susan stuck her head out the door of their house and shouted something Christian couldn't hear. Ronny Gold took off running, but Scott stayed behind with his dog.

Christian envied Sawyer. It had all been so easy for him. Abbey arrived with the kids, and within a month they'd decided to marry. No muss. No fuss. Easy as pie.

"Hiya, Uncle Christian."

Caught up in his misery, Christian hadn't noticed Scott's

approach. Now the ten-year-old was standing on the other side of the fence.

"Hello, Scott."

"What's the matter? You don't look so good."

Christian couldn't think of a way to explain his complicated, confused emotions to a child. He couldn't even explain them to himself.

Scott let himself into the yard and sat down on the step below Christian. "Does this have to do with Mariah leaving?"

Christian's eyes widened before he realized Scott must've heard Sawyer talking about the new secretary to Abbey. "Yeah, I guess you could say that."

"You want me to give you some advice on romance? I'm good at that."

"You?"

"Sure. I helped Sawyer before he asked my mom to marry him. I told him about those bath-oil beads that melt in the water."

Christian gently patted the boy's shoulder. It wouldn't be that simple with Mariah. Bath-oil beads weren't going to help *this* situation.

"Matt Caldwell asked me for advice on how to get Karen back, too."

"He did?" That surprised Christian. He'd always assumed Matt's reconciliation with his pregnant wife had been quick and effortless. She hadn't been back in Hard Luck long before they'd remarried. Every time he saw them lately, they behaved like newlyweds. It was hard to believe they'd ever been divorced.

"Matt bought an ice-cream bar for me," Scott told him. "My advice must've worked, 'cause he and Karen got married right after that."

"Good for you."

Scott leaned his back against the step. "You need any advice, I'll help you, too."

"Thanks for the offer, but what's going on between me and Mariah is different."

Scott cocked his head to look up at Christian. "How's that?"

"I really like Mariah."

"But you aren't sure you love her," Scott finished for him.

"Yes," Christian said, straightening. Scott's insight surprised him.

"I know what you mean," the boy said, sounding mature beyond his years. "It's like me and Chrissie Harris."

It took Christian a moment to remember that Chrissie was Mitch Harris's daughter. Mitch and Bethany had married that summer. "What about you and Chrissie?" he asked.

"Well," Scott said, propping his elbows on the step above. His look was thoughtful. "She's my little sister's best friend and she can be a real pest."

Clearly the boy knew women.

"But I like her," Scott continued with a heartfelt sigh.

Christian couldn't believe how adequately Scott had described his feelings about Mariah.

"But you know, sometimes I look at Chrissie and I think she's got the nicest eyes of any girl I've ever seen."

Christian thought Mariah's eyes were beautiful, too. The way they drifted shut at the precise moment he knew he needed to kiss her. How her long eyelashes brushed against the high arch of her cheek. How expressive they were, betraying every mood from anger to ecstasy. Her eyes. Oh, yes, she had beautiful eyes.

"Sometimes I think Chrissie's gotta be the prettiest girl in the world. Even with freckles."

That, too, accurately described Christian's feelings. He recalled the time he flew to Seattle and had dinner with Allison Reynolds. Outwardly she was a knockout, but he'd found her frivolous and superficial. Mariah, though…there wasn't an ounce of phoniness. "Mariah doesn't have freckles, but I know what you mean."

Scott grinned. "I thought you would." Then his expression turned serious. "I like Chrissie 'cause she's a good friend of Susan's. I don't know if Susan would've liked living in Hard Luck so much if it wasn't for Chrissie."

Christian mentally reviewed the women who'd come and gone in the past year. A number had stayed and settled in the community, and a number had left. Despite the hardships, despite the cold, Mariah had stayed. He'd misjudged her from the start, believing she'd be one of the first to pack her bags and go.

Scott's sigh was heartfelt. "One day I'll probably marry Chrissie Harris."

Christian winced at the word "marry"—it had always made him uncomfortable. "Don't you think you're a bit young to be talking about that sort of thing?"

"Sure, I've still got a lot of years, and Mom and Dad are already talking about me going to college."

Christian patted the boy's shoulder again, more vigorously this time, proud to call him nephew.

"But I've decided if I don't marry Chrissie, I want a girl like her."

"Scott!" Susan stood on the front porch across the street and hollered at the top of her lungs. "Dinner!"

"You should get going."

"Yeah. Mom's serving my favorite meat loaf tonight. She got the recipe out of the newspaper a long time ago from some lady who writes an advice column."

"Don't keep her waiting then." Christian might not know much about dealing with women, but he knew better than to let his dinner get cold.

"Did I help you any?" Scott asked.

"You did." It was true. "You should think about writing an advice column of your own."

Scott nodded thoughtfully. "I just might, you know. Someday Aunt Lanni wants to start a newspaper in Hard Luck. She might give me a column 'cause we're related."

"If you want, I'll put in a good word for you."

Scott beamed. "Great!"

Advice to the lovelorn from Scott O'Halloran, Hard Luck's hometown expert.

Smiling for the first time since Mariah had announced she was leaving, Christian stood up. His hand was on the front doorknob when something Scott had said suddenly struck him.

Scott wanted to marry a girl like Chrissie.

A woman like Mariah. That was what Christian wanted in his life. A woman like Mariah.

MARIAH HADN'T DECIDED what she'd do or where she'd live once Libby Bozeman was trained. The thought of leaving Hard Luck made her infinitely sad. But she had no choice if she wanted to avoid Christian O'Halloran.

Just thinking about that stubborn, obtuse man made her angry all over again. Angry enough to find it impossible to sit still. So, after dinner, she took a walk.

The sun was getting ready to set, and it wouldn't be long before dark, but she didn't let that deter her.

"I'll be back soon," she told Matt and Karen who sat in the swing on the front porch. Karen's head rested against her husband's shoulder, and Matt had one arm around her. Much as Mariah loved them both and delighted in their happiness, right now it was painful to watch.

Buttoning her sweater, collar pulled up around her ears, she walked briskly for about ten minutes.

Night descended faster than she'd expected, and not wanting to stumble about in the dark, she started to take a shortcut around the back of the Hard Luck Café.

Apparently Ben had just stepped outside, because the light from the open kitchen door spilled out, illuminating her path.

Mariah kept her head down, anxious to be on her way and avoid exchanging pleasantries.

She heard a muffled sound and paused to glance back. At first she saw nothing, then made out a shadowy form. It appeared to be a large animal on the ground, next to the garbage cans outside the back door. She hesitated, uncertain if she should venture closer. Lanni had once encountered a bear on the tundra, and just hearing the tale had given Mariah goose bumps.

She took a step, then two, before deciding it was ridiculous to run from her fears. If it was a bear in the shadows, he'd get far more interesting fare from Ben's garbage than she could provide.

As she approached the light, Mariah could tell it wasn't an animal down there in the shadows, but a person.

"Ben?" she whispered. "Ben!"

Ben didn't stir.

Chapter
10

"BEN." MARIAH FELL to her knees and pressed her finger against the artery in his neck. Again and again she tried to locate a pulse but found none. Her own accelerated at an alarming pace as she realized Ben Hamilton had probably suffered a heart attack.

She left him only long enough to race into the kitchen and call for help. She dialed Mitch's number. Hard as she tried to remain calm, her words were rushed and she felt close to panic.

Forcing herself to breathe deeply and think clearly, she returned to Ben's side and carefully rolled him onto his back. His head lolled to one side and his coloring was poor. She slid her hand behind his neck, then lifted his head and began to administer CPR. Luckily she'd taken a course in cardiopulmonary resuscitation in college and knew what needed to be done.

"Ben, oh, Ben," she said as she pressed the heel of her hand against his chest and pumped. He wasn't breathing on his own. His heart began again—erratically, but it was beating. She stopped to administer mouth-to-mouth.

She wasn't sure how long she worked, alternating between the breathing and pumping his heart. It seemed as though an eternity had passed before she heard footsteps behind her.

"What happened?" Mitch shouted.

"Heart attack," she panted. The two words required an inordinate amount of energy.

Mitch squatted down beside Ben and assisted her, taking over the breathing while she continued to work on the older man's heart.

Two emergency medical volunteers arrived at the scene and took over. A crowd started to gather, everyone whispering as Ben was loaded into the back of the ambulance and rushed to the health clinic.

"Mitch!" Bethany cried from behind him. "What's going on?"

Mariah watched Mitch gather his wife into his arms. "It's Ben," he whispered. Bethany's eyes immediately filled with tears.

"His heart?" Her voice trembled and she bit her lip. "I knew something wasn't right. He promised me he'd stop working so hard. He *promised*."

Mitch smoothed the hair away from Bethany's face in a gentle gesture of love and comfort.

"I just found him," Bethany sobbed in agony. "I can't lose him now."

"Are you okay, Mariah?" Sawyer O'Halloran arrived breathless, Abbey right behind him. "We were at Mitch's when you called."

Mariah felt as if she was in a daze, but she managed to nod. "Are you sure?"

"I'm fine." But she'd never felt this shaky. All at once her bones seemed to dissolve, and she slumped against the side of the building.

"I think you need to sit down," Abbey said, taking Mariah by the hand and leading her into the café. She steered Mariah to a chair, then quickly made a pot of tea.

"What's going to happen to Ben?" Mariah asked, praying her meager efforts had been enough to save him. She worried about whether she'd followed the procedure correctly. The CPR class had been years ago, and she might have forgotten something.

"Medical transport is on the way. A medical team will arrive by helicopter in just a little while," Sawyer explained. "Christian's on the radio with them now."

Abbey added a liberal amount of sugar to Mariah's tea and stirred it briskly. "Here," she said, "drink this."

"How'd you find him?" Sawyer wanted to know.

Mariah told them she'd gone out for a walk after dinner and was taking a shortcut back to the lodge because of the dark when she found Ben. She trembled as she spoke, remembering how she almost hadn't stopped to check. How she'd nearly given in to the fear of encountering a bear.

"Without you, Ben would've died."

Cupping the mug with both hands, Mariah drank deeply. It went without saying that Ben could still die.

By the time the distinctive sound of the helicopter could be heard in the distance, half the town had gathered by the airfield. Not that there was anything to see or do. People came to lend emotional support to one another, to show Ben that they cared and that he was an important part of their lives. To show him that Hard Luck wouldn't be the same without him. Even though Ben was unconscious, Mariah believed that all this love must touch him in some way.

As the emergency medical technicians wheeled Ben to the plane, the prayers and hopes of the community went with him.

"Any family?" a man called from inside the transport.

Bethany whispered something to Mitch, then hugged him and Chrissie and rushed to climb into the helicopter.

After the helicopter lifted off the runway, everyone started to talk at once. A number of the curious crowded around Mariah, and she repeated the story of how she'd discovered Ben. People were standing around Mitch, too, asking questions about Bethany's relationship with Ben. Mariah couldn't hear what he said and was too exhausted to wonder about it right now.

Karen and Matt walked back to the lodge with her. As she headed up the porch steps, Mariah saw Christian. He stood nearby, talking to Sawyer and Charles. His gaze left his brothers and moved to her. Their eyes met for a long moment, before she gained the strength to look away. Her heart was filled with a deep sadness as she turned and entered the lodge.

THE FOLLOWING MORNING Christian was the first to arrive at the Midnight Sons office. He'd spent most of the night tossing and turning, unable to sleep. Twice he'd called the hospital and talked to Bethany, and the news was good. Ben was stabilized, and the hospital had scheduled a number of tests. If all went as the doctors expected, Ben would be headed for open-heart surgery early that afternoon.

Worrying about Ben's condition wasn't all that had kept Christian awake. He'd given some thought to what he'd learned about his friend last night—that he was Bethany's natural father. Not surprisingly, it was all over town. People were shocked but more than that, they were genuinely pleased. Christian had also been thinking about Mariah.

He mulled over everything that had happened in the past fourteen months, everything he knew about her, from her courage in coming here to her skill and bravery last night. He considered her compassion, too, her honesty, her sense of humor. He'd misjudged her for so long. *A woman like Mariah.* The words wouldn't stop circling in his mind.

If he did marry, and eventually he intended to, he wanted a woman like Mariah. Not a fancy city girl like Allison. Or even one like Vickie, nice though she was. He wanted a woman like Mariah. But if he'd already found her, then—

The door to the office opened, cutting him off in midthought. Mariah walked in, and she looked as tired as Christian felt.

"Coffee's almost ready," he told her. He stood in front of the machine and waited for the liquid to finish filtering through, then poured them each a mug.

"Have you heard anything about Ben?" she asked, thanking him for the coffee with a weak smile.

Christian told her what he'd learned.

Mariah held the cup tightly with both hands. She was paler than he could remember, and the urge to take her in his arms and comfort her was strong. It hurt to realize she didn't want him.

"How'd you sleep?" he asked, perching on the corner of her desk.

"I didn't."

"Me, neither."

"I…don't know if I'm going to get much work done today," she murmured, avoiding his eyes.

The door opened again, and Sawyer entered. He paused when he saw Christian so close to Mariah. Christian started to tell him what he knew about Ben.

"I talked to Bethany myself," Sawyer said, interrupting him. "Charles and Lanni are flying into Fairbanks this morning to be with her. Mitch, too. They'll keep in close touch and let us know how he's doing."

"Good," Christian said. But he wished Sawyer hadn't arrived just then, because he wanted—needed—to talk to Mariah.

"I…I was telling Christian I don't know if I'll be much help around here today," Mariah said, sounding strangely fragile.

"Take the day off," Sawyer suggested. "I wouldn't be here myself if it wasn't necessary." He yawned loudly and rubbed his eyes. "I doubt anyone got any sleep last night. Abbey and I didn't, that's for sure, and the kids were up half the night, too."

"Everyone loves Ben," Christian said. "He—"

"The guy makes me mad," Sawyer broke in angrily. "He should've hired help a long time ago. Running the café alone is too much for him."

Christian felt the same kind of anger, but it was directed at himself. The symptoms had been there all along. The fatigue, shortness of breath—the very fact that he'd hired Mariah. He should have recognized Ben's increasing weakness. His guilt increased tenfold, knowing he'd taken Mariah away from Ben.

Mariah reached for her jacket. "Thank you. I'm sure I'll feel better tomorrow morning. When you find out about Ben's surgery, I'd appreciate hearing."

"I'll keep you posted," Sawyer promised.

"Thanks."

Christian didn't want Mariah to leave, not until he'd talked to her. "I'll walk you to the lodge," he said.

"Walk her to the lodge?" Sawyer repeated. "Trust me, little brother, she knows the way. Besides, I need you here. We're going to be shorthanded as it is."

Christian felt like groaning with frustration, but when he looked at Mariah, he noticed that she seemed relieved. She didn't want his company.

FIVE DAYS LATER Christian sat in the Fairbanks Memorial Hospital waiting room. He leaned forward, elbows resting on his knees. Twice he looked at his watch, wondering how much longer it would be before the nurse caring for Ben would let him into the room.

Ben was recovering from his surgery, which had taken place within twenty-four hours of his arrival. He was said to be wreaking all kinds of havoc with the staff. One nurse had claimed she'd rather care for a roomful of newborns than take another shift with Ben Hamilton.

Christian smiled just thinking about it.

"You can see Mr. Hamilton now."

Christian barely noticed the woman who spoke. He jumped out of his seat before she could change her mind and hurried toward Ben's room.

To Christian's surprise, his friend was sitting up in bed, and although he was pale, his coloring was decidedly better than before the surgery. Above all, Ben was alive.

Very much alive.

"Quit looking at me like you're viewing buzzard bait," he grumbled.

Christian burst out laughing. "Hey, it's good to see you."

"Yeah, well, I don't mind saying it's a pleasure to see you, too." Ben grinned, but the effort seemed to tax him. "I've been told that if it wasn't for Mariah I wouldn't be here now."

"That's right." Christian pulled a chair close to the bed and sat down.

"Speaking of Mariah," Ben said, dropping his head back against the pillow. "You still denying you're in love with her?"

A week earlier, Christian would have loudly denounced any such thing. What a difference this past week had made. "No," he answered flatly.

"So, is she staying in Hard Luck?"

"I don't know what her plans are at this point."

"For heaven's sake, are you going to marry her or not?"

Leave it to Ben to zero in on the one question that remained unanswered in his mind. It had taken him far longer than it should have to recognize the truth about his feelings for Mariah. In retrospect, he was embarrassed to admit how obtuse he'd been. He didn't know exactly when he'd come to care for her so deeply—sometime between the day of her arrival when she'd chased her underwear across the runway and the night she'd saved Ben's life.

Okay, he could admit he loved her, but did that mean he had to *do* something about it?

"I'm not ready for marriage," he declared.

Ben chuckled, the sound pitifully weak. "Have you talked it over with Mariah?"

"No." He hadn't even told her he loved her yet.

"What are you afraid of, son?"

Yeah, Ben always did have a way of getting right to the heart of the matter. "I don't know." It wasn't like he wanted to play the field; his dates with Vickie and particularly Allison had proved that. He'd gone out with one of the most beautiful women he'd ever met and spent the entire night wishing he was with Mariah.

Even Vickie, who used to be head-over-heels crazy about him, was ready to toss him to the wolves because he'd spent their date talking about Mariah. Other women bored him. He wanted a woman who was strong and funny and brave and sweet.

A woman like Mariah.

"Seems to me you don't know what you want," Ben said.

"I do know what I want," Christian responded. "My problem is I don't know what to do about it." He sat for several more minutes, thinking. When he looked up again he saw that Ben was asleep. He stood and gently squeezed his friend's arm. It was time he went back to Hard Luck, anyway.

Ben was going to be just fine.

MARIAH LOVED TO SIT out on the lodge's porch swing. The September afternoon was glorious with sunshine. Colors had started to change and the tundra was ablaze in orange and reds. Snow would come soon; in fact, there'd already been a light snowfall a few nights before. Before long the rivers would freeze, and daylight would be almost nonexistent.

She loved Hard Luck, loved Alaska, and didn't want to leave. She knew she needed to make a decision, but had delayed it.

Although Karen and Matt had offered to let her stay at the lodge indefinitely, Mariah had declined. Their generosity had touched her heart, but they had enough to do with the arrival of the baby and operating their tour business. An extra guest, even a paying one, would be a burden they didn't need.

That meant Mariah had to make a number of important decisions regarding her future.

It also meant she couldn't stay in Hard Luck.

And yet the thought of leaving filled her with unbearable sadness. Hard Luck was her home, more so than Seattle, where she'd been born and raised. Her friends were here.

Christian was here.

Moving the swing back and forth, she surveyed her options. She was so deep in thought she didn't hear Christian's approach.

"Mariah?" He stood on the top step and wrapped one arm around the support column.

Although his voice was soft, she nearly leaped off the swing, so great was her surprise. She could hardly believe he'd made it all the way to the porch without her noticing.

"Do you have a minute?"

He must've known she was searching for a plausible excuse to avoid him because he added, "I talked to Ben this morning."

"How is he?" she asked, eager for news.

"Resting comfortably. He sends his love."

"I'll try to get into Fairbanks this week to visit him myself," she said, realizing she sounded nervous. Well, she was. Being around Christian, especially outside the work environment, had always left her feeling tongue-tied and uneasy.

He walked across the porch and sat next to her on the swing. "I have something I'd like to discuss with you."

Mariah locked her fingers together, vowing to be strong. "I'm not coming back to work for you, Christian—no matter how much money you offer."

"This doesn't have anything to do with the office. This has to do with you and me."

Mariah felt as if the world went still, as if the wind stopped blowing, the sun ceased to shine and the whole world waited in silent suspension for him to continue.

"Us?" Her voice rose to a squeak. Resolutely she closed her mouth. Every time she talked to Christian, she seemed to say something stupid. Like raving about a salmon casserole. Or telling him to shut up because he was disturbing her fantasy. No wonder he sought out more sophisticated company. With her he got salmon casserole, she thought wryly; with Allison Reynolds it was T-bone steak.

"Yes, us," he repeated. "Actually I'd like to know what your plans are for the winter."

He wanted her gone. That was what this was leading up to. He was going to ask her to leave Hard Luck.

She remained silent.

"Matt told me you've decided not to stay at the lodge. That doesn't give you a lot of options, housing here being what it is."

"No," she admitted, and looked away as the pain burned a hole straight through her. "Let me make this easy for you. You're asking me to leave Hard Luck and I—"

"What?" he demanded, laughing as if what she'd just said was ludicrous.

Mariah didn't take kindly to his humor. She had nowhere to go except back to Seattle. Her parents would suffocate her with attention and *their* plans for her future. She felt too defeated, too discouraged, to make a new start in some new place. What hurt so terribly was that the man who held her heart in the palm of his hand was the one asking her to leave.

"I'll go without a fuss," she whispered.

"Mariah." Christian caught her by the shoulders and turned her so that she faced him squarely. "I'm not asking you to leave Hard Luck. Quite the opposite." His gaze pinned hers and she read the truth in his eyes. "I came to ask you to be my wife."

"Your wife?" she asked in confusion. "Is this a joke?"

"No man makes that kind of offer unless he's serious. And, Mariah, I've never been more serious in my life. I want to marry you."

Probably for the first time since her arrival in Alaska, Mariah was struck dumb.

"Say something," Christian urged.

She was touched by the uncertainty in his voice. After all this time, he still didn't know she was crazy in love with him.

"Kiss me," she said when she regained the ability to speak.

"Kiss you?" He glanced over his shoulder. "Right here? Now?"

"Yes," she said impatiently.

"This isn't another one of those fantasy things, is it? Because what I feel for you is real."

"This request is very real, too. Now shut up and kiss me."

"Just remember," he whispered as he reached for her, "you

asked for this." He brought her into his arms and slowly, methodically, lowered his mouth to hers.

In the beginning his kiss was gentle and tender, the way it had been the night of the dance. Soon it became more passionate. Mariah moaned softly, clinging fiercely to his arms. They quickly discovered that one kiss wasn't enough to satisfy either of them. They kissed again and again.

A sensation of weightlessness stole over her. She felt as if she could fly, float effortlessly through the heavens. Already her heart was soaring.

"Soon," Christian murmured, breaking off the kiss and burying his face in the curve of her neck.

"Soon?" she repeated.

"We're getting married very soon."

"But—"

"I don't know any man who could've behaved like a bigger fool than I have this past year. I love you, Mariah. I need you in my life."

Mariah brushed the tears from her face. "You're... sure about all this?" Loving him as much as she did, she couldn't bear it if he suddenly changed his mind.

"Oh, yes," he said, and kissed her again. "*Will* you marry me, Mariah?"

Smiling through her tears, she nodded eagerly.

Christian threw back his head and laughed.

"That wasn't supposed to be funny, Christian O'Halloran!"

"Not you, my love," he said, holding her more securely in his arms. "Us."

"*Us* is humorous?" If she wasn't so elated, so filled with joy, she could take offense at this.

"We're going to be very happy, Mariah." He kissed her once more in a way that left no doubt as to his feelings. "I've waited all my life for you."

"Christian! I swear you're the most oblivious man in the entire state of Alaska."

"I couldn't agree with you more," he said, gazing into her eyes. "It took me a while to figure things out, but I fully intend to make up for lost time."

Mariah laid her head on his shoulder and nestled into his embrace. "And I fully intend to let you."

"I meant what I said, Mariah. I want us to be married as soon as we can make the arrangements." He looked down at her as if he expected an argument, but Mariah didn't have any objections.

Not a single, solitary one.

ENDING IN MARRIAGE

Chapter
1

Late September 1996

TRACY SANTIAGO always cried at weddings. It embarrassed her because, for one thing, people might believe she wanted to be married herself. Yet nothing could be further from the truth. Tracy had high ideals; she also had strong opinions on a variety of subjects, most of which related to women's issues. Any man she got involved with would have to understand that. So far, the men in her life had been a severe disappointment.

"Dearly beloved, we are gathered together this day to celebrate the union of…"

Tracy lowered her head and struggled to hold back tears. She was standing near Reverend Wilson in the small community church of Hard Luck, Alaska, as her friend and former client, Mariah Douglas, exchanged marriage vows with Christian O'Halloran. Tracy was Mariah's maid of honor; his brother Sawyer was best man.

Almost two years before, the town had advertised for women—or, more accurately, had advertised jobs they'd hoped would bring women north. The O'Halloran brothers, owners and operators of a bush-plane business called Midnight Sons, had been the prime movers behind the plan.

In their eagerness to entice women to Alaska, they'd promised jobs, free housing and twenty acres of land if the applicants agreed to live and work in Hard Luck for one year.

"Do you, Mariah Mary Douglas, take…"

Tracy swallowed and tilted her chin, refusing to humiliate herself in front of the entire town—and even more importantly, in front of Duke Porter. The thought of him was enough to stiffen her spine and keep the tears at bay.

When she'd first read about the men in Hard Luck, Tracy had been suspicious. An article in the Seattle paper had described the proposal, which sounded too good to be true. Experience had taught her there was no such thing as a free lunch…or free land.

Her one fleeting thought that summer morning had been to hope that any woman who signed the contract would have an attorney look it over first. Heaven only knew what this rowdy crew of bush pilots was up to.

Little did Tracy think *she'd* be the attorney reviewing the contract.

A month later, Mr. and Mrs. Rudolph Douglas had made an appointment with the prestigious law firm where Tracy was employed. Tracy was assigned to meet with them.

It seemed the Douglases' daughter, Mariah, had been hired by the O'Hallorans as secretary for Midnight Sons, and the couple was worried. They'd asked Tracy to investigate the people responsible for luring their daughter north. They wanted her to study the contract, find a way to break it and bring Mariah safely home.

Tracy remembered how Mariah's parents had characterized their daughter—as gentle, fragile, naive and easily swayed by control-seeking men. They'd feared that Mariah had made a terrible mistake. Pride, they suspected, was the only thing that kept her in Alaska. Tracy believed the Douglases were justifiably worried.

Her voice shaking, Mrs. Douglas had talked about Mariah's decision to leave Seattle. Tracy was provoked to fury by the idea of a bunch of men taking advantage of young women, especially women like Mariah. She eagerly accepted the assignment and immediately made plans to investigate the matter. Within the week, she'd traveled to Hard Luck.

She'd been prepared to do battle for the rights of Mariah and the other hapless women, but nothing had gone quite as she'd expected. To her astonishment, what she'd discovered was a tight-knit community hard at work, forging a future for their families.

Tracy had interviewed the women who'd signed contracts with the O'Halloran brothers. She was more than a little surprised to find them content and even happy, despite the almost primitive living conditions.

The biggest surprise had been Mariah Douglas. The woman was nothing like her parents had described. Gentle and soft-hearted, yes. Gullible and easily swayed, no.

For her part, Mariah was embarrassed by her family's insistence that she return to Seattle. The very reason she'd applied for the job in Hard Luck was to escape her parents and their domineering ways. Alaska offered her the opportunity to create her own life without their constant interference.

The Douglases had wanted to file a lawsuit against the

O'Hallorans, but Mariah had refused to cooperate, so it became a moot point.

"Do you, Christian Anton O'Halloran, take as…"

Out of the corner of her eye, Tracy caught sight of Duke Porter. He'd positioned himself on the bride's side of the church just so he could fluster her. Tracy would've bet her grandmother's cameo on that.

It was during her first visit to Hard Luck that Tracy had met Duke Porter, one of the pilots employed by Midnight Sons. Duke epitomized everything she disliked about men. He was an opinionated, stubborn chauvinist who had no qualms about sharing his outdated views of women.

Duke referred to women as "the weaker sex." He was the type of man who resented any woman in a position of power. The aptly named *Duke* Porter might look like the rugged hero of an old-fashioned Western; the trouble was he sounded like one, too.

They'd clashed the minute they met.

The man was the worst redneck Tracy had encountered in *years*. Every time she thought about him, she gritted her teeth.

Instead of worrying about Duke, Tracy forced herself to concentrate on the wedding ceremony. The church was crowded with well-wishers as Mariah and Christian pledged their lives to each other.

Tracy didn't think she'd ever seen Mariah look more beautiful. She wore the serene expression of a woman who knows she's deeply loved. A woman cherished by the man to whom she's willingly surrendered her heart.

Mariah had loved Christian almost from the day she'd arrived in Hard Luck. It'd taken Christian well over a year to recognize that he loved Mariah, too. Once he had, though, it seemed the youngest O'Halloran brother was intent on making up for lost time.

The couple was married two weeks to the day after they'd become engaged. Their whirlwind courtship left Tracy's head spinning. Even if *she* wasn't a romantic, Tracy was charmed by the way Christian had rushed Mariah to the altar.

She didn't begrudge her friend's happiness. Or Christian's. But she firmly believed that kind of love wasn't meant for her, and the thought saddened her, although she wasn't completely sure why.

Christian O'Halloran hadn't been able to take his eyes off his bride from the moment Mariah had entered the church on her father's arm. The only word to describe Christian was *besotted,* and Tracy knew Mariah was giddy with happiness.

"Ladies and gentlemen, may I present to you Mr. and Mrs. Christian O'Halloran. Christian, you may kiss your bride."

There was applause as Christian drew Mariah into his arms and slowly brought his mouth to hers. The kiss lasted long enough for whistles and embarrassed giggles.

Following the ceremony, the wedding party moved on to the reception, which was being held in the largest building in the community—the Hard Luck school gymnasium.

Mariah had kept Tracy informed of the goings-on in town with her long newsy letters. Tracy suspected she knew more about Hard Luck than some of the town's residents did. Between her visits and Mariah's letters, she found herself falling in love with the state of Alaska. And specifically Hard Luck, the unique little town fifty miles north of the Arctic Circle.

As soon as she got to the gymnasium, Tracy stood in the reception line with the other members of the wedding party to greet the long row of guests. The first person to come through the line was Abbey O'Halloran, wearing an ivory-colored, lace-fringed maternity top.

"Tracy, it's so good to see you again," Abbey said, hugging her.

"You, too."

Abbey looked wonderful. Radiant. Tracy knew it was a cliché to describe a pregnant woman as radiant, but Abbey *was*. She simply glowed with health, happiness, excitement. In her last letter, Mariah had written that the ultrasound showed Sawyer and Abbey were having a daughter.

As the reception line progressed, Tracy was surprised by the number of people she recognized. Many she knew because of her visits, but others she remembered from Mariah's letters.

Just when Tracy was beginning to think she might escape Duke Porter, he stepped directly in front of her. He flashed her one of his cocky grins, the kind of grin that suggested she should be thrilled to see him.

She wasn't.

Tracy stiffened instinctively. "Hello, Duke," she managed to say.

"Tell me," he said, apparently not the least bit concerned that he was holding up the reception line, "were those *tears* I saw in your eyes during the ceremony?"

"I don't know what you're talking about," she returned tartly. The man possessed an innate talent for zeroing in on whatever made her the most uncomfortable.

"It seemed to me," he said thoughtfully, rubbing his hand over his clean-shaven chin, "that your eyes were suspiciously bright while Mariah and Christian exchanged their vows. Tears, Tracy? From a woman who's never been married? You must be close to thirty now, right?"

"I said you were mistaken," she said, leaning past him to greet the next person in line. Duke, however, stood his ground.

"You've never been married, have you, Tracy?" he said. "I wonder why. Judging by the tears, you must be wondering the same thing."

"As a matter of fact, I haven't given it a thought," she informed him coldly, angry with herself for rising to his bait.

He appeared to digest this information for a moment, then added, "It would take an unusual man to marry a woman who obviously hates men."

"I *don't* hate men," she said heatedly, then clenched her hands at her sides, furious that he'd done it to her again. Duke Porter knew precisely what to say to enrage her. What enraged her even more was how easily she allowed her control to slip with this… this bush pilot. Some of the best-known attorneys in the King County court system couldn't get a rise out of her nearly as fast.

He chuckled softly, clearly pleased with himself.

"You're holding up the reception line," she snapped in an effort to get him to leave.

Duke glanced over his shoulder. "You're right. We'll resume this discussion later. And there'll be no escape then, I promise you."

He leaned forward as if to kiss her, and she jerked her head back. But her action didn't disconcert him at all.

"Tracy?" he whispered for her ears alone. "Don't forget, I owe you one."

"Owe me?"

"For that kiss," he reminded her. He wiggled his eyebrows suggestively.

She opened her mouth to question his sanity. The last man on this earth she was interested in kissing was Duke Porter.

"The kiss," he said in calm tones, "that you had Mariah deliver. You owe me, you little troublemaker, and I intend to collect."

Tracy felt as if the floor had opened up and she was falling through open space.

Months earlier, she'd asked Mariah to kiss Duke on her behalf and to tell him it was from his favorite feminist. They'd meant the whole thing as a joke. And frankly she'd never expected to see Duke Porter again.

He smiled at her, but there was no amusement in his face. His expression said she was about to receive her due.

Tracy swallowed painfully. She had nothing to fear, she told herself. Duke was all bark and no bite. Her eyes held his, unwavering.

The person behind Duke cleared his throat, and Duke moved forward to offer his congratulations to the bride and groom.

Tracy's eyes followed him. She recalled the first time she'd met Duke and how she'd involuntarily reacted to the disturbing sight of his rugged sensuality. Duke was well over six feet, almost a full head taller than her own five-three.

He was muscular, as well, but she knew that his strength wasn't the result of working out at some gym with fancy equipment. He was a man who lived hard and worked harder.

His hair was straight and dark, a bit long in the back. He needed it trimmed, but then he had every time she'd seen him. From a distance his eyes looked dark, but on closer inspection she realized they were a deep shade of gray. Brooding eyes.

Tracy's were brown, and she wore her hair short and curly. With her court schedule what it was, she didn't have time to fuss with her appearance. She frowned on women who used beauty instead of intelligence to achieve their goals.

Her wardrobe consisted of business suits in grays and blues. A few casual clothes—jeans and sweaters. One fancier dress for those rare evenings when she participated in some charity function. And now, one rose silk maid-of-honor dress. Tracy would never have chosen such a traditionally feminine outfit for herself.

She'd always disdained feminine trappings, which she saw as pandering to men. From an early age she'd learned the disappointing truth—men were often intimidated by intelligent women. It hurt their pitifully fragile egos to admit that someone of the "weaker sex" might know more than they did. In her opinion, Duke was a classic example of this kind of man, and she refused to allow him to diminish her confidence. As the reception continued, Tracy managed to avoid him. She headed for the buffet and three of the pilots did verbal battle to see which one would have the honor of bringing her dinner. While the men argued, Tracy dished up her own plate. The three pilots watched openmouthed as she sat down and started to eat. The comedy went on as they rushed toward the buffet line, then hurried back to vie for a seat next to her.

Tracy had dated her share of men and been in several short-term relationships, but rarely had she had more requests than she could handle. This was certainly an aspect of life in Alaska she hadn't considered.

Just when she thought she was safe, Duke asked her to dance. Actually he didn't ask, he assumed. While her mind staggered, seeking excuses, he effortlessly guided her onto the dance floor.

Rather than cause a scene, Tracy let him take her in his arms.

"I was watching you just now," he said, and his voice was almost friendly. Almost, but not quite.

Tracy said nothing. She'd endure one turn around the dance floor and be done with him. She wondered if this was her punishment for asking Mariah to kiss him.

"I've finally figured out what you really need," he went on.

Tracy couldn't resist rolling her eyes. This should be good. To her surprise, he didn't seem in a hurry to tell her.

"You're one of those women who think because you've got a couple of college degrees you're better than a man."

Tracy opened to her mouth to argue, then hesitated. This time she wasn't going to be drawn into one of those no-win verbal exchanges. He could say what he wanted, and she'd keep her mouth shut.

"I bet you thought you were clever outsmarting Ted, Ralph and Jim, didn't you? I suspect you're used to having men compete for your attention."

Tracy wasn't going to correct him, that was for sure.

"It seems to me you're the kind of woman who needs to be tamed."

Despite her vow to keep her mouth closed, despite her determination not to become involved in a pointless argument, Tracy burst out, "Tamed? You think a woman needs to be *tamed?*"

"It won't be easy," Duke went on as if she hadn't spoken. "It'd take a real man, not one of those *sensitive* males you're accustomed to dating."

"I beg your pardon?" Fury poured through her like molten lava.

"I know just the type of man you date, too," he said smugly. "The ones who're trying to get in touch with their inner child."

"I'd like you to tell Gavin that."

"I take it Gavin's your boyfriend?"

"If you saw him you wouldn't call him a boy," she taunted as he led her around the dance floor.

"Really. Describe him to me."

She had no intention of doing so, but soon found herself mentally listing Gavin's virtues—even though she was a long stretch from being in love with her fellow lawyer. Gavin was witty and fun and they'd had a good time together, but it wasn't a serious relationship.

"A caring, sensitive guy, no doubt," Duke muttered.

"Gavin's a man of the nineties," she said curtly before she realized Duke had done it to her *again*.

Duke snorted. "A man of the nineties. I can picture him now."

"You've never even met Gavin," she snapped, quick to come to her friend's defense.

"I don't need to," Duke said. "I can see him already. He's just your type. Before he knows it, you'll have a ring through his nose and you'll be leading him around to show all your fancy friends how powerful you are. But once you're bored with him, it'll be bye-bye Gavin."

The effort it took not to respond sapped Tracy's energy. "I know what *your* problem is, Duke Porter," she announced evenly. "You're living in the Middle Ages. Talk about *me* being close to thirty and unmarried. What about you?"

"I don't have any desire to marry."

"Me, neither."

He snorted again as if he didn't believe her.

"That says a lot, doesn't it?" She mocked him openly. "It's perfectly acceptable for *you* to remain single, but you can't admit a woman might have those same feelings."

"Since the beginning of time, women have fought to control men."

"I see it the other way around," she argued. "Men seem to think it's their God-given right to dominate a woman."

"God created woman to please man."

"*What?*" Tracy groaned aloud. Duke Porter belonged not in the Middle Ages but back in the Dark Ages. "You mean pleasure him, don't you?"

That slow easy smile of his slid into place. "That, too."

"I don't believe it." Although the music hadn't stopped, Tracy pulled herself out of his embrace and walked off the dance floor.

Duke followed her. "Just a reminder," he said when they reached the far end of the room. "I still intend to collect my kiss."

"I didn't kiss you," she insisted.

"Yeah, but you wanted to. And you want it now."

"I'd rather kiss a rattlesnake," she assured him with her sweetest smile.

"No need," he returned flippantly. "You can kiss me, instead."

DUKE STEPPED BACK and watched as his friends buzzed around Tracy like bees around a rose in full bloom. It irritated him to see his fellow pilots, men he trusted and admired, taken in by a pretty face.

Tracy Santiago wasn't even that pretty. Cute, maybe, but that was about as far as he was willing to go. One thing he knew— he didn't like her.

Never had and never would.

Duke remembered when he'd first encountered the

attorney. He'd known instantly that Tracy wanted to make trouble for Midnight Sons and consequently for all of them. She was after the company, hoping to prove that his employers were exploiting women.

What a lie! Each and every woman who'd moved to Hard Luck had come of her own free will. True, the O'Halloran brothers had gone out of their way to give women incentives to move north, but there'd been no coercion, no sales pitch, no pressure. The women who'd stayed and become part of the community *wanted* to be here.

It hadn't taken long for the fancy Seattle attorney to show up, looking for an opportunity to ruin everything. Now, there was a woman with her own agenda!

Duke hadn't liked Tracy the first time they met. Afterward he should've simply forgotten her—yet he hadn't. Months after her visit, he was still dwelling on their fiery exchanges. No one had ever stood up to him like that, challenged him, and when he questioned her actions—well, to put it mildly, she gave as good as she got.

Their feud didn't end with her visit, either. Fate had pulled a trick on them both when he answered the office phone one afternoon and heard Tracy on the other end. The incident reminded him of everything he hated about her—and everything he *didn't* hate.

Mariah seemed to take pleasure in teasing him about his aversion to a certain female attorney. She tossed Tracy's name into conversations the way an enemy would toss a grenade.

Then there was the day Mariah had kissed him. Mariah! It hadn't taken Duke or any of the other pilots long to see the lay of the land when it came to *her*.

She'd set her sights on Christian the first day she arrived in

Hard Luck. So nothing could have shocked Duke more than the time she'd backed him into a corner and laid a lip-lock on him that had sent him spinning.

Then she had to go and ruin it by explaining that the kiss was actually from Tracy Santiago. If ever there was an ego buster, it was having that shrew get the upper hand.

What bothered Duke even more was that he hadn't been able to forget that kiss. He couldn't help wondering what it would've been like had it really been from Tracy. If they became romantically involved…

The truth was, that scared the living daylights out of him. Any relationship between them would be ludicrous. No man needed that kind of grief. Not that there was much chance of it happening to Duke, with her living in Seattle and him in Hard Luck.

His father had tried making a long-distance relationship work years earlier, and it had destroyed his family. His mother had hated Alaska. She'd stayed for several years, then moved to Texas, where she had family and friends. His father had remained in Alaska, and within a couple of years they'd divorced. Duke had hated Texas and was soon living with his dad. The two of them had gotten along well. John Porter had never remarried, and Duke didn't blame him.

John had died several years ago, and Duke rarely heard from his mother, who'd remarried and raised a second family. It was just as well, since they had little in common. He suspected he was an unhappy reminder of something she'd prefer to forget.

There was no denying that his own background had made him cautious—no, downright wary—about women and marriage.

Soon after the kissing incident, though, he'd let a friend in

Fairbanks set up a date for him. Generally he didn't bother with blind dates, but the daily flights to Fairbanks didn't give him enough time to meet women on his own. His reaction to Tracy had led him to forgo his usual caution.

Pretty soon he had something going with Laurie. She was divorced and had a couple of kids her husband took on weekends. They had a nice arrangement, he and Laurie. She wasn't interested in marrying again, she said, which suited Duke perfectly because marriage didn't interest him, either. He'd leave that to his friends.

No, sirree, Duke wasn't going to let any woman rule his life. He'd seen what could happen. But then again, he wasn't opposed to the sort of cozy setup he had with Laurie.

Unfortunately it hadn't lasted. A few weeks into their relationship, Duke realized she bored him. A perfectly good woman was crazy about him, and it was all he could do to feign interest. If he raised his voice, vented a little steam, Laurie cried. Real tears, too. Every now and then, he'd say something outrageous just to get a reaction out of her. She'd smile benignly and astonish him by agreeing.

Before long, Duke found himself making excuses not to see her. He even traded his flights a couple of times to avoid flying to Fairbanks.

When he figured he was being unfair to her, Duke dropped by her house to put a peaceable end to their relationship. He'd expected her to plead with him to stay, to weep and tell him how much she loved him.

Ending relationships had never been easy. Despite what some might say, he hated hurting a woman's feelings.

On the flight into town, he'd rehearsed a little speech. One in which he took all the blame for their breakup. He hoped she'd accept his apology and agree to let things drop. By the time he'd arrived at Laurie's, he'd felt ready for just about anything. But Laurie shocked him into realizing how unprepared he actually was.

As he stood outside her door, bearing flowers and looking like a fool, she offered him an embarrassed smile and introduced him to her new husband.

Duke was annoyed—and humiliated—to discover that all the while she was seeing *him,* she'd been involved with this other guy.

In retrospect, Duke found the situation funny, though at the time he hadn't been amused. He'd gotten angry, said things he later regretted and quickly left, stuffing his flowers into the nearest trash can.

In the air, on the return trip to Hard Luck, it occurred to Duke that Tracy would never lead a man on the way Laurie had. If she had something she wanted to say, it got said. Nor would she date a man on the sly.

Once he'd landed the plane and taxied into the hangar, Duke knew he'd come full circle. Tracy Santiago once again dominated his thoughts.

Just like she was doing today.

TRACY FELT as if she'd been granted a stay of execution. After the wedding dinner and dance, she escaped Duke and slipped into the back room to help Mariah change out of her wedding dress.

In an hour or less, the wedding couple would be on their way. Sawyer and Abbey would fly them into Fairbanks for their wedding night. The next morning the newlyweds would leave for California to board a ship for a two-week Caribbean cruise.

With tears in her eyes, Tracy hugged the woman who'd become her dearest friend.

"Dreams really do come true," Mariah whispered. "For so long I thought Christian would never realize he loved me."

"He's like all men," Tracy kidded. "He has no idea what's good for him."

"Oh, before I forget, I need to tell you about the flight that's been scheduled for you and my parents in the morning," Mariah said as she reached for her wool coat. "You should be down at the field by ten. And dress warmly."

"Don't worry, I will," Tracy said, not wanting to delay her friend.

"It might be September in Seattle, but here winter's setting in. The rivers haven't frozen yet, but we've already had plenty of snow."

All Tracy needed to do was look out the window to see that. Snow in September was foreign to her.

"Also," Mariah said, her eyes bright with happiness, "don't be surprised when I throw the bouquet in your direction. I expect you to catch it, too."

"What?" Tracy's eyes widened in mock horror. "Are you nuts?"

"Not at all. I want you to experience this kind of happiness, too."

Tracy's smile faded. As an attorney, she all too often witnessed marriages that came to bitter ends. She'd shied away from commitment, for that reason and plenty of others.

"Let one of the other women catch it," Tracy suggested.

"Not on your life. This one's for you."

Tracy wasn't sure she should thank her.

"One other thing," Mariah said quickly.

"What?"

"Don't be angry with me," Mariah said in a soft voice. "I didn't have anything to do with this."

"How could I possibly be angry with you?" Tracy said, and impulsively hugged her again.

Mariah's answering smile was wan. "Duke's the pilot who'll be flying you into Fairbanks tomorrow."

Chapter 2

"BEN, I THINK it's time we got you home," Bethany Harris said, sitting down in the vacant seat beside his. The wedding reception was winding down now that Christian and Mariah had left.

"Already?" Ben Hamilton muttered, frowning. He felt as though he'd just arrived. He wasn't accustomed to having anyone fuss over him. It took some getting used to, but at least he was back in his own bed, which was a heck of a lot better than the hospital in Fairbanks. A man could die in a place like that. The doctor said he needed plenty of rest; unfortunately he hadn't bothered to tell the nurses that. Ben swore they woke him up at all hours of the day and night for the most ridiculous reasons.

The open-heart surgery had left him weak. It used to be that he could run the Hard Luck Café from dawn to dusk and still have enough energy at night to play cards or read and watch a little television. Not anymore. Now he slept for much of the day.

The doctors and Bethany had assured him that he was recovering well and would soon be back on his feet. Ben hoped that was true, because he didn't make a good patient. Ask any of the nurses who'd been assigned to him!

"How are you feeling?" Bethany's question interrupted his thoughts.

"Fit as a fiddle," he said, gently patting her arm. He still found it difficult to believe he'd fathered this beautiful young woman. He hadn't known about her until she'd come to Hard Luck a year earlier. Talk about surprises! Learning he had a child had been the biggest shock of his life. Bethany had tracked him down and taken a job at the community school in order to meet him. She still taught there; she was married now and expecting her first baby—and she loved living in Hard Luck.

Ben was delighted with this opportunity to know his daughter. She was truly a gift, a miracle for a man who'd given up believing in such things a long time ago.

Until Ben's recent heart attack, only Mitch, Bethany's husband, had known of the special relationship between them. Ben had figured the O'Halloran brothers suspected something, but they'd never asked and he'd never said. Now, though, everyone knew. And that was fine with Ben.

"Let me walk you back to the café," Bethany suggested.

It was hard to have someone constantly watching over him. When he got out of the hospital he'd stayed with Bethany and Mitch for a few days. That was about as much tender loving care as he could take.

Over their protests, he'd insisted on returning to his own apartment above the café. Mitch had carried up his bags, and Bethany had prepared the place, vacuuming and changing linens, even arranging a bouquet of late-blooming wildflowers. She worried about the stairs that led up to his apartment, but he'd managed them without difficulty, taking it slow and easy.

True, he didn't make the trek down to the café very often, but he'd regain his strength in time and get back to work. It wouldn't be soon enough to suit him.

Ben's jaw tightened every time he thought about the revenue he was losing by keeping the café closed. More importantly, he knew folks around town depended on him for good food at a decent price.

Despite all the weddings taking place, the majority of men in town were unmarried, and many regularly came to the café for their meals. From the day it opened, Ben's place had been the social center of Hard Luck.

"You ready?" Bethany asked.

Ben would've liked to stay a bit longer and enjoy the festivities, but he didn't have the energy to argue. He stood and Bethany looped her arm through his.

"I'm thinking about opening the café," he said, and before she could object, he added, "part-time of course."

"No way."

He should've known a child of his would be stubborn, but he'd counted on her at least hearing him out.

"Just for dinner."

"Don't even think about it, Ben."

He recognized that tone of voice. It was the same one he used himself when he refused to budge. Yup, her stubbornness was definitely an inherited trait—inherited from him!

"What are you smiling about?" she asked.

He'd been found out. "Nothing," he muttered, toning down his grin.

As they left the reception, Bethany stopped to tell Mitch, her husband, where she was going. Chrissie, Bethany's stepdaughter, was busy with the other children, and after a brief conversation with the girl, Mitch joined his wife. One on either side of Ben.

Ben hated feeling helpless, but he let Bethany and Mitch support him until they got to the café. The place was empty and cold, a stark contrast to all the times it had been filled with the talk of men and the clatter of dishes. What Ben wouldn't give to crank up that grill and fry a few burgers!

Because he was drained from the afternoon's socializing, he took the stairs slowly, one at a time. He didn't like admitting how weak he felt, but Bethany and Mitch seemed to know without his saying a word.

"Sit down and make yourself at home," Mitch said, urging him toward his favorite recliner.

"I *am* at home," Ben snapped, then immediately regretted the outburst. "It feels good to have my own things around me. I—I appreciate your concern."

Mitch accepted the apology by giving him a pat on the shoulder.

There was a certain solace in being home, among his familiar comforts. The recliner. The television with its antenna, one spoke wrapped in aluminum foil. He'd gotten a satellite dish a few years back, but hadn't bothered to remove the antenna. You never knew when it might come in handy. His glance fell on the American flag framed and mounted on the wall. A small memento of more than twenty years in the navy.

It wasn't much, but this was home and the place he loved.

"Help yourself to a drink," he told Mitch, gesturing toward

the refrigerator in the compact kitchen. To his surprise Mitch took him up on the offer.

These days the couple generally stayed only long enough to make sure he was comfortable and then were on their way. Ben didn't blame them; their lives were busy. He didn't need anyone to tell him he wasn't good company.

Bethany claimed the chair across from him, and Mitch sat on the thick padded arm, his hand resting on his wife's shoulder. Come spring, Ben reminded himself, there'd be a brand-new baby at their house.

The thought of their child, his own grandchild, was one of the things that had helped him through the worst part of his recovery. He wanted to live to see Bethany's children. He'd missed out on the chance to be a father, and he looked forward to being a grandpa.

"Mitch and I wanted to talk to you about the café," Bethany said, glancing at her husband.

Ben tensed. He should've realized there was something coming. If these two thought they were going to convince him to retire and sell the café, they'd better think again.

"I'm not selling," he said, unwilling to let them even broach the subject.

"Sell the café?" Bethany repeated. "Ben, no, we'd never suggest that!"

His shoulders relaxed as relief flowed through him.

"We only want to encourage you to hire some help."

"I planned on doing that myself as soon as—"

"You got around to it," Bethany finished for him. "You've been saying that for months. Here you are, recuperating from open-heart surgery, and you're still just talking about it."

"Yes, well…"

"Look at you. You're barely out of the hospital and already you want to open the café."

"Part-time," he said under his breath, knowing they weren't really prepared to listen. They'd already made up their minds, just like he had.

"Just how long would that part-time business last?" Bethany asked in a knowing voice. Ben suspected she was right. He'd open up the café for dinner, and soon people would start wandering in around lunchtime, and before he knew it, he'd be back on the same old treadmill. But it was what he loved, what he did best. Fact was, he longed for his friends. People used to come in every day for coffee and conversation, and he missed that more than anything. Heck, he was downright lonely.

"People count on me," he said.

"We know that." At least Mitch agreed with him. "That's why we want you to hire someone to come and help *now*. Someone with plenty of experience you won't need to train."

"Just where do you suppose you'll find someone like that?" Ben asked. He wanted it known right then and there that he didn't think much of their idea. "Especially with the kind of wages I can afford." His thoughts went into overdrive. Another cook, especially one with plenty of seasoning, would run the place *his* way. Pretty soon Ben wouldn't belong in his own kitchen anymore!

"I've talked to Matt and Karen about taking in a boarder and—"

It hit him then. Strange how long it had taken him to catch on. Bethany and Mitch already had someone in mind.

"Who is it?" he asked outright, interrupting Mitch.

Once more the couple exchanged glances. "Mrs. Mc-Murphy," Mitch said.

"A woman?"

"Do you have something against a woman, Ben?" Bethany asked, challenge in her tone.

He opened his mouth to detail exactly why he *did* object to a woman working in his kitchen, then realized he couldn't say one word without offending Bethany.

"Where'd you find her?" he asked instead.

"In Fairbanks. She cooked at the Sourdough Café for years. Christian and Sawyer go there a lot, so they met her. She told them she's looking for a change of scene."

Ben knew the Sourdough Café had a reputation for good food. His objections started to dwindle. "She won't want to work here in Hard Luck," he muttered. The kids meant well, he knew.

"Why don't you meet her and ask her yourself?" Bethany suggested. "I talked to Sawyer, and he said Mrs. McMurphy could fly in with the mail run one day next week. If you don't like her, then no harm done."

He wasn't going to like her, but Ben didn't have the heart to burst the kids' bubble. Just because the woman could cook didn't mean he was comfortable letting a stranger into his kitchen.

"You'll at least meet her, won't you?" Bethany pressed.

"Okay, okay," Ben answered reluctantly. "But I'm not making any promises."

TRACY WAS out at the airfield by nine-thirty the next morning. Fat snowflakes drifted down from a leaden sky, and she wondered if the flight would be canceled because of the weather.

She lugged her suitcase into the mobile office for Midnight Sons, and the first person she saw was Duke. He appeared to be reading something on a clipboard; he didn't look up or acknowledge her. Not that she expected he would.

Sawyer O'Halloran was there, as well, talking into the radio; he was apparently collecting the latest weather data.

When he'd finished, he turned off the switch and swiveled around to greet Tracy. "Looks like it'll just be you and Duke."

This was not promising. "What happened to Mr. and Mrs. Douglas? We're supposed to be leaving together."

"They've decided to stay on another day," Sawyer explained. "Mrs. Douglas doesn't want to fly in the snow."

"Will the storm be a problem?" Tracy asked.

"Not as far as we can tell, and Duke's the best pilot in our fleet. You don't have anything to worry about," he said, then casually mentioned that the plane had recently been serviced. This, she suspected, was done to reassure her that everything was in good shape.

Duke's gaze met hers. "You want to wait with the Douglases?" he asked. Although there was nothing in his voice, a glint of challenge flashed from his cool gray eyes.

"No, I'll go," she said. Really she had no choice. Her court schedule was packed and she couldn't afford to miss any more work.

"What time's your flight out of Fairbanks?" Duke asked.

She told him, and he glanced at his watch. "Then let's leave now. If we're lucky we'll be able to avoid the worst of the storm."

She reached for her suitcase. Duke paused, his eyes holding hers. "You aren't afraid of a little snow, are you?"

"Of course not." Somehow, it seemed important not to let

him know she didn't entirely trust him *or* the weather. But the truth was, she'd prefer to fly when the weather was clear.

He nodded in approval. "You ready?" he asked, setting aside the clipboard.

"Sure," she said brightly, forcing some enthusiasm into her voice.

Duke headed out the door, and she guessed she was expected to follow him. But she didn't, not right away.

"Sawyer," she said, gripping her suitcase with both hands.

The middle O'Halloran brother looked up from his desk.

"I just wanted you to know that…that I think you've been completely fair with the women you've hired." This was more awkward than she'd thought. For some time now, she'd wanted to apologize, set the record straight, and this was the first real opportunity she'd had. "I realize we started off on the wrong foot, what with me arriving here the way I did. I couldn't be happier for Mariah and Christian, and the others."

He cracked a smile and dismissed her apology with a wave of his hand. "Don't worry about it. You were only doing your job. The Douglases are decent people, and they had every right to be concerned about Mariah."

Tracy felt better for having shared her regrets. They'd weighed on her mind all weekend. She'd meant the O'Hallorans no harm. Over the past year she'd come to respect the three brothers, and she didn't want there to be any hard feelings.

"I guess I should be on my way," she said, glancing over her shoulder toward the door. "I had a marvelous weekend. Thank you."

"We're glad you could make the wedding on such short notice."

It had taken a bit of finagling, but Tracy had managed to change her schedule, flying in on Friday afternoon. This was one wedding she hadn't wanted to miss, even though it meant traveling more than twenty-five hundred miles.

Duke was inspecting the exterior of the plane when Tracy joined him. "You can get in," he said absently.

"Thanks," she muttered, more certain than ever that this one-hour flight would feel like a lifetime. She'd taken Mariah's advice and dressed warmly in wool pants and a thick cable-knit sweater. Since the interior of the aircraft was heated, she couldn't decide if she wanted to keep her coat on or take it off.

Tracy was about to ask, but decided the less conversation between her and Duke, the better. Since he wore his jacket, she'd wear hers, too.

Once inside the aircraft, Tracy fastened her seat belt and held her breath. Flying didn't usually frighten her, but she'd rarely flown in a storm or in an aircraft this small. Neither Sawyer nor Duke had expressed any qualms, though, and they were the experts. Midnight Sons was proud of its safety record, and she was confident they wouldn't fly if conditions were hazardous.

Duke climbed into the plane and started the engine, which fired readily to life. Next he reached for the headset, adjusting it over his ears, and spoke into the small attached microphone. She could hardly hear him over the roar of the engine.

They taxied to the end of the runway, then turned around. She watched him do an equipment check, pushing various gauges and buttons. According to Sawyer, Duke was the best pilot they had. This ride wasn't going to be a lot of fun, with the snow coming down fast and furious, but the weather didn't seem to concern him, so Tracy resolved not to worry about it, either. Easier said than done, however...

The engine noise increased dramatically as Duke boosted the power and roared down the snow-covered gravel runway. Soon they were airborne. A few minutes later, he removed his headset and tucked it under her seat. After that, he looked in her direction once, as if to check on her.

"I'm fine," she shouted. But he must've known she was afraid from the way she kept her hands tightly clasped in her lap.

It came to her that if she was willing to put her differences with the O'Halloran brothers behind her, she should be willing to do the same with Duke. The words, however, stuck in her throat.

With Duke it was...personal. Duke felt a woman needed to be tamed. Indeed! It was time the man woke up and realized he lived in the twentieth century. Good grief, almost the twenty-first!

She supposed that nothing she could say or do would change his opinions, and it would be useless to even try.

Sighing, Tracy closed her eyes and tried to sleep. Not that it would be possible, but if Duke assumed she was asleep, he might ignore her.

Tracy wasn't sure when she noticed a difference, but at one point she became aware that something wasn't right. It seemed, to her uneducated ear, that the engine noise had altered slightly. She opened her eyes and straightened to find Duke studying the instrument panel.

"What is it?" she asked, studying the gauges herself.

He gave no outward indication that anything was wrong. She might not have known if it wasn't for the increasingly odd noises the engine made.

"Duke, don't play games with me!" she cried. This was no time to pay her back for that silly kiss—and yet she hoped that was exactly what he was doing.

He looked at her as if he didn't know what she meant.

"Okay, so I had Mariah kiss you," she said, and didn't care that she sounded frantic. "I admit it was a stupid thing to do. I…I don't know why I did it, but if you're trying to retaliate and frighten me, then I—"

It was as though he hadn't heard her. He cursed loudly.

"What's wrong?"

The engine sputtered, and there could be no denying they were experiencing some kind of trouble. Big trouble.

"We're losing—"

The engine faltered again.

"Start looking," he ordered tersely.

"For what?"

"A place to land. We're going down."

No sooner had he spoken than the engine quit completely.

CHRISTIAN AND MARIAH sat outside their gate at the Fairbanks airport waiting for their flight. Christian's arm was around his wife's shoulders.

His wife.

The realization took some getting used to, but it was a good kind of adjustment. Mariah tucked her head under his chin, and he stroked her hair contentedly.

"Our flight should be called soon," he told her. An entire two weeks on a cruise ship with his bride sounded like heaven. His life had been turned upside down in the past three weeks. A month ago he would've laughed at anyone who suggested he'd be married now. Yet here he was, and about as happy as any man had a right to be.

Mariah's eyes were closed, but she was smiling.

She had good reason to be tired—and happy. Their wedding night had been one of discovery and joy. Christian was still shocked that he'd been so clueless about his feelings for Mariah all these months. Once he'd recognized that he was in love with her, it was as if his whole world had expanded.

For the first year of their acquaintance, he'd barely been able to work in the same room with her, convinced she was nothing but trouble. Everyone else was crazy about her, but ironically, she *was* trouble—for Christian's heart.

He'd sensed that his self-contained emotional life was about to be blown wide open. Knowing he was in grave danger, he'd raised a protective barrier against her. He'd been ill-tempered, unreasonable and cantankerous, yet she'd put up with him day after day.

It would take him a lifetime to make up for the dreadful way he'd treated her, but it was a task he accepted willingly.

"Christian," she murmured, her eyes still closed. "Why'd you assign Duke to fly Tracy out of Hard Luck?"

Christian grinned. Tracy and Duke. Those two were like fire and ice. Complete and total opposites.

"They don't get along, you know," Mariah said, as if he wasn't already aware of it.

"Don't get along" was putting it mildly. He wouldn't be surprised if they argued the entire flight. He could picture it now. Duke would start the argument because he thrived on verbal battles. Christian suspected he particularly enjoyed getting Tracy riled up. Then she'd respond, and soon the fur would fly.

"It seems like cruel and unusual punishment to subject those two to each other for any length of time," Mariah said.

"Your parents will be there to mediate." He kissed the crown of her head. "Have I told you yet how much I love you?" he asked, changing the subject.

A slow, contented smile spread over her face. "As a matter of fact, you did. I love you, too."

His arm tightened briefly around her shoulders. "I know." Her love was one thing he'd never doubt.

"By the way," she said, raising her head to meet his gaze, "when did you start drinking your coffee black?"

Christian figured heaven would bless him for the restraint it required not to laugh outright. As his secretary, Mariah had served him coffee every morning for more than a year. Some days she added cream, others sugar, occasionally both, but only rarely did she get it right.

"Just recently," he answered.

His heart swelled with love, and he wondered if it would always be like this with him and Mariah. Sawyer seemed to indicate that it would. He'd married Abbey a year earlier and had never been happier. Charles, the oldest brother, had gotten married last spring.

At the time, Christian had felt light-years away from making a commitment to any woman, yet here he was, less than six months later, with his new wife by his side. The best part was how happy he was. He'd always thought that when it was time to get married, he'd go into the relationship with some reluctance, knowing his bachelor days were over. It hadn't been that way at all. He felt like the most fortunate man alive.

"You never did answer my question," Mariah said, nestling her head more securely against him.

"What question?" He was easily sidetracked these days.

"About assigning Duke to fly Tracy into town."

"I didn't assign him the flight," Christian murmured.

She lifted her head to meet his gaze, her eyes filled with unasked questions.

"It's true," Christian assured her.

"But I saw it on the schedule myself. I even warned Tracy and promised her it wasn't my doing, and now you're telling me Duke *isn't* flying her into town?"

"No," he said, and laughed smugly, "I'm telling you I didn't *give* Duke the assignment."

"Then how—"

"Duke requested it."

"He did?" Her wonderfully expressive face revealed her shock.

Christian nodded. "I thought it was a bit strange myself. But who am I to question such matters?"

"Really." Mariah's smile was back. "So Duke requested it. I'm beginning to suspect there's more going on with those two than meets the eye."

Christian opened his mouth to argue, then changed his mind. Everything he knew about love and romance he'd learned from his wife. She was the expert.

AVIATE. NAVIGATE. Communicate.

The words raced through Duke's mind at laser speed. His first response was to take whatever measures were needed to restart the plane's engine. From the way the oil pressure was falling, Duke guessed the line had ruptured. The engine sputtered to life once or twice, then died with a final spurt. Nothing he did could restart it, despite his continuous efforts.

"What do you mean we're going down?" Tracy sounded close to panic.

"We'll be making an off-field landing," he shouted. And then, because he knew she was frightened, he added, "They happen all the time."

"Maybe they do for you. You *have* done this before, haven't you?"

"Plenty of times." He hoped the lie would keep Tracy from panicking. The truth was, he'd made only one emergency landing, years earlier, in conditions a lot better than this.

He reached for his headset and began talking, linking with the air-traffic controller in Fairbanks, communicating his co-ordinates. He sounded calm, but his heart was beating so loudly he was sure it could be heard over the microphone.

As the plane descended through the clouds and snow, it became more and more difficult to make out the terrain below.

"Duke…" Tracy grabbed his arm, her grip tight. He felt her terror, experienced his own.

"Look around," he ordered. "We need to find a clearing where we can land."

September and March. Every pilot in Alaska knew those were the most dangerous months in which to crash. Snow on the ground, and the rivers and lakes had yet to freeze over.

In another week he could've settled this baby down on a frozen lake. If he tried that now, they'd both be dead in a matter of minutes.

Fact was, he didn't know what their chances were.

Not good, he decided. Not even promising.

Because of the snow and the wind, the plane glided. He worked the rudder, manipulating the aircraft any way he could, hoping to navigate it.

"I...I can't make out anything below," Tracy said.

Duke couldn't, either.

"What should I do?" she asked, and once more he heard the panic in her voice.

"Hold on as best you can."

"I'm already doing that!"

"You might pray," he suggested next.

"Pray? I don't think I know how. It's been a while."

He guessed they were both about to get a crash course in the art of prayer. Crash course. If it wasn't so terrifying, he would've laughed.

As they drifted down from the sky, Duke glanced at Tracy and winked. "Hold on tight, sweetheart."

He was beginning to make out the contours of the land, silently cursing when he saw trees. This was the worst possible scenario.

"Right before we land," he said, straining to sound cool and collected, "open your window and the door."

"I'll fall out."

"No, you won't." Although controlling the plane required his complete concentration, he reached over and grabbed the end of her seat belt. He yanked hard, making sure it was as tight as possible.

Then he did the same with his own.

Out of the driving snow, a small clearing appeared. Working as fast as his hands would let him, Duke shut down the plane's electrical system, including the rudders. The last thing they needed on impact was a spark to set off a fire.

"Hold on," he shouted as the aircraft slammed into the ground. A tree tore off the right wing, and Tracy screamed, covering her face with both hands.

The plane spun out of control, cartwheeling like a broken toy over the harsh landscape. Duke was nearly wrenched from his seat. A piercing pain stabbed his left arm as he felt the bone snap, and then he felt nothing.

Chapter
3

TRACY WAS VICIOUSLY jolted from side to side. The aircraft smashed against the side of a tree and spun around. The entire world became a blur, colors blending, lights blinking. The oxygen seemed to be sucked from the air.

Tracy heard Duke cry out and at the same moment felt something hit her head. Warm liquid trickled down her face. Blood? A scream froze in her throat. That was when she knew. She was going to die.

The incredible thing was that she felt no fear, no terror—nothing but a strange sense of peace.

Abruptly the tumbling aircraft hit something solid. The jolt was strong enough to nearly rip her seat from its hinges. The seat-belt restraints were the only thing that kept Tracy from being hurled through the front window.

Then there was silence. Absolute silence.

It hurt to breathe, and she struggled for each lungful of air.

Her chest felt as if a heavy weight was pressing against her. She managed a raspy breath and choked.

The seat belt kept Tracy in an upright position. It was painfully tight, and she realized that was the cause of her distress. She needed every ounce of strength she had to release it.

"Duke." Her voice was a hoarse whisper as she turned her head to look at her companion. Her distress increased tenfold when she saw him. Blood flowed freely from a gash on the side of his head.

Tentatively she reached out and touched his face, not knowing if he was dead or alive. "Please, oh, please don't be dead. Duke, be alive. Please be alive."

Although she felt as if her arms and legs had been jerked from their sockets, her fear propelled her into action. She located the pulse in his neck and nearly sobbed with relief.

Next she twisted around in her seat and applied pressure to Duke's wound, which continued to bleed profusely. The cut was jagged and very deep. Even to her inexperienced eye, it was obvious that he needed stitches.

Every time she moved, her body screamed with pain. But she maneuvered herself around so that she was kneeling on her seat. Then she pulled her scarf from her jacket and opened a package of tissues she found in her pocket; with these she constructed a makeshift bandage for Duke's head.

Judging by the odd position of his left arm, she assumed it was badly broken, perhaps a compound fracture. She leaned her forehead against his shoulder, struggling not to weep with frustration and fear.

Duke groaned and rolled his head to one side.

Tracy's relief was so great she brought both hands to her mouth. "Duke! We're alive. We're alive!"

He opened his eyes and smiled when he saw her kneeling next to him. "I told you this'd be a piece of cake," he murmured.

"Where's the first-aid kit?" she asked. "Your arm's—it looks like it's broken."

He nodded. "Feels like it, too." His face was deathly white. His eyes narrowed as he studied her. Raising his good arm, he touched her face, his hand gently caressing her cheek. "You're hurt."

"No," she countered, "I'm fine really. You're the one who's hurt."

His hand came away covered in blood. "You have a cut…" His voice started to fade. Tracy was afraid he might be going into shock.

"Duke, where's the first-aid kit?" she asked again. She tried to remember the emergency medical class she'd taken her first year in college, but worried she'd forgotten too much to be of any help to either of them.

Duke told her, and she scrambled into the back, digging through the emergency equipment. She found two sleeping bags and several packets of brown plastic bags. These, she discovered, were something called Meals Ready to Eat. Or so the package claimed.

The first-aid kit was the last item she pulled free. Tucking the plastic box under her arm, she squirmed forward. By the time she got back to her seat, she was breathless and weak.

Duke's face remained white with pain. She considered unwrapping one of the sleeping bags and covering him with that, but there was so little room. If only she could get to her suitcase.

"I've got the kit," she said, feeling triumphant for having

accomplished this one small feat. Then she went about treating his injuries.

She unwound her scarf and examined his cut, relieved to find the bleeding had slowed. She applied new tissues and retied the scarf.

Next she had to deal with his broken arm. She removed the inflatable splint from the first-aid kit, then shuffled through the box, looking for painkillers. She groaned in frustration. There didn't seem to be any.

Duke rested his head against the back of the seat and closed his eyes.

"I don't think you're supposed to sleep," she whispered. Her fears were rampant. At least the bleeding from her own cut seemed to have stopped. Her injuries appeared minor compared to Duke's.

"I'm going to have to do something about your arm."

He offered her a lopsided smile. "Have at it, sweetheart. Anything you do can't make it hurt any more than it already does."

Sweetheart. He'd called her that twice now, and with an unmistakable tone of affection. Always before, he'd said it in a caustic way, as if he meant to insult her.

"It'd probably be best if I got out of the plane and came around and worked on it from your side."

"No!" He spit out the word. "Don't leave the plane... If anything happened, I wouldn't be able to help you." His protest seemed to drain him of what little strength he had. His good hand clenched hers, cramping her fingers. "Promise me," he whispered breathlessly. "Promise me that no matter what happens, you'll stay right here."

"I promise," she said.

He closed his eyes again and sighed audibly.

"Your arm…"

"It'll be fine."

"No, let me do what I can. If I crawl behind your seat, I might be able to get the splint around it. Please, let me try."

"All right."

Tracy climbed into the narrow space behind him. In an effort to give herself more room, she climbed out his door and stood thigh-deep in the fallen snow. The cold and wind felt like tiny needles on her face and hands. She did the best she could to make Duke's arm comfortable, attaching the splint and inflating it, praying all the while that she wasn't hurting him more.

He bit off a groan.

"I'm so sorry," she whispered.

"Get back inside. Hurry now," he said. "It's too cold out there for you."

"I'm fine. It's you I'm worried about."

"I'll feel a lot better when you're right here beside me."

For the first time since the accident, Tracy smiled. Duke actually wanted her with him. From the very beginning, Duke had gone out of his way to challenge her, provoke her, tease her—and it had always worked. He irritated her faster than any man she'd ever known. But she realized now that she'd actually begun to look forward to their heated exchanges. Their arguments invigorated her. At the moment, though, an argument was the last thing she wanted.

By the time she clambered back inside the plane, she was shivering. Her fingers felt numb; she clenched and unclenched them in an effort to bring back feeling.

"I wish there was something I could give you for the pain."

"Don't worry," he whispered, dismissing her concern. "I'll be all right."

But she knew from his pale drawn face and harsh uneven breaths that he was in a great deal of discomfort.

"I have some pills—they're like aspirin—in my purse. Would that help?" she asked. She didn't mention that the medication was designed for menstrual cramps.

Duke closed his eyes and nodded. "Couldn't hurt."

After a few minutes of awkward searching, she located her purse. She dug around until she found the package, then fed him three tablets. He swallowed them without water.

"Where are we?" she asked. Snow covered the windshield, making it impossible to see out.

"Best I can figure, we're close to Kunuti Flats."

Not close enough, otherwise they would've missed the trees, Tracy mused. Swallowing hard, she asked the question that concerned her most. "How long will it take for someone to find us?"

"Don't know. Not to worry…emergency locator beam goes off immediately—links with a satellite network. They know where we are. Someone's on the way… Radio, need to contact them by radio…"

Tracy could see that he was struggling to remain conscious. "Duke!" she cried, reaching for his hand, gripping it in both of hers. His eyes rolled and he slumped forward.

Gently she eased him away from the plane's steering device. Never had Tracy felt so alone—so helpless and afraid. These were unfamiliar emotions for her, and she fought to regain a sense of control.

The radio. Before he passed out, Duke had said something about the radio. She didn't know how to use it. But she *had* to contact Fairbanks. When they took off, she'd watched Duke speak into the microphone attached to the headset. She could do that, couldn't she?

Careful not to disturb him, she removed the headset from him and placed it over her own head.

"Hello," she said, trying to control her voice. "Hello. Anyone there?"

Nothing.

In desperation she stared at the instrument panel. No lights showed, although she was sure they had earlier, before the crash. Obviously, damage to the plane had been severe. Now what?

Despite everything, she felt surprisingly calm. She knew there had to be a way to reach help and forced herself to think clearly. She studied the panel with all its gauges and instruments; they meant nothing to her.

A two-position switch caught her eye. *Battery*. Stretching forward, she flipped it up. Lights flashed across the panel and a sense of exhilaration filled her. Static popped in her ears.

"Mayday. Mayday. SOS. SOS!" she shouted into the tiny microphone.

The static cleared and a voice returned, "Fairbanks radio, Baron two, two, niner five hotel. I'm approximately five zero miles south-southwest of reported position of distressed aircraft."

The man didn't seem to be speaking the same English as Tracy. "This is Tracy Santiago. I'm a passenger with Duke Porter out of Hard Luck. Our plane is down—we crashed. Duke thinks we're near Kunuti Flats."

Tracy heard another voice respond and realized this man was talking to the one who'd spoken first. She was listening in on their conversation. The second man was on the radio in Fairbanks. But he didn't seem to want to talk to her. Once more, she started pushing buttons.

"Hello, hello. Help!"

A click sounded in her headset. She waited, suddenly remembering the old *Sky King* television reruns she'd watched as a child. She needed to press down and speak, then release the button for a reply.

She'd figured it out. A sense of jubilation shot through her. "Hello, someone answer me, please. Over." Sky King had always said "over."

"Radio calling, this is Fairbanks radio. You are on the emergency frequency."

She had the right place.

"Do you have an emergency?" the same voice asked.

"Do I ever! I'm with Duke Porter."

"Is your aircraft Cessna seven two eight bravo gulf?"

"How would I know?" she demanded impatiently. "How many planes do you people have that've crashed?"

"What's your status? Do you have injured?"

"Yes. The pilot's unconscious. Just get someone here, fast. I don't know how badly Duke's hurt."

"What are his injuries?"

She told him what she could, and then answered what seemed to be an endless list of irrelevant questions, about supplies and what they were wearing and how she felt. Not once did he answer her one major question— When would help arrive?

"We have your ELT signal. Suggest you turn off battery to conserve power," he instructed. "We had you on radar all the way down. Help will be dispatched, weather permitting."

"How long? Can't you at least tell me how *long* that'll be?" She prayed it would be soon, but she hadn't liked the gist of his questions, nor the suggestion that she turn off the battery to save power. His tone indicated she and Duke might be here for more than a few hours.

"Air Force Rescue copter will be dispatched as soon as weather permits," the man on the radio repeated.

"When will that be?" she cried, growing more frantic.

"Meteorological forecasts call for clearing in six to twelve hours. Conserve your warmth and battery power. This frequency will be monitored continuously should you require further assistance."

"Thank you—but please do what you can to get here soon," she pleaded, her heart sinking. Then she flipped the switch and severed her contact with the outside world.

The silence was intense.

A thousand questions bombarded her all at once. She could survive another six to twelve hours, but she didn't know about Duke. He was in terrible pain and she could do nothing to help.

Fear and loneliness returned full force. Soon she was shaking with cold. She reached for a sleeping bag and wrapped it around Duke and herself, then sat back, closed her eyes and tried to think positively.

Six to twelve hours. That wasn't so long—not really. They'd be fine for a few more hours, wouldn't they? Sure, it was cold and scary, but together they'd make it. Perhaps if she said it often enough, she'd come to believe it.

Tracy felt herself growing tired. Duke weaved in and out of consciousness; she knew that by the way he breathed and sometimes groaned. She wanted to stay awake for him, watch his vital signs, but the lure of sleep tugged at her.

If she was to die, she'd be with Duke.

Strangely the thought comforted her.

SAWYER DIDN'T THINK he'd ever experienced such frustration. Duke was down, and what information he'd received so far was sketchy at best. For hours now, he'd been sitting by the radio, waiting.

Despite the storm, every one of his available pilots was in the air. He hadn't asked them to track the emergency locator beam; they'd volunteered.

Sawyer knew that John, Ted, Ralph and the others felt as if they were searching for family. His pilots were a close-knit group, and Sawyer was fiercely proud of each and every man.

Duke was popular with the others, a natural leader. They looked up to him and often sought his advice. He'd been with Midnight Sons longer than almost anyone. Sawyer valued him as a colleague—and as a friend.

But recently they'd come close to losing Duke; he'd threatened to quit. Threatened, nothing. In a fit of righteous indignation, Duke had handed in his notice.

Christian had been at the heart of the trouble. His brother had grounded Duke for a single flight, and the pilot had been furious. To this day Sawyer didn't know what had happened between them, but Christian had gone over to the bunkhouse and they'd somehow settled their differences.

Sawyer shuddered at the thought of Duke's leaving. The fact was, he considered Duke his best pilot—certainly his most experienced. If anyone could get out of this alive, it was Duke Porter. But then, Sawyer was uncomfortably aware that these kinds of decisions often weren't in a pilot's hands.

More than ten years earlier Sawyer had gone down in a plane himself. He hadn't been alone, either; he'd been with his father. Weather conditions had been bad, but better than they were now.

Unfortunately that hadn't saved David O'Halloran. Before help could arrive, Sawyer's father had died in his arms.

Memories of that day flooded his mind, charged his senses back to those last moments when he'd watched the life ebb out of his father. The pain returned, as fresh now as it had been that afternoon. Sawyer rubbed his eyes, wanting to stop thinking, stop feeling. Forget.

Inhaling sharply as he tried to push the memories aside, he ignored the pain. But the scene remained steadfastly in his mind. Again and again it flickered like an old silent movie, frame after frame. Impotent rage and defeat came at him like a fist in the dark.

"Sawyer."

He gasped and whirled around to face his wife. His relief was instant. Abbey—his wife, his love, his salvation.

"Have you heard anything more?" she asked quietly. Her face was tight with worry.

"Nothing," he told her.

Abbey walked to his side and slipped her arm around his shoulders. Sawyer welcomed her touch, needed her tenderness to help erase the memories. His fears for Duke and Tracy were overwhelming.

Sawyer placed his arm around Abbey's thickening waist. Touching her gave him comfort no words could express. That she was pregnant with their child was a second miracle for a man who hadn't expected the first.

She bent down and kissed the top of his head. "Everything will be fine."

"I hope so," he said. "From what I understand, the rescue team won't be able to reach Duke and Tracy until the weather clears."

"You mean they'll be stuck out there?"

"It looks that way. We don't have any choice."

Abbey tensed. "Why?"

"The chopper can't get to them in this storm."

"Does anyone know if they're hurt—or how badly?"

That was the question that plagued Sawyer the most. Surviving in the cold for any length of time was difficult enough, but with their injuries… "Tracy talked to the controller herself."

"Tracy?"

He nodded, unsure how much to tell her. He didn't want to alarm Abbey unnecessarily. "Duke appears to have sustained the worst of it," he said finally. "Cuts, bruises, broken arm. But there's also the possibility of internal injuries."

She pressed her cheek to his. "There's nothing you can do."

"I know," Sawyer murmured. He had a gut full of anger mingled with guilt—for what, he didn't know. And fear. Yes. More than anything, fear.

It had been like this the day he'd lost his father, the day the light had gone out of his life. For years Sawyer had carried the guilt of that crash, although David had been piloting the plane. Afterward he was left to wonder if there'd been something, anything, he should have done, *could* have done, that might have spared his father's life.

He hadn't realized the extent of his emotional injuries until he'd met Abbey and married her. His wife's love had been a gift, a healing balm that eased away the self-recrimination.

"Tracy and Duke together," Abbey murmured. "Do you think they can last the night without killing each other?"

For the first time since he'd learned about the crash, Sawyer grinned. "You might have a point there."

WHEN TRACY AWOKE it was dark. Her eyes fluttered open and she noticed that her head was propped against Duke's shoulder. She felt warm and almost comfortable.

His good arm was around her.

"Duke?"

"So you're awake."

"You, too… I was so afraid. You passed out."

"You afraid?" She could hear the smile in his voice. "I didn't think you even knew the meaning of the word."

He must be feeling better if he was up to teasing her. "If I didn't know it before, I do now," she admitted shakily.

Concerned that she was hurting him by leaning against him, she shifted and attempted to sit upright.

"Stay," he said in a whisper.

Tracy wished she could see him properly. But if he was awake and not in obvious pain, that could only bode well.

"I'm not too heavy for you?"

"No." His face was so close his breath stirred the hair at her temple.

"Do you need any more…aspirin?"

"No, thanks. Save them for later. I'm about as comfortable as I'm likely to get."

Her arm rested against his middle, and her head remained on his shoulder. "It's already dark. How long did I sleep? What time is it?" she asked.

"Three, maybe."

"The helicopter won't come for a while. I figured out how to work the radio." She couldn't help being proud of this. "Fairbanks seemed to think it would be six to twelve hours."

"I guessed as much. We'll be fine."

"You blacked out on me. I got on the radio and—" To

Tracy's shock, her voice broke. She took a moment to compose herself, breathing deeply, but instead, her throat closed up and her eyes filled with tears.

"Tracy?"

She buried her face in his warmth and held back the emotion as long as she could. When it burst free, the sobs shook her entire body. "I thought you were dead! I didn't know what to do…alone. I was afraid of being alone."

His hand stroked her back. He murmured something, but so softly she couldn't make out what it was. But his message was clear; he offered her solace and comfort.

"I'm sorry," she whispered when the tears were spent. "I didn't mean to…" Embarrassed now, she wiped the moisture from her face.

"I was afraid, too."

"You?" Now *that* was something Tracy had trouble believing. The great Duke Porter. The man was fearless.

The wind howled outside the plane. From the side window, Tracy could tell that it had stopped snowing, but the sky was dark and ugly. She couldn't see any stars. The only light in the plane came from the moon reflecting off the snow.

"You okay now?"

"Yeah." But she wasn't.

"I've got a candy bar in my jacket. Want some?" he asked.

Now that he mentioned it, she realized she was hungry. "Sure."

In the dim moonlight, Duke retrieved the candy from inside his coat pocket and handed it to her. The chocolate bar was squashed and mangled.

"You might want to see if you can read the expiration

date," he suggested. "I have no idea how long I've been carrying it around."

At this point Tracy was too hungry to care. She peeled back the wrapper and broke off the top square. She gave it to him, then took a piece for herself.

Generally Tracy avoided sweets, and it'd been years since she'd had a candy bar. Right now, she thought it was the best thing she'd ever tasted.

"You called me sweetheart," she said, breaking off the next piece. Her fingers stilled abruptly. What had made her say that? She hesitated, wondering if he was going to pretend he hadn't heard her, hoping he would.

"Don't take it personally." His voice had stiffened noticeably.

"I didn't. We were going down and I was panicking and you...you didn't mean it. Besides, I wouldn't want to upset your girlfriend in Fairbanks."

She felt rather than saw his eyes bore into her.

Every time she opened her mouth, she seemed to drive her foot deeper into her throat. Whether he had a girlfriend in Fairbanks or anywhere else was none of her business.

"Forget I said that," she said hurriedly. Her face burned. Duke was a virile attractive man; it was logical that he'd be involved with someone. She'd be surprised if he wasn't.

"How'd you know about Laurie?" he asked, his voice cool.

"Uh..."

"Mariah." He supplied the answer himself.

She didn't bother to deny it.

A tense silence followed. "I haven't seen Laurie in some time," he told her.

Mortified beyond belief, Tracy felt it was important to clarify the situation. "I didn't ask, really I didn't. Mariah mentioned once—briefly, very briefly—that you had a friend you sometimes visited in town. She said it in passing."

"But you remembered?"

Tracy shrugged. She *had* remembered. The information had stuck in her mind for weeks. She hadn't questioned why. Now and again, she'd found herself wondering what kind of woman would interest a man like Duke. She'd wanted to think he was like other men she'd met who never looked beyond the size of a woman's breasts. But she'd always known that wasn't true of Duke. He might be a lot of things—a traditionalist, maybe even a chauvinist, a man who provoked her to anger—but he didn't see a woman as just a body.

"You were right about Gavin," she whispered. "He—he's hoping to find his inner child."

Duke laughed shortly.

Tracy found herself smiling.

"Laurie bored me."

"Bored you?" Tracy wanted details. The happy way her heart reacted to his words didn't bear considering.

"She agreed with me far too often," he said.

"The poor dear must have wanted to keep the peace," she teased.

Duke chuckled. "You, though—I could always count on you to challenge me."

"That's because you say the most outlandish things. Really, Duke, you've got to be more up-to-date."

"Nah," he returned. "And miss seeing your eyes spit fire at me? I've never known a woman who looks as pretty as you when she's roaring mad."

Pretty. It wasn't a word men used when they talked about

her. Smart, yes. Tough. Hardworking. A good attorney. But rarely did men view her as pretty.

Once again her throat tightened, and she struggled to hold back tears. She was lost somewhere in the Alaskan bush in a downed plane with an injured pilot beside her, and all she could think about was the fact that he thought she was pretty.

Chapter
4

As NIGHT CLOSED IN around them, Duke began to wonder if he'd make it. At times the pain in his arm was almost more than he could bear.

Tracy shivered at his side, but at least they were together. For a while, they talked, telling each other all kinds of things. Private things. Duke found it was like talking to his oldest and dearest friend. Comfortable. Comforting. He knew he was rambling but it didn't worry him, because he trusted her. He did worry about her bouts of shivering. As best they could, they conserved their body heat by cuddling together beneath the sleeping bag.

Duke's feet were in bad shape. The cold pierced through him like swords thrust into his legs. He'd dozed off, but the pain didn't let him sleep long. He'd lost feeling in his toes, which was, he supposed, a blessing of sorts. The relentless tingling sensation only added to his misery.

He was frightened for Tracy, who'd grown still and quiet.

"What if no one comes by morning?" she suddenly asked. It was the first time she'd spoken in at least an hour, he estimated. It was becoming more and more difficult to keep track of time.

"Don't worry, help'll be here soon." He sounded more confident than he felt. Duke had flown into plenty of storms and was well aware of their hazards. The last time he'd checked on the emergency frequency, there hadn't been any sign that the storm was breaking up. Apparently the cold front had moved directly over Fairbanks.

"Try to sleep," he urged. He couldn't sleep himself; the pain was too great to allow him the luxury of that escape.

Tracy rested her head against his shoulder, nestling into his warmth, sharing her own. A swell of tenderness washed over him. He was afraid of what would happen to her if he died.

Several minutes later, he gauged from the even measure of her breathing that she was asleep. If he was about to die, he decided, the time had come to think about his life—analyze his regrets. Somewhat to his surprise, he realized he didn't have many. To his way of thinking, his sins had been few, his mistakes plenty. He wished his relationship with his mother was better. The fault, if there was one, lay with him. He hadn't wanted to intrude on her life.

He'd never cheated anyone, rarely lied, and overall felt that he'd lived a good and decent life.

He wished he'd fathered a child. That came as a shock. A man didn't often consider his mortality. He dismissed the regret, certain it had occurred to him because of everything happening in Hard Luck. Weddings…and now babies. Karen Caldwell and Abbey O'Halloran were pregnant, and last he'd heard, so was Bethany Harris.

He didn't know what kind of father he'd be, but the thought of having a son or daughter appealed to him.

A house appeared in his mind—a house that didn't exist. He'd always hoped to build his own home someday. He figured he'd live in Hard Luck, close to his friends, be part of the community. He was sorry he'd never have a chance to build that house—if he was to die.

Tracy stirred, and he studied her in what little light the moon afforded him. He'd been astounded by the way she'd handled this crisis. He probably shouldn't have been, though; she was an incredible woman. Almost against his will, he found himself admiring her, grateful for her cool head and gentle touch.

One day Tracy Santiago would make some lucky son of a gun a great wife. She'd be a great mother, too; he felt it instinctively. He pressed a silent kiss to the top of her head, then closed his eyes. Yeah, she was one hell of a woman....

A whooshing sound disturbed him, and he made an effort to clear his mind. He must have slept. Night had become day.

The noise came again; it seemed to be some distance away.

"Duke, did you hear that?" Tracy lifted her head from his shoulder.

He opened his mouth to tell her he did, but couldn't find the strength to speak. He was glad she didn't seem to notice he was fading quickly.

"I need my suitcase!" she cried. "I know I promised not to get out of the plane, but I won't go far."

"No…"

"I'm going to get my red nightgown and climb onto the wing and wave it. Otherwise they might not see us in the snow. I'll be careful," she assured him, and then she did something totally unexpected.

She kissed him. Sweetly. Excitedly. On the lips.

"The helicopter's almost here." Her voice was giddy with relief.

Duke lacked the strength to tell her that the emergency locator beam would give the pilot their precise whereabouts. It was unnecessary for Tracy to climb onto the wing and signal. Even in his groggy state, he found the idea amusing.

The sound of the rescue chopper's approach sharpened as the aircraft drew near. Duke closed his eyes and whispered a prayer of thanksgiving.

Sounds began to mingle in his ears. The chopper, men's voices, Tracy's excited cries. Then someone was at his side and he was being extracted from the aircraft.

"Please be careful," Tracy shouted in the background. "Can't you see he's hurt?" Duke saw a flash of red and wondered if it was the nightgown she'd mentioned. Pity he'd never seen her in it.

Pain cut into his arm and he groaned as he was placed on a narrow stretcher.

"Don't touch his arm like that!" Tracy yelled. "What's the matter with you people? Can't you see he's in pain?"

Duke closed his eyes. Minutes must have passed before he opened them again, because when he did, he realized he was in the chopper and they were airborne. An emergency medical technician was taking his vital signs.

Tracy sat on the other side and held his hand between both of hers. She didn't look good, he thought. Dried blood matted her hair. The cut didn't appear to be serious, but he saw a lump on her head; he hadn't noticed it earlier.

Nor had he known how pale she was.

"Tracy." Her name was all he could manage.

Her eyes brightened with tears and a few spilled over. "You're going to be fine. We both are…. I don't know if we could've lasted much longer." She smeared the tears across her cheek, obviously embarrassed by them.

Although it required every bit of his strength, Duke brought her hand to his lips and kissed her knuckles.

He was barely aware of what followed. The next thing he knew, he was being wheeled down a hospital corridor. He couldn't remember landing or being taken from the rescue helicopter or driven in the ambulance. Nor did he know what had happened to Tracy. She'd been with him from the beginning of this ordeal, and he wanted her with him now. If he hadn't been so weak, he would've asked.

He heard raised voices and recognized a few. Sawyer was there; so were John, Ralph and a couple of the other guys. They all seemed to be talking at once. He tried to sit up to tell his friends that it'd take more than a little crash in a snowstorm to kill *him*. Unfortunately he didn't have enough energy to so much as move his head.

Where was Tracy?

"Tracy." He called her name, but it came out as a whisper.

A man in a white coat leaned over him. "You're asking about your friend?"

He nodded.

"You don't have a thing to worry about. She's fine—a few bruises, a couple of cuts, exposure. Dr. Davidson is examining her, but she's giving him all kinds of trouble." The physician grinned. "She's worried about you. I told Davidson to tell her you're going to be fine once we get that arm set. It's a compound fracture, which makes it more complicated. We'll be taking you into surgery within the hour. I've given you something for the pain, so you should be able to rest comfortably."

That was what he was feeling, Duke realized, the absence of pain. Tracy was all right; he could let go now.

SAWYER WAITED until he'd had a chance to see Duke and Tracy personally before he searched out a pay phone to call Abbey. He knew she'd be waiting anxiously to hear from him.

"They arrived twenty minutes ago," he said, and heard the relief in his voice.

"How's Tracy?"

"They're examining her now, but she looks great for having spent the night in a snowbank. The hospital probably won't even need to admit her."

Abbey's own relief was audible. "And Duke?"

"Duke wasn't as fortunate," Sawyer replied. He leaned against the wall, able to relax now that he'd seen his friend. "Compound fracture of his arm, possible internal injuries—they haven't told him that part."

"How bad?"

"We don't know yet." Perhaps he should've waited until he had all the details, but he'd wanted to call with the good news—Duke and Tracy were alive. Half of Hard Luck had stopped in at the office during the day, asking about them. Word of the crash had spread throughout the community.

"Will he be all right?" Abbey asked next.

"He's going in for surgery so the arm can be set. As for the other, it's too soon to tell. But my guess is Duke'll be just fine in a few weeks."

"Thank heaven."

"Yes," Sawyer murmured.

"The others are with you?" Abbey asked.

"Yeah. They're waiting for me in the cafeteria."

As soon as he'd heard that the snowstorm had cleared over Fairbanks, Sawyer had headed for the airfield, planning to assemble a rescue team and go after the missing couple.

Before he'd made it to the plane, however, Ralph had come running over with the news that they'd been rescued. He, John, Ted and three of the others asked if they could accompany Sawyer to Fairbanks. Nearly his entire crew had wanted to be at the hospital when Duke arrived.

Duke had friends. Good friends.

"I'll pass the word along," Abbey promised, sounding close to tears.

"Abbey, is everything all right?"

"Yes…yes, of course. It's just that I'm so relieved. Those two had me worried."

"You!" She'd been cool and controlled with him. Knowing how the crash had affected Sawyer, she must have figured she needed to be strong. He'd married himself quite a woman, Sawyer thought. A woman whose compassion and generosity humbled him even now.

TRACY WALKED into Duke's hospital room and felt the sudden urge to cry. She'd waited what seemed like hours for him to be brought out of recovery.

His head was bandaged, his arm was in a cast, and an IV bottle steadily dripped fluid into a needle imbedded in the back of his hand. Dark circles shadowed his eyes.

He was a mess.

The doctors had told her it would be a while before he

woke, but she didn't care. They'd been through too much together for her to desert him now.

She sat in the chair next to his bed, content to stay exactly where she was until he told her himself that he was all right. She didn't trust anyone else.

"Tracy?"

Sawyer O'Halloran walked into the room.

She gave him a weak smile. "That was some airplane ride," she teased.

He didn't smile. "I'll bet."

"You don't need to worry—I'm not going to sue."

He blinked in surprise. Obviously the thought had never occurred to him. But it probably had to others. After all, they'd figure, she *was* an attorney.

"How are you feeling?"

She smiled faintly. "Like I was in a plane crash." The cut on her head was held together with a butterfly bandage, and she'd suffered a slight concussion, but her injuries weren't life-threatening. No frostbite, even.

She must look a sight, but she didn't care. Nor was she willing to leave Duke's side until she knew for herself that he was going to pull through.

"Can I get you anything?"

"I'm fine, but thanks."

"I've booked a hotel room for you over at the Moose Suites," he said, and hesitated when she gave him an odd look. She couldn't help it. The Moose Suites?

"The place isn't as weird as it sounds. Clean rooms, reasonable rates. Ralph brought your suitcase there." Sawyer handed her a key.

"Thank you." Until he'd told her about the room, she hadn't

given a moment's thought to where she'd stay. Once Duke woke up, she'd take a taxi to the hotel, shower and sleep for a week.

"I took the liberty of contacting your law firm."

Her gaze shot to him and she blinked. "Oh, my, I forgot about work." Neither her law practice nor her life outside this hospital room seemed quite real at the moment.

"I spoke with Mr. Nelson."

"He's the senior partner." Tracy bit her lip. She'd pushed the entire matter of her career and her life in Seattle out of her mind. She tried to picture her work calendar and remembered that she had a brief due on Wednesday, a settlement hearing scheduled for Thursday and on Friday— Oh, dear, there was something important on Friday, but she couldn't remember what it was.

"Mr. Nelson was sorry to hear about the accident. He sends his personal regards and asked me to tell you to take as long as you need."

"Thank you, Sawyer." For a woman as disciplined and organized as she was, it astonished Tracy that she could actually forget about her work commitments.

"He asked if you'll give him a call when you're up to it."

"I…will." But not anytime soon, she thought.

"Until then," Sawyer continued, "you're not to worry. Mr. Nelson has everything covered."

She nodded, not knowing what to say. Her whole world was centered in this small hospital room with the man who'd saved her life.

This was no exaggeration, no survivor's gratitude run amuck, but simple fact. Tracy had heard the men talking as they'd pulled Duke from the plane. They'd found the ruptured fuel line and said the pattern the plane made as it went down showed that Duke had purposely steered it so that his side of the aircraft received the greater impact.

Duke's skillful handling of the plane had saved their lives. Again and again Tracy heard the investigators' comments to that effect.

A nurse had told her she was lucky to be alive, and Tracy had quickly corrected her. Luck had nothing to do with it. She was alive because of Duke Porter, and she wasn't going to forget it.

"Do you need me for anything else?" Sawyer asked.

"No…" She couldn't think, couldn't make sense of her incoherent impressions.

"Don't hesitate to phone if you or Duke need anything," he said.

"I won't."

He handed her his business card, and for the first time Tracy realized she didn't have her purse. Sawyer appeared to understand without her having to say a word.

"Your purse is with your suitcase in the hotel room. It's locked away safe and sound."

As she thanked him, Sawyer moved to the other side of the hospital bed and studied Duke. "He's going to come out of all this just fine. Don't you worry."

Tracy nodded, closing her eyes as she mentally reviewed the list of his injuries. His arm wouldn't heal overnight. It'd be months before he regained full use of it. The cut on his head, which had required twenty-five stitches to close, had been even meaner and deeper than she'd realized. The physician who'd sewn it shut had complimented her on the resourceful way she'd wrapped it.

As for his internal injuries, it was too soon to tell the extent of the damage. At best, his vital organs had been shaken up a bit. At worst… Well, at worst was something she didn't want to even consider.

"I'm leaving now," Sawyer told her.

She nodded.

"But I'll be back. Do you want me to bring you anything to eat?"

"Thanks, but no." The hospital had given her some warm broth, and she'd had tea and toast earlier. Food didn't appeal to her and probably wouldn't for some time.

"I shouldn't be gone more than a couple of hours."

"Okay."

Sawyer left the room.

Tracy pulled her chair as close to Duke's bed as possible. Because of the IV, she couldn't hold his hand, so she pressed her cheek against the side of the mattress and gently draped her fingers over his forearm.

She wasn't sure how much time had passed when she sensed that he was awake. Lifting her head, she noticed the way he ran his tongue over his lips, as if he was thirsty.

She stood and carefully poured ice water into a glass, adding a straw from a supply on the bedside table.

He rolled his head from side to side. "Tracy?"

"I'm here." She was inordinately pleased that hers was the first name he called.

His eyes fluttered open, and her heart filled with gratitude. She bent close to him. He raised his hand to her face and caressed her cheek.

Tracy battled the urge to weep and kissed the inside of his palm. "Sleep. Everything's wonderful. You're wonderful. I…am, too."

"Beautiful." The word rasped from his lips.

"Yeah, right." Tracy had no illusions about her looks. Especially now—she'd caught her reflection in the mirror.

She offered him the water and he sucked it greedily through the straw. The effort appeared to drain him, and he leaned back against the pillow and closed his eyes.

Content, Tracy sat down at his side and brushed the tears from her face.

BEN EXAMINED the dinner plate Bethany had carried up to his apartment. He grinned broadly when he lifted the lid and saw the hamburger bun. "Now this is more like it," he said, smiling up at her. He didn't know how many more of those healthy meals of hers he could stomach.

"Now listen, Ben, you've got to watch what you eat."

"I am, I am," he muttered. Not that he could avoid it, with Bethany standing guard over him every evening. He peeled back the bun and his heart sank with disappointment.

"What's this?" he demanded. He noticed that his raised voice didn't intimidate her.

"It's a veggie burger."

"A *what?*"

"You heard me."

He groaned. Bethany had set out to starve him to death, and she was succeeding. His own flesh and blood, no less.

"I've had more oat bran in the last three weeks than some horses," he said disgustedly.

"Ben—"

"You've shoveled more yogurt down me than any man should have to endure. I've put up with it, too, because… because you mean well. But now I'm putting my foot down.

Look at this," he said, pointing at his dinner plate. "You've ruined a perfectly good hamburger bun with this veggie... thing."

"Ben, you can't eat the way you used to. The least you can do is give this a taste. It's made with tofu and—"

"Tofu?" he cried, outraged. "Just what kind of man do you think I am? I hope to high heaven you didn't let anyone around here know you're feeding me *tofu!*"

"No—"

"I had bacon and eggs for breakfast." He tossed that out, knowing she wasn't going to like it.

"Who's the executor of your estate?"

"Don't get smart with your elders," he barked.

"What about lunch?" She folded her arms and glared at him. "Something tells me you didn't have the soup I set out."

"I made myself a pizza."

Bethany rolled her eyes. "I sincerely hope you've got your will made out. A pizza? Ben, really."

"I couldn't help it," he mumbled, feeling more than a little guilty. "Man does not live by bran alone." Although he had to admit he'd never been more regular—but he wasn't about to tell Bethany that. She might add even more to his diet.

"Just *try* the veggie burger."

Like he had much of a choice. Either he ate what she brought him or he waited until she left and made his way downstairs to rustle up some dinner. "All right," he said, but he knew he wasn't going to like it.

Bethany laughed unexpectedly. "I swear you're worse than a little kid. You'd think I'd brought you liver and onions."

"I like liver and onions." Now she was talking. Liver fried up in lots of bacon grease, not overcooked, either. He liked it tender, heaped with plenty of grilled onions. The thought of it set his mouth watering.

Bethany sat down across from him. "Remember, Mrs. McMurphy's coming for her interview tomorrow afternoon."

Ben wasn't likely to forget. The more he thought about letting a stranger into his kitchen, the more he was against the whole idea. He hadn't minded when Mariah worked for him, since she mostly stayed out of his way and let him cook. It'd been a luxury to have someone wait tables and collect dirty dishes.

But another cook! A woman, to boot. Not in *his* kitchen. Not while he lived and breathed. Well, it wouldn't take much to find fault with this cook Mitch and Bethany wanted him to meet.

"I talked with Mrs. McMurphy this afternoon," Bethany said. "She's excited to meet you."

"I'll just bet."

"She did a lot of the baking at the Sourdough Café and said she'd be willing to do that here, in addition to the other cooking."

"What'd she bake?" The way Ben figured, if he appeared interested and asked plenty of questions, Bethany might not realize he'd already made up his mind.

"Her specialty is strudel, although she said her cinnamon rolls were popular with the clientele."

Cinnamon rolls happened to be one of Ben's weaknesses. He'd never gotten the hang of baking them himself. He liked his rolls made with plenty of real butter and drizzled with icing. His gaze dropped to the veggie burger, and he decided he'd gladly give a year's profits for a single bite of warm, butter-oozing cinnamon roll.

"All I want you to do is give Mrs. McMurphy a chance."

"Of course I will." Ben reached for the glass of milk and took a swallow, afraid she might read the insincerity in his eyes. The milk tasted terrible, and he spit it back into the glass.

"What'd you do to my milk?"

Bethany pinched her lips together. "I didn't do anything to it."

Ben held his glass up to the light. "It's…blue."

"It's nonfat."

If anything was going to kill him, it was his daughter's attempt to manage his diet. "You can't spring nonfat milk on a man," he told her. "You should've warned me."

She crossed her arms. "Don't you think you're overreacting just a little?"

"No!" he insisted. "A veggie burger, skim milk, and a bran muffin for dessert. If I didn't know better, I'd swear you were trying to kill me."

"Ben!"

"All right, all right." He sighed. "Thank you for bringing over my…dinner." He used to eat more than this for his midnight snacks.

"Now, what about your meeting with Mrs. McMurphy?"

She wasn't going to let up on this, Ben could tell. "I'll be cordial and treat her real nice." That was what Bethany wanted to hear, and he wasn't telling a lie. He'd be cordial and polite when he showed her the door.

"Just to be on the safe side, I've asked Mrs. McMurphy to have dinner with Mitch and me following the interview," Bethany told him. "You're welcome to join us if you want."

Ben scowled. "It all depends on what you're cooking." Another night of veggie burgers, and he was likely to fade away to nothing.

DUKE AWOKE in the dim light and spent several minutes updating his memory. All he'd done for the better part of two days was sleep. Every time he opened his eyes, he discovered Tracy at his side. He wasn't disappointed this time, either. She'd curled up in the chair next to his bed and was sound asleep. Someone had covered her with a thin blanket.

At some point she must have showered and changed clothes, because she wore a sweater he couldn't remember seeing before. Having her here produced a warm feeling in the pit of his stomach. They'd been through a lot together. More than some people endured in a lifetime.

One thing was certain. Tracy was about the bravest woman he'd ever known. It couldn't have been easy for her, with him out of his mind with pain half the time.

He was proud of her, proud of the way she'd figured out how to work the radio and contact Fairbanks. The way she'd looked after him. She was cool and capable, the kind of woman who always found a solution, regardless of the problem. A woman who wouldn't give up when times got tough.

She'd kissed him.

The memory had a dreamlike quality to it. When they'd heard the rescue chopper's approach, she'd been so excited that she'd kissed him. It didn't mean anything, Duke told himself. The kiss had been an expression of joy, of relief. Nothing more.

He'd tried over and over to remind himself of that, but it hadn't worked. As brief as the kiss had been, as meaningless as he attempted to convince himself it was, he'd enjoyed it.

If he'd been able to, he would've wrapped her in his arms

and kissed her properly. His breath quickened just thinking about it. He'd take it slow and easy, making it a kiss neither of them would soon forget. His heart began to pound wildly.

Duke forced himself to look away. This was Tracy Santiago he was fantasizing about. The woman he'd fought with time and time again. On closer examination, he understood that he'd always been attracted to her. Well, opposites were said to attract, he thought, and they'd proved it. He actually enjoyed their verbal battles, even looked forward to them. A few had gotten out of hand, but he was more to blame for that than she was.

What he didn't like about Tracy, Duke realized, was that he felt out of control whenever he was with her. It occurred to him that he'd behaved around Tracy the way Christian had around Mariah. All the while he'd been complaining about his secretary, he'd been falling in love with her.

Love. Was it possible that he actually loved Tracy? The thought terrified him. He didn't *want* to feel this emotion, this…this vulnerability.

Damn it all, leave it to him to fall in love with some fancy, highfalutin Seattle attorney. A lot of good it would do either one of them.

Her life was in Seattle and his was in Hard Luck. Here it was, history repeating itself. His father had loved his mother enough to believe he could meld their worlds. In the end, they'd both been miserable.

Loving Tracy wasn't going to change a thing. He sure wasn't going to give up his life and follow her to the city. As far as he was concerned, *Fairbanks* was overcrowded. He couldn't imagine what life would be like in a city the size of Seattle.

And as for her moving to Hard Luck, tempting though it

sounded, Duke knew it wouldn't work. He couldn't ask a woman of Tracy's education and temperament to give up the bright lights of Seattle for some dinky town in the Arctic.

That didn't leave much room for their relationship.

It wouldn't be easy to let her go, not when she was looking at him with stars in her eyes. He knew what she was thinking, because he'd had those same thoughts.

But it wouldn't work.

Chapter 5

TRACY STIRRED in the chair at Duke's bedside. She raised her arms above her head and stretched, arching her back. Swallowing a yawn, she worked the stiff muscles of her shoulders. It took her a few minutes to notice that Duke was awake. He was sitting up in bed watching her.

"Hello," she said, surprised at how shy she felt around him. "How are you feeling?"

"Better than I did a couple of days ago. How about you?"

"None the worse for wear." She untucked her legs from beneath her and stood. "Any idea how long I've been asleep?"

"Don't know. I've only been awake for half an hour or so myself. Actually I didn't expect to find you still here."

She saw the look of disapproval in his eyes and stopped herself from telling him she'd only left his side for brief periods since their rescue.

"Shouldn't you be back in Seattle?" Duke asked. "It's been what? Two, three days now?"

"The…the senior law partner told me to take as long as I needed."

Duke's expression was grim. She could sense him shutting her out; it was like a gate closing, blocking her passage. Now that they were safe, now that they were back, he seemed to be saying he wanted nothing to do with her.

"How much more do you need?" he asked. The words weren't harsh, but their message was—she didn't have to stay in Alaska on his account. In fact, he'd prefer it if she left. "Nothing's keeping you here, is it?"

"No," she admitted reluctantly, averting her gaze.

"You'll make your flight reservations then?" She glanced up, and his eyes burned into hers.

Her heart constricted, but she refused to let him know how deeply he'd wounded her. "I'll call the airlines at the first opportunity." Her hand trembled as she folded the blanket and set it on the small pillow she'd been using. Her lips trembled as she faced him again.

She'd never been as intimate with a man as she'd been with Duke, and she wasn't referring to anything physical. The closeness they'd shared was emotional. They'd touched each other's lives in ways that went beyond the mundane. Together they'd stared death in the eye, clinging to hope and to each other.

He wanted her to leave, but she couldn't, not without thanking him. The words that formed so easily in her heart, however, stuck in her throat.

"I won't say it's been fun," she said, making a feeble attempt at humor.

"That's one thing it hasn't been," he agreed.

She stood by his bedside and resisted the urge to brush the hair from his forehead. Often while he'd slept she'd felt free to touch him, to offer small gestures of tenderness. She knew he wouldn't welcome the informality now that he was awake.

Finally she managed to say, "Before I return to Seattle I want to thank you."

"Hey, you seem to forget I was the one who brought that plane down."

"No," she corrected, "the ruptured oil line was responsible for that. Your skill as a pilot is what saved us both." Then, because she felt it was important, she added, "I know what you did."

Even as she said the words she realized he'd pretend ignorance and discount what the investigators had said. "You risked your own life to save mine."

"Nonsense."

Tracy hid a smile. She felt she knew Duke better than any man she'd ever dated.

"What's so funny?" he asked.

"You. I've talked to the men who investigated the crash site. They said that, from the evidence, you purposely put yourself at greater risk."

"That's ridiculous."

"Let's not argue," she said, knowing it would do no good to press the issue.

"Why not?" he asked, his eyes flashing with warmth and humor. "It's what you and I've done from the first. It feels right. You're a worthy adversary, Santiago."

She bowed her head, acknowledging the tribute. "I'll consider that a compliment."

His grin relaxed and he grew serious once more. "You did good," he said, his gray eyes dark and intense. "It wasn't any picnic out there, but you were a real trooper."

"I couldn't have done it without you." There wasn't a single doubt about that.

"Sure you would've," he countered swiftly. "You've got mettle and spirit. I was out of it most of the time and—"

"Not all." He'd held her and reassured her, when he was the one who'd sustained the worst injuries. She'd never forget that. The fear would've destroyed her if it hadn't been for the solace she'd found in his arms.

"I'll admit you surprised me," Duke said. "A city girl like you."

She wanted to tell him she wasn't any different from Mariah or the other women who'd moved to Hard Luck in the past two years. Something in his eyes told her she'd be wasting her breath. In the past they'd taken delight in waging verbal battles—but the time for that was over. They'd progressed far beyond quarreling to a level of mutual respect. A week earlier she would've responded with indignation; now she let the matter drop.

"You'll go back soon?" He made it sound like he couldn't be rid of her fast enough. Well, Duke never had been kind to her ego.

"Soon," she promised.

"If I ever need an attorney," he said brightly, "I'll know who to call."

Of all the things he might've said, this affected her the most. She bit her trembling lip in an effort to stall the emotion that burned just beneath the surface.

"Hey, what'd I say?"

"Nothing." Laughing a little, she shook her head. "You're one heck of a man, Duke Porter. I never thought I'd say this, but I'm going to miss you like crazy." Her heart hammered with the pain of the coming separation.

"I never thought I'd miss you, either." His face was pinched, his eyes shadowed. This time she knew it wasn't due to his injuries. Parting was as difficult for him as it was for her. But Tracy sensed that he wasn't keen on her knowing it, so she pretended not to notice.

"Take my advice," Duke said, "and ditch Gavin. You deserve a real man."

Unfortunately the only one who fell into that category was here in front of her—and he was sending her away. "I'd already decided that."

His gaze held hers, then he asked, "A kiss for luck?"

She smiled and nodded. He held his good arm out to her, and she came into his embrace. She assumed he only meant to hug her, perhaps give her a peck on the cheek.

But Duke gathered her close and directed her lips to his. The kiss was like the man. He held back nothing, twining his fingers into her hair, slanting his mouth over hers in a breath-stealing kiss. Her breath jammed in her lungs as her fingers dug into his shoulders.

She tasted his urgency, his hunger, experienced them herself. He wanted her and made no apologies.

The kiss might have gone on even longer if not for a noise in the hallway outside the partially closed door.

Duke released her with a reluctance that should have thrilled her, but didn't. With little more than a kiss, he was sending her out of his life.

"Goodbye, Tracy. Godspeed."

"Godspeed," she returned in a choked whisper. And then, while she could still hold back the tears, she walked hurriedly out of the room—and out of his life.

ENDING IN MARRIAGE 265

BEN HAD HIS EXCUSES neatly lined up in his mind. He'd meet Mrs. McMurphy and they'd exchange pleasantries. Next, he'd read over her résumé and ask half a dozen appropriate questions. Enough for her to believe he was giving her serious consideration. When the interview was over, he'd announce that he needed a couple of days to decide and would get back to her by the end of the week.

That was the way situations like this were handled. Ben possessed enough business savvy to know how to give a job applicant the brush-off.

He'd make sure Mrs. McMurphy and Bethany didn't know what he had up his sleeve. That would be a mistake. Instead, he'd play along, let both women assume he was satisfied with the interview. Then he'd sit down and have dinner with Bethany and her family. Socialize with Mrs. McMurphy.

Ben would lay odds that Bethany wasn't serving any tofu burgers this evening. Not with company. He was dreaming of Southern fried chicken, potatoes mashed with real butter, and sour-cream gravy. Dreaming—that was all he'd be doing, knowing Bethany.

Mrs. McMurphy was due any moment, so Ben slowly made his way downstairs. The café was empty and lifeless. He missed the old hustle and bustle. In the past, he'd sometimes gone an hour or two without a customer, but that was different. This kind of silence was downright eerie.

The grill was stone cold, but if he closed his eyes, he could hear the hiss of bacon and hash-brown potatoes frying in the pan.

Anticipating the woman's arrival, Ben put on a small pot of decaffeinated coffee—Bethany would approve—and pulled out a chair. As he sipped from his mug, he watched the Baron aircraft land. Sawyer was back—with the infamous Mrs. McMurphy.

Ben caught his first view of the cook and was surprised at how tall she was. She wore a long black wool coat and carried a wicker basket over her arm, like little Red Riding Hood come to visit the big bad wolf.

Sawyer escorted her to the café personally, but stayed only long enough to check that Ben was downstairs.

"So you're Mrs. McMurphy," Ben said after Sawyer left. "Ben Hamilton." He extended his hand.

"I'm very pleased to make your acquaintance," the tall slender woman said.

Years earlier Ben had seen a plaque that said never to trust a skinny cook. He was inclined to accept that advice.

"Come in and make yourself comfortable," he urged, motioning to the table where he'd been sitting. "May I take your coat?"

"Please." She slipped out of it; she wore a practical denim dress and boots. She put the basket down on the table and sat quickly, almost as if she feared her height would alarm him. Ben was a big man himself, well over six feet. It took more than a reed-thin woman to intimidate him.

"Could I get you a cup of coffee?" he asked, still playing politeness to the hilt.

"No, thank you."

She was prim, a bit shy, with friendly blue eyes that seemed to take up half her face. Her dark, gray-streaked hair was gathered in a loose bun at the nape of her neck. It was difficult to guess her age; she could be anywhere between forty and sixty. Plain. No rings, he noted. No jewelry at all, for that matter.

Ben pulled out his chair and sat down himself.

"I've enclosed some letters of recommendation," she said, retrieving an envelope from her purse. Her hand shook slightly.

She was nervous, Ben realized, and found that puzzling. If he raised his voice, as he tended to do, he'd scare the poor thing out of ten years of her life.

He peeled open the envelope and took out three single sheets of paper. It wasn't until he started reading that he noticed the most enticing scent. A blend of apples and spices. It distracted him so much that he couldn't finish the letters.

He hesitated and glanced at the wicker basket. His mouth watered. What was it Bethany had told him about Mrs. McMurphy's specialties? Oh, yeah—strudel and cinnamon rolls. Could it be possible…?

His eyes were riveted on the basket.

"I brought along an apple strudel," Mrs. McMurphy said, following his gaze. "Mrs. Harris was kind enough to invite me for dinner this evening, and this is my way of thanking her."

"Did you bring anything else?" Bethany wouldn't hesitate to drag him before a firing squad for asking.

"Cinnamon rolls," she said. "You're welcome to look over my résumé, of course, but I felt my rolls would speak for themselves. The recipe was my grandmother's."

"How thoughtful." Ben all but leaped from the table. He hadn't moved with this much agility for weeks.

Before another minute had passed he'd grabbed a plate and fork. His eyes feasted on the dish Mrs. McMurphy took from the basket.

Huge cinnamon rolls were piled high on the small platter. The frosting had melted over the top, just the way he liked.

"Please, Mr. Hamilton, help yourself."

Ben didn't need a second invitation. "I believe I'll have a

taste," he said, as if he felt morally obligated to sample her wares since she'd gone to the trouble of bringing them.

He placed the largest one on the plate and licked the sweetness from his fingertips. This was heaven. Forget all that nonsense about bran and tofu.

Trying to disguise his absolute delight, he read over her résumé as he took the first bite.

"As I explained earlier, the recipe was my grandmother's. Although it's more expensive, I use real butter." She said this hesitantly, her eyes studying him.

Butter. She used real butter.

"I've tried margarine," Mrs. McMurphy said with regret, "but the rolls don't have the same richness or full-bodied flavor. If I come to work for you, Mr. Hamilton, I insist on using the best ingredients, and that means baking with butter."

Ben licked his fingers clean. "Of course."

"If you'd like, you could try another," she said, gesturing to the plate. "I brought plenty."

"Don't mind if I do." He had to rearrange the stack in order to get the largest of the remaining four.

"I suppose you'd like me to tell you a bit about my background," she said after a moment. Ben was far too busy eating to ask her questions.

"Please." He gestured for her to continue.

She listed a number of restaurants where she'd been employed in the past twenty years.

Ben barely listened. His eyes were half-closed in ecstasy as he chewed and swallowed.

"I understand there's a housing shortage in Hard Luck at present," Mrs. McMurphy said next.

Oh, yes, that was something he'd wanted to bring up. A convenient excuse and, despite Bethany's interference, one he intended to use when he regretfully informed Mrs. McMurphy he wouldn't be able to hire her.

"I asked Mr. O'Halloran about the possibility of flying in from Fairbanks on a daily basis. Naturally it would depend on the hours you need me, and the flight schedule, but he seemed to think we could arrange something. Mrs. Harris also mentioned the lodge, and I called and spoke with Mr. Caldwell. They have a room I could rent during the week and then return to Fairbanks for the weekends."

Ben merely nodded and began to reach for a third roll.

"Perhaps you'd care to taste my strudel," Mrs. McMurphy suggested.

"Only if you insist." He shoved his empty plate toward her.

"I'm a widow," Mrs. McMurphy continued as she sliced off an ample portion of strudel and lifted it onto his plate. "My children are grown now, with lives of their own."

"Mrs. McMurphy—"

"Please, I'd be more comfortable if you called me Mary."

"All right—Mary," Ben said.

"The strudel is an old family recipe, as well," Mary said. "I don't think you'll be disappointed."

Ben slid a forkful into his mouth. If he'd been impressed with the cinnamon rolls, the apple strudel…well, the apple strudel was her triumph. The apples were tender and tart, and the delicate pastry seemed to dissolve on his tongue.

"Again, I use only real butter."

"Butter," he repeated, finishing the last exquisite bite.

"Yes. It's my one stipulation when it comes to baking. Seeing that you enjoy sweets, I wish I'd baked a cheesecake."

"I prefer the strudel." The first piece was gone so quickly he hardly knew where it'd disappeared. He helped himself to a second serving, taking a thinner slice this time.

"I imagine you're wondering why I left the Sourdough Café after five years," Mary said. Ben felt a little—only a little—embarrassed that she had to conduct her own interview. After all, he was checking out her qualifications and couldn't ask questions at the moment. His mouth was full. "It broke my heart to leave," she explained, "but the café recently changed hands, and the new owner was cutting corners."

"I see." Mary McMurphy might be thin as a rail, but the woman knew her way around a kitchen. That much Ben would say for her. But there was far more to running a café than slapping together an apple strudel, he thought righteously.

It was as if the woman could read his mind. "In addition to the baking, I'm an excellent short-order cook. I can see from your menu that you offer hamburgers and so on. But I also have a number of specialties, including Southern fried chicken. People have been telling me for years that mine's as good as any colonel's."

"Fried chicken?"

"I hope you aren't partial to instant potatoes. Now, I realize that up here in the Arctic real potatoes might be hard to come by at times. I'm not a stickler for this the way I am about using butter in my grandmother's recipes, but I do prefer to cook with real potatoes."

"Mashed with cream?"

"Does one mash them with anything else?" she asked, her large blue eyes wide and questioning.

"What about sour-cream gravy? Can you make that?" It was going to hurt like hell to tell this woman he wouldn't be able to hire her.

"I've never made sour-cream gravy, but if you have a recipe, I'm sure I could learn."

"I have the recipe."

Mary McMurphy smiled at him. She placed the leftover strudel and cinnamon rolls back in the wicker basket and draped the blue linen napkin over them.

"So it's not a problem to use butter?" She regarded him expectantly.

Before he could respond, the door opened and Bethany walked in.

"Butter?" he repeated. "I use it myself for all my baking."

"Wonderful!" Mary sounded genuinely pleased.

Slightly out of breath, Bethany approached the table. Ben knew she must have hurried over the minute school let out.

"Hello," Bethany greeted them, her face wreathed in a welcoming smile. "You must be Mrs. McMurphy. I can't tell you how pleased I am to meet you."

"The pleasure's mine," the woman said with shy politeness.

"So," Bethany said, looking from Mary to Ben, "how'd the interview go?"

Ben eyed the basket, praying Bethany wouldn't learn about his lapse.

"Very well," Mary said. "Ben's agreed to hire me, and furthermore he has no objection to my using butter in my recipes."

Hire her? Ben hadn't said one word about hiring her.

"Ben!" Bethany beamed with delight. "That's wonderful." She threw her arms around his neck and hugged him enthusiastically.

"I'll be able to start first thing Monday morning," Mary said, smiling broadly. "Now if you'll both excuse me, I'll go freshen up."

As soon as she left, Bethany took a chair. "I'm really happy about this, Ben. Mrs. McMurphy's a dear, isn't she?" She paused. "You'll have to forgive me for doubting you, Ben. I was so sure you were going to find some flimsy reason you couldn't hire her. I was all prepared to wage war with you. I left the school with my cannons loaded," she said, laughing lightly. "And to think it was all for naught."

October 1996

TRACY SAT STARING out her office window. Located on the top floor of a Seattle highrise, it had a view that was the envy of everyone who saw it. Puget Sound stretched out before her in all its splendor—deep blue water, islands thick with green firs, boats with bright billowing sails. A ferry sounded its horn as it pulled away from the pier, headed for Bainbridge Island.

October, as always, had brought warm Chinook winds, and while it was already winter in Hard Luck, Seattle enjoyed a lingering summer.

She'd been back a week, but it seemed more like a year. What had once been so familiar now felt strange and…a little pointless. Every night she hurried home, waiting for some word from Duke. A letter, a postcard, a message on her answering machine. She knew better than to hope, but she couldn't seem to make herself stop.

The only evidence of the sixteen hours she'd spent trapped in the downed plane was a thin red line on the left side of her forehead. And a heart that hungered for her pilot….

She could've disguised the scar with makeup, but didn't. It was like a badge of honor. A souvenir of those hours alone with Duke. Unfortunately her heart wouldn't heal as easily as her skin had.

She couldn't think of him and not get choked up. A friend, a fellow attorney, had taken her to lunch earlier that day and suggested Tracy see a counselor. Janice seemed to think that because Tracy wasn't interested in talking about the experience at every opportunity, she might require professional help.

Talk about it. That was all Tracy had done for days. She was sick of the subject. She'd told the story countless times, answered a million questions. What more did people expect of her?

True, she'd been vague about some of the details, but those details weren't meant to be shared. What had happened between her and Duke was special, and it belonged only to them.

She wondered if he, too, had been hounded with questions from his friends and what he'd told them about the time they'd shared.

Tracy had assumed—hoped, really—that once she was back to her normal life, she wouldn't think about Duke as much. It hadn't happened. He was with her day and night. With every waking thought. Every nonwaking one, too.

He often visited her dreams and she awoke feeling warm and happy, remembering the night she'd spent in his embrace. But the happiness never lasted. Maybe Janice was right. Maybe she did need to see a counselor. It probably wasn't normal to prefer a life-threatening plane crash to waking up safe in her own bed.

Filled with nervous energy, Tracy circled her desk. She picked up one of the greeting cards she'd bought that afternoon while walking along the waterfront. Some were humorous. Some sincere. Others blank. But they all had one thing in common.

They were meant for Duke.

The temptation to mail him a card now was almost too strong to resist. It'd be nothing more than a friendly gesture to ask how he was, how his arm was healing. Or so she told herself. Still, she hesitated.

Duke wasn't like any man she'd ever known. What applied to other relationships didn't work with him. Always before, Tracy had been the one in charge. She decided when they'd date. Where they'd go, and most importantly, how often they'd see each other. This time, Tracy couldn't set the rules. Duke was a man who followed his *own* rules.

The intercom buzzed. Tracy walked around her desk and leaned over to push the button. The receptionist's voice came on. The office was technically closed, and it was late to be receiving phone calls.

"Yes, Gloria?"

"I'm sorry to disturb you, Ms. Santiago. I was just putting on the answering service and the call came through. I can ask the caller to try you again tomorrow if you want."

"Who is it?"

"All I know is that the person's a friend of yours from Hard Luck."

Tracy literally fell into her chair. "Put him through." Her heart felt as if it was going to leap right out of her chest with happiness.

Duke.

"This is Tracy Santiago," she said, doing her best to sound nonchalant.

"Tracy, it's Mariah. Christian and I got back last night, and we just heard the news. How are you? It was such a shock to learn you and Duke were in a crash."

"I'm fine." Hiding her disappointment was more than she could manage.

"You don't sound so fine."

"I am, really."

"Christian and I leave for two weeks and it's like the whole world goes crazy while we're away. It must've been *terrible* for you."

"No," Tracy said honestly. "It wasn't so bad." Then, because she needed to know, she asked, "Have you talked to Duke lately?"

"Oh, yes, right away, as soon as we heard about the accident."

"How is he?"

"He looks good."

"His arm?" she asked anxiously. "Is it bothering him?"

"Not that he's said."

But then, Duke wasn't the type to complain. What she wanted, Tracy decided, was to hear Mariah say that Duke was pining away for want of her. But that would've been too much to expect.

"How was the honeymoon?" Tracy asked, needing to change the subject.

"Oh, Tracy, I'm so in love!"

"Christian's a good man," Tracy murmured.

"I wasn't talking about him." Mariah giggled. "I mean I'm crazy about cruising." Then she grew serious. "We had a marvelous time, and I'm more in love with my husband than ever."

Tracy wasn't surprised; those two were made for each other. Gathering her nerve, she said, "Listen, I need to get off the phone. The next time you see Duke, tell him I said hello, will you?"

"Sure." But Mariah sounded hesitant.

"You won't be seeing him?"

"Of course I will. He works with Christian, after all. He's grounded because of his arm."

Tracy had suspected he wouldn't be able to fly and knew that was probably the most difficult aspect of his recovery. Duke was more comfortable in the air than on land.

"He's been sort of a grouch lately," Mariah said.

That was understandable.

"If people ask him about the accident, he bites off their heads. I was in the office when Bill Landgrin made the mistake of mentioning how difficult it must've been for the two of you to be trapped in that plane together. Bill said something along the lines of you being a, uh, man-hater."

Tracy didn't hate men, although she'd been accused of it before. In fact, if she recalled correctly, it was Duke who'd made the accusation.

"Bill didn't mean anything by it," Mariah elaborated. "Everyone knows you and Duke have never gotten along. Neither one of you has made a secret of your feelings."

"True."

"Well, Duke went ballistic. Christian told me Duke shoved Bill up against the wall—and remember, he's only got one good arm."

"They…fought?"

"No, Christian broke it up."

"Good." Duke was in no condition to fight, especially with his left arm in a cast.

"But Sawyer and Christian talked it over and suggested maybe Duke should take some time off. He's arguing with anyone right now."

Tracy's inclination was to defend him. Duke had been

through a far rougher ordeal than she had. If ever he'd needed his friends, it was now.

"The next time you see him," Tracy said, chewing her lower lip, "tell him…" She didn't know what to say, or even if he wanted to hear from her. Dejected, she continued, "Tell him I said hello and…and that I hope he's feeling better."

"Sure thing," Mariah promised. "Take care, okay?"

"I will," Tracy promised, and replaced the receiver. She eyed the greeting cards on her desk and sorted through them, trying to decide which one she'd send Duke.

Chapter
6

JUDGING BY THE SOUNDS coming from downstairs, it seemed every available chair in the Hard Luck Café was taken. Nevertheless, Ben frowned. If he fired Mary McMurphy, he couldn't very well claim it was because business was slow. She'd been with him for several days now and had won more hearts than a beauty queen.

Ben swore every man in town had gained five pounds on Mary's cinnamon rolls. She baked a fresh batch every morning. He had it on good authority that his customers formed a line outside the café the minute she pulled those rolls from the oven. The aroma wafted through the cold morning air like nerve gas, attacking anyone within striking distance.

The café had done more business in the week since he'd hired Mary than in any seven-day period before that.

Ben had no cause for complaint—but the truth was, her popularity was a bit irksome. Soon folks would forget all about him. His biggest fear was that his long-time customers would prefer Mary's cooking to his own.

She'd proved to be so popular with his customers that he'd be in trouble if he laid her off now. He felt thwarted at every turn.

So he sat in his apartment above the kitchen, brooding.

Because he was officially still recovering from his heart surgery, he wasn't allowed to do any of the cooking yet. Nevertheless it drove him crazy to hear all the commotion going on below. In his very own café.

The noise gradually died down, but it would take more than dollar signs to sweeten his sour mood. How quickly he'd been forgotten. All his customers really cared about was their stomachs, he decided.

"Mr. Hamilton," Mary called from the foot of the stairs.

Ben ignored her.

"Mr. Hamilton," she tried again, her voice closer this time. She marched up to the top of the stairs and waited. Ben sat in his recliner, pretending to be asleep.

"I hope I'm not disturbing your rest," she said, despite his closed eyes. "There seems to be a lull, and I thought I'd bring you up a cup of coffee and the last cinnamon roll."

Ben's eyes snapped open. She'd brought him a cinnamon roll?

"I know Bethany's worried about your cholesterol, and I don't blame her, but if you watch what you eat the rest of the day, I don't think one little goodie would hurt you."

Ben couldn't agree more. It'd been downright painful smelling those rolls day in and day out without being able to taste one.

"I'll make sure everything in your diet balances out," Mary told him as she set the mug and plate on the small table next to the recliner. "I was hoping you'd come down this morning," she added hesitantly.

He grumbled a nonreply. No one wanted him around, not with Mary and her cinnamon rolls to satisfy them.

"Everyone's asking about you," she said.

Ben doubted that.

"I'm not nearly the conversationalist you are," she stated matter-of-factly. "The men miss talking to you. It's different having a woman there, they tell me."

Ben brightened somewhat. So his friends hadn't completely abandoned him. That was encouraging.

"Another thing," Mary said shyly. "I can't quite seem to get the sourdough hotcakes the right consistency. The customers like my rolls well enough, but they're going to get tired of those soon. Then they'll want their sourdough hotcakes, and I'm afraid I'm going to disappoint them."

So maybe the woman wasn't the paragon everyone assumed. "You'll learn," he assured her, feeling generous.

He sampled the roll and was reminded anew why his customers stood in the cold waiting for the café to open each morning. But Mary was right about her pastries being a novelty that would wear off, he thought smugly. She'd sell plenty, but there'd be a need for his hotcakes, same as always, within a week or two.

Mary lingered, nervously shifting her weight from foot to foot. "If it wouldn't be too much trouble, I'd like to go over the dinner menus with you."

"Sure. Now's as good a time as any." He motioned for her to sit. He couldn't very well keep her standing while he remained in his recliner.

"It won't take long, I promise."

"No problem," he muttered, and because it was true, he murmured, "I don't have anything better to do."

"I found a large prime rib in the freezer," Mary said, glancing over at him. "Were you saving it for something special? If not, I'd like to put it on the menu for Friday night."

"There're probably several in there. Sure, go ahead."

"Do you have any particular way of cooking your prime rib?" she asked, deferring to him again.

The last time he'd made one had been at least three months ago. "I slow-cook the roast in a bed of salt. Takes a few hours, but it's worth it."

"My, that sounds wonderful," Mary said, scribbling notes on her pad.

"I've got the recipe in the kitchen somewhere. Want me to get it for you?" He just hoped he could find it before Friday.

"That would be perfect." Her face glowed when she smiled. "If the rib is as good as you say, we might consider making it a regular Friday-night special."

"We might," he said, but he was unwilling to commit himself. In the past he'd saved those rib roasts for special occasions such as Founder's Day—commemorating the arrival of Adam O'Halloran in July 1931—and other important dates like Christmas and Easter. He hadn't thought about making it a weekly special. Hmm. She might be on to something.

"I should've started with Monday's dinner, instead of Friday's, shouldn't I?" Mary continued, raising a hand to tuck a few wisps of hair behind her ear. Ben found her nervousness rather endearing.

"What's for dinner this evening?" he asked, pulling his attention back to the matter at hand.

"Shrimp linguine with lemon sauce," she said. "If that suits you?"

Actually it sounded great. With all his cooking experience,

Ben had never gotten the hang of preparing shellfish. He made a fairly decent shrimp Creole, but that was about it.

"I think you'll like the linguine," Mary said, "and I promise you won't even suspect it's low-fat."

Ben frowned; he sure hoped Mrs. McMurphy hadn't turned into another Bethany. He didn't know if he could tolerate any more veggie burgers.

"I promise you'll never guess," she repeated, giving him a bright smile. He noticed that her back stiffened at his skeptical look. "I'm a woman of my word, Mr. Hamilton. If you find the linguine unsatisfactory, I'll cook you the meal of your choice. Agreed?"

He didn't hesitate, because he knew what he wanted. A cheeseburger. It'd been weeks, no, *months,* since he'd last sunk his teeth into a good old-fashioned burger. "Agreed."

As she'd said, Mary was a woman of her word. Ben ate two helpings of shrimp linguine and would've asked for more, but she ran out. It seemed the dish was as popular with his customers as it was with him.

Midmorning the following day, Ben walked carefully down the stairs. It was the first time he'd made the trip when Mary was actually cooking. She must have heard him, because she turned around, spoon in hand. When she saw it was Ben, she smiled broadly.

"Why, Mr. Hamilton, this is a pleasant surprise."

He grumbled something about being bored. He noticed several cookbooks spread across the counter and wondered what she was doing now. No cook he'd ever known cooked from a book, except on rare occasions.

"You couldn't have come at a more opportune time," she said. "Would you mind testing something for me?"

He couldn't think of a reason to refuse, and his breakfast of yogurt and fresh fruit had worn off long ago. "I suppose."

The next thing he knew, he was sitting at the counter. Soon Mary appeared with a filled hamburger bun divided into fourths. She wore an apprehensive look. "I'm having my first taste of this, as well."

"Hamburger?"

"No…it's something different."

He let Mary try hers first, watching as she took a bite. Her face remained expressionless for several seconds, then she smiled and nodded. "This isn't bad."

"What is it?" Ben felt a man had a right to know what he was tasting.

"Just try it," she urged.

He would've refused if he wasn't so hungry. He bit tentatively into the bun. He wasn't sure exactly what was in the filling, but whatever it was tasted…exotic. In fact, it was downright flavorful.

"Not bad," he agreed. "What is it?"

Mary McMurphy smiled. "A veggie burger. I combined several recipes and added a few ingredients of my own."

Ben wouldn't have believed anyone could make vegetables appetizing enough to serve on a hamburger bun, but she'd done it. He polished off the first quarter and reached for the second.

"Do you like it?" she asked eagerly.

He probably should've played it cool, let her think the food was just passable, but her eyes were so wide and hopeful. For the life of him, Ben couldn't dash her spirits. "It's good enough to eat, which is more than I can say about Bethany's. That stuff could kill a man's appetite for years to come."

Happiness radiated from her smile. "Thank you, Ben."

To the best of his knowledge, this was the first time Mary McMurphy had called him anything other than Mr. Hamilton.

DUKE STOPPED and checked his mailbox at the Hard Luck post office once a week or so. He hardly ever received more than bills. Occasionally he got a letter from his mother, but that only happened a few times a year.

He unlocked Box E and retrieved one envelope. The first thing he noticed was the handwriting. Not a bill; his bills were computer-generated. As soon as he saw the return address— in Seattle—he knew the letter was from Tracy.

He resisted the temptation to rip it open then and there. Back at the bunkhouse, he sat on the end of his bed and tugged open the flap. Inside was a business card, with her name scrawled across the front in bold letters, and a greeting card, with a note inside. He read it eagerly:

Hello, Duke,
Just a note to check up on my knight in shining armor. How's the arm doing?
     I'm back into the swing of things here, busy as ever.
     You said that if you were ever in need of an attorney, you'd call on me. I hope you meant that. I've taken the liberty of enclosing my business card.
     Mariah said you'd had a run-in with Bill Landgrin. I hate all the questions, too. I still think of you.

Fondly,
Tracy Santiago

Fondly. What did that mean? *I still think of you.* What was she saying? Duke read the card a second time and then a third. He scowled, wondering exactly what Mariah had told her about his clash with Bill. He hoped she didn't know how angry and aggressive he'd been, how much he'd overreacted. Losing control was out of character for him. Granted, Landgrin was a jerk, but a verbal putdown or two would've sufficed. No, Duke had lashed out for only one reason—he missed Tracy.

For days now he'd been fighting memories of her. And losing the fight. This kind of weakness was foreign to Duke, but he was beginning to realize he couldn't ignore the effect she'd had on his heart. Even his mind was playing tricks on him. Thoughts of her invaded his sleep. Night after night, she was there to greet him when he closed his eyes.

He missed her. He missed her smile and the way the corners of her mouth turned up ever so slightly, as if she didn't want him to see how amused she was. He missed her sarcasm and her opinionated ideas. He even missed their verbal battles, although he was no longer interested in finding fault with her.

Reading the card she'd sent intensified the feeling of emptiness a hundredfold.

The amount of time he spent thinking about Tracy contradicted all his beliefs about personal discipline. He couldn't *stop* thinking about her. He wondered if she'd taken his advice and broken off her relationship with that "sensitive" character she'd been dating. He wondered if she lay awake at nights remembering the kiss they'd shared. That woman really packed a wallop.

Unsure how to respond to Tracy's card, Duke tucked it inside his locker. Because he needed to think, he wandered over to the Hard Luck Café for a cup of coffee.

Ben Hamilton was up and around a little more these days, and if Duke was lucky, he might find Ben alone. He wanted a chance to talk with him for a few minutes. Privately.

Ralph and Ted were sitting at the counter when Duke walked in. He hadn't expected to find his fellow pilots lingering over coffee this late in the morning. It was quite obvious that they weren't any happier to see him than he was to run into them.

"Duke, good to see you," Ben greeted him. At least one person in Hard Luck hadn't turned traitor. "How's the arm?"

"Don't ask," Ralph advised the cook. "He's liable to chew your head off."

Duke didn't take the bait. While it might be true that he'd been a bit short-tempered lately, he didn't think his friends should hold it against him. He was a pilot, after all, and any pilot would react badly to being grounded.

"How about coffee and a cinnamon roll?" Ben invited.

"Sure thing," Duke said, purposely sitting several seats down from the other men.

Ben brought over the coffee and pastry, and Duke glanced at the men he'd once considered his friends. In retrospect, though, he didn't blame them. He *had* been in a foul mood since his release from the hospital. His inability to fly wasn't their fault—and it wasn't the only reason for his bad temper. If he was looking for something—or someone—to blame, it would be Tracy.

"I imagine you're feeling…restless these days," Ben said, leaning casually against the counter.

"Yeah, you could say Duke's restless," Ralph muttered, his elbows propped on the counter while he held his mug with both hands. His eyes seemed riveted straight ahead.

Duke's jaw tightened. He and Ralph had argued just the other morning; Duke really couldn't remember why. Over something trivial, no doubt.

He wasn't accustomed to having this much free time. He'd thought he could work in the office during his convalescence, but all he seemed to do was get in the way. Mariah's replacement had been trained, and everything was under control there. Sawyer took pity on him, now and then offering him some menial administrative task. On a good day he could count on killing an hour, maybe two, in the Midnight Sons office.

The rest of the time he was on his own. He'd read more books in the past couple of weeks than in the entire previous year. Television didn't hold his attention; never had. So he'd been reduced to playing solitaire. He'd played for hours yesterday—then realized he was a card short.

That was what his argument with Ralph had been about, he recalled. Ralph had lent him the deck, and Duke had accused his friend of knowingly holding back that one card. Okay, so maybe he'd overreacted.

Duke remembered how Ralph and the other pilots had risked their own safety to search for his downed plane, and he felt an immediate surge of regret. Next time he was in Fairbanks, he'd pick up a new deck of cards for Ralph. No need to say anything; his friend would get the message.

"I hope this guy isn't being too ornery, Ben," Ted said as they paid their tab.

Again Duke held his tongue. He waited until the two pilots had left the café, then expelled his breath.

"So…you've been a bit out of sorts lately," Ben said, grabbing the coffee pot. He pulled up a stool and sat on the opposite side of the counter.

"Maybe," was all Duke would admit. "I've got too much time on my hands."

"Know what you mean," Ben said. "You're talking to a man

who's spent the last month twiddling his thumbs. All I got to say is it's no wonder our country has problems, with daytime TV as bad as it is."

Even though Ben was half-serious, Duke couldn't help laughing. He was still chuckling when the door opened and Sawyer strolled inside.

"Howdy, Ben," Sawyer said, sliding onto the stool beside Duke's. "How's it going, Duke?" He turned over his mug.

Although he would've preferred a few more minutes alone with Ben, Duke smiled. Shrugging, he said, "Oh, not bad, considering."

"Where's Mrs. McMurphy?" Sawyer asked next.

Duke had been wondering the same thing.

"She decided to organize the storeroom," Ben explained, reaching for the coffee pot and filling Sawyer's mug. "I've been meaning to do that myself, but I kept putting it off. I feel guilty letting her do it by herself, but she insisted. I did make her promise to call me if she had any problems."

"Leave it to a woman to get a person organized," Sawyer said, with a year's worth of marriage behind him. "Abbey and I hadn't been married a month before she emptied every closet in the house. She found a few things that turned out to be worth a pretty penny, too."

"Like what?" Ben asked just as Christian entered the café.

"A couple of old baseball cards I had as a kid. I gave them to Scott for his birthday, and you'd think I'd handed the boy a piece of gold. He loved them."

"Trust me, the only thing Mary's going to find in that storeroom has long expired," Ben said. He looked at Christian, who'd joined the other two men at the counter. "What's Mariah up to these days?"

"Organizing," he said with a wide grin, "what else? She's getting the house set up, but that shouldn't take long. Last I heard, she was talking to Matt and Karen about capitalizing on the tourist business."

Duke sipped his coffee. Who would've believed women would have such a strong impact on the community? From the first, he'd known there'd be changes when they arrived, but he hadn't been sure they'd be *positive* changes. Now he had to acknowledge that they were.

"I imagine you're getting fidgety," Sawyer said to Duke.

That had to be the understatement of the century. "A little."

"Personally I don't know what you're hanging around Hard Luck for," Ben said.

"He's right," Sawyer put in. "You've got plenty of sick leave, plus your vacation time. Why don't you do some traveling?"

"Good plan," Christian murmured as Ben poured his coffee.

"Any idea where I should take this vacation?" Duke asked.

"Yeah," Sawyer said slowly.

"I have a suggestion," Ben added.

"Me, too," Christian said.

"Well, let's hear it."

"Seattle," all three of them said at the same moment.

They stared at each other, then laughed uproariously. They were still laughing as Duke hurried out.

AS SHE SORTED through the mail, Tracy noticed there was nothing from Duke. By her best estimate, he'd received her greeting card a week earlier. In that time she hadn't heard a thing from him. Tracy sighed; she'd been a fool to send the card. He'd made it plain when she left that he didn't want anything more to do with her.

Determinedly she pulled her gaze away from her desk calendar. With a court case coming to trial—and jury selection that morning—she had far more important subjects to occupy her mind.

She checked her watch and realized she was due in court in less than twenty minutes. She was never late, especially for court.

Just as she was about to place her file in her briefcase, Gloria buzzed her on the office intercom. "There's a call for you on line two."

"I don't have time for it now. I've got to get over to the courthouse," she said. "Would you take a message, Gloria?" This case was an important one, and Tracy had thought long and hard about the best way to approach the jury.

"I'll get Mr. Porter's number and—"

Tracy dropped her file. "I'll take the call," she said. She closed her eyes and drew a deep breath before she reached for the receiver. "This is Tracy Santiago."

"Hello, Tracy."

He sounded wonderful, vibrant, healthy. *Close.* As if he was in the room next door, instead of several thousand miles north.

"Duke." She kept her eyes fixed on the small Waterford crystal clock on the corner of her desk. "It's *so* good to hear from you." She knew she sounded thrilled; it didn't matter. She couldn't hide her feelings from him, and she wasn't even going to try.

"I thought I'd call to thank you for the card."

"My pleasure. Listen, Duke, I really am pleased to hear from you. I don't want you to think I'm giving you the brush-off, but I have to be in court in a few minutes. If you'll give me your phone number, I'll call you back as soon as I'm free."

He hesitated.

"Duke? Your phone number?"

"I've always been taught that the man should call the woman."

She groaned out loud. "I don't have time to debate protocol. Just give me your number."

"I'll call you. Now hurry up or you'll be late."

"Duke, you're being unreasonable!"

He chuckled. "Give 'em hell, sweetheart."

Before she could respond, the line went dead.

"Duke," she cried in frustration. *Weeks,* she'd waited weeks to hear his voice, and now she *still* had to wait. And all because of some archaic rule he'd learned as a boy!

Well, she didn't have time to worry about it now. Grabbing her briefcase, she hurried out the door. When she returned, though, she'd move heaven and earth to find that man's number.

DUKE SAT ON THE BED in the fancy Seattle hotel room and sighed. He'd come a long way, and even now he wasn't sure he'd done the right thing.

Oh, he'd found plenty of reasons to visit Seattle. None of which had anything to do with Tracy. But he wasn't going to kid himself.

The purpose of this trip wasn't to take a vacation. It wasn't even to look over house plans or arrange for building materials to be shipped to Hard Luck. It didn't have to do with the list of plane parts Sawyer had asked him to look into, either.

The reason he was sitting on a bed costing him a hundred and fifty bucks a night was Tracy Santiago. He'd come to see her because he hadn't been able to stay away.

"Court," Duke repeated. She was a career woman, he reminded himself. She wasn't going to drop everything just because he was in town for a few days. She didn't even *know* he was in town. He hadn't gotten around to telling her he was in Seattle. She'd find out soon enough.

But he wasn't staying long. Not at these prices.

He walked over to the desk and picked up the room-service menu. One glance assured him he'd prefer to dine out.

Tucking the room key securely in his pocket, he left the hotel and walked onto the street outside. More people occupied the sidewalk in this one square block of Seattle than walked through Hard Luck in a year.

All the activity made Duke nervous. He didn't know how people could ever get used to this kind of racket. Cars, buses, horns and sirens...

The noise level didn't improve as Duke walked downhill toward the Seattle waterfront and Pike Place Market. If anything, it got worse. Even Anchorage wasn't this crowded.

Realizing he was hungry, Duke waited in line for ten minutes to order some fish and chips from one of the stands that dotted the piers. The deep-fried fish was tasty, and he enjoyed it so much he got back in line to buy a second order.

As he ate he gazed around him. The snow-capped mountaintops of the Olympics appeared in the distance. The scenery was very nice, he observed, but nothing he couldn't see in his own state.

When he passed the aquarium, he decided to go in. It was well worth the fee, and he wandered around for an hour or so. He figured that should be enough time for Tracy to finish at court and be back in her office.

He pulled out her business card, located Fourth Avenue on his map and walked down the street until he came to her building.

He stood across the street and counted the floors until he found the twenty-first. He wondered if she had an office with a window and suspected she did. She wasn't a partner yet, but he didn't doubt she'd become one in time. She was ambitious and dedicated.

He felt a sense of pride—and a kind of fear. Their lives, their careers, couldn't possibly coexist. There was no common ground. Except...love? But love, no matter how strong, wasn't enough to wipe out the differences. Damn, he wanted to see her, though.

The fact that he happened to spot her on the crowded Seattle sidewalk could be nothing less than fate. All at once she was on the other side of the street, walking at a clipped pace, presumably back from her lunch break. Checking his watch, he saw that it was almost one. She must be heading over to the courthouse. Her briefcase was in her hand and her steps were filled with purpose.

"Tracy," he shouted, but she didn't hear.

He tried again, running down the sidewalk.

She paused and glanced over her shoulder, not realizing he was on the other side of the street.

She looked good. Her hair bounced ever so slightly as she walked. He'd forgotten what a beautiful woman she was. He must have been blind earlier. Long shapely legs, a tiny waist and hips that—

He walked straight into a little old lady who glared at him as if she was sure she recognized his picture from a post-office "wanted" poster.

"I beg your pardon, ma'am."

"You might look where you're walking, young man," she scolded.

"Please forgive me," he said, but his gaze followed Tracy. She was going up a flight of steps into the King County Courthouse.

"Don't let it happen again," the woman said.

"I won't," Duke promised, sidling over to the curb. He looked both ways, then quickly jogged across the street. A horn blared a warning, which he ignored.

"Tracy!" He tried calling her again, hurrying into the building just as she stepped into an empty elevator. Because he had to walk through the metal detector, he missed it and was forced to wait. Not knowing which floor she was going to, he waited until her elevator stopped and noted it was the fifth.

As soon as the next elevator returned to the lobby, he stepped inside and pushed the button for five.

The fifth-floor hallway seemed even busier than the street. Duke edged his way into the courtroom and looked around. Apparently this was a high-interest case, judging by the media coverage.

Duke slipped into a row near the back and sat down.

Within a couple of minutes, the bailiff instructed everyone in the courtroom to rise. The judge, dressed in flowing black robes, entered the room and took his position. The jury was already seated.

"Are you ready for your opening statement, Ms. Santiago?" Judge Kingsley asked Tracy.

She stood. "Yes, Your Honor, I am."

Duke strained to see her client. He appeared to be a man

in his thirties, perhaps younger. For no reason he cared to examine, Duke experienced a twinge of jealousy. No doubt Tracy was a popular attorney. She was sharp, decisive, thorough. And beautiful. What jury could refuse her? If he was the prosecutor, Duke knew he'd be worried.

Tracy stood slowly and walked toward the jury box. She smiled at the twelve men and women, her pose relaxed.

"Ladies and gentlemen," she began confidently, "I'm here today to prove to you beyond a shadow of a doubt that my client is not guilty. As this case unfolds, you will be assured that Jack Makepeace acted purely in self-defense. He—"

She turned and faced the courtroom, and by some fluke her gaze landed on Duke.

She stopped, and faltered slightly.

Her arms dropped. Her eyes widened. Duke could see the muscles work in her throat.

"Ms. Santiago," the judge asked, "are you all right?"

She walked over to the table and poured herself a glass of water. "I'm fine, Your Honor," she said, glaring at Duke.

Maybe she wasn't as pleased to see him as he'd hoped.

Chapter 7

TRACY TOOK another swallow of water and waited for her heart to stop pounding. *Duke was in Seattle.* A small matter he hadn't bothered to disclose when they spoke earlier.

She looked at him a second time and frowned openly, letting him know she was furious. How dared he do this to her in the middle of her opening statement?

"Ms. Santiago, is there a problem?" the judge asked a little impatiently.

"I beg the court's indulgence," Tracy said. "I...needed a sip of water." She made an effort to compose herself and walked toward the jury box, hoping the twelve men and women were more forgiving than the judge.

Through sheer willpower and years of practice, Tracy was able to finish her presentation without further incident. She dared not look at the court observers again, for fear Duke would distract her. Nevertheless, she was aware of his scrutiny as she spoke. She could almost hear him tell her to "give 'em hell." She might have done it, too, if she hadn't been so shaken by his unexpected appearance. Because of it, she was afraid she hadn't made any substantial progress in proving her client's innocence.

When the trial recessed at four, Tracy spoke briefly with her client, then reeled around to confront Duke. The minute they were alone, she fully intended to give *him* hell.

He was gone.

Had he been a figment of her overactive imagination? Perhaps the phone call had been responsible for making her think she'd seen him when she hadn't. Maybe, just maybe, she was losing whatever sanity she still possessed.

Taking her briefcase, she headed out of the courtroom and back to her office. The minute she got there, she'd phone Hard Luck to get the name of his hotel. She was in the hallway walking toward the elevator when she saw him leaning indolently against the wall. He flashed her an easy smile.

The color remained high in Tracy's cheeks, and she scowled at him with the full force of her annoyance, which by this time was considerable. But despite her outrage, simmering just below the surface, was joy. Absolute joy.

"You might have told me you were in Seattle," she snapped, not knowing which emotion to express first.

"You were on your way to court," he reminded her.

"But you might have said *something*," she returned.

He looked healthy and vital. Whole. His left arm, cast and all, was supported by a sling, but it didn't distract from his strong masculine appeal. Almost against her will, she felt herself moving toward him. Tracy wasn't sure if she should slap him silly or hurl herself into his arms and *kiss* him silly.

Duke made the decision for her. Without saying a word, he stretched out his right arm, inviting her into his embrace.

Nothing could have kept her away. She bolted across the corridor and wrapped both her arms around his waist. A small cry emerged from her throat as she buried her head in his shoulder.

Duke's good arm came around her, and Tracy felt a sense of peace, a happiness she'd never experienced before.

His cheek moved against her hair, as if he savored the feel of her in his arms. "You're right," he whispered, and his voice didn't sound anything like normal. "I should've told you."

"I nearly had a heart attack when I turned around and saw you in the room."

"I know. I saw that right away. Obviously I wasn't thinking when I went in."

"Then you were gone."

"I meant to leave as soon as I realized what was happening to you, but then you seemed to recover. So I waited till it was nearly over and came out here."

She nodded, breathing in his scent. He wore a bay-rum aftershave that made her think whimsically of pirates with rakish smiles and sparkling Caribbean seas.

"You're good, sweetheart. I always knew you could argue better than any woman I'd ever met—or any man for that matter—but when you're standing in front of a jury box, you're something to behold."

She was tempted to laugh *and* weep. "You certainly know how to sweet-talk a woman when you have to, Duke."

"That's no bull, Trace. You're a good attorney."

"Thank you." But she hadn't even gotten up to half speed! If he could see her when she really hit her stride...

"Will you go to dinner with me?" he asked.

"When?"

"Tonight?"

"Yes," she answered, unable to hide her eagerness. "If you want, you can pick me up at my office. I generally don't get out of there until after six."

"Fine. I'll see you then." He kissed her forehead. His lips lingered against her skin. When he released her, it seemed hard for him to let her go.

Evening couldn't come soon enough to suit Tracy.

"I'll be there by six," Duke promised.

Tracy knew that their embrace had attracted attention. Many of the people who knew her stared with undisguised curiosity, but Tracy didn't care.

Duke started toward the elevator.

"Duke," she called, and he turned around. "It's great to see you."

He grinned and brushed the hair from his brow. "You, too."

She watched him board the elevator while her mind spun with gleeful excitement. Duke in Seattle. And she'd be seeing him again that very evening.

"Who's the hunk?" Janice Cooper, her friend and colleague, had strolled to her side.

"A friend."

"He must be some friend if you practically run into his arms. Weren't you the one who insisted all men are animals but some of them make nice pets?"

"This one's special," was all Tracy would admit. To say anything more would be to give herself away. Although she supposed she'd already done that...

"He must be," Janice added with a hefty sigh of envy. "I don't think I've ever seen you look this happy."

So it showed. Well, Tracy mused, she obviously wasn't very good at hiding her feelings. Somehow she didn't care.

"He looks the rough-and-ready type," Janice continued, "not the type you usually go for, like Gavin. What makes this one so special?"

"You mean other than the fact that he saved my life?"

Janice whistled. "*That* was Duke Porter?"

"The one and only."

"But I thought he lived in Alaska."

"He does."

"I suggest you find whatever it is that man's got so we can bottle it. Most of the men I've met in the past ten years could use a solid dose of this guy."

Tracy chuckled, but Janice was right. The men she'd dated fell sadly short on the masculinity index. Duke's muscles weren't built in any gym and what was left of his tan came from the sun. He had the instincts and the natural confidence to cope with any situation. He had courage. He knew who he was, without needing psychiatrists, self-help manuals or courses on finding his inner child.

Duke Porter was as genuine as they came.

DUKE STUDIED his reflection in the store mirror and barely recognized himself. He couldn't recall the last time he'd worn a suit. His father's funeral, probably, more than fifteen years ago. It was the same suit he'd worn to his graduation. And his mother's second wedding.

"What do you think?" The salesman circled him like a

buzzard, closing in for the kill. The man knew a sale when he smelled one.

Duke checked the price tag dangling from the end of the jacket sleeve. And groaned. Five hundred bucks for a suit seemed an awful lot just to be properly dressed to take Tracy out to dinner. When he'd called to make reservations at the hotel's fancy dining room, he'd been informed a tie was required "for the gentlemen." A tie? For dinner? He wondered what they served that was so almighty special that a man was expected to dress up for the experience.

"You can have the alterations finished in an hour?" Duke asked. The sale was contingent on that.

"Yes, of course, for a small fee."

Duke would bet the fee was anything but small, but he had no choice. A man didn't take a city girl like Tracy to dinner just anywhere. For reasons he didn't want to question, he found it important to prove he was as classy as any of the men she routinely dated. True, he preferred to eat at a comfortable place like the Hard Luck Café, but he could hold his own in her sophisticated big-city world.

By the time five-thirty rolled around, Duke Porter's new look was complete. A woman in a beauty shop had cut and blow-dried his hair—Duke hoped the guys back in Hard Luck didn't hear about that. He'd shaved and splashed on some new cologne—a lot of lawyers bought it, the saleswoman told him. If his clean-cut looks didn't affect Tracy, then maybe the cologne would do the trick. He was wearing his new suit and silk tie, his new shoes, and carrying a lightweight raincoat over his right arm. Assessing himself in the hotel mirror, Duke decided he looked good. Like a million bucks—but then he'd invested nearly that much in the cause. Tracy was worth it, though. He trusted she'd appreciate the effort.

He arrived at her office building. The outside might have been a bit stark and forbidding, but the interior was posh, richly decorated in mauves and grays. The way Duke figured it, if they could afford to put leather sofas in the waiting room, the firm would be too pricey for the likes of him.

A smartly dressed receptionist unlocked the door and smiled at him. She wore her coat and looked ready to leave for the night.

"I'm here for Tracy Santiago," he said.

"Mr. Porter?" she asked.

He nodded.

"She's waiting for you."

Duke followed the receptionist down the narrow hallway to Tracy's office. She glanced back at him several times.

"Mr. Porter's here," the woman announced to Tracy, then left—reluctantly, it seemed to Duke.

Tracy rose from her desk with a welcoming smile. But the minute her eyes landed on him her grin faded and her jaw dropped. "Duke?" she asked, squinting. "Is that you?"

"Hey, I thought you'd like my fancy duds." He held out his right arm and rotated, giving her an eyeful of what five-hundred-plus bucks could buy in this town.

"I can't believe… You look so different," she murmured. Shaking her head, she brought her hands to her mouth. "I can't believe it."

"You mean you don't like it?" He'd be pretty disappointed if that was the case.

"Like it—yes, of course. It's just that you don't…look like you."

He frowned. "Then who *do* I look like?" He'd never known Tracy to be flustered—other than this afternoon, when he'd surprised her in court. Now that he thought about it, he wasn't exactly sure how he'd expected her to react. She wasn't the type to gush all over him, although, in a way, he supposed he would've liked that.

She walked around from behind her desk. "You're probably the handsomest best-dressed man I've ever seen."

The tension eased from Duke's shoulders. Handsomest, best-dressed—now, those were compliments he could live with.

"You look pretty good yourself, sweetheart."

If he didn't know better, Duke would've sworn Tracy blushed. He peered at her carefully—yup, she was definitely blushing. He hadn't thought the man existed who was capable of cracking this woman's composure, least of all him.

The blush added a tinge of pink to her cheeks, and before he could consider the wisdom of kissing her, Duke stepped closer and lowered his mouth to hers. Tracy angled her head and moaned softly.

Duke's heart boomed like thunder, and he deepened the kiss. After a moment he drew back, trying to clear his head. This wasn't the time or the place for kissing her. "I made dinner reservations," he said in a hoarse voice.

Tracy moistened her lips and lowered her eyes. "I'll get my purse and be ready in just a minute." She reached for her jacket, but Duke took it from her hands.

"Allow me," he said, awkwardly holding it open for her.

She smiled and slipped her arms into the sleeves. "Thank you."

He nodded and resisted the urge to kiss her again. The

evening was going to be a test of his restraint if they continued like this. The fact was, he'd prefer to skip dinner altogether and spend the evening making love to her. He found the picture that came to his mind so enticing he had to stop and inhale several deep breaths.

Tracy's office was close to the hotel, so they walked the short distance, holding hands. When he mentioned the name of the restaurant, she arched her brows. "The Rose Garden is one of the most elegant places in town."

"I figured it must be," he said nonchalantly.

The restaurant was on the top floor of the hotel. They rode the elevator up the outside of the building and watched Seattle grow smaller. Tracy pointed out Elliot Bay and Puget Sound.

"I've only been here once," Tracy said. "The food was great, but—" she hesitated and dropped her voice "—very expensive."

"Don't worry," he whispered, "I can afford it."

He nearly changed his mind when he read the prices listed on the menu. Even Alaska didn't charge a man ten bucks for a cup of coffee. He wasn't sure he liked the atmosphere, either. Men running around in fancy dress was one thing, but having the waiter place his napkin in his lap was another. There were some things a man preferred to do on his own.

"What are you having?" Tracy asked. Her eyes met his above the menu.

Duke was a meat-and-potatoes kind of guy. Always had been, always would be. He read the list of dishes offered and couldn't find anything he'd seriously consider eating. Alligator. Pheasant. Frog's legs. Snails. Duck. The one item that interested him was salmon, but he could have that in Alaska anytime he wanted without paying an exorbitant price. Good grief, there were only so many ways to cook a fish.

"Have you decided?" he asked.

A waiter stiffly approached their table, his nose leveled toward the ceiling. He held a pen and pad in his hand and looked distinctly unfriendly. "The special this evening is *palomillo à la parrilla*." He paused. "And may I ask the wine steward to discuss our wine list with you?"

"I believe we'll need a few more minutes," Duke said. "And no, thanks, to the wine—I'll just have a beer."

"Me, too," Tracy said, mentioning the name of a local microbrewery.

The waiter seemed not to hear them.

With precision movements, he pivoted and walked away.

"I wouldn't mind a salad," Tracy said.

Duke thought he'd be safe if he ordered the same thing. "That sounds good," he said, and set aside the menu.

Tracy ordered the *salade printanière Monte Carlo.*

"I'd like a salad, as well," he said, looking the waiter in the eye although he nearly had to stand on the seat of his chair to do so. "But all I want is some lettuce and maybe a few other vegetables sliced over it."

"Celery and radishes?" the waiter suggested.

"Fine." Duke was easy to please.

"Alfalfa sprouts?"

"That's fine, too," he said, and smiled over at Tracy.

"Asparagus?"

Duke nodded.

"In other words you'll have the *salade printanière Monte Carlo?*"

"Exactly," Duke said as if he'd known that all along. He was beginning to think this waiter wasn't interested in receiving a tip.

"Very well, sir."

Duke returned his attention to Tracy.

"Might I suggest the *scallion vinaigrette* dressing for your salads?" the man continued.

"Please," Tracy answered.

"I prefer ranch dressing."

The man's nose angled even higher. "I'm afraid we don't carry ranch dressing."

"Blue cheese then."

The waiter sighed, clearly disapproving of Duke's choice. "As you wish."

As soon as he left the table, Tracy smothered a laugh. "I'm sorry," she said. "I was just thinking of that waiter working at the Hard Luck Café." She giggled. "He wouldn't last five minutes."

Duke grinned. "At least Ben serves ranch dressing."

"Speaking of Ben, how is he?"

"Doing great. He recently hired a chef, Mrs. McMurphy—"

"A woman?" Tracy asked, elevating an eyebrow.

"Is there something wrong with that?" Duke asked.

"Of course not! It just surprises me. I didn't think Ben was the type who'd let another person in his kitchen—particularly not a woman."

"We Alaska men are a lot more fair-minded than you give us credit for," Duke said, pretending to be insulted. But his eyes caught hers, and soon they were both smiling.

A few minutes later, their drinks came in crystal glasses and their salads arrived under silver-domed lids. Duke had eaten plenty of lettuce in his day, but he'd never seen anything so artfully arranged. The asparagus fanned out like a starburst in the middle of the plate. It looked almost too pretty to eat.

"No wonder the prices are so high," he murmured, staring at the vegetables on the gold-rimmed china plate.

"It tastes even better than it looks," Tracy promised, and she was right.

But it wasn't enough. Duke recognized that even as he paid the bill. Once he'd dropped Tracy off at her home, he'd head to the closest hamburger joint and get himself a real dinner.

"How about a walk along the waterfront?" Tracy said on the elevator ride down.

"Sure." Duke didn't want their evening to end so soon, even if he felt half-starved.

"I love the Seattle waterfront," Tracy said as they strolled downhill toward Elliot Bay. Friday-night traffic filled the streets, and Duke stared at it, still overwhelmed by the noise and the number of people. He didn't mention that he'd spent much of the day sightseeing. He'd been particularly impressed by the waterfront area—Pike Place Market, the fish market and the produce stands. Why, there were fruits and vegetables he'd never even heard of before!

Before he returned to Hard Luck, Duke decided, he'd buy a few of the delicacies he'd discovered for his friends. Seedless watermelon would be a sure hit with the youngsters.

"Tell me about everyone," Tracy said as they walked to the end of the pier. The wind whipped her hair about her face. She leaned against the railing, staring out over the choppy green waters. The evening had begun to fade, and the street-lights had come on, casting a warm glow over the area.

"Karen's really looking pregnant these days," Duke commented. "Abbey, too, come to think of it." Tracy had seen both women when she was in town for Mariah and Christian's wedding. It hardly seemed possible that it was only weeks ago; it felt like a lifetime. He'd changed in those weeks. So had she.

"Ben's getting more ornery every day," Duke said with a chuckle. They'd reached the end of the pier.

"Dotty, Sally and Angie?"

"Doing just fine. They send their love." His voice fell on the word *love*.

He had no intention of kissing her with people milling about, but it was asking too much not to hold her. He'd dreamed of little else for too long not to give in to the temptation. Later, he promised himself. Later, he'd kiss her.

With only one good arm, holding her proved to be slightly difficult. He moved closer and slid his arm about her waist.

Tracy placed her hand against his chest, and Duke suddenly decided he didn't want to wait. Slowly he leaned forward and kissed her. He reasoned that it was evening and there weren't *that* many people. Anyone who didn't like it could look elsewhere.

Duke almost lost himself in that kiss. Somewhere deep inside, he managed to find the restraint to break away.

Tracy trembled, her eyes wide and uncertain. "When…will you be going back?"

That was the sixty-four-thousand-dollar question. Duke didn't know. The way he felt just then, it wouldn't be anytime soon.

"How long are you staying? A few days?"

He heard the dread in her voice and nearly kissed her again. What they were doing wasn't smart; Duke realized that at the same time he realized he didn't care. Some might call him selfish, and he'd be the first to agree, but right now, he needed her. He needed this.

"I don't know," he said.

"Longer than a week?" she prompted.

Because he couldn't answer her question, he kissed the delicate curve of her neck. It felt so good to touch her like this.

"Duke?"

"More than a few days," he whispered.

"A week? Longer?"

Her scent intoxicated him. "Yes," he whispered.

She exhaled softly, and his heart constricted. All these years he'd assumed he had to be ten-thousand feet above the earth to get this high. He'd never known a man could experience this exhilaration with a woman.

Tracy was teaching him things he'd never discovered. Never suspected.

The sound of children giggling pulled them apart. Duke took her hand and together they strolled back up the pier.

"There's so much I want to show you," she said.

They passed a fish-and-chip place, and the smoky scent of grilled salmon was enough to make Duke's stomach growl with hunger. Tracy might be satisfied with a mere salad, but a bunch of fancy lettuce decorated with alfalfa sprouts simply didn't fill him.

"You're hungry," Tracy accused.

He shrugged. "A little."

Her eyes lit up with excitement. "I know a fabulous Mexican restaurant that's just four or five blocks from here. There's not much ambience, but the food is terrific. You game?"

He chuckled and nodded. "What about you?"

"I'm starving," she admitted, smiling broadly.

"Then lead the way."

"One thing first," she said. "You'll be in town tomorrow evening?"

Duke nodded.

"Then I'll treat you to dinner."

Duke stiffened. "I don't know how men and women do it here, but in Alaska a man buys."

Disagreement flashed in her eyes, but Tracy didn't argue with him. "What if I cooked the meal myself?"

He hadn't considered that. "You cook?"

She grinned. "You haven't eaten until you've tasted my cooking."

This woman was full of surprises. "I'll be there. Just tell me where and when."

BEN WAS ASTONISHED at how well the Friday-night special went over with the married folks in Hard Luck. Mary sold out of the prime rib during the first hour. This Friday she'd decided to cook two complete roasts, using his recipe.

For years Ben had catered primarily to the men on Friday evenings. Some of the pipeline workers always flew in for a little rest and relaxation. The guys got a chance to catch up with each other, talk, share a few laughs. It wasn't uncommon for them to play pinochle or bridge, either.

Ben hadn't given much consideration to what the married couples in town did for entertainment. He knew from Bethany that Mitch usually rented a movie from Pete Livengood's store or had one of the pilots pick up a video in Fairbanks. They spent the early part of Friday night in front of the television with a big bowl of popcorn before Mitch, a public-safety officer, went out on patrol.

"You sure we're going to sell enough of the specials to use up both these roasts?" Ben asked Mary.

She nodded. "We could have doubled our sales last Friday, and I've been advertising all week. Don't you worry. If there're leftovers, I'll make roast-beef sandwiches the lunchtime special on Saturday."

Ben didn't have much of an argument. He'd come to trust Mary's judgment and was willing to give her free rein in most culinary matters.

At six that evening, Sawyer and Abbey showed up, holding hands.

"We're on a date," Sawyer told Ben, and winked at his wife. "The kids insist they're old enough to stay on their own and we're giving them a chance to prove it."

Abbey slid into the booth, and Sawyer sat next to her. Abbey's tummy was growing nice and round these days, Ben noticed. She looked prettier than he'd ever seen her, and he suspected the pregnancy had something to do with that.

No sooner had Abbey and Sawyer seated themselves than Christian and Mariah walked into the café.

"You meet up with the nicest people at Ben's," Abbey teased.

"Do you mind if we join you?" Christian asked.

The two brothers sat across from each other, their wives at their sides. The sight produced a sense of rightness in Ben.

There'd been a time not so long ago that he'd assumed the two older O'Halloran boys would remain bachelors. For some reason, Ben had always assumed Christian would marry, but not his older brothers.

Ben was well aware that the women moving to town were responsible for the vast changes in Hard Luck. It astonished him every time he thought about it. Why, their community was growing by leaps and bounds. They'd become a real family town, a good place to raise kids—and to grow old.

Ben spent the evening helping out where he could. He found himself busy, pleasantly so, but not overworked. With his permission, Mary had hired two part-time employees, a couple of high school girls who were excited about the job. She'd trained them herself.

He wasn't sure what it was, but Mary McMurphy had a way about her he didn't quite understand. She'd approach him about some issue he adamantly opposed, and then—before he knew how she'd managed it—he'd find himself agreeing.

Hiring the two part-time waitresses was a perfect example. When she suggested that they needed serving staff, he'd decided he'd take on one and only one waitress. The funny part was that Mary had accepted his decision and even agreed with it. But before long she'd brought up a number of excellent points on the advantages of hiring additional help. The next thing Ben knew, he had two part-time employees, just what Mary had suggested in the beginning.

The evening went well, and as she predicted, Mary sold out of both roasts. One of the things he liked best about her was that she didn't gloat.

"I'll finish this," he told her when he found her washing up the last of the pans. "You've been here all day."

"Actually," Mary said, drying her hands on a clean towel, "I…waited because I had something important to ask you."

Ben noticed that her eyes didn't meet his. The woman hadn't worked for him a month and she was going to ask for a raise. Ben could see it coming.

She'd planned this all along, he'd bet. She'd made herself

indispensable just so she could turn around and demand all kinds of unreasonable things. He braced himself for the worst.

"What is it?" he asked gruffly.

Mary's head jerked at his tone, and her eyes filled with shock. "I—I wanted to know if you'd mind if I used your kitchen to bake my cinnamon rolls for the Caldwells," she blurted out. "I'd be willing to pay you whatever you felt was fair for the use of the electricity and all."

It was then that Ben saw tears shining in her eyes.

"Never mind," she said, reaching for her coat. "I should've realized that would be unfair to you. Forgive me, Ben." And she was out the back door before he could stop her.

Chapter
8

Tracy stood in the middle of her small kitchen and closed her eyes, groaning aloud. Here it was, almost seven on Saturday night, and she was nowhere near ready. She didn't know what she could've been thinking when she invited Duke to dinner. Especially a dinner she'd made herself.

She didn't cook. She'd never cooked an entire meal in her life—at least, not one people could actually eat.

When she'd so blithely said Duke hadn't lived until he'd tasted one of her dinners, she'd been challenging the fates. Opening her eyes, she regarded her normally spotless kitchen and wanted to weep. The room was a disaster. Every pan she owned was filled with one abandoned effort or another.

Sauces—she'd supposed that if she followed a recipe, she could make a decent sauce, not this foul-smelling stuff burned to the bottom of her brand-new saucepan. But the only reason she'd ever used her stove before was to light candles when she couldn't find matches. Well, that was a slight exaggeration; she'd boiled water and heated canned soup. All her other meals were delivered or came in a package she warmed up in her microwave.

She checked her watch and groaned again. Duke would arrive soon, and she didn't know what to do. The sirloin-tip roast had sounded so easy. The butcher had been kind enough to give her detailed directions—a little salt, a dash of pepper, rub it with a garlic clove, then slap it in the oven. The same with the woman at the Pike Place Market where she'd picked up the fresh asparagus. A little water, she'd said, and a pinch of salt. Why, even a child could cook asparagus.

Tracy had paid a king's ransom for these culinary jewels, but the hollandaise sauce she'd intended to pour over them was an unmitigated disaster. She'd really wanted to dazzle Duke with that sauce.

The mashed potatoes were…disgusting. She'd wanted everything to be perfect for Duke, so she'd peeled, boiled and mashed the real thing. Her mistake had come when she'd put in too much milk. Then, in desperation, she'd attempted to fix her mistake by adding instant potato flakes. Now the whole sorry mess looked as if it would be better used as wallpaper paste.

As for gravy, hers resembled a watered-down drink from some sleazy bar. Not a thick rich sauce redolent of an expensive cut of meat.

The one bright spot was dessert. She'd been smart enough to pick up a strawberry torte at the bakery. It sat safe and protected on the bottom shelf of her refrigerator.

Her table, set with china and crystal, looked elegant, Tracy willingly admitted. She'd bought a book that showed how to fold linen napkins and spent a good hour learning how to turn each one into a bird. They sat, poised for flight, on her china plates.

Tracy barely had time to change out of her jeans and into slacks and a silk blouse when the doorbell chimed. She slipped her feet into shoes and looped gold earrings into her earlobes as she hurried to the front door.

Taking an extra second to survey her condominium, she noticed that a magazine had been left out. She raced across the room and hid it under a pillow.

"Duke, hello." She greeted him as though she'd been lazing around all day. Little did he know that she'd spent her entire Saturday on this disastrous dinner, agonizing over each and every detail.

He stepped inside and handed her a bouquet of flowers and a bottle of merlot. "How sweet," she said, bringing the rose-buds to her nose. Their scent was light and delicate. Tracy hoped it was enough to overpower the aroma of the scorched egg mixture she'd attempted to turn into hollandaise sauce.

"Make yourself at home," she said, draping the roses across one arm like a beauty queen and tucking the bottle under the other.

He stepped farther into the room and looked around. "Nice digs."

Tracy was proud of her home. The high-rise condominium offered a fabulous view of the islands that dotted Puget Sound. The rooms were spacious, giving the place a wide-open feel. She'd purchased it shortly after her first visit to Alaska and realized only later why it had appealed to her so much. The land in Alaska seemed to stretch on forever, and she'd wanted to capture that same sense of freedom in her own home.

Duke walked over to the chrome-and-glass dining-room table and the black lacquered chairs. The table setting was indeed lovely, if she did say so herself.

"Wait here," she said, backing away from him, "and I'll get a vase for the roses." She didn't dare let him anywhere near her kitchen. The second he saw the mess she'd created, he'd know the truth.

She opened the swinging door just enough to squeeze through and returned a few minutes later. The roses were the perfect complement to her beautiful table.

"Wine?" she asked.

"Please."

Tracy poured them each a glass, then set the open bottle in an ice bucket on the buffet. With a slightly manic smile, she led the way into the living room.

She sat down in the chair across from him, balancing her wineglass. Tracy feared her perfume hadn't completely covered the scent of smoke in her hair. If Duke got close enough to catch a whiff of that, he'd guess that she'd nearly set her kitchen on fire.

Duke leaned toward her as if he felt the distance between them was too great.

"What's for dinner?" he asked enthusiastically. "I'm starved."

Tracy's heart sank, and she swallowed her rising sense of dread. Doing her best to appear calm and serene, she listed her menu in detail. Duke's eyes grew more appreciative with each item.

"I have to admit, you surprise me."

"I do?" she asked, feeling giddy.

"You must've spent all day in the kitchen."

"Nah," she said and gestured weakly with her hand. She sipped her wine, wondering just how she was going to escape this nightmare she'd created. Sooner or later—probably sooner—he'd learn the truth.

"How'd you spend your day?" she asked.

Duke studied his wine. "I went to a house designer in Tacoma and looked at plans."

"You're building a home? In Hard Luck?"

He nodded. "It's one of the things I've been wanting to do for a long time now, but kept putting off. The accident made me realize how much I was looking forward to building it with my own two hands."

"You must know a great deal about carpentry, since your father worked in the trade."

Duke was very quiet for a moment. "How'd you know that?" He looked at her intently.

Tracy boldly met his stare. "How do you think I'd know? You told me."

"When?"

"While we were waiting for the rescue helicopter."

Slowly Duke eased against the back of the chair. "Did I by chance mention anything else?"

"Oh, yes."

"Like what?"

"Well, for one thing, your real name is John Wayne Porter, which is how you came to be called Duke."

He sprang to his feet so fast that Tracy's neck snapped up, following his movements.

"I told you that?"

"Is it a deep dark secret you don't want anyone to know?" That seemed downright silly to her.

"Yes...no." He rammed the fingers of his right hand through his hair. "Is there anything else...I said?" He turned and glared at Tracy, as if he wasn't sure he could trust her.

She shook her head, not mentioning what he'd said about

his parents. Instead, she swallowed hard. Silence fell between them while she composed her thoughts. Plainly Duke didn't want her knowing these things about him.

"We were alone, and I was miserably cold and more afraid than I'd ever been in my life," she whispered. Despite her efforts, her voice trembled. "When night fell, I never realized how black and…and suffocating it can feel. You were obviously hurt, and my greatest fear was that you might die before we could be rescued. I felt so…so utterly helpless."

Tracy held back the emotion, but with difficulty, taking a moment to calm herself before she continued. "You seemed to sense my panic. When you were conscious, you calmed me with words. You…" She paused and moistened her lips. "You told me about your dad and growing up in Homer and about the time you were ten and decided to play Superman. You tied a bathroom towel around your neck and flew out the upstairs bedroom window."

"I nearly broke my fool neck," he said with a rueful grin.

"But you didn't. You broke your leg, instead."

Duke laughed softly. "It sounds like I developed foot-in-mouth disease out there."

"You don't remember any of it?" How could he have forgotten? It was during those times he'd held her close, sharing not only his body heat, but a part of himself. In retrospect, Tracy didn't know which had brought her more comfort, his warmth or his words.

"I remember very little," he answered starkly.

"You don't need to worry, Duke," she assured him, meeting his gaze. "Your confidences are safe with me."

He relaxed. "Not even the O'Hallorans know my real name is John Wayne."

"It's a perfectly good name."

Duke frowned, apparently disagreeing with her. "I suppose I should be grateful I didn't do or say anything really embarrassing."

"You mean like telling me about the women in your life?"

Duke's eyes narrowed.

"You did mention Laurie. And Maureen," she said, despite knowing she should keep her mouth closed.

Duke went pale. "I told you about Maureen?"

"Your first love…er, lover."

"Isn't it time for dinner?"

"We can wait. I've got everything warming in the oven."

"Tracy…"

"All right, all right," she said. "I'll shut up, but I promise you have nothing to fear. Like I said, your secrets are safe with me—mostly safe." She set aside her wineglass, got up and headed for the kitchen.

"Did I happen, uh, to say anything about you?" He was addressing her back.

"About me?" She turned, pressing one hand dramatically to her chest. Briefly enjoying herself, she let her eyes grow huge. "As a matter of fact, you did."

He waited expectantly.

Once she felt he'd suffered enough, she answered his question. "You claimed I was the sassiest, most opinionated woman you'd ever met."

His shoulders went slack with relief. "You are, no argument there."

"Then you said I had the best-looking legs of any woman you know." Having said that, she disappeared into the kitchen, leaving the door to swing in her wake.

Her smile died as she viewed the room. She left the sliced meat and mashed potatoes in a warm oven and took the green salad from the refrigerator. This part of dinner should be edible. She'd bought one of those packages that had the vegetables already sliced in with the lettuce. She'd wanted to impress Duke with a homemade dressing, but that was a lost cause. The bottled stuff would have to do. She dumped some on and tossed vigorously, splashing the sides of the crystal bowl. At least it was ranch dressing.

She carried the salad into the dining room. "Would you like to start with this?" she asked.

"Sounds like a good idea."

Tracy smiled sweetly and prayed he'd fill up on salad, because everything else was a mess. She tried to delay the inevitable, but Duke made it clear that he was eager for the main course.

Her heart beating with trepidation, Tracy delivered the meat, potatoes, limp asparagus and gravy to the table. Duke's smile revealed his anticipation.

"I have to admit," he began, reaching for the meat platter, "that I was skeptical when you said you cooked. As far as I'm concerned, keeping a home is becoming a lost art. Too many women—and men, too, I suppose—don't value domestic skills anymore." He helped himself to a generous portion of sliced roast.

Silently Tracy forked one thin slice onto her own plate.

Next he piled a mound of mashed potatoes on his plate and liberally poured gravy over both.

Tracy held her breath when he sliced into the meat and sampled his first bite. He winked at her and chewed.

And chewed.

And chewed.

An eternity passed before he swallowed, and when he did, she saw the lump slowly move down his throat.

"I—I hope the roast isn't too tough," she said.

"Not a bit," he assured her, but she noticed that he reached for his water glass and drank until it was empty.

Filling her fork with mashed potatoes and gravy, Tracy tried her first taste of the dinner. The potatoes stuck to the roof of her mouth and the burned taste of gravy, which she'd tried to cover with powdered garlic, was so awful it brought tears to her eyes.

Duke was about to take a bite.

"Stop!" she cried, as if the mashed potatoes were laced with arsenic. She stood up, plate in hand.

He hesitated, fork poised in front of his mouth.

"Don't eat that," she shouted, then raced around to his side of the table. He stared at her in shock. Tracy grabbed his plate and rushed into the kitchen to scrape the contents of both plates in the garbage.

The time had come to tell the truth.

Duke was still seated at her beautifully set table when she returned. Rarely had Tracy felt like such a failure—and rarely had she felt so dishonest.

"What you were saying earlier—about women who lack domestic skills," she said weakly. "I'm… I'm afraid I'm one of them."

Tracy expected Duke to laugh and taunt her. What she didn't expect was silence.

Duke dropped his napkin on the table and slowly exhaled.

"Say something," she pleaded.

"Chinese or pizza?" he asked after another moment.

Tracy didn't hesitate. "Chinese."

He grinned. "You know, I would've eaten every bite, then complimented you on your efforts."

"And died in the process," she added. "I don't require that kind of sacrifice from you."

Duke looked away, and Tracy saw that he was struggling not to laugh.

"You knew, didn't you?" she said, figuring out the source of his amusement.

"I guessed."

"You might've said something," she muttered, fighting down an attack of righteous indignation. "Instead, you let me make a fool of myself and—"

"What could I say?"

She didn't know. Sighing, she shook her head.

"I'm honored you were willing to put yourself through this on my behalf," he said. "Not every woman would've gone to all this trouble."

"I wanted to impress you."

"You have."

"Sure, with how big a fool I can be."

"No," he countered swiftly. He wrapped his good arm around her waist and pulled her onto his lap. Her heart thumped, and a quivery feeling took hold of her stomach. It was like this every time he touched her.

"You know," she said wistfully, "I've never told anyone this, but I always wanted to be a whiz in the kitchen." Publicly she'd scorned cooking as a reactionary pursuit, something that repressed women. And yet, secretly, she'd found it rather fascinating, although she'd firmly believed she couldn't afford to indulge in traditional female activities. Her rebellious nature had kept her out of the kitchen. Until now.

No man had ever mattered to her more than Duke. Over the years she'd dated lots of men, but she'd never wanted to impress any of them with her culinary talents. Only Duke.

She'd learn, she decided, and feel good about it. She understood now that preparing a meal for someone you loved wasn't demeaning or repressive at all. It was another way of showing your love. *Not* that she'd be trading in her briefcase for an apron on a full-time basis!

MONDAY MORNING Ben came down the stairs from his apartment to find Mary with her arms elbow-deep in bread dough.

"Mornin'," he greeted in the same gruff tone he generally used.

"Mornin'." Mary didn't turn to look at him.

Ben exhaled sharply. They hadn't spoken since she'd rushed out of the café Friday evening. He was a crusty old bachelor who'd somehow managed to offer the men who sought his help advice on romance. But for himself, he wasn't sure how to even *talk* to a woman.

He poured himself a cup of coffee and eyed Mary, wondering where to start. Normally he planned the day's menu, and they worked companionably together.

"Looks like snow," he said, although he hadn't so much as glanced at the sky.

"Good chance," she returned.

"One year at the beginning of October we got twenty inches in a single day."

Mary made no comment, but continued to knead the dough with practiced hands.

Ben waited—for what, he didn't know. "Damn it, Mary!" he barked.

She jumped at the sound of his voice, increasing his sense of guilt.

"Say something," he ordered.

She finally turned to face him, her eyes flashing fire. "And just what do you want me to say?"

"You wanted to talk to me about baking your rolls for the Caldwells, right?"

"Yes," she said huffily, "but you made it plain you weren't interested, so I dropped the matter."

"I thought you were going to ask me to give you a raise. I don't want to sound cheap or anything, but you've barely started working here and—"

"A raise?" she cried as if he'd insulted her.

"What else was I to think?"

Mary planted her hands on her hips and glared at him.

Ben knew he owed her an explanation, but he felt awkward making it. He wasn't accustomed to explaining his actions, and it bothered him that he needed to do it now. "I haven't had many employees over the years."

"So I gathered," she said, and it seemed to him that her voice was a bit less exasperated. "I wasn't asking for any raise, Ben Hamilton. All I wanted to know was whether you'd mind if I baked an extra batch or two of my cinnamon rolls for the Caldwells' guests, come winter."

Ben nodded, indicating she should continue.

"Naturally I wouldn't bake during the hours I'd be working for you."

"Naturally," he echoed.

"It would mean staying in town one weekend a month and using the ovens on Saturday mornings. I'll miss visiting my grandchildren, but that can't be helped."

Ben often used the ovens himself on the weekend.

"Of course, I'd bake in the morning so you'd have free use of the ovens later in the day."

Ben could see she'd thought everything through.

"Since I'd be using your kitchen and your ovens," she went on, "I'd be willing to pay you whatever you felt was fair."

"I see. Are the Caldwells supplying the ingredients?"

"No, I'll pay for those myself."

Ben could see a problem in the making. He didn't know how they were going to keep everything separate. Her flour, his flour. Her butter, his butter.

He mentioned this.

"I hadn't thought about that," she murmured.

"Perhaps we could sell the cinnamon rolls as a Hard Luck Café specialty. You could bake while you're on duty here, and we'd divide the profits." As far as Ben could see, his idea was advantageous to them both.

Their eyes met and Mary smiled shyly. "That sounds good."

"Does that mean you agree?" he asked.

"Yes. Thank you, Ben," she said, and returned to her dough.

The woman might be skinny, but she knew how to cook. And bake. Furthermore, she seemed to know just how to bend his will to her own. And for the first time in his life, Ben didn't object to bending a little.

He'd stopped thinking of Mary as a nuisance. To his surprise, they worked well together. He no longer minded sharing his kitchen with another cook, and the fact that Mary was a woman hardly bothered him at all.

NOT ONCE in the week that followed did Duke say anything about returning to Hard Luck. Tracy didn't press him for fear he'd think she'd grown tired of his company. Nothing could be further from the truth. If anything, she'd come to rely on spending all her spare time with him.

He brought her the plans he'd had drawn up for his house, and together they'd gone over each detail. It astonished her that anyone would undertake such a project, but Duke seemed to know what he was doing. At any rate, he revealed no qualms. According to what he'd told her, he could have the project completed the next summer. True, he'd need help with certain aspects of the construction, but he'd already lined that up.

Tracy was working on a project of her own. She was teaching herself to cook. With the guidance of a basic cookbook, she practiced making a number of uncomplicated recipes. She didn't let Duke know what she was doing, hoping to surprise him in the near future.

Janice stopped off at Tracy's office just before five-thirty one day.

"You seeing your friend again this weekend?" she asked.

Tracy, fresh from the courthouse, was eager to escape. To her great relief, the trial had ended that afternoon; to her even greater relief, she'd won. Now she looked forward to seeing Duke with no distractions or obligations to worry about. Before his visit she'd always been one of the last to leave the building. Not anymore.

"Yes," she said, slipping some papers she needed to read into her briefcase. "We're driving to Leavenworth early Saturday morning and spending the day there." Tracy looked forward to the trip with childlike excitement.

"Are you getting serious about this guy?" Janice pressed.

"Yes," Tracy replied. She *was* serious, very serious. Neither one had discussed it, but Tracy knew Duke felt the same way about her.

He must.

Janice crossed her arms and leaned against the side of Tracy's desk. "Gavin asked about you the other day," she said casually.

Gavin seemed like a stranger. Tracy could hardly believe the two of them had once dated—or that she'd ever seen him as more than a friend.

Gavin took pride in being sensitive to a woman's needs; he always agreed with Tracy on social, political and sexual issues. He kept current on the latest trends and "correct" ideas. He never *argued* with her, never expressed an outrageous opinion. He was a good person, but compared to Duke, he was boring.

Duke wasn't insensitive, Tracy had discovered. The things he'd said and done in the past had been part of a game with him. He'd looked for ways to irritate her, enjoyed sparring with her, delighted in provoking her. Granted, he was a traditionalist and they'd never agree on everything. That, she figured, should keep life interesting for both of them. She understood now that she'd willingly participated in their volleys, that they were an effective way of dealing with her attraction to him. And vice versa, she strongly suspected.

"Tell Gavin I said hello the next time you see him," Tracy replied without giving the matter much thought.

"He asked me out," Janice announced. She seemed to be waiting for Tracy to object.

"I hope you accepted," she said, snapping her briefcase shut.

"I thought I should talk to you first," her friend said, sounding awkward and unsure. "I mean…I know you like Duke, but eventually he's going to leave, and then there'll be Gavin again." She flung a stray lock off her shoulder in a gesture that looked like a challenge.

"There'll be Gavin again," Tracy repeated.

"He's crazy about you."

"No, he isn't," Tracy said, almost laughing. "You just think he is. Listen, Janice, I haven't got time to talk now—I'm meeting Duke. If you want my permission to date Gavin, you've got it."

Janice didn't say anything for a moment. "You're sure?"

"Absolutely positive."

"What…what if things don't work out between you and Duke?"

"They will," she said with utmost confidence. Duke might not know it yet, but he'd find out soon enough. She reached for her briefcase and smiled. "As for Gavin—go get him, Jan. He's all yours."

Her friend returned a brilliant smile. "Thanks, Trace."

"No problem," she said on her way out the door. She should've recognized that Janice was interested in Gavin much sooner, and was sorry it had taken her so long. She had an excuse, though: love had blinded her.

THE FOLLOWING MORNING Duke and Tracy headed out of Seattle on their way to the German town of Leavenworth. Duke drove her car. Tracy had packed a picnic lunch full of goodies from the deli, and the day stretched before them like an unplanned adventure.

"You're going to love this," Tracy assured him. "The entire town celebrates Octoberfest."

"The only Leavenworth I've ever heard of is a prison," he mumbled, and took his eye off the road long enough to glance her way.

"This is no prison," Tracy said, then went on to describe the town with its elaborate old-European buildings. "It's like stepping into a fairy tale," she concluded.

Duke frowned. "A fairy tale. We're driving three hours for that?"

"A fairy tale with beer," she amended.

Duke grinned. "Now you're talkin'."

Tracy rested her head against his shoulder. "The most amazing thing happened to me last night," she said, remembering her short conversation with Janice.

"Oh?"

"My friend—a good friend, at that—asked me if I minded if she went out with Gavin."

"Mr. Sensitive?"

"Right."

"What did you tell her?"

Tracy thought she heard an edge in Duke's voice. Was he jealous? "There's no need to worry."

"I'm not worried," he insisted. But when she didn't continue the conversation, he prodded her. "Aren't you going to tell me your answer?"

"I thought you weren't worried."

"I'm not, but I'll admit to being mildly curious. After all, this is the very man you used to toss in my face as a paragon of virtue."

"Oh, hardly."

"You most certainly did," he said with ill-disguised impatience.

"As far as I'm concerned, Janice can do whatever she wants with Gavin."

Duke gave her a cocky smile. "That's what I thought you'd say."

"Oh, are we getting overconfident or what?" she teased.

"No," he answered simply. "I don't have any hold on you. You can see anyone you please. It just so happens that *I* please you."

At one time, not so distant, his words would have inflamed her. Now they amused her.

She was surprised when Duke grew quiet. She enjoyed the playful banter they often exchanged.

"Tracy," he said, his voice harsh with regret, "I have to get back to Hard Luck."

She opened her mouth to protest and knew it would do no good. He'd already stayed far longer than she'd had any right to hope.

"Trust me, sweetheart, I don't want to go, but I have to."

"When?" she asked, trying to hide her dread.

"Soon. In a couple of days."

"When will I see you again?"

He shook his head. "I don't know. I don't get down this way very often."

"I probably won't be able to fly up to Hard Luck until spring." And spring seemed a million years away. Tracy couldn't bear the thought of waiting until the ice broke on the rivers before she saw Duke again.

The silence between them grew oppressive. "There's one option," she said.

"You mean meeting halfway? I've thought about that and—"

"No." She cut him off, thinking fast. Her eyes rounded with excitement. "There's another way."

"I've thought about it over and over," Duke said, sounding discouraged, "and I can't come up with anything."

"But, Duke, did you ever consider the obvious?" She paused. "We could get married!"

Chapter

9

"MARRIED?" DUKE ALMOST drove off the road. He couldn't believe his ears. Married? Him? To Tracy? The woman needed her head examined.

First, he wasn't the marrying kind. Never had been, never would be. Second, Tracy? And *him?* A polished city woman and an outdoors guy? A sophisticated attorney and a down-and-dirty Alaskan bush pilot? Forget it!

"Well?" Tracy said excitedly, studying him. "What do you think?"

Duke opened his mouth, but no sound came out. Myriad objections tangled themselves on the end of his tongue. Then, because he couldn't formulate a clear response, he said tartly, "In case you need reminding, there are certain things the man does in a relationship, and proposing marriage is one of them."

"Fine. I'm listening." She laid her head on his shoulder, and the warm feelings he'd experienced every time they were together, every time they touched, continued. As soon as he saw the stars in her eyes, he should've realized what was going on in that brilliant mind of hers. He wanted to slap himself upside the head for even making this trip to Seattle. All he'd managed to do was set them up for trouble.

Marriage. That was how a woman's mind worked. Duke had assumed, had hoped, that a career-oriented woman like Tracy would be different. She wasn't.

"I'm waiting," she said, and smiled up at him, her eyes so bright they nearly blinded him.

Duke swallowed uncomfortably. "Sweetheart, you don't know what you're saying."

"I most certainly do," she insisted.

Duke knew he was walking onto a tightrope without a safety net, but he also knew he couldn't avoid the subject. "It's only natural that you should feel close to me, seeing what we've been through. But it's not enough to…" He let his words trail off. Yes, they shared a closeness that went beyond the usual male-female relationship. They'd faced death and had bonded in ways that took most folks years to achieve. And while it was true that he harbored few of the resentments he'd originally felt toward Tracy, he wasn't anywhere close to considering marriage.

"In other words, you don't feel anything special for me, even though—"

"I didn't say that," he interrupted.

"Then explain yourself, Duke Porter." She raised her head from his shoulder, and sat up straight as a pool cue, sliding closer to the passenger door.

"Let's discuss this later," he suggested, wanting to delay the argument until they'd both had time to give the subject some rational thought. But he knew that no matter how much thinking he did, he wasn't going to change his mind. Any kind of long-term arrangement between them was impossible. For many reasons.

"I'd prefer that we talk about it now," Tracy persisted.

He should've known she wasn't going to let it drop this easily. Figuring it would be impossible to talk about this *and* drive safely, he exited the freeway. He didn't know the name of this city, only that it was north of Seattle. He followed the signs to a city park.

Neither spoke until he pulled into the parking lot and turned off the engine. There were trees everywhere, their leaves brilliant shades of orange and red, but Duke barely noticed.

"All right," he said, and expelled his breath slowly, dreading what was sure to come. "Since you insist, let's air this here and now."

"You make it sound like we're about to put up our dukes and fight." She paused and smiled thinly. "No pun intended."

Grateful for her light remark, Duke grinned. Maybe they could both laugh off the marriage suggestion. It would save her pride and his freedom.

Sure he loved her; he was willing to admit that. He loved her as much as he did any woman, possibly more. All right, *definitely* more, but that still didn't mean he was ready to settle down for the rest of his life.

"Marriage? Can't you see that it'd be a disaster with us?"

"No," she answered fiercely.

"Sweetheart, think about it. You and me? We're different people."

"I should hope so."

This wasn't going well. Not well at all. Already he could feel the noose tightening around his neck, and he wasn't going to let that happen. He tried a different approach.

"We live in different worlds. I don't fit in yours, and you sure don't fit in mine."

"I love Hard Luck," she said, her tone heartfelt.

"Sure, it's a great town—I couldn't agree with you more. But your work is here and mine is there. I've enjoyed my time in Seattle, but if you didn't live here, I'd've left within a couple of days." He took a deep breath. "I don't deal well with this many people around me twenty-four hours a day. I need elbow room, and lots of it."

"I'm not asking you to move to Seattle," she said.

"You're not suggesting you move to Hard Luck, are you?" Try as he might, Duke couldn't picture Tracy living in the Arctic.

"That's exactly what I'm saying."

"Tracy," he said, laughing softly, "have you lost your mind?"

Her eyes held his for a long time. "No," she whispered. "I've lost my heart. I love you, Duke. I want to spend the rest of my life with you. I want to help you build that house you've planned, and then, God willing, I want us to fill those bedrooms with children. Our children."

Her words fell like a sword, cutting him to the bone. His mind immediately filled with the sound of children's laughter, and the allure was so strong he was forced to close his eyes and concentrate in order to banish it.

Home. Children. She sure was good, but then Duke knew that; after all, he'd seen her in action in a courtroom.

But it wouldn't work, not this time. If she didn't recognize that, then he did.

Duke had tried to be part of her world, and it had cost him five hundred dollars for a suit he'd probably never wear again. He'd been snubbed by an arrogant waiter because he preferred ranch dressing. He'd never paid more for a few leaves of lettuce, even in Alaska, than he had in that fancy restaurant. He'd done all that in an effort to impress Tracy, and the only thing he'd gained—he suspected it was a bargain—was the realization that he'd never be comfortable in the big city.

For her part, Tracy had tried to fit into his life, too. If he'd ever doubted she loved him, all he had to do was remember the dinner she'd slaved over on his behalf.

If he didn't love her as much as he did, he would've laughed himself silly that night. As it was, he'd been determined to chew every bite, smile and compliment her even if it killed him. And if the first taste was a sample of what was to follow, it just might have.

Tracy living in Hard Luck? As much as Duke enjoyed the notion, he was smart enough to realize it wouldn't work. Besides, there were other more obvious considerations.

"Your career is here in Seattle," he reminded her.

"I can get licensed to practice law in Alaska."

He didn't want to argue with her. It seemed pointless to tell her there wasn't enough work to keep even one attorney employed in Hard Luck. And any cases there were would be minor stuff—wills, maybe a few contracts—not the exciting criminal cases she'd trained for.

She might assume she loved him now, especially in light of what they'd been through together, but that attraction would soon wear off. Once she was subjected to everyday life during an Arctic winter, she'd grow bored and restless. The last thing he wanted was for Tracy to marry him and regret it later.

As gently as he could, Duke said, "It won't work. I wish I was different, but I'm not. I can't move to Seattle, and you'd never be happy in Hard Luck."

She opened her mouth to argue, but he stopped her. "Hear me out. If I was ever tempted to marry anyone, it would be you. But you're missing the entire point.

"I believe in family, but I like my life just the way it is. I'm free to go where I want, when I want, without the responsibility of a wife or kids. And frankly that's the way it's going to stay."

"I don't intend to lock you away in a closet for the rest of your life," she snapped.

Duke could see he was waging a battle of words with an expert. Tracy was capable of swaying a twelve-person jury with her arguments. He didn't stand a chance if he continued.

"Listen," he said, his voice gaining strength and conviction, "you took it upon yourself to ask, although I see that as the man's prerogative. Okay, then I suggest you be 'man' enough to accept my answer, and that answer is no. I don't *want* to be married, and I'm not going to let you persuade me otherwise. Understand?"

"Perfectly," she answered in a clipped voice.

Duke immediately regretted the harsh words. "I didn't mean to hurt you." He wanted to kick himself for flying to Seattle and giving in to the need to see Tracy. If anyone was to blame for this fiasco, he knew where to look.

The mirror.

LANNI O'HALLORAN was as nervous as she was excited. Charles was due home that afternoon after three weeks in the field.

She'd known long before they were married that, as a geologist, he was required to make these trips. The first few months of their marriage he'd managed to get home every few days.

Not this time. Charles had been gone a full twenty-one days, and it'd felt like that many years to Lanni.

In an effort to exhaust her emotional energy, she cleaned house and planned a gourmet dinner. But it wasn't food Charles would be thinking about when he walked in that door, and Lanni knew it.

A soft smile touched her lips.

So much had happened in the time he'd been away. She'd sold another article, this one to a glossy women's magazine. With extra hours on her hands, she'd dabbled in writing fiction. She wasn't sure how successful it was. But her sister-in-law Karen had read the short story and liked it.

There was far more important news than her most recent sale, though. News she couldn't wait to tell her husband.

Lanni glanced at the clock and sighed, wishing the hands would move faster.

Every time a car drove past the house she found herself racing to the front window, hoping it was Charles.

Her news wouldn't keep much longer. She felt it would burst forth the minute he walked in. It wasn't every day a wife could announce she was pregnant.

She'd kept the information to herself a full seven days now, and she was finding secrecy more and more difficult. But it didn't seem fair to share her excitement with her friends when her own husband didn't know.

Charles had wanted to wait until they were married for a year before she became pregnant, and Lanni had agreed. But eight months was *close* to a year.

Their original plan had sounded good—until Karen had come to Hard Luck, pregnant, and Lanni found herself longing for a baby, too.

Her brother, Matt, and Karen had been divorced at the time Karen discovered she was carrying Matt's baby. She'd served as Lanni's maid of honor at the wedding, and things had progressed from there. Really, everything had worked out beautifully. There was no telling how long it would've taken those two to come to their senses if not for the pregnancy.

Within a couple of months, Matt and Karen were back together and they'd remarried soon afterward.

No sooner had Lanni heard the happy news about Karen's baby than Charles's brother Sawyer informed them Abbey was pregnant.

Sawyer and Abbey were ecstatic. Sawyer was still walking two inches above the ground and had from the minute Abbey told him the news. The last Lanni had heard, Sawyer had purchased a case of cigars and was handing them out to his friends. Their daughter wasn't born yet!

Charles had been pleased for his brother and Abbey, but he'd still felt they should wait the full year.

Waiting wasn't Lanni's strong suit. She'd agreed to postpone the wedding for eight painful months while she finished her apprenticeship with the Anchorage paper. Charles didn't want her to regret their marriage and had insisted she complete the program. She'd done it, but had been miserable a lot of that time, missing him terribly.

The door swung open. Lanni couldn't believe she hadn't heard the truck. Charles stood just inside their living room, as compellingly virile and handsome as ever. No, more so.

"Charles!"

He dropped his backpack onto the carpet and held out his arms. Lanni didn't need any further encouragement. She ran across the room and hurled herself into them. Even after eight months of marriage, her heart felt as if it would explode with joy at the love she saw in his eyes.

Charles gathered her close. Before she could speak, his mouth met hers in a kiss potent enough to buckle her knees. He told her with that one kiss how lonely he'd been, how much he'd missed her, how glad he was to be home.

The kiss went on and on, and probably would've lasted even longer if Lanni hadn't been bursting with news.

She pulled her lips from his. "Charles, I've got wonderful news!"

"Later," he said, lifting her from the floor and bringing her mouth level with his. "What have you done to me, woman?" he whispered, kissing her repeatedly. "I've never missed anyone so much in my life."

"Good. Now you know how I've felt."

"I need a shower," he said, bringing his arms around her waist.

"Dinner's in the oven."

"It's not food that interests me," he said, and chuckled.

"I've been your wife long enough to know exactly where your interests lie, Charles O'Halloran." She braced her hands against his shoulders. "Now, look at me, because I've got something important to tell you."

"You made another sale?" he guessed.

"Yes, but that's not it." Tears of joy filled her eyes and she cupped his face with her hands. "I...we're going to have a baby."

Apparently her news shocked him, because his hold slackened and he released her. She slid down and landed with a thud on her own two feet. Dismay widened his eyes.

"I know you wanted to wait a year," she rushed to say, "but we've been married over eight months."

Charles walked to the ottoman and slumped onto it. "Pregnant?" Almost immediately he was back on his feet. "I need a drink." He walked into the kitchen and brought down a whiskey bottle from the cupboard above the stove.

Lanni followed him, nervously rubbing her palms. "I…I thought you'd be happy."

He looked at her as if he hadn't heard a word she'd said, then poured a liberal amount of the amber liquid into a glass. He tossed it back. "A baby?"

Lanni nodded. "Don't look so shocked. We've been playing Russian roulette with birth control for weeks. What did you expect would happen?"

"Who else knows about this?"

"No one yet. I wanted to tell you first. I thought you'd be happy," she said again.

He shook his head. "I am. It's just that…"

"Just what?" she challenged.

"A shock."

"Well, maybe you should receive another!" Whirling around, she grabbed her coat and rushed out of the house.

"Lanni!"

She heard him call her name, but ignored it and ran down the street. She'd only gone a short distance when Mariah, driving Christian's truck, pulled up alongside her. She rolled down the window on the driver's side.

"Lanni," she asked, "is everything all right? I thought Charles would be home by now."

"He is."

"What are you doing out in this cold with just a jacket?"

Lanni looked at her sister-in-law and burst into tears. Unable to speak, she wrapped her arms around herself and sobbed.

"You'd better come with me," Mariah said quietly. Leaning over, she opened the passenger door.

Lanni climbed into the truck just in time to avoid Charles, who'd come running after her. She heard his frantic cry, but ignored him.

"Lanni?" Mariah asked gently when she pulled up in front of the house she shared with Christian.

"How about a cup of tea?" Lanni asked, wiping the tears from her face.

"Tea?" Mariah glanced over her shoulder. "Sure. Come inside and you can tell me what's made you so unhappy."

"Unhappy? Me?" Lanni cried. "I couldn't be happier! Charles and I are going to have a baby." Then she started to weep all over again.

CHARLES FIGURED he'd give Lanni a half hour before he went after her. He'd seen her climb into Mariah's truck. Right this moment, she was probably telling Mariah and Christian what a jerk he was, and she'd be right.

A baby. Lanni pregnant. It still didn't seem real.

What Lanni had said about playing Russian roulette with birth control was true, but she'd never made a secret of the fact that she wanted a baby. Maybe he was being selfish, but Charles had wanted to keep Lanni to himself for a while longer.

He rubbed a hand across his eyes and thought about what he'd done. Lanni was hurt and confused. Hey, so was he.

Charles had never expected to fall in love. When he did, he fell for the granddaughter of the woman who'd spent a large part of her life working to destroy his family. He hadn't known that at first, though. When he *had* learned the truth about her, Charles had turned his back and walked away.

He'd soon learned that was a mistake. He loved her, and with his mother's help and Lanni's persistence, he was able to put aside his doubts. Lanni's love was the greatest gift of his life.

Once again, Charles thought in near-despair, he'd found a way to destroy what he wanted most. After an hour it was clear that Lanni wasn't coming back. He'd have to swallow his pride and go after her. But before he made another colossal mistake, he decided to do what he always did when he needed advice. He visited Ben Hamilton at the Hard Luck Café.

Ben was busy in the kitchen when Charles arrived.

"Long time, no see," Ben greeted him when Charles sat on a stool at the counter. It surprised him how busy the place was. In the past there'd been times Charles would stop in and be the only customer.

Today Ben actually had a waitress there, and furthermore, he needed her.

"What can I get you?"

"How about a psychiatrist?"

Ben laughed and automatically filled Charles's mug with coffee. "What happened?"

"Lanni's pregnant."

Ben eyed him speculatively. "That's great news, isn't it?"

Charles nodded without a lot of enthusiasm.

"You don't look too sure," Ben said, leaning against the counter.

"I don't know that I'm ready for a family. Darn it, Ben, I love my wife and I wanted her to myself for a few more months." He wasn't going to be the type of father Sawyer was, Charles realized. His brother had wanted to get Abbey pregnant from the moment he'd slipped a ring on her finger.

"Are you saying the baby's due this week?" Ben asked. "I know you're a real go-getter, but this kind of thing usually takes a few months, doesn't it?"

"Yes, but— Oh, I suppose you're right. Anyway, I didn't throw my arms into the air and leap for joy the way Lanni expected, and now she's spitting nails she's so mad at me."

"What are you going to do about it?" Ben asked.

Charles stared into his coffee. "The only thing I *can* do. Throw myself at her feet and beg forgiveness."

"I've noticed," Ben said thoughtfully, "that the longer you wait to apologize, the more difficult it becomes. After a while, the words tend to stick in your throat. Trust me, the sooner you do it, the better for both of you."

Charles agreed. He glanced at his watch and headed over to Christian's house. He parked out front and sat with his hands resting on the steering wheel while he rehearsed what he intended to say.

Ben was right. The sooner he apologized the better. With a certain reluctance, he climbed out of the truck and knocked on the door.

Christian answered, looking at Charles as if he should be arrested. "I wondered how long it'd take you to get here." His brother unlatched the screen door and held it open.

Charles stepped inside. "Where's Lanni?"

"In the kitchen with Mariah. What did you say to her?" Christian demanded.

Charles glared at him. "That's between Lanni and me."

"Fine," Christian muttered, "then you go take care of it. She hasn't stopped crying since she got here."

Charles took a deep calming breath and made his way into the kitchen. Lanni sat at the table with her back to him;

Mariah sat across from her. He saw a teapot and two cups on the blue checked tablecloth.

"I'd like a word with my wife," Charles said to his sister-in-law. "Alone." It seemed Mariah was going to ignore him, but apparently she changed her mind, because she slipped silently out of the kitchen.

"Lanni," Charles whispered. She didn't respond. He walked over to where Mariah had been sitting and stood behind the chair, hands in his pants pockets.

Lanni's tear-streaked face made him realize he loved her beyond life itself. He'd wanted everything to be perfect for her, for them. Yet he was the one responsible for her unhappiness. He felt a surge of remorse.

"We're going to have a baby," he said. Now that the information was beginning to sink in, he found he rather liked the idea. A baby. His and Lanni's.

"I know you're not happy about this and—"

"I *am* happy," he insisted, cutting her off. "It just took some getting used to. We're going to have a baby," he repeated. Yes. This was *good* news.

Lanni gnawed on her lower lip. "You aren't angry?"

"Angry?" She'd thought he was angry? He moved around the table and knelt down in front of her. "Never that, honey. Surprised, shocked, but never angry. This is our baby, yours and mine. I'm sorry I reacted the way I did. Can you forgive me?" The words came straight from his heart.

Lanni nodded. "Yes! I'm so happy I could burst."

"I'm happy, too, because you are. The idea of being a father frightens me a little, I admit." But then, it had taken him a long time to get comfortable with the idea of loving Lanni. He knew he was going to love this child beyond reason, the same way he did his wife.

"I love you, Charles," Lanni whispered, throwing her arms around his neck. She rested her head against his shoulder. He didn't deserve her love, but he'd always known that.

Charles breathed in her fresh scent and buried his face in her neck. Everything was going to work out just fine. Next spring he'd be a father.

He smiled.

DUKE PUSHED the food around his plate with his fork, his appetite almost nonexistent. He'd been back in Hard Luck for more than two weeks, but it seemed more like two years.

If he couldn't fly soon, he'd be worthless.

"More coffee?" The young waitress Ben had hired approached his table.

"No, thanks." Duke shoved his plate aside.

"What's the matter, don't you like my spaghetti anymore?" Ben asked. He pulled out a chair and sat down. Before, Duke had always welcomed Ben's company, but these days he preferred his own.

"Guess I don't have much of an appetite," Duke muttered.

"I hear you've bought some land off the O'Hallorans."

Duke nodded. "I plan to start building next spring."

Ben's eyes showed his approval. "A man should have a place of his own."

"It's time I moved out of the bunkhouse," Duke said without further comment. He'd meant to leave a couple of years ago, but there'd been no compelling reason. Besides, he got along well with the other pilots. Or used to. Right now he didn't think anyone would regret his leaving, not after the last six weeks. He hadn't been good company.

"Seems like a mighty big house for just you. How many bedrooms?"

"Four," Duke answered. Bedrooms. He remembered Tracy's comment about filling those rooms with children and the two of them building a life together. When she'd first mentioned marriage, his hackles had gone up and he'd thought she was crazy. Married? Him? No way.

"Four bedrooms," Ben echoed. "What're you gonna do— open a boardinghouse?"

"No," Duke replied, annoyed. He wasn't sure *what* madness had possessed him to want a four-bedroom house when all he needed was one bedroom, possibly two.

Ben chuckled. "You got the look, pal."

"The look?" Duke asked.

"Misery. I know all about that broken arm of yours, but it's not physical pain I'm talking about."

"Ben, I appreciate—"

"No, you don't," Ben interrupted. "You're mad at me for saying anything, and frankly I don't blame you. I've been watching you ever since you got back from Seattle."

"I don't want to talk about Seattle," Duke said tightly. That was the last thing he wanted to talk about—his time with Tracy. She haunted him, every minute of every hour, asleep or awake. It was even worse now than before he'd gone to see her.

"No," Ben agreed, "I don't suppose you do want me to mention your visit to Seattle."

"Furthermore, I'm not the marrying kind."

"That's what Sawyer said, remember? Charles, too, if you recall."

"Well, sure," Duke said, "but they didn't fall in love with successful big-city attorneys. It isn't going to work between Tracy and me, and the sooner everyone accepts that, the better."

He knew he sounded angry—but he was. It might seem straightforward enough from the outside looking in, but Duke had seen Tracy in her element, and it was a lot more impressive than anything he could offer her in Hard Luck.

"You sure about that?"

"Of course I am," Duke said. He shoved back his chair and stood. "Listen, Ben, I appreciate what you're trying to do, but this time it won't work. Besides, if you're such an expert on romance, you should keep track of what's happening in your own backyard."

Ben frowned. "What do you mean?"

Duke picked up his tab. "Anyone with eyes in his head can see what's going on with you and Mary McMurphy."

Ben's jaw sagged open so far it nearly hit the countertop. "You're out of your mind."

Duke chuckled. "If you say so."

"Me and Mary McMurphy?" Ben managed a laugh, but it sounded false. "I'm not in love with her."

"If you say so," Duke repeated, walking toward the cashier and paying his bill.

"I don't want you spreading rumors, you hear me?" Ben warned. "The last thing I want is someone embarrassing Mary with that kind of talk."

"My lips are sealed, Ben. But I have to tell you, I don't think this is much of a secret. The entire town's talking about you two, and everyone's happy for you."

"Mary McMurphy?" the cook scoffed loudly, causing

several patrons to turn and stare at him. "There's nothing between her and me!"

At that moment Mary stepped out from the kitchen. Her gaze met Ben's, and even Duke could read the fury and betrayal in her eyes. Then she whirled around and returned to the kitchen. Ben swallowed uncomfortably as he glanced longingly in her direction. "A woman like Mary McMurphy is better off without the likes of me," he muttered.

All love did, Duke decided as he walked out the door, was make people miserable. He wanted nothing more to do with it.

Chapter
10

MARY TOLD HERSELF she was nothing but an old fool. Certainly she'd never intended to fall in love with Ben Hamilton. That old sea dog wouldn't know love if it smacked him right between the eyes.

Which it had.

Ben had all but shouted his lack of feelings for her to the entire restaurant, humiliating her. Well, at least now she knew exactly where she stood with the man.

Everything they'd shared these past weeks meant nothing. It had seemed to her that they'd come far, but apparently not. She slammed the oven door shut, angry with herself for losing control of her heart when she was old enough to know better.

In the beginning Ben had resented her. He'd made it quite clear that he didn't want her anywhere near his precious kitchen. Gradually his attitude had improved, but it had taken weeks to gain his trust and admiration.

At first, aware of how he felt about her, Mary had tiptoed

around his ego, being careful not to take matters into her own capable hands. She knew a thing or two, seeing that she'd been in the restaurant business for well over twenty years. But each and every step of the way, she'd gone to him, seeking his counsel and approval before making changes.

After a while Ben had come to value her suggestions. Her idea of serving prime rib on Friday nights had been a huge success. He'd allowed her to test a few of her other ideas, too. Even though he didn't feel the café had enough business to justify hiring two part-time waitresses, he'd agreed to give it a try. Business had increased dramatically, and he'd soon recognized the wisdom of adding staff.

It wasn't that Ben didn't appreciate her. Mary knew otherwise. His voice was often gruff, but he had a kind and generous heart. It was when she realized this that she'd gradually lowered her guard. That, unfortunately, had been a mistake, because she'd gone and done something foolish. She'd fallen in love with Ben Hamilton.

She'd been a widow for nearly fifteen years now. She was content with her life, but she would've welcomed a companion. A partner.

Her children were grown and didn't need her, so she'd hoped to relax. Maybe travel some. Fanciful dreams, she mused sadly. That was all they were. Dreams.

"Mary."

She continued washing the last of the pots and pans. Forcing a smile to her lips, she turned to greet Ben as if nothing was amiss.

"Maybe you and I should sit down and talk," he said hoarsely.

You didn't spend this much time with a person and not know him, and Mary sensed Ben's reluctance.

"I can't this evening," she returned stiffly. "Perhaps another night."

His shoulders sagged with relief. "Good. I mean, that's okay. Whenever you've got a free moment."

Mary resumed her task, scrubbing the pots with enough force to rub holes right through them. Her elbow made jerky movements as she expended her anger. And angry she was. Not at Ben. She knew he was uncomfortable with emotion, particularly if it related directly to him. No, she was angry at herself.

Ben cleared his throat and addressed her back. "I did think," he said, "that it was time we discussed giving you a raise."

"I haven't been with you very long," she said dismissively, not bothering to turn around.

"I know that," he snapped, then gentled his voice. "But you've made some good suggestions. Business is better than it's ever been. Your prime-rib special on Friday nights was a lot more successful than my frequent-eater program."

She rolled her eyes. Frequent eaters! My heavens, what had the man been thinking?

"I believe a ten-percent increase would be fitting."

Mary was well aware that the raise had been prompted by nothing more than good old-fashioned guilt. He was sorry for embarrassing her.

"Thanks for the offer," she told him firmly, her back still to him, "but no, thanks."

"You're turning down a raise?" Ben sounded incredulous.

"Yes." Mary was sure he'd never heard of such a thing, and in fact, she'd never refused a raise before. But she did now with good reason.

"Why in tarnation would anyone turn down a raise?" Ben demanded.

Mary pulled the plug in the sink, and the water gurgled down the pipe. Peeling the rubber gloves from her hands, she turned to face him, but kept her gaze lowered.

"Is there anything wrong with my money?" he asked in the same impatient tone he'd used earlier.

"No, except when you're using it as a substitute for an apology."

"What do I have to apologize for?" he asked, his voice rising. "You try to do something nice for someone, and what do you get?"

"Now listen here, Ben Hamilton, it's a free country, and I can choose what I will and won't accept as a wage," she said, squaring her shoulders and boldly meeting his look. His face was flushed, and she was sure that losing his temper couldn't be good for his heart condition.

Ben ripped the apron from his waist and flung it aside. "What do you want from me?"

His question took her by surprise. "What makes you think I want anything?"

"Because that's how women are."

"Really, Ben," she said dryly. "And since when did you become such an expert on women?"

He took a deep breath, which he slowly released, his cheeks billowing out. "I suppose you're going to hand in your notice now."

She'd considered it, but had quickly changed her mind. She'd come to enjoy life in Hard Luck, to love the town and its people. Weeknights were spent at the Caldwells' lodge, and she'd formed friendships with several of the older women in town. "I see no reason to quit—unless you don't want me around anymore."

"I do," Ben admitted gruffly. "Want you around, that is."

The tension left Mary's shoulders and she smiled softly. "Thank you for that."

Ben shifted his weight from foot to foot. "I'd miss you if you decided to move on," he said, his gaze holding hers. "I never thought I'd say that, but it's the truth."

"I'd…miss working with you, too."

The expression in his eyes grew warm. "I've never been married."

"I know." She'd asked Bethany about his marital status the first week she'd come to work with him.

"I, uh, never gave the matter of marriage much thought," he went on, his gaze skirting hers. "Women these days want to be romanced. Hell, I'm too old and fat for that sort of thing. And if the truth be told, I don't know a thing about love."

"You most certainly are not old and fat," Mary said heatedly. "You're a fine-looking man. And you say you don't know about love, but that's simply untrue. You're a generous, giving human being. Why, this entire community loves you!" She paused. "Your café's the heart of the town. When folks have a problem, you're the person they seek out for advice."

"Maybe," he agreed reluctantly, "but no woman would ever love a man like me."

"Nonsense." Mary felt like stamping her foot. "That's the most ridiculous thing I've ever heard you say."

Ben studied her, his eyes intense. "What about someone like you, Mary? Could you…love me? Would you be willing to marry me?"

"Of course I would! But marriage is more than romance— it's a partnership. It's working together, sharing each other's joys and sorrows. It's building dreams and—" She stopped abruptly when she realized what he'd asked. "What did you say just now?" Her heart felt light with wonder.

Ben drew in a deep breath. "I asked if you'd marry a man like me."

"Is that a proposal, Ben Hamilton?"

He frowned and said nothing.

"You asked if I'd marry a man like you, right?" she prompted irritably.

He still looked stunned. "Did I?"

"Don't worry, Ben, I didn't take you seriously."

"But what you said, about marriage being a partnership, that's true, isn't it?"

"Of course."

"And you said you *would* marry me." He grinned now, obviously taking to the idea.

"I did?"

"I heard you with my own ears." His smile faded, and he cleared his throat. "Would you be my wife, Mary McMurphy? My partner not only here at the café but in life?"

Mary felt tears crowd her eyes. She didn't need to think about her response; she already knew. She nodded. "Yes. Oh, yes, Ben."

His face broke into a big smile, and he held his arms open wide for her. Mary felt young all over again as she walked into his embrace. Ben tightened his arms around her and sighed deeply. To Mary, it was the most romantic sound she'd ever heard.

TRACY GAVE DUKE two weeks. She figured that within that time, he'd come to his senses and realize they were meant to be together. She marked Halloween on her calendar and waited impatiently to hear from him. But she hadn't.

The man's pride was a formidable thing, she thought as she unlocked her front door and stepped inside. Now it was Halloween night, and the only visitors she could expect were trick-or-treaters. In the morning she'd decide what to do next.

She glanced through her mail and tossed the junk and the bills on her desktop. Mariah had written her a long newsy letter earlier in the week, which Tracy had read a dozen times or more. Duke's cast was off and the people of Hard Luck had breathed a collective sigh of relief. Everyone hoped his bad mood would end soon. Once Duke was able to fly again, his friends all said, his spirits would improve. Mariah said she doubted it, knowing the source of his discontent.

Mariah also wrote that Duke had never mentioned Tracy or talked about his time in Seattle—but that didn't mean he wasn't thinking about her. Tracy would've been shocked if he *had* said anything. That wasn't Duke's way.

He hadn't forgotten her. She'd wager she was on his mind every minute of every day, just like he was on hers. How long he'd cling to his stubborn pride she could only speculate.

The doorbell chimed. Kids already? She picked up the candy bowl and answered.

Two goblins smiled up at her and screeched, "Trick or treat!"

"And who might this be?" Tracy asked, squatting down and letting the youngsters paw through the bowl filled with boxed raisins and granola bars.

"Thanks, Tracy," her neighbor Marilyn Gardener said as she steered her two daughters down the hallway.

Tracy closed the door and set the bowl on a nearby table. Walking to her fridge, she removed the casserole she'd assembled that morning and put it in the oven. When Duke did come back, she had a real surprise for him. She could cook. Not just one or two recipes, either, but a whole repertoire. Her mother would be proud of her; Sharon Santiago had raised five daughters, and each had become an accomplished cook—with one exception. Tracy grinned to herself. What could she say? She was a late bloomer—and everything seemed to hit her at once. Until she'd fallen in love with Duke, she'd avoided thinking about marriage and children. She'd been perfectly content to play the role of indulgent aunt.

Duke. Tracy had a great deal to thank him for. Mostly he'd awakened her to life. Her views had been so narrow, her focus solely on her career. Then she and Duke had crashed, and all the things she'd pushed into the background had suddenly sprung free.

Duke. She'd been so confident he'd return....

Why she'd chosen Halloween as her day of reckoning she couldn't explain. Two weeks was an optimistic estimate, she supposed. It was just that she missed him so much and she'd been positive he missed her, too.

Apparently not.

Struggling against a bout of melancholy, Tracy changed out of her business suit and into jeans and a sweater.

The doorbell chimed, and once more Tracy picked up the bowl and opened the door. More neighbor children, looking for a handout.

No sooner had she closed the door than the bell chimed again. This time, however, it was Duke. "Trick or treat," he said, grinning sheepishly.

All she could do was stare at him.

"Raisins? Granola? Sweetheart, you're going to disappoint

those poor kids. They want candy and chocolates, the gooier the better."

Happiness bubbled up inside her. "Oh, Duke!" If he didn't reach for her soon, she was throwing caution to the winds and leaping into his arms.

Without waiting for her invitation, he stepped into her living room and closed the door. The teasing light faded from his deep gray eyes as he studied her.

"Sit," he ordered, and Tracy was in no state to argue. She sank onto the sofa, clasping her hands together in her lap. Once she was seated, Duke began to pace in front of her.

"From the moment we met," he said, "you seemed to be of the opinion that you can do anything a man can do."

"Well, for the most part I can," she returned evenly.

"As you've taken great delight in proving to me," he muttered. "Well, surprise, surprise, Ms. Attorney, there are certain matters best left in the hands of a man."

"If you've come all this way to argue with me, then—"

"I didn't."

She stood. "I think—"

"Please listen," Duke barked.

Because she was so shocked, she sat back down, snapped her mouth shut and did as he asked.

"When it comes to a marriage proposal, you need to learn that a man prefers to do the asking."

Tracy almost swallowed her tongue. "A…marriage proposal?"

"You heard me."

"If you're upset about me bringing up the subject first, then you should know I just got tired of waiting. I love you, Duke, and you love me."

"You're doing it again."

She pressed her fingers to her lips. "Sorry."

He continued pacing.

"Well?" she prompted when he didn't immediately speak.

"I'm thinking."

"That's the problem," she insisted, scrambling onto her knees on the sofa. "You think too much." If he didn't stand still long enough to kiss her, she was going to do it herself.

"What makes you think you'll be happy in Hard Luck?" he demanded.

"You're there," she answered simply.

He didn't allow her response to sway him. "What about your career?"

"Yes, well, that's a concern, but I've thought it through. I'll set up my own practice. True, there probably won't be enough clients to keep me busy full-time in the beginning, but—"

"At least you're willing to admit it. How do you propose to fill your time? I know you, Tracy, and you won't be content sitting on your duff."

"Actually, not having a full-time practice suits my purposes perfectly."

His eyes narrowed. "How's that?"

"I want children, and I believe we should start on the project right away."

Duke's gaze seemed riveted to hers. "Now, just one minute…" He rubbed the back of his neck as he took in her words. "You really know how to throw a man off center, I'll say that. I haven't so much as proposed, and you're already talking children."

"I want a big family. I have four sisters, you know."

"Would you kindly stop jumping the gun?"

"I'd like three, possibly four of my own and—"

"Four kids, in this day and age?" he said, aghast. "You're not thinking clearly. Couples can't afford to clothe and educate that many children."

"We'll do fine." The man was nothing if not obstinate.

"I haven't agreed to anything yet."

She pretended not to hear him. "I feel it's important that we be young enough to enjoy them."

"Tracy," he said, obviously exasperated.

"Am I answering your questions?"

"You make our marriage sound like a foregone conclusion."

"You mean it isn't?" She batted her eyelashes, teasing him. She'd never be a pliant woman who would bend easily to his will—but for the sake of his ego she supposed she could bend every now and then.

"No way!"

She sighed impatiently. "I'm going to tell our children this, you know."

"Tell them what?"

"That I was the one who proposed."

"The heck you will!"

Tracy nearly laughed out loud. Instead, she held out her arms. "Just how long is it going to take you to kiss me?"

"In a minute," he said, "but first I have to figure out how I'm going to do this."

"Do what?"

He walked over to the sofa and got down on one knee.

Her eyes widened with surprise. Duke was going to propose on bended knee. *Duke?* But then, he'd always been a traditionalist, so it made sense that he'd do this the old-fashioned way.

"Promise me you won't say a word until I've finished," he said.

"I promise," she said breathlessly. Duke was actually going to propose. At last. She pressed her lips together hard to show him her sincerity.

"I didn't want to fall in love with you, and God knows it wasn't what I planned. You're gutsy, stubborn, insolent, hardheaded— and special." His voice lowered to a whisper. "So very special."

She blinked back sudden tears.

"In addition to all of that, you seem to think you love me."

She nodded vigorously. The need to talk was so strong she had to bite her lip.

"I don't know *why* you love me, but frankly I've given up trying to figure it out. I'm crazy about you. Yes, I love you. There, I've said it."

She rewarded him by kissing her fingertips and touching them to his lips.

"I don't understand why you'd sacrifice all this for life in Hard Luck, but you seem to have it squared away."

Once more she nodded.

"Three kids, possibly four," he groaned. "Knowing you, you'll probably talk me into ten."

She held up four fingers.

He closed his eyes, shaking his head. "I'm not agreeing to any more than two for now." He paused and grinned. "That's advice a good attorney would give."

She smiled and shrugged. Not speaking was difficult, but she'd promised.

"So you think we should get married."

She held her breath.

"I'm beginning to believe you're right."

Tracy couldn't help it—she threw her arms around his neck and cried joyfully, "Oh, Duke, what took you so long?"

A grimace of doubt tightened his face. "I'm not good enough for you—"

"Don't you dare say that," she interrupted. "You're the best thing that's ever happened to me, Duke Porter, and don't you forget it."

"Me?"

"Without you, I'd have spent the rest of my days defending my rights as a woman, pushing love out the door, arguing until I had no voice left while I stood on my soapbox. Without you, life would've passed me by. I would've missed so many pleasures. I would've been so lonely." She paused, her eyes solemn. "I've learned that I can have my principles and love, too. I need you, Duke."

He blinked, as if he wasn't sure he should believe her. They faced each other. His love in all its depth shone in his eyes, and it was a reflection of what she felt for him.

"We're going to fight like crazy," he whispered.

"And make love like crazy."

A smile edged up one side of his mouth. "I love you, Tracy." His arms circled her waist. He kissed her eyes and nose and cheeks and chin, unable to get enough of her. Her senses reeled; her heart raced.

It'd been so long since he'd last held her. She loved the way his eyes darkened before he kissed her. The way his hands moved gently over her body, and the sound of his voice when he whispered her name.

They were going to be very happy—of that Tracy had no doubt. She'd found her man, and he'd found her. A man to love for the rest of her life.

Epilogue

SCOTT O'HALLORAN sat in front of the fireplace at the Caldwells' lodge. Dinner was over and the adults had gathered in the front room, planning a reception for Duke and Tracy. The other kids were watching a video upstairs; Scott, however, had declined the opportunity to see *Snow White*. He'd decided to stay down here with his dog instead. Eagle Catcher rested peacefully on the braided rug next to him, snoring softly as Scott stroked his fur. With a quiet moment to himself, Scott was considering the changes that had come to Hard Luck since his own arrival a couple of years ago.

"I still can't believe it," he told the husky. "Duke married Tracy." He shook his head, feeling wiser than his years. People tended to see him as "just a kid"—and he couldn't very well deny it—but he was smarter than some folks seemed to think.

For instance, Scott knew long before his mother and Sawyer did that they were in love. Sawyer had insisted the other bush pilots leave Abbey alone—and then found all kinds of excuses to spend time with her himself. But he'd almost blown it with that flippant marriage proposal. If it hadn't been for Susan and him running away with Eagle Catcher, Scott didn't know *what* would have happened. He didn't like to think about it.

His mom had married Sawyer, and now there was little Anna. When they'd learned Anna was a girl, Scott had been sorely disappointed. He'd wanted a little brother real bad, but now that she was born and everything, he was glad to have another sister. Not that he'd let Susan know. Susan was a pest. But Anna was all soft and sweet, and when he held her he felt happy and proud. Scott hoped for a brother someday, but if that didn't happen, he'd accept another sister.

After his mother and Sawyer got married, it hadn't taken him long to figure out how things were between Charles and Lanni. The day he and Susan had gone looking for wildflowers with Lanni and encountered the bear proved exactly how much Charles liked Lanni.

Charles had been so relieved when he found them that he'd kissed Lanni right then and there. Scott never did understand why they waited so long to decide to get married. Lanni had to move away, and then Charles moped around Hard Luck for weeks until he finally saw the light.

Scott had felt downright sorry for Charles. He'd wanted to say something, but he'd overheard his parents talking, and they seemed to think it was best to let Charles and Lanni sort out their differences themselves. They must've been right, because a little while after that, Scott learned Charles and Lanni were getting married the following spring.

Eagle Catcher stretched out his legs and yawned loudly. Scott felt tired, too, but he kind of liked sitting here by the fireplace while the adults talked in the other room. Duke and

Tracy's wedding had taken place in Seattle two weeks earlier, and they were due back in Hard Luck the day after tomorrow, so folks wanted to give them a special welcome.

He had to admit those two had taken him by surprise. But Mitch and Bethany hadn't. Scott smiled to himself. He'd seen the look that came into the teacher's eyes whenever Mitch stopped by the schoolhouse. It was the same look he'd seen in his mother's eyes after Sawyer kissed her the first time.

Susan and Chrissie, Mitch's daughter, had played match-maker—and it had worked, not that Scott approved of their methods. To his way of thinking, Mitch had married Bethany *despite* Susan and Chrissie's schemes. They all seemed happy, though. He'd heard that Bethany's baby was due a couple of months before Lanni's. At this rate, the Hard Luck school was going to need more than two teachers.

Matt and Karen's little boy was born a week before Anna. Clay Caldwell. His daddy was crazy about him. So was his mother.

Scott felt a little smug about Matt and Karen. He took full credit for those two patching up their relationship. He figured it was his advice that had helped Matt win Karen back.

Not only that, he'd helped Christian and Mariah. He remembered the evening he'd come across Christian sitting on his front porch, looking downright miserable—like he'd lost his wallet or something. The "something" turned out to be his secretary. Scott liked to think he'd helped his uncle that night, but at the time he wasn't sure Christian had heard a word he'd said. Now Christian and Mariah were married, too, and he suspected it wouldn't be long before they started having children.

Then there were the surprises. First Ben Hamilton and Mrs. McMurphy. Scott hadn't known people that old could

fall in love. Ben's behavior—the way he watched Mrs.
McMurphy and the way he snapped at everyone—had made
Scott suspicious. He'd talked it over with Eagle Catcher and
even his canine friend was skeptical, but Scott knew what he'd
seen. Sure enough, a month later, he heard that Ben and Mary
McMurphy were getting hitched.

By this time, Scott had been to more weddings than some
ministers. He'd wondered what kind of bride Mrs. McMurphy
would make, seeing that she was practically as old as his grandmother. What had surprised him was how pretty she looked.
Not pretty like his mother or Lanni or Mariah, but different.

Ben, too, although the cook would probably be offended if
Scott called him pretty. Ben was a cool guy. Since marrying Mrs.
McMurphy he was even more fun. He actually let Eagle
Catcher into the café now and then, and his cooking was better
than ever.

The other surprise came when Scott learned that Duke was
marrying Tracy. He'd been worried when their plane went
down in a storm. Not just worried about their injuries, but
about the two of them killing each other. Boy, had he been
wrong. Next thing he knew, Duke was in Seattle visiting
Tracy. Now they were married, and Tracy was going to open
up a law office in Hard Luck.

Lots of other people were starting new businesses. Last he
heard, Pete Livengood was planning to put in a hardware
place. There was even talk about a video store—a whole
store—not just a few shelves at the back of Pete's grocery.
That'd be great. A friend of Karen's from California was
moving north to set up a beauty shop, but this would be a place
where both men and women got their hair cut. Scott preferred
the video store. Oh, and Lanni was starting a newspaper—

maybe she'd let him have his own advice column. "Ask Scott," he'd call it. He grinned to himself.

Yup, Hard Luck had changed since the day he'd arrived. It wasn't just a town fifty miles north of the Arctic Circle anymore. Hard Luck was home.

MIDNIGHT SONS AND DAUGHTERS

Chapter
1

The Present

THE FIRST THING Chrissie Harris intended to do when she saw Scott O'Halloran was slap his face—hard. She might even have the opportunity today, she thought, reluctant to get out of bed on this clear August morning. The man had broken her heart, not once but twice—and she'd *let* him!

The first time she'd been sixteen, and she'd stood at the Midnight Sons airstrip one frigid winter morning and watched him fly out of Hard Luck, Alaska. Unable to get along with his mother and stepfather, Scott had enlisted in the army. Chrissie had thought her whole world would cave in without Scott. She'd been crazy about him from the time she was in grade school, when his mother had moved to Hard Luck with him and his sister and married Sawyer O'Halloran. In third grade Chrissie had decided that as soon as they were grown-ups, she'd marry Scott; she'd been so sure he loved her, too—a belief she'd maintained for the next decade.

She'd been wrong.

A year out of high school he'd clashed with his father and promptly volunteered three years of his life to Uncle Sam. Chrissie had moped around for weeks, missing him dreadfully but pretending otherwise. In retrospect she realized she hadn't fooled anyone. Least of all Susan, her best friend and Scott's sister.

Every afternoon Chrissie had beaten a path to the post office, eager for a letter. Every night she'd poured out her heart to him in long missives. In the beginning Scott did write. Boot camp was hell, he'd told her. Following graduation he'd volunteered for Airborne Ranger School in Fort Benning, Georgia. Eventually his letters became less and less frequent. Finally they stopped altogether.

What hurt most was that Scott had asked his *sister* to break the news. As gently as possible, Susan let Chrissie know that Scott had met someone else.

That was the first time he'd broken her heart.

The next time happened the year Chrissie and Susan graduated from college. The two families had thrown a huge celebration party in Hard Luck, which half the town attended. Who should unexpectedly show up but Scott O'Halloran? He'd occasionally come home during the intervening years, but Chrissie had always avoided him. After the heartless way he'd dumped her, it was what he deserved. But at twenty-one she was older, more mature. Smart, too. She hadn't graduated magna cum laude for nothing.

But Chrissie wasn't nearly as savvy as she'd assumed. It took Scott less than a week to maneuver himself back into her life.

He told her how much he'd missed her, how he regretted the way he'd treated her. He'd gone on to claim that every woman he'd met since paled compared to her. Blah, blah, blah.

Chrissie had swallowed his lies, every one of them. She was so in love with him her brain had virtually ceased to function. Then Farrah Warner had arrived and declared herself Scott's fiancée. Scott had tried to explain, to apologize, but Chrissie had refused to listen. Before another day passed, Scott and Farrah had flown out of Hard Luck, leaving everyone, including his own family, upset and confused.

Chrissie vowed that was the second and *last* time he'd ever break her heart.

Recently she'd heard that Scott was returning to Hard Luck permanently as a partner in Midnight Sons, the bush plane service owned by his father and his uncle Christian. Chrissie swore she wouldn't allow Scott O'Halloran anywhere near her. She would *not* give him the opportunity to break her heart a third time.

That determined, she rolled over and turned off her clock radio before the alarm could buzz. Sitting up, she rubbed the sleep—what little she'd managed to catch—from her eyes. She'd spent most of the night reviewing her history with Scott, going over and over his betrayals, hardening her resolve. At twenty-five, she wasn't a schoolgirl anymore. The law degree hanging in the office she shared with Tracy Santiago Porter said as much.

When the phone pealed at five minutes after seven, it jolted Chrissie so badly she nearly fell off the bed.

"Yes," she snapped.

"Scott's flight is due in at ten," Susan cheerfully informed her. Despite everything, her best friend continued to believe that Scott and Chrissie were meant to be together. As far as Chrissie was concerned, it wouldn't happen in this or any other lifetime.

"Oh, Scott's coming home?" Chrissie asked, hoping she sounded bored and uninterested. "Is that today?"

"You know it is."

"Yes," Chrissie said, faking a yawn. "I suppose I did."

"This time it's for good. My brother's here to stay."

"Really?" Chrissie feigned a second yawn as if she couldn't care less. She cared, all right, but only because she wanted to tell him he was lower than a tundra rat—and then follow that with a resounding slap to his face.

"Mom and Dad are thrilled."

Chrissie tensed, struggling to hide her reaction.

"He's going to be flying for Midnight Sons. Mom and Dad have been wanting this for years. With Anna and Ryan older now, Dad's hoping to cut back his hours and… Oh, Chrissie, this is what we've *all* wanted!"

Chrissie knew that, but she wasn't sure Hard Luck was big enough for both of them. Fine, she could deal with Scott living in Hard Luck. It wasn't as though her world revolved around him. Not anymore. Whether he stayed or moved on didn't make one iota of difference to Chrissie.

She could certainly be civil if she ran into him, although that wasn't likely to happen often. Hard Luck wasn't as small a town as it had once been. Back in the nineties, the population was around fifty—mostly cantankerous men in need of women. The O'Halloran brothers hadn't been able to hold on to their staff of professional pilots and were losing them at an alarming rate to other commuter-airline companies in Fairbanks and Anchorage. Something had to be done, and quickly.

The best way to keep their pilots, the brothers had decided, was to lure women north.

Their plan had worked, too. Surprisingly well. Abbey, Scott and Susan's mother, was the first woman to arrive, and a number of others had come soon afterward. In the years since, Hard Luck had expanded, and its population had reached a robust three hundred and counting. More families moved in every year.

Susan's husband, Ron Gold, and his partner, Matt Caldwell, did a booming winter tourist business, which involved dog-sledding, camping and more. Midnight Sons flew in the adventure-seeking sightseers. But that was only part of their business; they also functioned as a commuter airline and courier company. Actually, they had a corner on the market, because the only way to get to Hard Luck was by plane.

It wouldn't be long now before the next group of visitors showed up. The last days of summer lingered on, but in early September the weather would start to turn chilly; snow would come by October—and with it, the winter tourists.

"Chrissie! Have you heard *anything* I said?"

"Sorry," Chrissie muttered. "I kind of drifted off."

"I want you to be pleased Scott's moving home," Susan insisted. "You two make such a perfect couple."

Chrissie snickered. She couldn't help it. She and Scott? Not anymore. She didn't trust him, couldn't make her heart vulnerable to him again. The first two times had hurt too much. No, she was a sensible attorney now, a woman who wouldn't be swayed by a glib tongue and a pair of baby blues, even if they did belong to the one and only man she'd ever truly loved.

"Scott could move next door and it wouldn't make any difference to me," Chrissie said in as matter-of-fact a tone as she could muster.

"You sure about that?"

"Positive." Leave it to Susan and her romantic inclinations. But then, Chrissie supposed Susan was entitled to feel optimistic on that score; the year she graduated from college, she'd married the boy she'd loved half her life. "Listen, I've still got to shower," Chrissie said. Knowing Susan wouldn't be satisfied until she had her way, she added, "When you see Scott, tell him hello for me." As soon as the words left her lips, she realized her mistake. Scott might consider that an invitation to look her up, and there was nothing she wanted less. Quickly she said, "No, don't. In fact, I'd rather you didn't mention my name at all."

"You know Scott's going to ask about you."

"Well, if he does, tell him I'm totally content without him in my life."

Susan laughed outright. "That sounds like a crock to me."

"Well, it isn't," Chrissie said, praying she wasn't giving herself away. Hiding her true feelings from her best friend was something she found difficult. But the truth was, she fully intended to keep her distance from Scott.

Resolved to push all thoughts of him from her mind, Chrissie got into the office early. She refused to look at her clock, refused to remember that at ten that very morning, Scott O'Halloran was flying back into Hard Luck—and into her well-ordered life.

At eleven-thirty, just as she was about to break for lunch, Kate, the secretary she shared with Tracy, called her. "Scott O'Halloran is here to see you. Shall I send him in?"

Already? Chrissie's heart began to race, pounding so hard she had to catch her breath. Scott was here? *Now?*

"Ms. Harris?"

Forcing her heart to slow down, Chrissie took a deep breath. "Send him in," she said.

Half a minute later Scott strolled into her small office. He hadn't changed. He was still better-looking than any man had a right to be. He'd always had a real presence—a confident quality and a sense of life that invariably attracted people. Especially women. Chrissie made herself stand and meet him eye to eye. For one wild moment all she could do was stare. Furious at her reaction, she lowered her hands to her desk for support.

"Hello, Scott," she managed to say, proud of revealing no emotion. To all appearances, he might have been a stranger.

"Chrissie." He sent her a smile bright enough to rival the summer sun.

She inhaled and held her breath. With hardly any effort, he was tearing down her defenses. And, no doubt, he knew exactly the effect he had on her, hide it though she might.

"You're looking good," he murmured with a nod of approval.

"Yes, I know," she said in blithe tones, wanting him to realize she wouldn't be won over by a bit of flattery and some practiced charm. Not this time. He could fall at her feet and beg her forgiveness, and she'd look down at him and feel nothing but contempt.

"Do you have a few minutes?" he asked.

"Actually I don't." How *dared* he assume he could saunter into her office and pretend nothing had happened? He had nerve, she'd say that for him. Well, so did she. "Perhaps it'd be best if we cleared the air now," she said aggressively.

"Cleared the air?"

"If you think you can walk back into my life again, you're

wrong. I'm older now. Wiser, too. You made a fool of me twice. There isn't going to be a third time."

Scott's lips quivered with a smile.

"You find this amusing?"

"If you'd give me a chance to explain…" he began.

She laughed lightly, breezily, as if to suggest she had no interest in anything he had to say. "Explain *what?* You're the one who claimed to be in love with me—and all the while you were engaged to another woman! Frankly, I'm not interested in hearing any explanations." With great aplomb, she walked around her desk to her chair. Sitting down, her back very straight, she reached for her pen and glanced casually upward. "I think you should leave now."

"Well, the truth is, Chrissie, I didn't stop by to rehash old times. I was planning to hire you to draw up some legal papers, since I'm becoming a full partner in Midnight Sons."

"Oh." Mortified beyond words, Chrissie wanted to crawl under her desk.

"But that's okay. I'll make an appointment with Tracy."

"Ah…" she blubbered, then nodded, implying she thought this was probably the best idea.

"Good to see you again," he said on his way out the door, closing it behind him.

Chrissie dropped her forehead to her desk. What was it about Scott O'Halloran that turned her into a complete idiot every time she saw him?

Chapter 2

ABBEY O'HALLORAN was ecstatic. As she shelved books at the Hard Luck library, she reflected on the reason for her happiness. She'd been waiting a long time for this day. Her son was home. Years ago, divorced and raising two children alone, she'd moved to Hard Luck and, after a whirlwind courtship, had married Sawyer O'Halloran. They had a good marriage and had added Ryan and Anna, now seventeen and nineteen respectively, to their family. Sawyer had adopted Scott and Susan, and loved and nurtured her children as his own. Scott, however, had gone through a difficult period of teenage rebellion that had left Abbey and Sawyer at a loss.

It'd all started his last year of high school, when he had a couple of minor run-ins with Mitch Harris, the sheriff and Chrissie's father. Mitch assured Sawyer and Abbey that Scott wasn't a bad boy and the pranks he'd pulled were typical of many teenagers. Skipping school and painting graffiti on the community-center wall were small infractions, ones Abbey had been willing to overlook. What she couldn't excuse was Scott's lack of respect for Sawyer. Her husband had been nothing but warm and loving to both Scott and Susan. Scott, though, had become an increasingly angry young man, and he'd vented that anger against Sawyer. Abbey had never understood why her son seemed so resentful, why he'd felt such rage. His unpleasant behavior had escalated during his high-school years and later, too, when Scott had briefly worked for Midnight Sons. Although Sawyer had never complained, Abbey knew he'd been deeply hurt by the things Scott had said and done.

Then one day, without a word to anyone, Scott had enlisted in the army. Not that Abbey or Sawyer would have objected. By this point it was obvious that Scott had problems he needed to resolve. As his mother, she'd longed to help him deal with his past, yearned to answer his doubts, but she couldn't help what she didn't understand. Watching Scott fly out of Hard Luck for boot camp was, without question, one of the most difficult moments she'd ever experienced.

She'd known someday he'd return. She just hadn't known when that day would come. And now…it finally had.

The library door opened and Sawyer walked in. Even after all these years of marriage, she felt a rush of joy at the sight of him. His hair had started to gray and the laugh lines around his eyes were more pronounced, but he was as handsome and vital as when they'd first met.

"What are you doing here?" she asked, surprised to see him.

"Hey, I've got a library card."

His eyes held a warm teasing light and she smiled in response. She loved this man and had borne him two children. They'd made a good life together in Hard Luck and looked forward to when they could officially retire and travel, the way they'd planned. As Sawyer often reminded her, there was an entire world for them to explore. But no matter where they went, Alaska would always be home.

"I thought you were with Scott." She placed the latest Janet Evanovich mystery back on the shelf, then turned and kissed her husband.

"Hey, what's that for?"

"I'm just so happy I can barely hold it inside. Scott's home! And this time it's for good."

Sawyer grinned with equal delight. "He's grown up, Abbey."

"I know."

"The years away have had a positive effect. He's lost all that anger. He's made peace with himself and he's ready to step into the business." Sawyer moved toward her desk and perched on the corner. "Did you hear he's found a place to rent?"

"Already?" Abbey couldn't help being disappointed. She'd hoped to fuss over her son for the first couple of weeks.

"He wants to make his own way, and I can't say I blame him," Sawyer said in Scott's defense. "Matt and Karen are renting him one of the cabins they renovated this summer." Their good friends, the Caldwells, owned and operated Hard Luck Lodge; they'd always been fond of Scott. Their primary business was providing accommodation for the tourists who flew in with Arctic Experiences, the tour company run by Matt and their son-in-law, Ron Gold.

Now that Abbey thought about it, one of those cabins was ideal. There was also a touch of irony attached to it. She'd come here in response to an advertisement offering jobs to women willing to move to Hard Luck, fifty miles north of the

Arctic Circle. Hoping to attract qualified applicants, Midnight Sons had included a cabin and twenty acres of land. What the brothers hadn't bothered to disclose was that the cabins were dilapidated one-room shacks, desperately in need of repair. If *that* wasn't insult enough, the twenty acres they'd so generously thrown in were nowhere near Hard Luck or the cabins. For the most part they were only accessible by air.

"Matt's done a good job with those cabins," Sawyer remarked.

Abbey agreed. The original shacks were torn down years ago and larger, better-equipped cabins had been built. The Caldwells had begun an extensive process of renovation and Scott would be renting one of the newly upgraded cabins.

"Scott's had a busy afternoon," Sawyer continued. "He was in to see Tracy about having the papers drawn up."

"Not Chrissie?" Abbey asked.

Sawyer shook his head. "Apparently not. My guess is, he knows he's got some fences to mend."

Abbey nodded slowly. As Scott's mother she could think of no better wife for her son than Chrissie Harris. Although Scott had never discussed his feelings for Chrissie, Abbey knew he'd loved her as a teenager, and she strongly suspected he loved her still.

That morning when he'd arrived, Abbey noticed the way Scott's gaze had moved over the crowd gathered to greet him. He'd been searching for Chrissie; she was sure of it. And practically the first stop he'd made in town was the attorneys' office. Yes, there were some legal papers to be drawn up, but there certainly wasn't any rush.

"Abbey?"

She glanced up to find her husband watching her.

"You've got that look in your eye."

Abbey played dumb. "What look?"

"The one that tells me you're up to no good."

She frowned with indignation. "You haven't got a clue what I'm thinking, Sawyer O'Halloran."

"That's where you're wrong," her husband challenged, leaving her desk to sink into an overstuffed chair. Abbey sat on the chair arm beside him. "I do know what you're thinking," he told her. "You're thinking about Scott and Chrissie."

Abbey considered arguing with him, but he was right and he knew it. "Don't you remember how badly Scott wanted us to get married?" she asked, the years rolling away with the memory. Sawyer had originally proposed for what Abbey believed to be all the wrong reasons. It'd nearly broken her heart to turn him down, but with one failed marriage behind her, she couldn't afford to make a second mistake. She'd already fallen in love with him, but his proposal had been motivated more by his fear that someone else might ask her first. Or so it had seemed to her. Loving him the way she did, afraid he didn't really love her, she'd felt the only sensible option was to protect her family—and her emotions. She'd decided to leave Hard Luck. Then Scott and Susan had disappeared. Abbey had never known such panic as she'd felt that night.

Her husband reached for her hand, gently squeezing her fingers. "If not for Scott and Susan running away, I might have lost you. I was crazy about you then and I'm even crazier about you now."

Abbey pressed her head to his shoulder, savoring the feel of his arms around her.

"Only, back then I didn't know how to tell you," Sawyer said, the frustration and anguish of that night evident even after all these years. "I didn't know how to persuade you to stay."

Abbey kept her head against her husband's shoulder. "Now Scott needs our help," she whispered.

"With Chrissie?"

Abbey nodded. "I'm afraid he's more like you than you realize. He loves Chrissie, but he's not sure what to do."

"Are you suggesting I give him advice?" Sawyer asked, looking aghast at the prospect.

Abbey giggled. "Hardly. The situation calls for diplomacy."

Her husband's frown cut deep grooves in his forehead. "Like what?" he asked warily. "And please note that I'm ignoring the slur on my diplomatic abilities."

Abbey smiled. "Let's hold a welcome-home party for him. Next Friday—a week from tonight. We have a lot to celebrate, don't you think?"

"We do indeed." Sawyer's face relaxed. "And there's a certain someone you're going to invite, isn't there?"

"Shh." Abbey brought her index finger to her lips. "I don't want to be obvious about it."

"Right," Sawyer said, sounding amused. "We wouldn't want to be obvious."

"We'll make it a surprise party."

"A surprise party?" Sawyer echoed. "But who do you intend to surprise? Scott or Chrissie?"

IT WAS ALMOST FOUR-THIRTY when Scott walked into the Hard Luck Café—too early for the dinner crowd. The restaurant hadn't changed much over the years, and neither had Ben. To Scott's eyes, Ben Hamilton had aged barely a year in the past ten. He was in his sixties now, his hair a little thinner on top but his welcoming smile as warm as always.

"Scott!" Ben greeted him with unconcealed delight. "Hey, boy, you're a sight for sore eyes."

The two men exchanged hearty handshakes and then impulsively hugged.

"So you're moving back to Hard Luck?" Ben asked.

"I am," Scott confirmed, and slid onto a stool at the counter. He picked up a menu, although he wasn't planning to order a meal. The menu was a lot more professional-looking than it used to be with its smudged type and cracked plastic coating. But fancy menus or not, the Hard Luck Café had been his favorite restaurant for years, and in his time away he hadn't found any he liked better.

"We got salmon on special. Mary poaches it in a lemon sauce that's out of this world." Ben kissed his fingertips extravagantly as he spoke.

In the old days, Ben had served everything loaded down with fat and extra calories. No more; his wife, Mary, had seen to that. Healthy food choices had started appearing on the menu when Ben married her, although the changes had been surprisingly subtle.

"Salmon sounds good, but Mom's cooking me a feast." He closed the menu and tucked it behind the sugar canister. Ben automatically poured him a mug of coffee.

"So I hear you're going to be flying with your dad and Christian."

"I am." His hands cupped the mug. Scott had earned his pilot's license when he was sixteen. Whereas most teens hungered for their driver's license, Scott had been far more interested in learning to fly. After his stint in the army, he'd worked for a flight service out of Utah, flying tourists over the Canyonlands. He'd been content, enjoying his freedom and earning decent money. He'd had friends, lots of them, and a number of women he saw on a regular basis—but these relationships were all casual, without depth or commitment. He'd also been engaged once, but that had turned into a spectacular mess, and he hadn't repeated the experience. Then, a month ago, he'd suddenly realized he'd been running away from what he wanted most, and that was his home and family. He missed Alaska, regretted the anger of his youth and the pain he'd brought his parents. It was time to make amends.

And then there was Chrissie.

He smiled thinking about their encounter that morning. When he announced that he'd merely come for legal advice, she'd looked like she wanted to crawl into a hole. He'd managed not to laugh then but couldn't restrain his amusement now. He chuckled, replaying the scene in his mind.

"Did I miss something funny?" Ben asked, sidling up to the counter and leaning against it just as he had for so many years.

"Not really," Scott told him. "Just something that happened this morning, soon after I got here."

"Oh."

Scott had stopped by Chrissie's office on business, but he was willing to admit there was more to it than that. He'd wanted to see her and, in fact, had been anticipating their meeting for weeks.

Chrissie was one of the reasons he'd stayed away from Hard Luck and one of the reasons he'd come home.

"Seems just like the old days seeing you again," Ben said.

"The old days," Scott repeated. Back then, the Hard Luck Café had been the gathering place for the entire community.

The men, in particular, used to meet at Ben's. Not only that, many people in the community, if not most, had come to Ben at one time or another to talk through their problems. Scott suspected they continued to do so.

"Remember that frequent-eater program?" Scott asked.

"Yeah," Ben answered with a grin. It was a short-lived program. "Don't need gimmicks like that," he said. "I got more business than I know what to do with."

Scott nodded; he wasn't surprised that Ben's remained popular. He knew that in the last ten years a couple of other restaurants had opened, but the Hard Luck Café was—and deserved to be—everyone's favorite. Ben was officially retired; however, he couldn't quite keep his hands out of the business.

"I remember you as a youngster, sitting on one of those stools," Ben said with genuine fondness. "Only seems right to see you here now."

"It used to be I could talk to you about anything," Scott recalled.

"Still can, if you've got a hankering," Ben assured him.

Scott was tempted. Many a time he'd discussed his problems with Ben Hamilton. Many a time he'd felt as if the world was against him. Few people knew that Ben was the one who'd suggested Scott consider enlisting in the military. A former navy man, he'd been disappointed when Scott chose the army. But not as disappointed as Sawyer that he hadn't decided on the air force.

Back then, Scott had been downright contrary. Angry, too, only he didn't know why or at what. Eventually he'd recognized that it wasn't Sawyer he hated. Scott knew he'd been old enough at the time of his parents' separation to be aware of his biological father's rejection and to be seriously hurt by it, to wonder if he was somehow to blame. The teen years had become increasingly difficult, especially when he'd secretly contacted his father at fifteen—and been rejected a second time. Then Eagle Catcher, his husky, had died. The grief he'd felt over the loss of his dog had deepened his anger. Hardly understanding himself, he'd lashed out at those he loved most. The things he'd said and done embarrassed him now.

"Anything you want to discuss?" Ben asked, sounding eager. "It stays right here. Nothing you tell me goes any further."

Scott hesitated, then decided to ask about Chrissie. Really, there wasn't anyone else he *could* ask. Not Susan, who was guaranteed to run to her friend and repeat every word. Not the other pilots, either, or his uncles or aunts. No one in his extended family, that was for sure.

"Is Chrissie seeing anyone special?" he blurted out before he could stop to ponder the wisdom of showing his hand like this.

"Chrissie Harris?" Ben asked as if there were two Chrissies in Hard Luck. He averted his gaze. "As a matter of fact, she is."

"I see." So Chrissie *was* involved. It made sense that she would be. Ridiculous though it was, considering their history, he'd hoped she'd be as interested in renewing their relationship as he was.

"I've never met him, mind you," Ben was saying.

"He's in Fairbanks?"

"So I understand."

"You hear anything else?"

"Some." Ben was less forthcoming than usual.

Scott waited patiently.

"I don't know who he is. I'm probably speaking out of turn by telling you anything."

"I'd like to know," Scott said. "I *need* to know," he thought to himself.

"She visits Joel every second weekend. That's all I know—Joel, Fairbanks, twice a month. Okay?"

"Does Joel have a last name?" Not that it mattered, but Scott was curious.

"Must have, but no one's ever told me."

There'd been a Joel Higgins a year behind him in school—a good athlete, well liked and well adjusted. Needless to say, Scott hadn't cared for him and dismissed him as a male Goody Two-Shoes.

"Every other Saturday morning, Chrissie flies into Fairbanks and doesn't return until Sunday afternoon. Generally she comes in here for a bite to eat before heading home. Once in a while she mentions Joel, but she's pretty closemouthed about him. Let me add one more thing, though," he said, and paused, frowning heavily. "By the time she steps off that plane, she's really dragging."

Scott didn't need Ben to say another word; he got the picture. Chrissie spent weekends with Joel and arrived back in Hard Luck exhausted. He didn't need to guess the reason, either. No wonder his sister hadn't mentioned Chrissie's involvement with someone else.

Sure as anything she knew, but she hadn't so much as dropped a hint—because his finding out would ruin everything. Susan, the hopeless romantic, refused to let go of the idea that Scott and Chrissie belonged together.

"Ask her," Ben advised.

"Ask *Chrissie*? You have to be kidding!"

"Why not?" Ben demanded. "Nothing works better than the direct approach. According to Mary, that's what women want these days. None of this second-guessing stuff. That went out with the seventies. If nothing else, Chrissie will respect you for being forthright enough to ask."

"I'll think about it," he said reluctantly.

Scott finished his coffee, but when he went to pay, Ben told him it was on the house. His old friend's generosity hadn't changed. In addition to a good cup of coffee, he'd given Scott something to think about.

THE NEXT FEW DAYS passed quickly. School had begun again on Tuesday. Wednesday afternoon Scott had an appointment at the law office. He was in the waiting room when Chrissie walked into the reception area. She halted midstep the instant she saw him.

"Hello, Scott," she said, her voice cool and even.

"Chrissie." He nodded. Then, feeling the need to explain the purpose of his visit, he added, "I have an appointment with Tracy."

"Yes, I know." She held a folder in both hands and wore a slightly puzzled expression, as if she'd forgotten why she'd come out of her office. "I, uh, gather everything's going very well for you at Midnight Sons."

"I'm enjoying myself."

"Everyone's pleased to have you home."

"Everyone?" he asked, wondering if she included herself.

"Your family, certainly." This came after a slight hesitation.

"I had coffee at Ben's the other day," he said casually, hoping to ease into a more comfortable conversation. "I swear he hasn't changed at all."

"He's wonderful. So is Mary."

A short silence followed, which Chrissie broke. "I understand Matt and Karen rented you one of the renovated cabins."

So she'd been checking up on him. That was encouraging. Maybe, just maybe, she still cared. That thought gave him the courage to ask her out. "I was thinking you and I might have a drink one afternoon," he suggested.

Her eyes widened and her hands tightened on the folder.

"A drink," she repeated slowly. "At Ben's?"

He nodded. "Or dinner, if you prefer."

She squared her shoulders and chewed her lower lip before answering. "I don't think so."

He shrugged, as if her refusal was of little consequence to him. "That's too bad. I had a few things I wanted to discuss with you."

Chrissie's expressive eyes had always told him what was on her mind before she uttered a word.

"You had something you wanted to talk to me about?" she finally said.

"Yeah."

She worried her lower lip further. "Maybe…" She hesitated, then seemed to regain her resolve. "I don't think so, Scott," she said again. "Thanks, anyway." She turned away to enter her office.

"How long do you intend to avoid me?" he called after her.

At his question, she turned back. "Avoid you? Don't flatter yourself. What I *intend* to do is live my life just the way I am now."

"You obviously have every intention of avoiding me."

"I have *every intention* of not seeking you out. That's not the same thing."

"I see."

"Apparently you don't," she returned in her best lawyer voice. "You're out of my life, Scott. That was your choice, not mine."

"People change, Chrissie. They——"

"Oh, no, you don't," she interrupted, waving her finger at him. "You're not going to do this to me. Not again."

"I asked you out for a drink. I wasn't proposing we move in together."

"Oh, sure, a drink—for old times' sake."

"No," he corrected. "A drink to clear the air. I deserve that much, don't I?"

Her eyes flared with outrage. "What you deserve, Scott O'Halloran, is a slap across the face." She raised her chin so high she threatened to put her neck out of joint. "All right," she said abruptly. "Fine. As a matter of fairness I'll have a drink with you."

Scott felt a surge of hope. "When?"

"Friday night at the party."

Scott frowned. "What party?"

"The party your parents are——" She bit off the rest of the sentence.

"Chrissie?"

Squeezing her eyes shut, she slowly exhaled. "Oh, darn, it's supposed to be a surprise."

Chapter 3

THURSDAY MORNING Karen Caldwell poured her husband a second cup of coffee, then joined him in the massive kitchen at the Hard Luck Lodge. Working as a team, they'd built the lodge into one of the most popular tourist destinations in the state. It'd taken fifteen years of blood, sweat and tears. They were equal partners, Karen and Matt, not only in business, but in life.

During those years they'd also had three children and managed to create a warm nurturing home for their family.

Clay, their eldest, had been the best surprise of their lives, conceived while they were divorced and living apart. The pregnancy was what had brought them back to their senses. Clay was in high school now. The girls, Jill and Emily, were nine and eleven respectively.

Clay was a lot like Karen—steady and capable. Jill and Emily were more like Matt—creative but a bit unfocused. The focus part would come in time, the way it had with their father, Karen believed.

"What are you thinking about?" Matt asked when Karen sat down across from him at the table. In a flurry of activity and near-panic, the girls had flown out the door for school. After the long summer break they were having trouble resuming the discipline of waking up early. Only a few minutes ago, Jill had been searching for her misplaced backpack. While her sister dashed frantically about, Emily had slapped together lunch for both of them. Now, with the girls gone, blessed silence enveloped the kitchen.

"It's not what, it's who," she told him. "I'm thinking about Scott."

"It's good to see him again, isn't it?"

Karen knew Matt was pleased about renting out one of the cabins on a long-term basis, especially to Scott, whom they both liked. "He's still hung up on Chrissie, isn't he?" Karen asked, knowing her husband had talked to Scott a number of times.

Matt shrugged, and Karen rolled her eyes. In her opinion, most men were hopeless when it came to romance; Matt was no exception. And Scott—well, as a kid he'd had delusions of romantic expertise.

"Don't you remember what Scott told us just before Clay was born?" she asked her husband.

Matt chuckled. "That was a lot of years ago."

Karen's memory was good, and this particular incident had stayed with her. She smiled, recalling the day the young boy had stood resolutely before her. "He said he was responsible for bringing the two of us back together. In fact, he felt we owed our reconciliation to him."

Matt burst out laughing. "Scott's the one who said I should take you camping."

"In order to wine and dine me, right?" Karen muttered. Scott's idea of creating a romantic mood was that Matt should drag her and all the necessary and assorted gear to his favorite fishing place. Apparently Scott believed that sleeping on the ground, battling off mosquito attacks, plus catching, cleaning and cooking all their meals would rekindle their love. All this when Karen was several months pregnant with Clay. What a disaster *that* had been.

For one thing, fishing had never been her forte, and Matt had been furious when she'd nearly lost his favorite rod and pole. Then she'd fallen in the river and gotten drenched from head to toe. Matt had managed to catch fish after fish, and all she'd caught was a miserable cold, as if pregnancy hadn't made her uncomfortable enough. By the time she returned to Hard Luck, it was a miracle they were even speaking to each other.

"Scott used to see himself as quite the matchmaker, didn't he?"

They exchanged smiles across the table, smiles that quickly turned into laughter as the memories continued to surface.

"You know what I think?" Karen said, reaching for her coffee. She held the mug in front of her lips as she mulled over her idea. "Turnabout is fair play."

Matt stared at her. "Oh, I don't know about that.... Anyway, this is none of our business. They—"

Karen went on as though he hadn't spoken. "We could arrange for Scott to take Chrissie someplace he once considered wildly romantic...like, I don't know, the garbage dump? Didn't he suggest we go out there and watch the bears?"

Matt chuckled. "*Scott* will think that's fun, but I'm not so sure about Chrissie."

"True," Karen agreed. "Hmm. All we need to do is figure how to get the two of them alone. Given a little time, I bet they'd work everything out."

"At the garbage dump?"

Karen rolled her eyes again. "Someplace else. *You* come up with a spot. You're the creative one in the family."

"Karen, be sensible. First of all, you don't have any real evidence that Chrissie still feels the same way about Scott."

"She does," Karen said. "I'm positive."

"Okay, so they went together for a while, but that was ages ago."

"Chrissie's loved Scott from the time she was a kid."

Matt seemed to require a moment to think about that. "All right, Chrissie loves Scott. But how will Mitch feel about all this? I didn't get the impression he's too thrilled to have Scott back in town."

Her husband had a point. Mitch Harris was Chrissie's father and represented the law in Hard Luck. Scott wasn't a bad kid, but he and Mitch had clashed a number of times when Scott was in his teens. Not that the boy's misdemeanors were anything new in Hard Luck; other teens were guilty of similar behavior. The difference was Chrissie's relationship with him. Father and daughter had argued over Scott more than once. Mitch had refused to make allowances for his daughter's boy- friend, regardless of her desperate pleas. Karen knew Mitch had breathed a sigh of relief when Scott left Hard Luck, despite Chrissie's broken heart.

"Mitch never disliked Scott," Matt said. "If anything, he was doing him a favor by making him accountable for his actions."

"I know, but…"

Studying her, Matt set his mug aside. "What's gotten into you? I've never known you to meddle in anyone's love life before. Why now?"

Karen sighed and realized her husband was right; this wasn't her usual style. Still, what had happened between Scott and Chrissie bothered her for some reason, bothered her a lot, and she felt a mother's urge to fix things. Maybe she was being fanciful, but Karen saw in Chrissie the same kind of pain she herself had once felt.

"If Scott and Chrissie are meant to be together," Matt said, relaxing in his chair, "then it'll happen without any interference from us."

"Don't be so sure," she murmured.

"Karen!"

"I can't help myself," she protested. "I've seen the look on Chrissie's face when anyone mentions Scott's name. And the same is true of Scott. I know what it's like to love someone so much that the hurt only seems to get worse. When we got divorced, it just about killed me."

"Me, too," Matt said quietly, his gaze sobering.

"We were both stubborn and afraid and in pain." Those weren't times Karen ever wanted to relive. Pregnant and alone in California, afraid to tell Matt about the baby, afraid not to.

"And both of us in love."

"Not that it helped us communicate any better." They'd been defensive and bitter. In those days it'd been impossible to talk without their discussions erupting into arguments.

Matt reached across the table and squeezed her hand. "The part about me loving you hasn't changed. All these years together proves it."

On rare occasions, her husband could actually be romantic. And it was more meaningful because Karen knew it was genuine and heart-deep, never a mere gesture.

"So you want to help Scott get back together with Chrissie?" he asked, sounding resigned.

"If we can," she said. "But we can't tell anyone." Whatever they did would have to be on the sly. Maybe a private conversation between Matt and Scott? Or a little confidential "girls' talk"? They'd have to figure out the best approach.

"It'll be our secret," Matt agreed.

They emptied their leftover coffee in the sink and then, with a quick kiss, went about their busy days.

CHRISSIE ARRIVED at Scott's "surprise party" early Friday evening. His mother opened the door, and Chrissie instantly lowered her gaze, feeling dreadful that she'd been the one to spoil the surprise. Immediately following her second run-in with Scott, Chrissie had called Abbey and confessed her faux pas. As always, Abbey had been gracious and forgiven her mistake.

"Chrissie, would you stop?" Abbey said now, leading her into the large family home. "A surprise party was a ridiculous idea, anyway. I'm glad Scott knows, because it took away the pressure. Come inside and make yourself comfortable."

Chrissie didn't think that was possible. If not for Susan, she'd have found a convenient excuse to miss this event. Susan, however, wouldn't have let her live it down.

Neither would Scott.

She'd say one thing about Scott O'Halloran—he was determined. That morning, when she got to work, she'd found a lovely bouquet of roses. Not just any roses, but red ones—a dozen perfectly formed buds. The card had read simply *Scott*.

Chrissie suspected he'd purchased them in Fairbanks the day before. Not that she was about to let a few beautiful roses sway her decision—although they must have cost a fortune.

It would take more than flowers. A lot more! As soon as

the thought went through her mind, Chrissie tensed. No. She refused to even *consider* any kind of reconciliation. She refused to give Scott the power—or the opportunity—to hurt her again. He wasn't going to find himself back in her good graces. No way! She'd be civil, but that was it. He was part of her past, not her future.

With a quick detour to exchange hugs with Christian and Mariah O'Halloran, Chrissie headed straight for Susan, who was in the kitchen fussing with a variety of hors d'oeuvres. She slid them, hot from the oven, onto large ceramic platters. "Chrissie!" she cried when she saw her. "I *knew* you'd come."

Grumbling, Chrissie reached for a green olive and munched on that, rather than argue. There was no point in explaining that she was here only under protest.

"Have you seen Scott?" Susan asked.

"No." As much as possible, Chrissie planned to spend the night avoiding him—which was exactly what he'd accused her of. Too bad, she told herself firmly. She had no choice. Anyway, his opinion of her behavior was irrelevant.

"He is the guest of honor, you know."

Chrissie sent her friend a dirty look and Susan laughed good-naturedly. Susan was pregnant and although the apron barely fit around her extended belly, she looked beautiful and healthy—and very happy. Ron was in the family room, chatting with friends. Chrissie caught a glimpse of him as he glanced at his wife. A pang of envy shot through her at the love, the adoration, she saw in his eyes.

"Let me take those mushrooms out for you," Chrissie said, and Susan handed her the oven mitts. Keeping busy was the key, she decided. Standing around making idle chatter, wondering where Scott was—and how to stay out of his vicinity—

would quickly drive her insane. She had to ignore the fact that he was somewhere in this crowded room…and probably watching her.

Picking up the large platter required two hands. A moment later, she was walking into the family room, balancing it carefully, when without warning Scott appeared directly in front of her.

Chrissie couldn't think of a thing to say. Not a single thing. She stood there, doing an excellent imitation of an ice sculpture—cold and unmoving.

"Did you like the roses?" he asked.

"They were very nice." She kept her voice expressionless.

"Thoughtful, too, don't you agree?" He turned toward his sister and winked.

Obviously the flowers had been Susan's idea. Chrissie should've known her friend had put him up to this.

She purposely hardened her heart and stared at him, her composure intact. "I'm afraid you wasted your money." Then she sidestepped him and marched into the other room, her tray of mushrooms aloft.

This wasn't the first time Scott had sought her out at a party; the last occasion had been after her college graduation. He'd pulled her aside and told her a batch of lies about how much he'd missed her and wanted her back in his life. She'd been so crazy in love with him she'd believed every word. The memory chilled her blood. She'd been gullible and naive, but she wasn't anymore.

The O'Halloran home was crowded, and Chrissie wove her way in and out, smiling, chatting, offering hors d'oeuvres to the guests while Abbey welcomed late arrivals. These included Chrissie's dad, Mitch Harris, and her stepmother, Bethany. She paused, still holding her tray, and kissed both of them in greeting. She and Bethany chatted for a few minutes as Mitch moved toward Sawyer, then Chrissie resumed her duties. It might've been her imagination, but she sensed that everyone was watching her. She had the definite suspicion that all the interest she was generating had nothing to do with crab-stuffed mushroom caps.

She was about to return to the kitchen when Scott sneaked up behind her. "We were going to have a talk, remember?"

"No, I don't remember! I didn't agree to that," she informed him stiffly. "As far as I'm concerned, there's nothing to discuss."

"I want to clear the air," Scott persisted.

"The air's as clear as it's going to get." She edged away.

Scott followed. "Not from where I'm standing."

He was making this awfully hard. Chrissie could feel herself weakening; she couldn't allow that to happen.

"Could I have everyone's attention?" Sawyer called as he stepped into the center of the room. He held a bottle of champagne in one hand and a flute glass in the other. Abbey, Mariah and several other people appeared with champagne bottles and trays of glasses, pouring drinks for all the guests.

"We'll continue this discussion later," Scott said in a low voice.

"I told you before—there's nothing to discuss," Chrissie insisted, her voice carrying farther than she would've liked. A number of people turned to look in their direction.

"Our son is home to stay," Abbey said, tears of happiness brightening her eyes.

Sawyer slipped his arm around Abbey's waist. "And he's now a full partner in Midnight Sons." He raised his champagne glass. "I'd like to propose a toast. To Scott. Welcome home, son."

"Hear, hear!" Matt Caldwell yelled, and his words echoed around the room as glasses were lifted in Scott's honor.

"Speech, speech," Ryan, Scott's half brother, shouted.

Scott groaned, but his objections were quickly overruled when his family and friends took up the cry. He moved closer to his parents and grabbed Ryan by the shoulders, squeezing hard. "Thanks a lot, little brother," he muttered.

Everyone laughed. Scott looked a bit uncomfortable and obviously needed a moment to gather his thoughts. "I'd like to thank everyone for this wonderful *surprise* party," he began.

The entire room erupted into laughter, and several people grinned at Chrissie. If it hadn't been in poor taste, she would have walked out right then and there. Scott had knowingly set out to embarrass her. She fumed and said nothing, refusing to acknowledge his statement.

"If I've learned anything from the last few years, it's that we all make mistakes, say and do things we later regret. I've certainly committed my share of those, and will probably be guilty of more during the course of my life."

"As will we all," Mitch Harris inserted. Bethany stood beside him, smiling; she sought out her stepdaughter, who tried to look away.

From across the room her father's eyes connected with Chrissie's, too, as though to remind her that he'd long ago forgiven Scott—and so should she. Chrissie broke eye contact.

"As most of you know," Scott continued, "I had something of a…rebellious youth."

Mitch Harris saluted the comment with a raised champagne glass, and a few guests chuckled.

"I said and did things that caused grief for those I love. I know I've hurt my family, but despite everything, they never lost faith in me."

"Not once," Sawyer said in agreement.

"My family and friends have put up with a lot," Scott added, and glanced toward Chrissie. Almost immediately he turned back to his parents. "It's good to be home, Mom and Dad."

A chorus of "Welcome Home" followed from everyone in the room, and again, the family and friends of Scott O'Halloran toasted his return.

There was a surge of chatter then, and Chrissie went to the kitchen to assemble another platter of hors d'oeuvres. Susan came in shortly afterward and stared at Chrissie, obviously waiting for her to say something.

"What?" she snapped, glaring at her friend.

"Scott was talking to *you* just now."

"I know. He was talking to you, too. He was talking to everybody."

"Doesn't that mean anything? What he said about past mistakes and regrets and all?"

Chrissie was saved from having to answer when Abbey walked in. Grateful for the escape, Chrissie edged her way out of the kitchen. Her relief was short-lived, however. No sooner had she entered the family room than Scott joined her.

"We were having a discussion…"

"Yes," she said with an exasperated sigh. "As I recall, it was about air quality."

Scott grinned, which made his classic features even more handsome and appealing. Chrissie doubted hers was the only heart he'd broken since leaving Hard Luck.

His eyes grew solemn. "I meant what I said. I made a lot of mistakes, and I want you to know I'm sorry for the pain I caused you."

Chrissie dropped her own eyes, rather than let him see how deeply his words affected her. She'd never expected Scott to apologize, and it took her a while to respond. "Apology accepted," she whispered.

"Can you really forgive me?" He clasped her shoulders and compelled her to look at him.

Chrissie knew what he was asking, but she wasn't sure she could say what he wanted her to. "I *have* forgiven you. I put everything behind me years ago, Scott." That was true—and yet it wasn't. She'd made the conscious decision to let his past actions go, but she couldn't excuse or forget them.

He expelled an enormous sigh as if he'd been waiting a long time to hear that. For an uncomfortable moment he gazed into her face. Then he said, "I'd like to see you again."

"See me?"

"Go out with you," he corrected. "As in date. I'd like us to start again."

She was definitely tempted. Where she found the courage to refuse him, Chrissie would never know. Slowly she shook her head.

"I did say I'd forgiven you, Scott," she said. "But there are consequences to one's behavior. Nothing you say now will ever undo the past. I wish you well, Scott, I really do, but I'm not going to risk letting you hurt me again."

He didn't say anything for a few seconds, then finally let his hands fall. "I can understand that," he said quietly.

He turned away, and she didn't stop him.

Chapter
4

BETHANY HARRIS sat cross-legged on the bed, waiting impatiently for her husband to return from his late-evening rounds. Her thoughts were confused, and she wanted to discuss the O'Halloran party with him. When they'd left, Mitch had dropped her off at the house, then stopped in at the station to check with the night dispatcher, a habit he'd developed during his many years in law enforcement. He wouldn't be long, she knew, but she was eager to talk about the events of the evening. Especially the exchange she'd witnessed between Chrissie and Scott.

The sound of the door closing propelled Bethany off the bed. "I'm glad you're back," she said, greeting her husband in the kitchen. She was barefoot, her eyelet cotton gown reaching nearly to the floor.

"Are the boys in bed?" he asked.

"Both of them," she said. Jack, their youngest, was eleven. Their older son, Jeremy, attended the local high school. "Did you notice Chrissie tonight?" she asked.

"She was helping serve, remember?" Mitch reminded his wife absently. He moved into the living room, unbuttoning his shirt as he walked.

"What Chrissie was doing," Bethany told him, "was avoiding Scott." She knew her stepdaughter well enough to recognize that Chrissie was keeping herself occupied all evening in an effort to elude Scott—not that her plan had worked.

Mitch frowned and sank into his favorite chair in front of the television. "I thought she was over Scott. I assumed she was willing to forgive him and ready to move on."

"I'm sure she *has* forgiven him, but…" Sitting on the arm of his chair, Bethany shrugged. "As for being over him, forget it." Half the night she'd had to resist the urge to throw her arms around her stepdaughter and comfort her. How well she understood the doubts and uncertainties Chrissie felt; it was like seeing history repeat itself.

"I'd better have a talk with her," Mitch said, still frowning.

"About *what?*" Bethany demanded, wondering if her husband knew something she didn't. When it came to police matters, Mitch was closemouthed. As he should be. Bethany respected his discretion. But he sometimes kept private fears and concerns to himself, too. If he had information regarding Scott and Chrissie, she wanted to hear it.

Mitch's gaze clouded with indecision. "I'm not keeping any secrets, if that's what you're thinking. It's just—" He abruptly changed his mind about whatever he'd planned to say. "Actually, Chrissie may want to talk to me about Scott, and I was hoping you'd give me a few suggestions—unless, of course, *you'd* prefer to talk to her."

"I'd gladly talk to Chrissie," Bethany told him quietly, "if I knew what to say."

They were both silent for a moment. "I think very highly of Scott for publicly apologizing to his family," Mitch said. "That couldn't have been easy."

"It was a generous thing to do," Bethany agreed. Scott's admission of his faults had taken maturity and inner strength; so had his decision to seek his family's forgiveness, especially in a roomful of people. Part of his speech, Bethany realized, had been directed at Chrissie.

Her stepdaughter was a warmhearted woman who'd already forgiven Scott—of that much Bethany was sure. But apparently forgiveness didn't extend to resuming their relationship.

Bethany had seen Chrissie leave the party soon after Scott's speech, unable to hide her misery; Bethany had desperately wanted to follow her out. She sensed that Chrissie loved Scott, yet—despite her feelings—refused to take another risk on the man who'd hurt her twice.

"There's something I never told you." Her husband's eyes sparked with hidden laughter. "Just before our wedding, Scott came to talk to me."

"*Scott* did? He was what—twelve?"

"I think so. And he sounded sincere as can be."

Bethany could only imagine what he'd had to say.

Mitch rubbed the side of his jaw. "Scott felt I needed to know you were in love with me long before I ever noticed."

Bethany, who'd moved to sit across from her husband, knees tucked beneath her chin, lifted her head. "He didn't!"

Mitch raised his hand. "I swear it's true. Scott said he recognized the *look*. According to him, Abbey looked at Sawyer the same way you looked at me. He asked me if love made people act dumb because that was how his mother and Sawyer behaved. He wondered if that would happen to us."

Pressing her forehead against her knees, Bethany couldn't suppress a laugh.

"Apparently he didn't approve of what his sister and Chrissie had done to get us together, either."

"I don't believe this."

"Then he recommended I marry you in spite of Chrissie and Susan's matchmaking, and congratulated me on seeing through their ploys." Her husband's smile was delighted as he reminisced. "I could talk to Scott," he finally suggested. "Just like he spoke to me."

Bethany considered that, but instinctively knew Chrissie would resent her family's intrusion. "You've already had a number of talks with Scott. Over the years, I mean."

Mitch's smile disappeared and he nodded. "He was an angry teenager, but nothing I said helped him."

"Don't be so sure."

Mitch leaned forward. "I've seen other kids like Scott. He was never vicious or even all that bad. First, there was the pain of losing his dog and then…well, this is what I started to tell you. He contacted his father when he was fifteen. He never told Abbey and Sawyer."

"But *Sawyer's* his father."

"By adoption, true, but Scott had things to resolve with his birth father—and it didn't really happen. The bastard out-and-out rejected him. His own kid!"

"You never told me this before."

Mitch's eyes avoided hers. "I know. He asked me to keep it confidential. But I tried to help him…."

"I think you *did* help him, although Chrissie didn't understand that at the time."

Mitch shook his head. "Scott hurt her the same way he hurt

himself. Now he's back and she doesn't trust him, and really, can you blame her?"

"No…" Still, Bethany wished a reconciliation was possible.

"Maybe you *should* talk to Chrissie." Mitch glanced hopefully in her direction. "Maybe that would be the best approach, after all."

"And say what?" Bethany asked.

Her husband hesitated. "I don't know. Something inspiring. Hey—you could always ask Ben for advice. Seems to me he has a knack for knowing the right thing to say."

In theory Mitch's idea sounded good, but this was a delicate situation, one that required sensitive handling. Chrissie might take offense at her family's meddling in her affairs. In fact, Bethany could amost guarantee it. Besides, knowing Ben, his solution would probably be to lock Chrissie and Scott in a room together and refuse to release them until they'd sorted everything out.

"You think we *should* ask for Ben's opinion?" Mitch murmured.

Bethany gave a pensive shrug and laughed softly at the idea of leaving her stepdaughter's love life in the hands of crusty, outspoken Ben—the man who also happened to be Bethany's birth father and the reason she'd moved to Hard Luck in the first place. "I think we should let Chrissie make her own decisions. Although, I suppose, if the right opportunity presents itself…"

Mitch took a moment to mull that over. Then he nodded. "You're right. And you never know—one of them might actually *ask* for our advice. In which case, we'll be happy to give it. Come on," he said, stretching his arm toward her. "It's past my bedtime."

CHRISSIE AROSE EARLY Saturday morning and dressed warmly for her bimonthly flight into Fairbanks. As she ate some toast, she filled her backpack for the weekend, then walked to the Midnight Sons landing strip. Duke Porter, her law partner's husband, generally flew her into town. They'd gotten to be good friends over the past few months, since she'd started the mentoring program arranged through a Fairbanks social-service agency. Joelle Harmon was a twelve-year-old foster child at risk. Abandoned by her mother, father unknown, Joelle had been in six foster homes in four months, until she was accepted into the experimental group home. Chrissie had spent months building a relationship with the girl.

Her breath formed small clouds as she hurried toward the Midnight Sons office to check in for her regularly scheduled flight. It would turn bitterly cold soon enough. Within the month, snow would fall and winter would set in with such ferocity that just the thought of it sent shivers down her spine. Despite that, Chrissie loved Alaska; she'd lived here almost her entire life and couldn't imagine settling anywhere else.

Opening the door, she stepped into the office. "Duke, I—" She stopped as soon as she realized it wasn't Duke standing there, but Scott O'Halloran.

"Morning," he greeted her cheerfully. He was pouring himself a cup of coffee and didn't bother to look up.

Her smile faded. "Where's Duke?"

"Sleeping in, I assume." Scott finally glanced up. "I'm taking the morning flight."

Chrissie hesitated, unsure what to do.

He reached for a clipboard and headed out the door. He paused when she didn't follow. "You coming or not?" he asked. "I'm leaving now. I have some deliveries to make in Fairbanks."

Chrissie figured she didn't have any choice. She might as well get used to being around Scott, no matter how uncomfortable he made her feel.

Climbing into the plane, she was relieved when Scott immediately placed a pair of headphones over his ears. Making polite conversation would've been difficult, and at least he'd circumvented any requirement to do so. He ran through a flight-check list before starting the engine of the Lake LA4 amphibious plane. He could've been flying alone for all the attention he paid her.

Frankly, that was the way Chrissie wanted it. Yet when they soared into the endless blue skies toward Fairbanks, she found herself wishing circumstances could have been different. This wasn't the first time she'd flown with Scott; she'd been in the air with him dozens of times. In Hard Luck planes were equivalent to cars anywhere else. More than one summer afternoon had been spent flying to nearby lakes for a refreshing swim.

The first time he'd ever kissed her had been underwater. They'd done plenty of kissing above water, too. Chrissie closed her eyes, trying not to remember.

As they approached Fairbanks, she relaxed, grateful to be close to her destination and away from the confines of the plane. Away from Scott. His landing was smooth, a "greaser" as the pilots called it, and the aircraft came down gently, touching the tarmac with barely a jolt.

"Nice landing," Chrissie said when Scott removed the headphones.

"Thanks."

"Will you be flying me back tomorrow afternoon?" Not that it mattered, but she wanted to know.

"My name's on the schedule." He unlatched the door and climbed out, his jaw noticeably tight—as though her question had angered him.

Refusing to let his mood intimidate her, Chrissie opened her own door and climbed down the wing, shaking her head at Scott's offer of assistance. Once she was firmly on the ground, she slipped her backpack over her shoulders and straightened. "See you tomorrow, then."

He nodded curtly.

Without another word, Chrissie turned and started toward the terminal.

"Have fun with your boyfriend," he called after her, his voice dripping with sarcasm.

Boyfriend? She couldn't imagine where he got that idea. Chrissie thought about explaining that she was mentoring a twelve-year-old girl, then changed her mind. Perhaps it was for the best if Scott believed she was seeing another man. Not many people knew about her work with the experimental foster-care program. Her parents, of course, and Tracy. She'd briefly mentioned it to Ben's wife, too, but none of the details; she'd only referred to visiting Joelle on a particular weekend.

This foster-care program, being tested by the state, placed school-age children in a situation similar to a boarding-school facility. Each student was assigned a volunteer mentor from the community, who spent time with the child, encouraging and listening.

Chrissie had grown to love the quiet soft-spoken child. At first it was all Chrissie could do to get the painfully shy girl to speak above a whisper. Gradually, thanks to the support of the group home and the trust Chrissie had built, Joelle grew more confident. Chrissie hardly recognized the child she'd first met in the smiling chattering girl Joelle had become.

"I leave at four o'clock sharp," Scott shouted.

"I'll be here," Chrissie responded, tossing the words over her shoulder.

"See that you are," he snapped, "or I'll leave without you."

His parting shot annoyed her, and she jerked open the heavy glass door leading to the terminal. Her frown changed to a smile as Joelle ran toward her. "Chrissie, Chrissie!" the girl shouted. "Guess what? I got an A on my essay for English!"

Chrissie enveloped the girl in a hug as a surge of joy and triumph rushed through her. Joelle had come so far, and Chrissie couldn't help feeling a personal pride in the progress she'd made. Every accomplishment was significant; every accomplishment took her further from her disadvantaged past and toward a hopeful future.

"Oh, Joelle, I'm *so* proud of you." Those simple words, spoken with heartfelt sincerity, brought a huge smile to the girl's face.

"I've got a busy weekend planned for us," Chrissie told her.

Joelle wrapped an arm around Chrissie's waist. "I brought my paper if you want to read it."

"You bet I do," she told her, and they walked out of the terminal together.

FOUR O'CLOCK SUNDAY afternoon, as promised, Chrissie was back at the airport. After two days with Joelle, she was exhausted. A friend who worked as a flight attendant for one of the airlines let Chrissie use her apartment. The arrangement worked well for them both. Jackie usually had weekend assignments, and whenever she was on duty, Chrissie watered her plants and looked after the place.

Scott was waiting for her. "We may have trouble with the weather," he said by way of greeting.

"What kind of trouble?"

"A storm front's headed toward us. Would you understand the meteorological details if I explained them?"

"Probably, but I'll just take your word for it," she said. "Are we stuck in Fairbanks?"

"Not if I can help it. I've been on the phone for the last thirty minutes. If we leave now, we can squeak through. Ready to go?"

"Of course."

"Then let's get this show on the road." He led her to the plane and Chrissie dutifully followed him and climbed inside, fastening the seat belt. Although she knew they were in a hurry, she was reassured that Scott took the time to go over the preflight checklist thoroughly.

It was nearly dusk when they soared into the sky, which was clear and cloudless. Those conditions, however, didn't last. About halfway between Fairbanks and Hard Luck, they hit thick cloud cover and heavy winds, and the plane pitched and heaved. Rain and sleet lashed them from all directions, and ice started to build up on the wings. Chrissie didn't need to be a pilot to know how dangerous that was.

Although she'd flown in every type of weather, the rough-and-tumble ride unsettled her. During one particularly bad stretch, she closed her eyes and bit her lip.

"You okay?" Scott asked.

"Uh-huh."

Talking into his headset, Scott was busy for several minutes. "We're going down," he suddenly announced, his voice emotionless.

Adrenaline bolted through her. "We're landing? Where?" It was nearly nightfall and raining. She could barely make out the landscape below.

Scott, however, was concentrating on the radio, reporting the details of where they were, and he didn't answer her.

Chrissie clenched her hands tightly as he circled the area and slowly made his descent. By the time the lake came into view, her nerves were shot. Just as flawlessly as he'd landed the day before, Scott guided the plane onto the water's surface and cut the engine, gliding it toward shore.

"Where are we?" she asked once her heart had stopped pounding.

Scott took off his headphones. "Lake Abbey," he said brusquely. "We'll wait out the storm here."

Terrific, just terrific; he'd chosen the very lake where he'd first kissed her. The lake Sawyer O'Halloran had named after his wife.

Chapter
5

SCOTT MANEUVERED the plane as close to shore as possible, all the while feeling Chrissie's glare. The woman was in a rage, which was ridiculous. It wasn't as though he'd created this storm, although to tell the truth, he wasn't really complaining. It gave him the opportunity to talk to Chrissie without her dashing off.

"You did this on purpose," she accused him. "Why don't you just admit it?"

"If you want something to blame, I suggest you look at the weather," Scott replied.

"The storm's only an excuse, and you know it. We never should've left Fairbanks."

She had him there, but he'd honestly believed they could slide in before the cold front hit. Rather than argue with her, he said calmly, "My family built a cabin here." He cringed at how convenient that sounded; she already knew about the cabin, so she probably figured he'd planned this all along.

"I suppose you're going to suggest we wait out the storm there," she said in a scathing voice.

"Well, yes…" No wonder she doubted him, but the truth was, he *hadn't* planned it.

"I'm well aware of your parents' cabin," Chrissie returned defiantly, crossing her arms.

"You're welcome to spend the night in the plane," he said nonchalantly. She couldn't—he wouldn't allow it—but she didn't know that. He'd make his way to the cabin, build a fire, and if she hadn't shown up by the time he finished, he'd go back for her.

"That's exactly what I intend to do."

Scott should have expected it. "Fine. I'm going to the cabin," he told her, opening the aircraft door. A bone-chilling blast of Arctic wind shook him, and he gasped at the shock of it.

"I have plenty of blankets here," she told him, sounding less sure of herself now.

"If you need anything, just holler." He closed the door, wondering if he should drag her out of the plane right then and there. She was being ridiculous—again. But he assumed that after Chrissie had spent thirty minutes sitting in the frigid plane, her attitude would soften.

Edging along the pontoon, Scott leaped onto the shore. Luckily his boots protected his feet from the icy water. A flashlight led him toward the cabin through a night as black as he'd ever seen. Moon and stars were hidden by dark clouds, and there was no snow to provide even a tiny bit of reflection. The rain still pelted down.

He reached the cabin without incident. Scott's parents, Sawyer and Abbey, had built the log structure about twelve years earlier, with plenty of help from family and friends. It'd been quite a feat and required careful planning. Naturally the cabin had no modern conveniences, but it'd served as a family vacation home ever since.

As soon as he was inside, Scott lit the lantern and set it in the window, making sure the light was visible for Chrissie, in case she decided to join him. He couldn't keep from looking out, although it was difficult to see anything more than a faint silhouette of the plane.

His next challenge was to get a fire going. Luckily everything he needed—logs, kindling and matches—had been left within easy access for just such an emergency. Once he got the wood burning, Scott checked the cupboards. Again, his family had provided an adequate supply of canned goods. He and Chrissie shouldn't be trapped here long, four or five hours at most. The worst of the storm would pass by then, and they'd be able to land safely in Hard Luck early tomorrow morning.

He had the coffeepot brewing on the woodstove when he thought he heard a noise outside. It was probably just the wind, but in case it was Chrissie, he wanted to appear as relaxed as possible. If she happened to peek inside, he wanted her to think he didn't have a care in the world. Throwing himself down in the big chair, he leaned back his head and closed his eyes.

Ten minutes later his patience was gone, along with the pretense of relaxation. Chrissie was an idiot if she thought he was going to leave her in the plane while he sat, warm and cozy, inside the cabin. He grabbed his coat, determined to trudge back to the lake.

The wind was now mixed with ice and snow, and it stung his face when he opened the door. He shone the beam of light on the narrow footpath leading to the water's edge. Shoulders hunched against the wind and rain, he kept his gaze down. The flashlight guided his steps, illuminating the walkway a few feet at a time. Scott paused when the light fell on a pair of wet boots. Chrissie.

"I…I changed my mind," she announced.

Scott bit off any chastisement, although he had plenty he wanted to say. Instead, he held out his hand.

She hesitated before slipping her gloved hand in his. "Thank you."

She moved close to his side, and his arm went about her waist as he helped her to the cabin. With the wind behind them, propelling them forward, they were at the door within minutes.

The cabin was warm, comfortable and surprisingly intimate, despite its size. At first Chrissie stayed near the door, as if she feared what might happen if she advanced completely into the large open room.

"How about a cup of coffee?" Scott asked, his back to her.

"Please."

He dared not turn around for fear she'd see the amusement in his eyes. Judging by the way she maintained her distance, she apparently expected him to ravish her any minute.

"You were able to let someone know where we are?" she asked, rubbing her hands together as she stood in front of the fire, which was now burning well. The wood crackled and flames leaped merrily, casting warmth throughout the room.

"Duke took the message." Her lack of trust bothered him, and the situation seemed a lot less amusing.

"Good," she said briskly.

He poured them each a steaming cup of fresh coffee. He

found sugar but no creamer; there was, however, a bottle of whiskey, and he doctored his coffee with that. Might as well get comfort where he could. She declined.

Scott sat down in the big overstuffed chair Sawyer favored. If Chrissie wanted to act like a piece of cardboard, that was fine by him, but *he* intended to relax. Despite the impression he'd given, landing the plane during the storm had been a stressful experience. "I haven't been here in years," he said, glancing around.

"Me...neither."

"The last time—" He stopped abruptly the second he realized exactly when that had been. It was the summer she'd graduated from college.

"The last time you were here was with me, wasn't it?" Chrissie asked. She sat on the sofa across from him, huddled over her cup as though it was something that required her protection. Her boots and socks were off and drying by the fireplace. She sat with her bare feet tucked beneath her.

"Seems like a lifetime ago," he said, his voice a little hoarse. He'd watched Chrissie that day and he'd remembered everything he'd spent the past few years trying to forget. Even after he'd hurt her, she'd been trusting and sweet. The teenage girl he'd left behind had matured into a woman. That afternoon had been one of the most wonderful of his life; it'd opened his eyes to what he really wanted. All this time he'd been running away—from his family, his town, the people he'd known—and until that afternoon he hadn't realized how much he missed Chrissie, how much he needed her.

His original plan had been to fly into Hard Luck, attend the graduation party, then head out immediately afterward. His relationship with his mother and Sawyer was strained at the time, and he hadn't wanted to overstay his welcome. During his years away, he'd made a new life for himself, first in the military and after that, in Utah. He'd hurt his parents, embarrassed them. It seemed better for everyone involved if he kept out of their lives.

To his surprise, Sawyer and his mother had been genuinely delighted to see him, and willing to put the past behind them. He'd loved spending time with Susan, Anna and Ryan, and he'd remained in Hard Luck for ten days. His reluctance to leave, however, was due to more than his family. Scott had lingered in town because of Chrissie.

With Sawyer's permission, he'd borrowed the Cessna, had Ben pack him a lunch and then taken off with Chrissie for an afternoon of swimming and fun. As soon as he could manage it, Scott had Chrissie back in his arms again.

The minute they'd kissed, those years apart had dissolved and it was as if he'd never left. Every time they kissed, he had another reason to stay. Every time they touched, he felt a sense of rightness. This was home. This was Chrissie, the first girl he'd ever loved, the only girl he'd ever loved....

"Are you tired?" he asked, wanting to cut off his memories before they took him into territory best left undisturbed.

"Exhausted," Chrissie admitted, sounding more relaxed now that she'd had a warm drink.

"I'll scrounge up some blankets from the loft." He was anxious to do something, preferably something that required movement. Sitting around reminiscing about the one summer afternoon he most wanted to forget wouldn't help matters. Unfortunately it was the same summer afternoon he most wanted to remember.

He straightened the ladder that went to the loft. His parents used the upper area for storage in case bears broke into the cabin. Climbing up, he discovered that Abbey had packed everything neatly away for the winter, but it didn't take him long to find extra bedding.

Grabbing several blankets, he carried them down for Chrissie. She'd finished her coffee and placed her mug in the sink.

"If you want, you can sleep down here on the sofa close to the fire," he suggested.

She nodded.

"I'll take the loft."

She nodded again.

"Good night, Chrissie."

"Night," she muttered, her voice low.

Scott started up the ladder, then stopped. "Chrissie?" he asked, uncertain what had changed. Clearly something had. He heard it in her voice, although she kept her head averted and he couldn't see her expression.

"Yes?" She sounded cheerful again.

He stepped off the rung and moved toward her. "Is everything...all right?"

Turning to face him, still in the shadows, she said, "Listen, I know I was out of line earlier. I'm sorry for what I said."

"That's okay."

"You can't control the weather." They stood no more than a few feet apart, tension electrifying the air between them. Scott didn't know what to make of it. Part of him wanted to shout that it was time to put aside the hurts of the past and talk honestly. He opened his mouth to say as much but saw her stiffen and knew it was useless. She wouldn't lower the emotional barricades she'd erected against him. Nor could he forget that there was another man in her life now. A man she visited in Fairbanks at least twice a month.

"Good night," he said again, unnecessarily. After he'd stacked extra wood by the fireplace, he climbed the ladder to the loft.

He made up his bed, and when he lay down, he could see Chrissie below. She'd piled blankets on the sofa, then turned off the lantern. The only light in the cabin came from the flames dancing in the fireplace, throwing shadows about the room. The wind moaned outside the door. Another time the low whistle might have lulled him to sleep, but not tonight. Not with Chrissie only a few feet below…

Closing his eyes, he was beseiged by the memory of her kisses—the taste of her mouth against his, her eager response to him, the need she created in him with a single touch.

"Scott?"

Her soft voice startled him and he opened his eyes. "Yeah?"

"Are you asleep?"

"No."

"Do you mind if I ask you something?"

Anything would be better than this stilted politeness. "Sure, ask away."

"Do you remember that last summer we were here?"

He almost groaned aloud. "I'm not likely to forget."

"I wondered…" Her voice broke.

"What did you wonder, Chrissie?"

"I need to know if what Farrah said was true. Back then. *Were* you engaged to marry her?" She paused, then added, "Was it true?"

He'd been lying on his stomach, his head resting on his folded arms. He rolled onto his back and stared blankly at the ceiling. He opened his mouth to tell her, to explain it all away—but he couldn't. Yes, he had excuses and justifications for that day they'd spent on the lake, when he had, in fact, been engaged to another woman. He could tell Chrissie how he'd finally understood that Hard Luck was his home, that she held his heart. He'd *wanted* to tell her, but his hands had been tied. It would've been unfair to Farrah, and he owed her that one kindness before he broke off the engagement.

"Your silence is answer enough."

"I don't have any excuses, but—"

"There's always a but, isn't there?" Her voice had an edge he'd never heard before.

"Chrissie—"

"No, listen, it's all right, really. I shouldn't have asked. I knew, but I needed to hear you say it."

At that moment he would have given anything for the ability to lie to her. But he couldn't make himself do it. "I didn't marry her."

"I noticed," she said sarcastically. "She dumped you, huh? I don't blame her. No woman in her right mind would marry a man who—" She choked off the rest, took a moment to compose herself, then continued. "A man who gave her an engagement ring and then got involved with a high-school flame. Farrah dumped you," she repeated, "and you deserved it."

Scott could hardly keep himself from saying that not marrying Farrah was *his* decision—and the smartest move he'd ever made. He thanked God that he'd come to his senses in time to save them both untold heartache. They'd fallen conveniently in love, and getting married had seemed the inevitable next step. Not until he'd seen Chrissie again did he realize his mistake.

He'd wanted to tell her the truth about Farrah that summer day. He'd intended to break off the engagement once he returned to Utah and then, as soon as he was free, come back to Hard Luck and plead with Chrissie to marry him. So much for the best-laid plans. The matter of his engagement had blown up in his face when Farrah unexpectedly flew up to see him; she'd arrived with great fanfare and announced to everyone within earshot that she was his fiancée. Scott had seen the look his parents exchanged. His mother had been confused, especially after all the time he'd spent with Chrissie. Sawyer had been angry and they'd argued. Soon afterward, without a word to Chrissie, Scott had left Hard Luck.

He owed her an apology, and more. "I know it comes too late," he ventured, "but I am genuinely sorry."

His words appeared to fall on deaf ears. Then, "Is the apology meant for me or Farrah?" she asked.

"Both."

"It must've given you a real thrill to have two women in love with you at the same time."

He let the comment slide. "I'd settle for just one," he said quietly.

The fire popped, then briefly flamed, spreading a warm glow around the room. Scott watched as Chrissie threw aside the blankets and leaped to her feet. "Oh, no, you don't!"

"Don't what?" he asked, sitting up. He couldn't imagine what he'd said that she found so offensive.

"Let's get something straight. You think you can bring me back to Lake Abbey, stir up a few old memories and then weasel your way back into my life. Well, I'm here to tell you it isn't going to happen!"

"Chrissie—"

She covered both ears and started to hum. "I'm not listening. I'm not listening. Nothing you say will make one bit of difference."

If she hadn't looked and sounded so silly, Scott might have let the moment pass. Not now. Climbing down the ladder, he marched over and sat on the sofa beside her.

Taking her by the wrists, Scott looked directly into her eyes. The flickering light from the fire revealed her astonished expression. "Nothing I say will make any difference?" he asked. "Then try this on for size. I love you, Chrissie Harris. I've loved you half my life."

Chapter
6

DUKE PORTER WAITED until he knew Scott and Chrissie had landed safely on Lake Abbey before he left the Midnight Sons office. As he walked through his front door, taking off his wet jacket, he inhaled deeply. The scent of sage and his favorite chicken dish drifted through the house. He could hear sounds of laughter from his youngest daughter, Sarah Lynn.

"Are Scott and Chrissie okay?" Tracy asked, carrying a chicken casserole to the dining-room table.

"Yes and no," Duke told her, helping himself to a black olive.

"Daddy!" Sarah playfully slapped his hand. "You're supposed to wait until dinner."

"Sorry, I forgot," he said, and winked at his middle daughter who stood a short distance away, a frown of disgust on her face. Shortly after turning thirteen, Leah had, without any warning, completely lost her sense of humor. Almost overnight, his fun-loving outgoing daughter had turned into a morose and sullen teenager. Her twin sister, Shannon, hadn't changed. Although that might still happen, he thought wryly, but he hoped not. Two at one time was more than he could handle.

"What do you mean? Did Scott land safely or not?" Tracy demanded.

"He landed," Duke explained, "only it wasn't in Hard Luck."

"He's all right, isn't he?" Leah asked, her brown eyes wide with concern.

She had a major crush on Scott O'Halloran. "I presume so. He thought he could beat the storm system coming our way, but he couldn't. So he decided that, rather than risk it, he'd touch down on Lake Abbey."

"All alone?"

"Chrissie's with him."

Leah slouched in the kitchen chair and pouted. "Some women have all the luck."

Tracy returned to the dining room with a pitcher of water and placed it in the center of the table. When she looked up, her eyes connected with Duke's. "How long will they stay there?"

"Overnight, I expect, perhaps longer. Depends on the weather."

Tracy's bold smile triggered a responding one from Duke.

"What?" Leah asked, glancing first at her mother and then her father.

"Nothing," Tracy muttered.

"Never mind," Duke said.

"Oh, puh-leeze," Leah groaned, and rolled her eyes. She nudged her younger sister. "Cover your eyes. Mom and Dad are going mushy on us."

"Shannon! Dinner's ready." Tracy called their other daughter from her room.

Shannon appeared promptly. Both girls looked so much like Tracy that even now it took Duke by surprise. When he'd married her, he'd envisioned a houseful of rough-and-rowdy sons; instead, he had three beautiful daughters. Not once, not for a single second, had he been disappointed. His life was full and he adored his wife. In fact, marriage was the best thing that had ever happened to him.

They all sat down and joined hands for grace. Before the completion of the "amen," Duke had reached for the serving spoon and leaned toward the casserole. His wife cast him a disapproving look, which he ignored.

"Did I hear someone mention Scott and Chrissie?" Shannon asked.

"He's stranded with Chrissie up at Lake Abbey," Leah complained. "Can you imagine getting stuck in a storm with a hunk like that? Why can't it happen to me?" Still bemoaning her sorry lot, she stretched across the table for the plate of biscuits and helped herself to one.

Duke quickly grabbed a biscuit before he got shortchanged; it'd been known to occur. To his astonishment, Tracy had turned out to be a excellent cook. He'd had his doubts when he first married her, and with good reason. Once, during their brief courtship, he'd visited her in Seattle and she'd insisted on making dinner. The meal had darn near killed him. But soon after that, she'd started practicing. And once they were married, she'd taken cooking lessons from Mary Hamilton and proved to be an apt pupil.

Duke had to give all due credit: His wife was a marvel. She'd gone into this marriage convinced she could do it all and have it all. She'd claimed she could maintain her career as an attorney and keep up with the ever-increasing demands of being a wife and mother. And for the most part, she had. They'd planned the first pregnancy and she'd managed, even with twins. It wasn't until Sarah Lynn was born that Tracy took a leave of absence from the law firm. With infinite wisdom— and with advancing age—she'd declared that yes, she *could* have it all, just not at the same time. When Sarah Lynn started kindergarten, Tracy put on her attorney's suit again. Chrissie Harris had joined the law office, after working there during her summer vacations from law school, and had become a valuable addition.

Within ten minutes, all three girls had eaten and vanished. Duke and Tracy lingered over their coffee.

"So…Scott and Chrissie are stuck up at Lake Abbey," Tracy said.

"Bring back any memories?" Duke teased.

She smiled. Years earlier Duke and Tracy had been involved in a fairly serious airplane crash. Tracy had been living in Seattle at the time, and she'd flown up to Hard Luck to attend Mariah's wedding. Duke had been scheduled to fly her into Fairbanks for her connecting flight to Seattle. The two of them had clashed from the moment they'd met. Tracy Santiago was everything Duke disliked in a woman; he found her bossy, independent and headstrong. He'd derived pleasure from baiting her and soon discovered that she could more than hold her own. Tracy had viewed him as an unreasonable male chauvinist pig—one of the few men who really fit that now-dated expression. Their arguments and dislike of each other had been legendary.

Then the plane had gone down, and Duke was badly hurt.

He'd broken his arm and sustained internal injuries. During the long hours before the rescue team arrived, Tracy had shown herself to be both capable and compassionate. While she confidently dealt with the crisis at hand, caring for him and guiding the rescue party to the downed plane, Duke realized he'd done something very foolish. He'd fallen in love with her.

Tracy loved him, too, and had the wisdom to recognize that although they were vastly different, they had everything necessary to make a good life together. Duke had just needed some time and distance to figure out what Tracy already knew.

He'd claimed, in the days before Tracy, that he wanted a conventional wife. One who'd stay home with the children, bake cookies and do other wifely things. None of that interested Tracy. He'd married her, assuming he'd survive on frozen dinners the rest of his life, but by then he'd loved her too much to care. Over the years there'd been some bad meals, but many more fabulous ones. Some of the inedible dinners he'd cooked himself. Tracy wasn't the only one who'd changed; he'd done his fair share, too.

"Are you remembering the crash?" Tracy asked.

Duke nodded. "I think it's poetic justice that Scott and Chrissie are stranded up there together. He loves her, don't you think?"

"I don't know about Scott," Tracy said with a thoughtful look, "but I certainly know how Chrissie feels."

So the two women had talked about Chrissie's relationship with Scott. It shouldn't surprise him; after all, they worked together. "When did Chrissie mention Scott? What did she have to say?"

"Actually she didn't say a word," his wife told him, standing. "We don't generally discuss our personal lives at the office."

"But you just said…" Duke trailed her into the kitchen. "How do you know what Chrissie's feelings are if she didn't mention Scott?"

"The way I always know," Tracy said casually, putting the butter dish back in the refrigerator. "It's what people *don't* say that's more informative."

"Girls!" Duke shouted to his three daughters. "Dishes."

His order was followed by a chorus of protesting groans, all coming from different parts of the house. Duke ignored them, as did Tracy.

They both retired to the living room and Tracy reached for the mystery novel she was reading. Normally Duke would turn on the television, but he left it off this evening.

"I hope Scott and Chrissie can work it out," he said.

Tracy glanced up. "So do I."

"Anything interesting on television tonight?"

Tracy continued to read. "There's a documentary on Discovery I was hoping to catch. About Australia."

"It's not on too late, is it?"

"Why?" She raised her eyes to meet his.

"I was thinking of making an early night of it."

"Oh?" Tracy returned to her book. "Any particular reason?"

"Yes." It was a test of his determination not to laugh. Tracy knew full well what he had in mind. After being married to him all these years, how could she *not* know?

"You coming to bed early or not?" he asked.

"Oh, I'll be there," she said, the corner of her mouth quivering. "I wouldn't miss it for the world."

THE CABIN HAD BEEN quiet for more than a hour, and Chrissie was sure Scott had gone to sleep. His breathing was regular and even. She wished the sound of it would lull her to sleep, too, but so far it hadn't. She envied his ability to drift off like this, especially after their heated discussion.

Scott had claimed he loved her—and she'd laughed at him. That probably wasn't the most tactful response, but she couldn't help herself. He didn't expect her to believe him, did he?

No man who loved a woman treated her the way Scott O'Halloran had treated her. They'd both said some things tonight that would've been better left unsaid, and then he'd stalked away, climbed into the loft and promptly fallen asleep.

His ability to put their discussion behind him so quickly only went to prove that she was right. Otherwise how could he possibly sleep now? It made no sense. Not when she was lying there, reliving their argument, the anger and resentment churning inside her. If he *did* love her as he'd said, then he should be upset, too; he should care. Clearly he didn't.

Their argument, however, was only part of what was keeping Chrissie awake. Hunger contributed its own pangs to her sleepless state. She and Joelle had eaten a late breakfast, but that was almost twelve hours ago. If she read her watch correctly, it was now 10:00 p.m. She squinted down at her wrist, trying to make out the miniature numbers on her uselessly elegant watch. Maybe it was only nine, she thought; nevertheless, she was famished.

The way she figured it, she had two options. She could stay up, seethe with resentment toward Scott and listen to her stomach growl, or she could be angry with Scott and quietly investigate the canned goods in the kitchen.

The second option held more appeal. As silently as possible, she threw aside the quilts and tiptoed toward the kitchen. The latch on the cupboard door was tricky and she couldn't see to get it open, no matter what she tried. She felt so frustrated she wanted to slam her fist against it.

"You have to be smarter than the average bear," Scott said from behind her.

Chrissie whirled around. "I thought you were asleep!"

"I wasn't."

"Oh." She sighed heavily, wanting to avoid another confrontation with him—although she wouldn't back down if he started one. Gone was the shy teenage girl he'd jilted and the young college graduate whose heart he'd broken. She was a woman now, and perfectly able to deal with the likes of him.

"You're hungry."

Chrissie's nod was stiff, distrustful.

"Breakfast in bed, was it?" he asked in a sarcastic tone.

At first Chrissie was going to disabuse him of that idea, then decided she should let him believe what he wanted. He didn't know her, and time had proved he never *had* known her. Not really. "Something like that." She said the words flippantly.

He reached behind her, his hand grazing her ear, and twisted the cupboard knob. The door instantly sprang open. The top of her ear, where his finger had inadvertently touched, burned hotly. She didn't want his touch to affect her like this.

"You can leave now, thank you very much," she muttered fiercely.

"I'm hungry, too," he said. Leaning forward, he grabbed a can from the shelf. Wanting to avoid any chance of further contact with him, Chrissie stepped to one side, but all she managed to do was position herself more securely in his arms.

His ability to fluster her just irritated her more. She stiffened, and Scott's brows arched when he noticed her reaction.

"I'll get out of your way," she offered, eager to escape.

He didn't respond, nor did he move.

She watched as his eyes narrowed. Wondering how much he could see in the firelight, she prayed that not a hint of what she really felt was reflected on her face. Her heartbeat was out of control, and her mouth had gone completely dry.

"Scott…let me go." She waited for him to release her.

He did so with obvious reluctance, dropping his arms to his sides. He stepped away, and she saw his eyes harden—and then he did something so unexpected, so underhanded, that for one shocking moment, Chrissie couldn't believe it.

He kissed her.

Not in the sweet gentle way she remembered. Not the cherished kisses of their youth, the memory of which she'd carried with her all these years. Instead, his mouth was hard on hers, the kiss wild and dangerous, stealing the very breath from her lungs.

Chrissie gasped and would have protested further if Scott had allowed it. Pinned against the cupboard, Chrissie had no means of escape. She tried to break it off, tried not to enjoy the familiar taste of him. It'd been so long since he'd kissed her…. She shouldn't remember, shouldn't savor his touch. She was strong and capable. Yes, she was. But one kiss, and she could feel herself weakening. He'd hurt her deeply, but she found herself thinking there was probably a legitimate reason for the things he'd done. Already she was making excuses for him!

"No!" She wrenched away.

He hesitated, eyes puzzled. "Why did you…?"

Oh, what the heck. But if he was going to kiss her, it would be on her terms, not his. Clutching his shirt collar, she jerked his face toward hers. If he wanted to kiss, then it would be a kiss he wouldn't soon forget.

Scott gave a deep growl and half lifted her from the floor. Her feet dangled several inches off the ground, but by this point a little thing like suspended animation wasn't going to distract her. The kiss was unrestrained, intense, and Chrissie let it continue, wanting to make sure he knew she hadn't been lying home at night wondering about him.

When he ended it, his breathing was ragged. Hers, too. Chrissie pressed the back of her hand to her lips and boldly met his look.

"I hope that answers your questions," she said as pleasantly as she could.

"Well...not really."

He reached for her, but she was quick enough to sidestep him. "No, that was a mistake, and one that won't happen again."

"Or what?" he demanded. "You'll take me to court?" Scott returned to the main part of the cabin, dropped into the chair, then leaned forward and ran his fingers through his hair. "Tell me about him," he said.

"Who?"

"Joel."

Chrissie could hardly believe her ears. "Joel! You want to hear about Joel?"

His response was to glare at her from across the room.

Outraged, Chrissie glared right back. "Is that why you kissed me, because you couldn't bear the thought of me being with another man?" Whatever appetite she'd experienced earlier faded away, and she merely felt hollow, not hungry. Her legs weren't all that steady, either. Shocked and a little disoriented, she sank onto the far end of the sofa.

This explained it all. He was jealous. Everything he'd said

and done had been prompted by his fear that she was involved with someone else. The minute he learned Joel was really Joelle, his interest would wane. It was all a game to him.

A game Chrissie refused to play. "For your information, it isn't Joel I go to see, it's Joelle."

Frowning, he looked up. "Joelle?"

"She's twelve, and I'm her mentor."

"Are you saying—" he spoke slowly, deliberately "—it isn't a *man* you fly out to spend time with every other weekend?"

"That's precisely what I'm saying. Not a man. A twelve-year-old girl."

"But you said—"

"I said nothing. All right," she added, wanting to be as fair as possible, "I might have let you believe it was a man, but you were the one who suggested it in the first place. I don't know who gave you that impression, but—"

"Ben," he muttered, his frown deepening.

Chrissie closed her eyes and shook her head. She'd mentioned Joelle once to Mary, who must have told Ben. Clearly he'd either misheard or jumped to the wrong conclusion or both.

"You talked to Ben about me?" she asked suddenly. She didn't like the idea of Scott discussing her—with Ben or anyone else. That angered her even more. "You have some nerve, I'll say that for you."

"Chrissie—"

"Don't Chrissie me! I'm not a naive sixteen-year-old, nor do I have stars in my eyes. I know exactly the kind of man you are."

He stared at her. "You *don't* know me," he snapped. "If you did—"

"I know all I want to know."

"Fine."

Refusing to give him the last word, she muttered, "Fine with me, too."

It seemed a sad way to end their conversation, if indeed it could be called a conversation. Scott returned to the loft with an opened can of beans and a fork; she jerked the blankets over her shoulders. Wordlessly she sat and guarded the fire, trying to forget Scott's kisses.

Chapter 7

"WELL?" MARIAH O'HALLORAN glanced up from the secretary's desk, where she filled in one day a week at the Midnight Sons office. Years earlier she'd been one of the first women to respond to the O'Hallorans' advertisement; she'd accepted the position of secretary and ended up marrying her boss.

Christian gently closed the door and slumped into the chair nearest her desk. Her husband had a strange look on his face, and Mariah didn't know what to think. "Scott and Chrissie are back, aren't they?"

"They're back."

"And?" She hated it when Christian made her dig for every little detail. He knew that she and half the residents of Hard Luck were dying to hear what had happened between Scott and Chrissie. Everyone hoped the two of them would mend their differences while they were stranded on Lake Abbey.

In her eyes the situation was ideal. They were alone together while the storm raged outside. Christian claimed she was an incurable romantic, but if that was true, then so was almost everyone in Hard Luck. "I want to know about Scott and Chrissie."

"You and the rest of the town. There must've been a hundred people at the airfield this morning when they landed."

Mariah leaned forward. "Did it look like everything's okay with them?" she asked.

"Hardly," Christian said with a shake of his head. "The minute the engine stopped, Chrissie had the door open and was scrambling out. Seemed to me she was in an awful rush."

"Oh." This wasn't encouraging. "What about Scott? Did he go after Chrissie?"

"No." Christian frowned. "He took off in the opposite direction. Now that I think about it, he seemed to be in a rush himself."

"Oh, dear."

"It's too bad, isn't it?"

Her husband's comment surprised her, since he rarely showed any interest in other people's romantic problems.

"I think the world of Scott," Christian went on to say.

"I know you do," Mariah said.

"He's a good guy—turned out well. I know he had a few problems as a teenager, but lots of boys do. I certainly don't hold it against him. Hey—remember when he read Susan's diary and wrote comments in the margins?"

"I sure do," Mariah said, grinning. She agreed that Scott had turned out well. She'd watched him, Susan and Chrissie mature into young adults. From the time Scott and Chrissie were in high school, she'd known they shared a special bond. Like almost everyone in Hard Luck, she'd assumed that one day they'd marry. But she'd apparently assumed wrong, and that saddened her.

"Years ago," Christian said, stretching out his legs, "before we got married, Scott and I had a talk…about women."

Mariah managed to hold back a smile. She didn't even want to *think* what he might've had to say on that subject.

"Scott offered me some advice," Christian said, grinning broadly, "having to do with romance and the two of us."

"Don't you dare tell me after all these years that you married me on the advice of a fifth-grade boy!"

Christian's eyes avoided hers. "It wasn't exactly *advice*."

"You'd better tell me."

"Well, Scott bragged about the help he'd given other guys— like Sawyer and Matt Caldwell and even Mitch Harris—when it came to love and marriage." Christian shook his head, a half-amused grimace on his face. "He suggested he could help us, too."

"Did he, now?"

"He did, but I would've come to the right conclusion— eventually." He paused. "You'd decided to leave Hard Luck, and I was pretty depressed about it."

In Mariah's opinion, Christian's memory was a bit flawed. "You fired me, if I remember correctly."

"Yeah, but that's because I was crazy about you. I thought if you were gone, then— But I don't want to get sidetracked here. All I can remember is how bad I felt when I realized you were actually going to leave. Nothing was working out the way I expected." His eyes held hers for an extra-long moment. "The fact is, I'm as crazy about you now as I was then."

Mariah resisted the urge to walk around her desk and kiss her husband—but only because she wanted to hear the rest of his story.

"You remember what it was like back then, don't you?"

"I'm not likely to forget." She wouldn't, either. Christian claimed he'd been depressed, but it didn't compare to how she'd felt. The weeks after she'd left her position at Midnight Sons had been some of the bleakest of her life. To this day, Mariah didn't know what she would have done without her friends. Matt and Karen had provided housing and encouragement. Abbey, Lanni O'Halloran, Bethany—they'd all rallied around, offering comfort and advice when all she'd wanted, all she'd ever wanted, was for Christian to love her.

"It seems odd to remember a conversation I had with a kid almost fifteen years ago," Christian admitted, "but in some ways, it's as if it took place yesterday. That's how clearly I remember Scott giving me his advice to the lovelorn—and talking about Chrissie."

"What did he say?"

"He told me that one day he was going to marry her, freckles and all."

Mariah smiled. "That boy had sense even then."

"Unfortunately he appears to have lost it," Christian said. He checked his watch, and looked surprised when he noted the time. Leaping to his feet, he said, "Gotta go. Are you picking up the boys from soccer practice this afternoon or am I?"

"I'll do it," she said, and grinned at his look of relief. Both their sons were enthusiastic about indoor soccer.

"I'll be glad when they can drive themselves," he said on his way out the door.

"Me, too," she agreed. Their two boys, born thirteen months apart, were ten and eleven. They were wonderful kids, both crazy about sports. The oldest, Tyler, loved to fly and often accompanied Christian on his scheduled flights. He was a sociable, gregarious boy. The younger, Travis, while as athletic as his brother, was more of an introvert.

"See you tonight, then," Christian called.

Mariah went to the door and watched her husband leave. She hadn't quite made it back to her desk when the door opened a second time, and to her astonishment Scott O'Halloran walked in. He looked none too pleased.

"Christian here?"

"He just left," Mariah told him. "If you hurry, you can catch him."

"That's okay, thanks." Scott began to head out. "I'll see him later."

"We were just talking about you," Mariah said, and regretted it the instant the words were out of her mouth.

"Me?" Scott hesitated at the door.

"Christian was remembering some advice you once gave him about romance."

Scott seemed puzzled. "I gave Christian advice?"

"It's not surprising that you've forgotten," she said, making light of it, "especially since you were only a kid."

"What did I say?"

She thought for a moment, then decided it wouldn't do any harm for him to know. "You were quite the matchmaker in those days."

"Not me," he said, smiling for the first time. "I left that to Susan and Chrissie."

"That's not the way I remember it," Mariah said.

"Those really were the good old days." He sighed. "Now that I think about it, maybe you're right. When I was twelve or so, I toyed with the idea of writing an advice column. I even talked to Lanni about putting it in her paper."

"Pretty enterprising of you."

"Especially when you consider what a hopeless mess my own love life is."

"Scott, that's not true." Mariah felt sorry for him. "I'm sure things aren't hopeless."

"It is true," Scott countered.

He seemed utterly defeated, and Mariah suddenly wanted to throw her arms around him, as though he were one of her sons. "Christian seemed to think you got *him* thinking in the right direction," she said bracingly.

Scott's expression was incredulous.

"Whatever you told Christian worked. We have a successful marriage to prove it." She had his interest now. "If you love Chrissie—"

"Mariah, let me stop you here. It's over. Chrissie isn't interested."

"Don't you believe it."

He shook his head. "I'm afraid you're wrong. She as much as told me so this weekend. And I think it's probably for the best."

THE OFFICE FELL QUIET when Chrissie entered. Everyone stared at her as she walked in. The secretary, Kate, jumped up from her desk immediately, clutching a handful of files, and followed her down the short hallway.

"We were all worried when we heard you'd been held up by the storm," Kate told her.

"There was nothing to worry about," Chrissie muttered, wanting to avoid the subject. She reached for the stack of mail on her desk, shuffling through it.

"I have your appointment calendar for the day."

"You can leave it with me," Chrissie said. In other circumstances, she would've headed directly home, soaked in a hot tub and slept through the day. Mondays, however, were often hectic. She had appointments all morning, and it was too late to reschedule them now.

No sooner had she sat down at her desk than there was a polite knock at her door.

"Come in."

"Hi." Tracy stuck her head in. "Glad you got here safe and sound."

"Thanks."

"Everything go all right?"

Chrissie wasn't sure how to answer. "Reasonably well, I guess."

The worst of the storm hadn't passed until daylight, and by the time she and Scott returned, the entire town of Hard Luck had heard about their predicament. If that wasn't bad enough, their families, friends and neighbors had all rushed to the airstrip, eager to welcome them back. Unfortunately, at that stage, Chrissie and Scott were barely on speaking terms.

Everyone, her parents included, had stared at them with great anticipation, obviously expecting their engagement to be announced on the spot.

"Are you *sure* you're all right?" Tracy asked.

"I'm fine, really. Just tired."

"If you need anything, let me know."

"I will," Chrissie promised. "Listen…there's something I want to talk over with you later."

Tracy frowned.

"I'd explain it now, but there isn't time. My first appointment's due in ten minutes and I have to read through his file. Can we talk this afternoon?"

Tracy nodded. "Of course. Whatever you need."

"Thanks," Chrissie whispered as Tracy quietly closed the door.

Chrissie buried her face in her hands. It didn't help that she was exhausted, not having slept all night. How could she, with Scott only a few feet away? She doubted he'd gotten any more sleep than she had.

Scott had left the cabin before dawn and gone to the plane. At first she'd panicked, fearing he'd fly off without her, but then reason had reasserted itself, and she'd acknowledged that, for all his faults, he wouldn't abandon her. Apparently he'd made radio contact and received the latest weather information. In thirty minutes or so, he returned and told her they'd fly out at first light.

During the trip back she might as well have been sitting next to a robot. He didn't speak to her. For that matter, she didn't have anything to say to him, either. The situation was dreadful and destined to grow worse. Until this weekend misadventure, they'd at least been cordial with each other. Now even that was gone.

It was clear to her, if not to him, that they couldn't both stay in Hard Luck. One of them had to go. Leaning back in her chair, Chrissie tried to think about it rationally. Since he'd only recently come home and was now a partner in the family business, it didn't seem right that Scott should leave.

She was the one who'd have to go. Tears threatened again, but she refused to give in to self-pity. She'd move to Fairbanks, she decided. Get out of Scott's way.

That decision made, there was only one thing left to do.

Tell Tracy and her parents. Then Scott.

Chapter
8

SCOTT HADN'T SLEPT all night, and he suspected Chrissie hadn't, either. He was bushed. After a visit to the office to drop off his flight bag and chat briefly with Mariah, he headed home. He genuinely sympathized with Chrissie, having to work all day. But the sad fact was, she didn't want his sympathy or, unfortunately, anything else to do with him.

When he made a quick stop at the Hard Luck Lodge, Matt and Karen were openly curious about what had happened between him and Chrissie, but they accepted his vague explanation—or seemed to, anyway. Once in his cabin, he stood under a long hot shower and then collapsed on his bed, falling instantly asleep.

A pounding on his door woke him. Sunlight came into the bedroom's one window and he glanced at his clock radio, astonished to see that it was already midafternoon.

"Just a minute," he growled. Grabbing a pair of jeans, he

hurriedly pulled them on, along with a sweatshirt. He padded barefoot to the door, yawning as he went.

Seeing Chrissie on the other side was a shock. He froze, his yawn half-completed.

"Do you have a minute?" she asked stiffly.

"Sure," he said, and stepped aside. From the tight lines around her eyes and mouth, he could tell she hadn't had a good day. There were dark shadows beneath her eyes, and she looked in desperate need of sleep. He wondered what was so important that it couldn't wait.

Chrissie peered inside the small cabin and shook her head. "Not here."

"Where, then?" he asked, not quite concealing his irritation.

"Can you meet me at the Hard Luck Café in fifteen minutes?"

He hesitated, thinking this probably wasn't the optimal time for them to discuss anything. Not with her so tired she could barely keep her eyes open and with him feeling so on edge. Despite that, he was curious. "I'll be there," he said briskly.

"I'll get us a booth."

He closed the door, then rubbed his face. Something was up, and he was about to learn what. It took him almost the full fifteen minutes to find his shoes, socks and gather his scattered wits.

The September wind cut into him as he hurried toward the café. As promised, Chrissie was sitting in a corner booth, her hands clutching a mug. The lunch crowd had disappeared, with only one or two stragglers. Ben and Mary stared at him, their curiosity as keen as his own.

"She's been here all of five minutes," Ben whispered when Scott stopped to collect his own coffee.

"Looking at her watch every few seconds," Mary added.

"She wants to talk to me," Scott muttered.

"We'll see that you have as much privacy as you need," Mary assured him.

"You settle this once and for all," Ben said. "You're both miserable, and the whole town with you."

Scott had to grin. "I'll do my best."

He carried his coffee to the booth and slid in across from Chrissie. "You have something to say?"

"I do." Her back was ramrod-straight, her arms unbending as she held her coffee away from her, both hands still clamped around the mug.

Scott waited for several minutes, his patience wearing thin when she didn't speak.

"Are you aware," she finally said, keeping her gaze focused on the table, "that we have a problem?"

"What do you mean?" He wasn't being sarcastic, just inquisitive.

"Did you notice how everyone was there at the airfield?"

He'd noticed, all right.

"How did that make you feel?" she asked.

He shrugged, wondering if there was a correct answer. "Uncomfortable, I guess."

"Embarrassed?"

"Yeah."

"Me, too." Her look softened perceptibly.

"Everyone was expecting something from us."

"They weren't interested in your American Express card," he said in a weak attempt at a joke.

"No," she told him, with not even a hint of humor. "What they were looking for was some *sign* from us."

"True," he admitted, refusing to sound defensive, "and we gave it to them, don't you think?"

"Oh, we sure did," she returned.

"So what's the problem?"

She glared at him as though he should have figured it out long ago. "The problem is, we've disappointed the whole town."

His friends and family weren't nearly as disappointed as Scott was himself, but he didn't mention that. As far as he was concerned, he'd already laid his heart on the line. He'd told Chrissie he loved her and she'd laughed in his face. His pride had reached its quota for abuse; he wasn't willing to accept more.

"I feel that we can't both remain in Hard Luck," she announced.

"What?"

"Just as I said. One of us has to leave."

So *this* was what her meeting was all about. She wanted him out of Hard Luck. Well, it wasn't going to happen. This was his home, his life, and he wouldn't let Chrissie screw it up. Not when he'd done such a stellar job of that himself. He wasn't going anywhere. He'd only recently found his way back.

His face hardened and so did his heart. "You're asking me to leave."

Chrissie's eyes widened. "No!"

Her answer perplexed him. "What do you want, then?"

"I…I'd never ask that of you, Scott. I'll be the one to move. I've been thinking about it all day, and it makes perfect sense for me to leave town. I have connections in Fairbanks and then there's Joelle and…"

She rattled on, but the longer she spoke the more Scott realized how close she was to tears.

"Chrissie," he said, interrupting her, "why are you doing this?"

She stopped abruptly. "Isn't it obvious?"

Tears glistened in her eyes, and she blinked in an effort to hide them. Scott's frustration and anger melted away, and he resisted the impulse to reach across the table and touch her cheek, comfort her somehow. What prevented him was knowing she'd resent any display of affection. He clenched his hands into fists and said, "You're not thinking straight. Listen, go home, get some sleep, and we can talk about this later."

"No. My mind's made up. One of us has to leave, and it has to be me."

"You're overreacting." After a good night's sleep she'd see that and regret this entire conversation. "This is an important decision. Let's sleep on it before you—or I—do something rash."

"No," she said again, her voice gaining strength. "You don't understand."

"What I understand is that you've gone thirty hours without sleep, and now isn't the time to make such a critical decision."

"But I know exactly what I'm doing," she insisted.

"Why should *you* be the one to move?" he demanded, completely losing his patience. "You've lived here your whole life. This is your home. If anyone goes, it should be me."

Chrissie closed her eyes and shook her head. "I can't let you do that."

"Why not?"

"Because I love you," she whispered. "I won't let you leave."

Scott was sure he'd misunderstood her. "You…love me?"

Her eyes flared as though she didn't realize what she'd said. "You've just come back. It's been a long time, and…and you can't. You're a partner in Midnight Sons. The papers have been drawn up and…" She shrugged. "It just makes sense that I be the one to go."

"What has any of that got to do with you loving me?" He wasn't about to drop the subject, no matter how hard she tried to talk around it.

She ignored the question and continued. "I'm getting to the point in my career where my practice is growing. I fly into Fairbanks regularly on business. It's logical that I live there, so I'll go."

"You didn't answer my question."

"It…was a slip of the tongue," she said through gritted teeth. "I didn't mean it."

Scott relaxed against the vinyl cushion and slowly smiled. "You never were much good at lying."

Her eyes grew wide and her face reddened as she sputtered, "But…but—"

"You love me, Chrissie. You've always loved me."

She shook her head, refusing to respond.

"I should've known it when I kissed you. I would have, too, if I hadn't been so caught up in what was happening. It was all I could do to keep from making love to you right then and there."

"As if I'd let you," she sniffed.

She seemed ready to slide out of the booth, and Scott reached across the table and grabbed her hand.

Chrissie's gaze shot to his.

"I have a better suggestion about how to settle this. A compromise." He had her attention now. "One in which neither of us has to move away from Hard Luck."

She didn't ask what he meant, but he sensed her interest.

He hesitated, debating the wisdom of what he was about to do. Experience had taught him to be wary with Chrissie—but then, she had a right to mistrust him.

"Marry me," he said simply.

She didn't say anything for a moment. "Marry you?" she echoed at last.

"I love you." He wouldn't add any embellishments, nor would he offer her unnecessary compliments. If she couldn't already see that he was speaking from his heart, then anything else he had to say wouldn't help his cause.

"Scott...like you said, we need to sleep on it. We're both tired. It was an exhausting night—"

"I don't need to sleep on it. I love you, Chrissie. I want to make you my wife. I want us both to live here in Hard Luck, to raise our children here, to grow old here. Together."

She swallowed hard.

"There's no one else waiting in the wings, either. Only you."

As though she didn't trust her voice, she shook her head again and slipped out of the booth. Without a word, she started to walk away.

So that was his answer. The burden of his disappointment seemed too much to bear. He propped his elbows on the table and covered his face with his hands.

"I'll pack up my things and be gone by morning," he told her, his voice raw.

She stood with her back to him, but at his words, she whirled around. "I told you I'll move."

"No, I said I'd go." He took his first and last sip of coffee, left the mug on the table and got out of the booth. He hadn't gone more than a few feet when Chrissie stopped him.

"All right!" she shouted. "All right."

Frowning, he faced her. "I'll be out of Hard Luck by morning."

"I…I wasn't agreeing to that. I meant, I'll marry you."

Mary stood in the background, both hands over her mouth as though to keep from shouting with glee. Scott cast her a warning glance, and her eyes twinkled with sheer delight.

"Why would you marry me?" he demanded. "Other than the fact that I asked you to."

"First…" She lowered her gaze to the floor. "I…love you. I've loved you for as long as I can remember."

"I want a woman's love, not a schoolgirl crush."

"Give me a chance, and you'll see how much of woman I am."

He grinned. "Any other reason?"

She nodded. "I couldn't let you walk away from me again. It nearly killed me the first two times."

"It's not going to happen, sweetheart." He held open his arms, and she flew into his embrace. His hold was so strong he practically lifted her from the floor, then her lips were on his. She kissed him in a way that left him in no doubt of her feelings. And in no doubt that she was every inch the woman she'd claimed.

"This is wonderful news!" Mary cried from behind them.

Scott heard the honking sound of Ben blowing his nose and recognized that his friend was shedding a tear of shared happiness.

Scott broke off the kiss, afraid to believe Chrissie was actually in his arms. "You aren't going to wake up tomorrow morning and change your mind, are you?"

Her smile told him there was no chance of that. Her expression sobered and she sighed. "I promised myself I wouldn't let this happen, but, Scott, oh, Scott, I'm so happy it did. I've always loved you."

He continued to hold her. "Don't make any more promises to yourself, okay?"

"I won't," she whispered with a laugh.

And then she kissed him again.

From the *Hard Luck Gazette*
By Lanni O'Halloran, Editor

It's official! I don't suppose I'm the only one who's noticed that Chrissie Harris is sporting an engagement ring. I spoke with the soon-to-be mother-of-the-bride, Bethany Harris, early this afternoon and Bethany confirmed that Scott O'Halloran and Chrissie have set their wedding date for New Year's Eve.

Bethany and Mitch proudly claim credit for having brought this couple together as a result of some timely advice to the bride. However, this conflicts with what Matt and Karen Caldwell recently told me, which suggests that *they* were the ones who'd played a major role in the wedding plans—although when pressed Matt insisted their part in furthering the romance would remain his and Karen's secret.

The new Mrs. O'Halloran will continue practicing law with Tracy Porter, while Scott's duties with Midnight Sons will expand, particularly since his father, Sawyer O'Halloran, intends to retire. Sawyer and Abbey have already booked a trip to New York and are looking forward to a second honeymoon.

As a "Welcome Back to Hard Luck" gift, Sawyer has given his son a purebred Alaskan husky, related to Scott's beloved Eagle Catcher, whom many of our readers will remember. Scott and Chrissie have both expressed their delight.

A bridal shower will be hosted by Scott's sister,

Susan Gold, and will be held at the Hard Luck Community Center the sixth of November. On the same night, Ben Hamilton will host a bachelor party at the Hard Luck Café.

As a wedding gift, my husband, Charles O'Halloran, and I, together with Mariah and Christian O'Halloran, as well as Scott's parents, have presented the engaged couple with twenty acres of land—and a cabin. Kind of goes full circle, doesn't it?

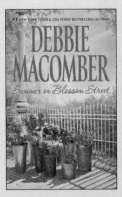

#1 *New York Times* and *USA TODAY* bestselling author

DEBBIE MACOMBER

The wedding dress, made years ago,
came with a promise:

The First Man You Meet...

Shelly Hansen's great-aunt's wedding dress has arrived—
which means, according to family legend, she is destined
to marry the next man she meets. Then she trips and
falls into Mark Brady's arms, and starts seeing him
everywhere.... *Coincidence?*

is *The Man You'll Marry*

After her own wedding, Shelly sends the dress to her
best friend, Jill Morrison, in Hawaii. But the man she sat
beside on the plane—gorgeous grouch Jordan Wilcox—
can't be the man in question, can he? She met him
before the dress arrived!

The Man You'll Marry

Available wherever books are sold.

MIRA®

www.MIRABooks.com

MDM2783TR

#1 *NEW YORK TIMES* BESTSELLING AUTHOR

DEBBIE MACOMBER

Father's Day

Robin Masterson's ten-year-old son, Jeff, wants a dog.
And there just happens to be one right next door!
But the friendly black Lab belongs to Cole Camden,
the *unfriendliest* man in the neighborhood. Still,
Jeff persists…and soon Robin and Cole are looking
at each other differently.

The Courtship of Carol Sommars

Peter Sommars is fifteen and needs a little more
independence. Which is why he'd like his mom, Carol,
to start dating. He even knows the perfect man—
Alex Preston, his best friend's dad. Alex is interested,
but Carol keeps sidestepping his pursuit. Which only
makes Alex—and the boys—more determined!

Right Next Door

Available wherever books are sold!

MIRA®

MDM2700TRR